*Love in wartime is always sister to trag-
edy — and never more poignant than in
the bitterest of wars, when loyalties and
divisions cut through the very hearth-
stones, when brothers became foes and
friendship was expendable. . . .*

# The
# Outlawed Banner

## BY GARLAND ROARK

In this new historical novel of the Civil
War, Garland Roark tells the exciting
story of two close friends who were made
enemies and drawn into a duel at sea by
forces that split a nation.

On the eve of the Civil War, Lieutenant
James Hillyer, U.S.N., was visiting the
Alabama plantation of his best friend,
Lieutenant Adam Cutler. It was there
that he met and fell in love with Adam's
lovely sister, Adria. But when the war
came, James remained with the North,
while Adria and her fiery brother found
their loyalty lay with the South.

Adam became an officer on the famous
rebel raider, *Alabama,* whose lethal blows
against Northern shipping from the Gulf
to the coast of France made her a prime
target for the U. S. Navy. James's duty,
as an officer on the *Kearsage,* was to destroy the *Alabama.* Following the hunter
and the hunted went the hopes and prayers of the girls they left behind.

THE OUTLAWED BANNER is a powerful,
absorbing novel that not only captures
the spectacular drama of battle at sea,
but creates a vivid and moving portrait
of a decaying — but proud — civilization.

# THE OUTLAWED BANNER

BY GARLAND ROARK

BY GARLAND ROARK

# The Outlawed Banner

DOUBLEDAY & COMPANY, INC., GARDEN CITY, NEW YORK, 1956

LIBRARY OF CONGRESS CATALOG CARD NUMBER 56–5964
COPYRIGHT ©, 1956, BY GARLAND ROARK
ALL RIGHTS RESERVED
PRINTED IN THE UNITED STATES OF AMERICA AT
THE COUNTRY LIFE PRESS, GARDEN CITY, N.Y.
FIRST EDITION

AGAIN—WITH DEVOTION

*To Leola*

# FOREWORD

In this tale based on the struggle between the Federal Union and the Confederate States, it is the writer's aim to draw aside the time-mellowed curtain and present a way of life in all its glory and tragedy over sand and wave; and in the process to focus attention on the little-known and understood decisive naval war.

Despite the great engagements on water at Hampton Roads, the lower Mississippi and Mobile Bay, military events on land so overshadowed the war at sea that history all too briefly records the daring exploits of the commerce destroyers, blockade-runners and even the blockade itself, which slowly but surely sealed the fate of the Confederacy.

A study and review of sea power and its use by both sides compels not a few historians and observers to believe that had any of these Southerners, Semmes, Maffitt, Maury, Tattnall or Buchanan, under a resolute government commanded a fleet anywhere near the size of Farragut's, the blockade of the Confederacy would have failed at the outset and a navy-supported South would have won the war late in 1862.

This story begins on land, where all ships are born, and though it takes the reader aboard famous Confederate ships and Federal cruisers in chase and in battle until the "Stainless Banner" became the outlawed banner, seldom does it stray too far from the ladies of Bay Oaks, an imaginary Southern mansion near Mobile.

I deem it necessary to explain to the reader that none of the fictional characters in this book are based on actual persons living or dead, that all historical events herein are the result of careful study of accounts prepared by both sides and relieved of partisanship, and that the story was written, let me say, with controlled bias.

My sources of information, too numerous to list in full, include the following: *Memoirs of Service Afloat during the War between the States,* by Admiral Raphael Semmes; *Two Years on the* Alabama, Sinclair; *The Gallant Rebel,* Horn; Miller's *Photographic History of the Civil War* (the navies); *Confederate Blockade Running,* Vandiver; *Century War Book,* Pictorial Edition, Battles and Leaders of the Civil War; *Confederate Veteran Magazine,* issues of 1928–29; Fleming's *War and Reconstruction in Alabama;* Coulter's *Confederate States of America,* 1861–65; *The French Quarter,* Asbury.

I am especially indebted to my friend and student of the War between the States, Mr. Jack McKinney, for the use of his rare books, to Miss Mildred Wyatt, and her staff, of Stephen F. Austin College Library, and to Miss Virgie Sanders, all of Nacogdoches, Texas; and to Mrs. J. Balfour Miller and the ladies of Natchez, Mississippi, for their true Southern hospitality in giving me the "Old South," for the exterior of Bay Oaks in this story is patterned after gracious Miss Myra Smith's Natchez mansion, D'Evereux; and to my wife Leola, for her faith and patience and assistance in the preparation of this book.

GARLAND ROARK

*Nacogdoches, Texas*
*September 14, 1955*

# CONTENTS

BOOK ONE

# The Sovereign States

GARLAND ROARK is the well-known author of such out-
standing novels of the sea as *Slant of the Wild Wind, The
Wreck of the Running Gale,* and his recent story of the
Texas Navy, *Star in the Rigging.*

# 1.   A Holly Tree

1

THE PEACEFUL WATERS OF MOBILE BAY under a clear December sky seemed nothing short of a good omen to Adria. She had never quite outgrown a childhood fancy handed down by Mammy Rose. Redbird, wild violet, or a V of geese on the wing, to mention a few, were signs of good fortune. Despite the fact that she had never gone to the trouble of checking the results of this kind of daydreaming, she found it as fascinating at nineteen as she had when she was nine.

On this bright morning Adria sat the saddle of a blooded chestnut mare. From the wooded bluffs, where smells of pine cleansed the air of harbor odors, the view was excellent. Long and wide, the bay stretched from Fort Morgan on the southern sand spit, far out of sight under the horizon, up to the broad oaks of Mobile, planted more than a century ago by the French and Spanish colonists. Creeping down the Mobile River like toys on a make-believe stream, cotton barges propelled by a river packet moved to a rendezvous with English and Yankee ships. Gulls caterwauled, dipped and rose in a poetry of motion, as if they alone were in charge of the Alabama port.

A sigh of contentment escaped Adria. Then she became suddenly aware of her reason for being here. Erasmus and another slave were waiting for her to select a yule tree for the annual Christmas ball at Bay Oaks. The event would take place tomorrow evening, seven days earlier this year, due to business calling her father to New Orleans. But she would not be hurried. Not with the morning air so fine and so many happy thoughts of holiday parties crowding her mind.

It seemed that tomorrow, Thursday, December 20, 1860, would never come. Adam had written from Baltimore that he would arrive in time for the ball. Her handsome brother, Lieutenant Adam Sheridan Cutler, U.S.N., was relatively unimportant. However, he seemed very necessary in the scheme of things, for he was bringing a guest, his closest friend and shipmate, Lieutenant James Hillyer of Maryland.

Adria's dreamy gaze turned speculative. The long lashes framing brown and amber eyes moved restlessly as her mouth, full-lipped and red, curved into a smile that was anything but childlike. Thinking of Adam's friend, a perfect stranger to her, she was planning a campaign with all her prettiness and charm, which she had long ago learned were far more than average.

Adria had heard of the Hillyer family while attending the female academy up in Virginia, though she was no more impressed now than then by anyone whose sole claim to eligibility emanated from the blood coursing his veins. Southern aristocrats were plentiful, and most of them knew how to dance and squire a lady. She was searching for something more than mere prerequisites. Perhaps Adam had not intended to provoke her curiosity to the bursting point, though he had done just that. And now she suspected him of deliberately penning a challenge in the somewhat hasty note enclosed in a letter to her parents.

Dear Temple:

Jim Hillyer is tall, sandy-haired, and much too serious for you to charm and drop like the others. Was with me under Captain Tattnall last year when we went to the aid of the English in their brush with Chinese forts, after which "Tatt" excused himself for breaking American neutrality with a classic remark: "Blood is thicker than water." But about Jim—

His family is four generations Old Navy, steeped in tradition, gold-plated Annapolis, so he's not apt to take sides in all this talk about free versus slave states, or states' rights. Convince our most zealous father of this (as only you can) and don't say I didn't warn you if you go after his heart and lose your own.

Love,
Adam.

There he went addressing her as Temple again. Though it was a part of her name, her mother a Temple of the Mississippi Temples, it rang boyish; and she supposed Adam would introduce her to the lieutenant as "My sister Temple." Oh, Adam would have his fun. But he should know better than to challenge her.

Adria's high, full breasts rose and fell as she breathed a sigh. "James Hillyer," she said in a whisper.

All at once she remembered a promise to the seamstress from

Mobile to be at home by eleven to try on the ball gown. "Erasmus!" she cried. "Hurry and find a tree."

"They ain't no mo' holly than they is watermelons. Tole yo' dat. 'Sides it am pow'ful bad luck to bring holly inside de house befo' Chris'mas Eve."

"A silly superstition," she scoffed. "Like putting your hat on back-wards if a rabbit crosses your path, or tying hair on top of your head with a string to cure a sore throat, or sweeping after dark."

"Jes' de same, chile, don't fetch no holly to de house now. Ain't pine a heap purtier?"

Adria flashed the old slave a hostile glance, which fell short of conveying threat. She had never been able to deceive Erasmus. On the other hand, he had never been able to refuse her anything.

"If you don't find a big holly with lots of red berries, I do declare you'll have only lye hominy for Christmas dinner."

Big lips spread wide in a coal-black face. "Yas'm. Reckin dat mought be mos' turrible thing could happen to dis heah nigger."

She rode ahead, toward Bay Oaks, thinking of dresses, dances, decorations, and the hundred and one little things needing attention before tomorrow evening. My, but she prayed the weather would hold clear, though not so warm.

The sound of hoofbeats at full gallop claimed their attention. A lean rider soon emerged from the pines standing in the stirrups. He waved a creamy planter's hat and reined his black charger in their direction, drawing from Erasmus: "Purties' hoss in sebben states, and Mistuh Law'nce sholy can ride him."

That he could, Adria mused, watching how straight and graceful he sat the saddle. But then the only son of Leland Jarvis of Brier-lane, the largest plantation up in Marengo County, should excel in many things. As he rode up, with gray eyes flashing in a dark, hand-some face, bits of gossip about him popped into mind: wild as a Texan; fiery-tempered gambler; amiable gentleman until the fourth bourbon. But how he could dance and pay compliments to a lady. She gave him a smile.

"Pray tell me just why you're 'way down here, Lawrence Jarvis."

"Is there any doubt about it, Adria? I swear you're harder to track down than that old red fox from the bottom land. Was on my way to Mobile when I spotted a bobcat. Went to borrow Adam's hounds and learned you were down this way. The cat can wait."

"Bless me, the way you dote on hunting it's a wonder you ever got through the university. I hope to goodness you don't stumble over an old fox before my ball tomorrow evening."

"Ha!" He leaned toward her, pressing her hand in his. "If I do, I'll tip my hat and say, 'Sorry, suh. Now could I meet you here, say, come tomorrow?' "

"And if the fox knew how big your head usually is the day after a party, he'd agree to be there."

"How you talk!" His laugh rang pleasantly. "You'd think a man of twenty-three needed a guardian."

"Just a guide, dear Lawrence—to lead you away from the sideboard." Head cocked sidewise, she scolded by a mere quirk of her mouth and an instant's glance.

"I could use a right pretty guide. Permanently. Just when am I going to be honored with an answer to my question, honey?"

Making a pretense of deliberating the question, she replied, "In Southampton, England, last winter, a customs man said to Father, 'Sire, 'tis said patience is a law of the universe.' "

"Is that old peckerwood of an earl of something or other still penning you love poems?" At her taunting nod, he asked again when she would reply to his important question.

"Maybe New Year's Eve. Maybe during Mardi Gras, or—perhaps tomorrow night."

Her eyes narrowed on him, then fell to the saddle horn, purposely. Her lashes lifted innocently, inquiringly, to find in his face a mounting excitement which she chose to keep alive.

"Now be off, Lawrence. You make me forget almost what I'm here for." As he beamed under her pretty show of annoyance, she urged her horse into a walk. "And if you get your face bruised arguing about that old Abe Lincoln again, as on election night, I'll give the first dance to the ugliest man there."

Erasmus laughed when Lawrence rode off whistling. "Lawdy, she put him in a spirrut. He a good catch, all right, and she know he am, same as Marse Joseph know."

The slave scratched his white kinky head and felt right proud of Miss Adria. He remembered the day she arrived in this world as if it were only yesterday. Mammy Rose delivered her at three in the morning of July twenty-second back in 'forty-one. "Miss Annabel doin' fine," she beamed, and Marse Joseph poured good brandy for everyone, including the household slaves, all the while arguing with Miss Annabel's testy sister Eugenia over the name his daughter should bear. How they had badgered back and forth, with "Tut tuts," and "Preposterous! Perfectly horrible" from her, and no end of "dammit alls" from him. By six that morning Marse Joseph stalked the floor half drunk and his sister-in-law sat with arms folded across her chest glaring at him. At seven she said, "All right, you stubborn ox, we'll compromise." "Like hell we will, ma'am!" At eight they shook hands, he having his way with "Adria," she with "Temple." And eight-year-old Adam ran to tell his mother all about it. "Adria? Temple?" she said, gazing weakly at the pink baby bearing down on black Felicity's full udder. "Why, I had in mind Claribel. It means brightly fair in Latin." Fat Mammy Rose laughed so she shook like jelly. "Shuckin's, ma'am, we's in Alabamy. 'Sides, what rights yo'all got? All yo' done was born dat chile."

Erasmus had watched Adria grow up; pretty like her mother, headstrong like her father, everybody's pet. She ruled over Bay Oaks with smile and temper and guile; she turned pouting into an art even before the time she won over Aunt Eugenia and gave a party for Mammy Rose and Uncle Erasmus on their fiftieth birthdays. At fifteen she seemed mature. When she turned sixteen, Erasmus and Rose knew their little mistress had grown up.

There had been other changes at Bay Oaks. The loss of Mr. Adam, proclaimed the most ardent coon, cat, and fox hunter for his age in the county, to the bluestocking university at Tuscaloosa was felt all over the plantation. The expressions of sadness in his hounds' eyes entered his father's. But as long as cotton still came down the river there was hope that Marse Adam would return to stay. They waited, and time went by, and Bay Oaks under the sun witnessed plantings and harvestings, the coming of mills and factories that turned out shoes and furniture and plows and steamboats in God's own Alabama. But old cotton was still king, and Marse Adam had gone on to Annapolis and to the sea. "Dat ole ocean and him a land man, Rose!" The golden days were on the wane. When Miss Adria went off to school, Erasmus thought the flowers would never bloom again in the gardens of Bay Oaks. Then Miss Eugenia moved off to Galveston, Texas, and the hounds grew old, and Marse Joseph was getting so lonely he hadn't a temper any more—until someone would mention politics and the "money-lovin' Yankees" who wished to free the slaves. Only the mistress, beloved Annabel Cutler, remained the same in those prosperous but lonely years. It seemed she had enough patience for everyone.

Then Miss Adria returned, and Erasmus compared the change in the tempo of life at Bay Oaks to the coming of a palatial river boat, with string bands and steam calliopes playing the sweetest music this side of heaven. Life began anew. Young gentlemen came to pay call in elegant carriages. The big parties came again, and Marse Joseph shed his years, complained of this and that as though he meant it, and began losing his temper more often.

Grinning now, Erasmus remembered how he had beamed in his burgundy claw-hammer coat as he moved among the guests with trays of wine.

"Better peel your eyes for a holly," Adria called back.

"I is. I sholy is." Only the mule heard his chuckle and low-voiced elation. "T'morrer night yo' wears a new green coat, Erasmus Brown. Yassuh, at the mos' hifalutinest party ever throwed round Mobile!" His voice lifted with:

"Look over yonder, Miss Adria, at dat fat 'n' fine holly tree!"

She whirled her chestnut horse and circled the tree. "Splendid. I knew you'd find one," she said.

"Simply prayed dat tree up outen de groun', missy—on 'count I is already starvin' on hominy fo' Christmas. But it am bad luck to put it in de house yet."

Adria gave the mare free rein and raced ahead of the tree bearers toward the wide ornate iron gates of Bay Oaks. Great live oaks with long gray festoons of Spanish moss lined the driveway, which wound through gardens famous for their beauty in season to one of the most attractive homes in Mobile County. Stately white Doric columns supported the upper-story gallery that ran the full length of the house and shaded large green-shuttered windows, and a massive carved door crowned with intricately wrought fanlight and flanked by matching side lights. The entrance design was duplicated on the second floor, and the door opened on a lacy wrought-iron balcony where the family usually gathered to watch the traditional Christmas hunt. The presents were hidden on the front lawn and the excited slaves searched for them. Surmounting the mansion and sloping green roof, a white cupola, or observation tower, surrounded by a banistered "widow's walk," glistened in the tempered sunlight.

Adria rode on thinking of the party. Formal invitations had been issued. Tomorrow evening long lines of carriages would move up to the lighted front gallery, and thousands of candles would blaze in the long hall, the double parlors, which would be turned into a ballroom, and the banquet room. There would be laughter, much curtsying by belles in gorgeous silks. The ladies would be pretty, the men engaging, and all sociable and correct and bound by ties of kindness.

Oh, Bay Oaks was the greatest place in the world. Cotton was

wonderful. It made planters like her father and Leland Jarvis great
fortunes. Of course, the big cotton plantation was not near gay
Mobile, but upriver in Clarke County. At the Bay Oaks plantation
her father raised sugar cane, a little cotton, and some tobacco.
Rather, the Cutlers lived and entertained here in lavish style. When
they tired of it, they traveled here and there and, with other planters, made the European grand tour.

At the back of the house Adria gave the horse to a groom and
rushed up the steps and down the back gallery. She entered by a
side door, only to find Mammy Rose with hands at rest on broad
hips and a stern look on her face.

"She waitin', all right. Ain't I done teach you punctual? Ain't I?
Sho, yo' wants a dress what's elegant, but yo' don't wont——"

"Rattle! Rattle!" Adria retorted, disappearing hurriedly up a narrow back stairway. She raced down a long hall to her room, where
she stood panting a full minute before getting out of her clothes.
By the time she was ready to bathe, Mammy Rose entered the
room.

"Do' wide open and yo'all standin' nekkid as the day yo' was
born." She fussed about, bringing perfumed soap and towels. "Had
wa'm water waitin'. If it's cold now, 'tain't my fault."

Adria smiled absently, stepped to the fireplace, and began mas-
saging her waist where stays and petticoats had etched red lines
on her pink-white skin. Half listening to her mammy's mumbling,
she twisted her lithe young body defiantly and turned her back
to the fireplace a moment. When the door slammed shut, she walked
to a mirror and gazed at her own figure with exciting appraisal as
she saw herself in imagination the most beautifully dressed woman
at the ball.

The very thought caused her blood to warm and mount from her
loins to her throat. Her full, rounded breasts seemed to tingle and
her cheeks were flushed and hot. It was a delicious moment. Then
it was gone, completely evanescent, and she felt chilled and
ashamed, for every detail of her body, from the slope of her belly
to the mole on her neck, was revealed. Her breathing quickened.
Grimacing unduly, she loosed her wavy brown hair and tossed it
back in an impulsive gesture. It shone like silk against the smooth
magnolia-white skin of her shoulders. From some opening, perhaps
the fireplace as the wind shifted, a breath of cool air caused goose
flesh to cover her. Chilled and sobered, she shook her head as
though suddenly very tired.

"Fiddlesticks!" Looking up at Mammy Rose, she blurted forth, "I honestly do believe all this excitement and suspense is wearing me to a frazzle."

"Lawdy, chile, if that was so, you'd a spent most yo' life sick abed."

Adria smiled dreamily at the flowery chintz curtains. "I wonder if he's as handsome as Adam lets on he is."

"Hush up and put somethin' round yo'self. That seamstress woman ain't got the patience I is. There, she knockin' now."

Heavens alive, here she was nude! Hastily she clad herself in undergarments and stepped into one petticoat after another. The door opened upon a tall, bony-faced spinster with hair so black it seemed to further bleach her too white skin. But in her hands was a creation that took one's breath away. Miss Sally Drexel was a dear; that she was, despite her stern eyes, for she had fashioned a thing of beauty.

"Lawdy!" Mammy Rose simply stared in wonder when Adria stood in a ball gown of ashen-rose silk sprinkled with small bouquets of pink roses, the leaves and stems of palest green. "Bless me, honey!" Festoons of artificial silk roses to match the gorgeous print bordered a full skirt. Why, with elbow-length kid gloves and real roses at her waist, no one in all the Southland could hold a candle to Adria Temple Cutler.

"Raise de neck," Mammy ordered, eyes rolling and determined. "I say raise de neck." She went unnoticed. "I says raise it. 'Tain't safe not to!"

Adria had no ear for her; nothing but eyes for her lovely image in the mirror, that and the unseen gloved hand of a naval officer whom she had never met about her slim waist.

## 2.   And Mistletoe

1

"DEVIL take it all, Annabel, if them niggers don't show up soon with the cigars, I'll greet the menfolk with a face red as a turkey's wattle." Pausing before the fire with long figure stooped noticeably, a sure sign of sudden wrath, Joseph alternately fingered a red mustache tip and cast sidewise glances at his wife.

Her large eyes lifted and fell quickly, conveying some secret amusement; just like Adria's, he observed, except that Annabel had the wisdom of maturity to mask her thoughts with expressions of tolerance. He had no sooner shaped such a comparison than she proved again she was her daughter's mother.

"It's already that red, dear." Nor would she so much as glance up from the tuck she was taking in his best muslin shirt to witness his look of indignation. Bushy brows met. He walked away and back again, murmuring unintelligibly, but thinking: Annabel was damned attractive for her years. Now take the mistress of Magnolia Hill Plantation—younger than Annabel, provocative, very exciting, though shallow by comparison. She would be here, of course, and oddly enough he was looking forward to the widow's visit.

The downstairs seethed like a beehive with shining-eyed domestics engaged in numerous last-minute chores. A black boy stacked firewood, since the chill air warned of low temperatures, and Erasmus, in green claw tails so new the store smell lingered, white silk waistcoat, and dark pantaloons, passed out final instructions to his black ushers. Others unlimbered trays, polished tiny spots from silver service, busied themselves replacing and lighting candles throughout the house, while back in the kitchen cooks basted ducks and turkeys and shelled fat oysters for skewering later in the evening. Boys merrily at work chipping New England ice into tubs filled with bottles of imported champagne got underfoot all too often.

"Time Adam arrived, don't you think, Annabel?"

"He'll get here. Abel's waiting at the dock."

"This Lieutenant Hillyer—do you suppose he's our kind of Southerner? Maryland is somewhat Yankee-minded, you know. In fact——" A commotion outside claimed his attention. "Adam, maybe," he said, excited. It turned out to be Monsieur Perrone and his seven-piece Negro orchestra from New Orleans.

"As I was saying in this madhouse—— Now what? Oh, thank you, 'Rasmus. Just what I needed. Be sure there's plenty more on the sideboard." Dashing off the bourbon with a smack of his lips, he stared thoughtfully at the fire. "Better go dress." He looked at his spouse, adding, "I suppose."

"There," she said with relief, extending the shirt.

"God 'lmighty, Annabel, how can you be so calm at a time like this?"

Her mouth curved into a smile that he could only describe as being devilish, especially when her large eyes were full upon him, as now.

She took his arm and guided him to the front of the house. "We'll take a last look before dressing. By that time Adam should——" Pausing, with lower lip drawn under her teeth, she was a woman in critical judgment of decorations that appeared in perfect arrangement to her husband. "Place that vase on the marble-topped table, Joseph dear." He obeyed. "That's better," she said, and he frowned approvingly. "Joseph, I suggest you warn Erasmus to delay extra servings of hard liquor to Mr. Lawton. Remember the last two occasions?" He remembered well Lawton's behavior. "Also, I trust you haven't forgotten that Nellie Sisson can't turn a leg to any tune."

Joseph made a wry smile, not quite covering the deviltry in his eye as he admitted silently to enjoying the time spent in teaching her this step and that.

The broad hallway was flooded in mellow candlelight emanating from sconces and a single chandelier that hung from an arch midway between the fanlights. Two fluted Doric columns supported the arch on each side and at the right rear of the hall a stairway curved gracefully to a landing. Here and there holly sprays and ornaments gaily announced the season, while twin vases of yellow flowers near the columns seemed to proclaim a yearlong welcome.

Joseph and Annabel had patterned Bay Oaks after a great house in Natchez, Mississippi, and watched it rise into a structure of rare beauty in 1847.

The rich years that followed were not measured by Annabel in terms of land, slaves, and cotton. Family, friends, and events seasoned the great halls and drawing rooms of Bay Oaks. There was always activity of one kind or another. People, friends or relatives, came to "spend the day" or week. There were formal and informal parties, and often the hunters and hounds commenced a day at dawn. Actually, it seemed quite lonely when no extra horses appeared at the mounting block.

Just thinking of the good times caused Annabel's eyes to mist over and the tip of her nose to redden.

Taking his cue from her nose, Joseph decided that this was another of her emotional flurries that went with a change of life, no doubt, and proceeded to usher her hurriedly up the stairs. At the landing she seemed herself again—dammit all, never lacking in surprises—for she turned on him with:

"I hope you didn't invite that schoonerman Sherrod here tonight. Is it true that he hired a crew of niggers in New York and sold them in Mobile?"

"Northern propaganda, nothing more, even though I don't like the man. You know as well as I do that what they say in England is true, that New York is the slave capital of the world. Only Yankee ships run slaves."

"Yes, I know all that, but did you invite Captain Sherrod here tonight?"

"I did not. He's too notorious for——"

"And just this once, Joseph dear, don't corner Leland Jarvis with talk about a match between Adria and Lawrence."

He stiffened. "Madam, I don't think she could do better. I'm ready to give my consent tonight or any other time three thousand acres of cotton land is thrown at my daughter's feet."

"Of course, Joseph, it's only that I wish you'd refrain from helping Leland and Lawrence throw it." She moved on without even turning her head.

He stared after her. Angry, he thought of a dozen replies, but too late. A confounding woman, Annabel, but a remarkable one. As he passed her room, the door opened suddenly a few inches and she placed a note in her voice that caused his heart to skip a beat: "Joseph."

He entered and slowly closed the door. She was a handsome woman, one obviously doing her utmost to avoid his glance. Small wonder Adria was half guile. But who would imagine this female he had taken as a bride on her sixteenth birthday was the mother of a son going on twenty-eight? Dark hair cascading down over her bared shoulders, fine mature bosom gently heaving, a single petticoat veiling her small figure—by thunder, she was stronger than bourbon! She kissed him lightly, and said something about not wishing to offend him down at the landing, though there was absolutely nothing of what she was saying in her eyes.

"Better get dressed, dear, if we're to meet Adam downstairs." She added, "But you'll have to help me out of the dress after the ball. Heavens, I'll be lucky to get into it!"

In the hall Joseph raised his voice to Erasmus. "A glass of champagne for my wife! Hear me?"

Hear him? Joseph chuckled. Hell, there was little doubt that the order was heard as far away as the Mobile docks.

2

The shining candle lamps on each side of the Cutler coach-and-four evoked excitement that penetrated the slave quarters in swift seconds. Before the matched sorrel horses reached the gate, the cry "Marse Adam!" preceded a wholesale exodus into the open. Fat mammies collided with barefoot youngsters and old men hobbling along with the aid of hickory canes. One slave had the presence of mind to lead old Jupiter on a chain to a reunion of master and favorite hound. "Dat po' ole houn' dog so toothless he puff out his cheeks to bark." "Shut up, woman. Once he see Marse Adam he sprout a whole new set." Big Abel, in tail coat and black silk top hat, sat high in the driver's seat. With eyes and teeth gleaming, he very importantly ordered the "niggers" to get out of the way. Marse Adam was home. The porch filled, and the doors of the house opened just as a pair of tall men in navy blue stepped from the carriage.

"Adam!" Joseph ran ahead of Annabel, who stood at the steps taking in her son with eager eyes. My, how brown and stalwart he appeared. Why had they fetched the hound? Now his dirty paws were all over Adam's chest. And Adam didn't seem to object; rather, he hugged the creature and twisted his long ears affectionately. The clamoring slaves all sought Adam's attention, some succeeding. A few heard their names called and beamed under the honor.

Presently she felt his searching glance, the sudden arresting of the blood in her veins and subsequent quickening of her pulses. She saw the melting softness come into his dark eyes, and she felt him already in her arms, locked in her heart, before he took a step in her direction. Moments later he was tilting her chin and smiling down upon her.

"Hello, pink nose," he said softly.

"It is not! Besides, you hugged Jupiter first."

"He got there first." He kissed her then.

Erect, broad-shouldered Lieutenant James Hillyer stood near a front carriage wheel. Although he seemed entirely abandoned, the set grin on his full, sun-reddened face pushed up friendly wrinkles about his eyes, which, under raised brows, squinted approval of all he saw. He removed his cap in perfunctory manner, revealing close-cropped, curly hair the color of sand, and looked up at the rows of columns highlighted on the inner side. Soon his wandering eyes came to an abrupt halt on a small balcony above the entrance where a vision in pale rose silk caught and held his attention.

Instantly aware that she was engaged in unabashed study of him, and inwardly embarrassed at being caught thus, he tensed and stiffened. This would be Temple, of course, he decided, meeting her intent gaze. Adam's remarks flashed through his mind: "Queen of all she surveys, tyrant, wheedler, a good one to have on your side, grandest sister in the world." The porch lights threw shadows of her bosom and face upward, creating an untrue picture that left him curiously unsatisfied.

However, he was not blind to the demands she made upon him. Some gesture was due. Although he did not relish the devilishly awkward feeling of being taken apart piece by piece, it was something else to be found wanting in common grace.

He made his bow and felt amply rewarded by her brief smile and curtsy. Then Adam was leading him to the porch.

When he looked up again, the balcony was empty. Ushered inside, he found himself under the polite scrutiny of Adam's parents, whose genuine welcome surpassed even his fondest expectations. In the whirl of his mind were appreciation of the beauty of Bay Oaks, the irresistible charm of Adam's mother, reminding him in a way of his maternal parent, the sincere hospitality of Joseph Cutler, who made it evident that by sheer power of will or prior command he withheld questions that had to do with the seething political issues of the time. Not the least in his mind was the girl on the balcony, and perhaps his glances at doorways revealed his secret, for the hostess advised that he might not meet Adria before she stood in the receiving line. Warmed with welcome, he was shown to his room. A half hour later Adam, in naval dress uniform, entered swinging a liquor bottle. Pouring, he said:

"Fortify yourself, sir, before ordering the beat to quarters. Aye, for my sister Temple just walked down the stairs rigged out for conquest."

They touched glasses, drank lightly. "Adam, your mother called her Adria."

"Her name is Adria Temple. She despises the Adria."

"I rather like it."

"You're to be congratulated, Jim. My sister should have been my little brother. She's the outdoor girl, horses, hounds, good eye for horseflesh or crops, and all that. Why, the greatest cross Mother bore was Temple's disregard of bonnets and gloves to ward off the burning Alabama sun. No eye for gentlemen, none whatever."

"Odd. Odd indeed. But the devil with you, Adam! Seems you're ribbing me. Didn't you say she was rigged out for conquest?"

"That I did." Adam looked solemn. "I meant acres of good land, not men." Endeavoring to hide the humor forcing its way into his expression, he said in wishful tones, "Now maybe you could change all that. Damned if you wouldn't earn Mother's everlasting gratitude."

Lieutenant Hillyer frowned and tugged at the sandy growth of his upper lip before turning on his friend. "Look here, Adam Cutler. Did you steer me into this port for that reason? If you did, 'twas a damned treacherous thing to do."

"Keep your voice down, sailor. Here, have a cigar." When James stiffened a trifle and refused, Adam brought a disarming smile into play. "Course I didn't invite you here for that, though it's deserving of earnest consideration. Aye, that it is."

Thinking now, as he had a dozen times aboard ship, that dear Jim must have been a grown man even in childhood, Adam forced a thawing grin from his guest with a friendly slap on the shoulder before masking challenge with banter.

"Come along, Admiral Co-Co, and see how long you can stay afloat without striking the colors."

The first glimpse of Adria under tawny candlelight caused the Marylander a sudden start. He became lost to all else as he stood in his tracks staring in open amazement at a girl of medium height with lustrous brown hair and the smallest waist he had ever set eyes upon. Lord above, Adam was surely blind, for here was a contradiction of all the brother had implied. His breath quickened in appreciation of the exquisite curves of her young but mature figure, which seemed more revealed than hidden by a shimmering ball gown, though it was her face that held him in a state of pleasant shock. Her forehead was smooth and rather noble, with natural eyebrows delicately arched above restless brown eyes. The word "vibrant" seemed to adequately describe her, though there was doubt in his mind that any one word could do her justice.

He became suddenly aware of her regard. It was more a hasty glance of appraisal, briefly upon him, now swinging away as more guests arrived to compel her attention. Then her intense eyes met his, and her small but full mouth, after assuming all sorts of gracious expressions of welcome, magically curved into a sultry smile that he had seldom received from a woman in her high position. He felt the blood leaping warm at his temples and neck as she surveyed him down the length of his dress uniform and up again.

Summoning composure, he said, "Adam, she's too wonderfully fair to fit your description." He looked over his shoulder to find himself alone, though when he turned to face her again, Joseph Cutler was reaching for his arm, saying:

"Adam should hang from a yardarm. Disgraceful manners on his part, sir, you a whole hour in our house without having met my daughter. Now, here . . ."

Standing before her, hearing introductions as though over a horizon, James felt her challenge sweeping like a tropic gale clear through him. Her very nearness and a scent of perfume were like wine suddenly reaching up to consume him.

How his heart hammered when her bright red lips parted over even white teeth and she addressed him with, "I've looked forward to this meeting, Lieutenant Hillyer. And it seems I've heard so much about you that you've become James. You won't mind, will you?"

Managing a proper reply and nod, James stepped briskly in search of something fiery to slow his fast heartbeat.

For James the occasion presented one thrill after another, all minor by comparison to the big one, of course. But Adam seemed genuinely proud to present him, even to proposing a toast to "my shipmate" in the company of gentlemen who proved beyond any doubt that Southern hospitality was as much in evidence in Alabama as in Virginia. Maryland could hardly qualify as a paragon due to her divided sympathies on paramount issues. Strangely, a young planter was asking which way the lieutenant's home state would go if the "nigger lovers" forced a decision. James did not know. Conversations ran toward hunting and hounds, the price of cotton, slaves and whisky, returning always to the strained relations between the North and South.

Plantation owner Jarvis remarked upon Yankee shrewdness with feeling. "They're disguising the real issue by circulating all sorts of tales about our cruelty to the niggers. Mind yo', Lieutenant Hillyer, the real or trumped-up beatings and rape of our niggers which we're accused of are a blind to the No'th's aim to strangle our prosperity. The gentlemen from New England covet our wealth and cheap labor. Afraid we'll start manufacturing shoes and machinery on a big scale." The planter added, looking straight at James, "Suh, you've kindly put up with my harangue, so I'd be right proud to listen to your opinions."

"Indeed. So would I," Joseph Cutler put in eagerly.

James felt the unwelcome pressure of respectful silence. Wincing under the attention of the half dozen or more dyed-in-the-wool Southerners, Adam no exception, he sought to temporize.

"Being a naval man, and no scholar in the science of economics, I can only remark on a fact so pertinent it's often overlooked. In bad times the plantation owner is forced to feed and clothe his slaves, whereas the Northern manufacturer simply lays off his hands. I doubt if he'd trade places with any of you."

"A fact," Jarvis responded with zeal. "I never thought of it that way, did you, Joseph? So who's brutal, the plantation man or the Yankee moneygrubber? Lieutenant, suh, my compliments to a true Southerner."

Adam smiled wisely while James breathed with relief, pleased to have gotten out of it so easily. His true sympathies were better left unvoiced here; or so he was thinking, when a handsome young man with an impetuous look in his eye addressed him.

"How do you feel about secession, suh?"

Jarvis said, "My son Lawrence, Lieutenant. My apologies to both of you. Reckon I thought you two had met."

For a minute or so James thought he had escaped the issue, for a large man with great mustaches was launching forth with some justification, James admitted, into the worn subject of states' rights. "Since 1816, gentlemen, the fat Southern goose has been plucked by Yankee tariffs. And now we are told by Northern papers, and from a thousand pulpits up there, that the issue is a moral one—slavery. The whole thing is trumped up to hide a purely political matter. Where's mah drink?"

"In yo' hand, Sam." A laugh followed.

"Beggin' pardon, Ralph, mah glass is. But it's empty, like the Yankees want our pockets. To prove it, the North exports practically nothing, while the exports of the South are the basis for Federal revenue.

"Did you know, gentlemen, that Virginia, the C'linas, and Georgia alone defray more than half the annual expense of supporting the Federal Gov'ment? Do you doubt it, Lieutenant Hillyer?"

"I'm sure the facts will bear you out, sir," James replied to this unwanted attention.

"Damn right. And small wonder President Buchanan denied a

state the right of secession in his speech to Congress on the third of this month."

"Sam is right," Joseph said. "It's a matter of money and politics. But say this for Buchanan, he said in the same speech the Constitution gave him no right to coercion."

Lawrence Jarvis once more placed his question. How did James feel about a state's right to secede?

James pondered the question less than his reply. Smiling rather painfully, he said, "Begging your pardon, sir, we in the naval service consider it imprudent to air our opinions."

Adam intervened when the face of young Jarvis underwent a change. "Jim didn't mean to sound stiff, Lawrence. But it so happens that he spoke the truth, and it applies here the same as in the Brooklyn Navy Yard." His hand fell to Lawrence's shoulder. "Saves us a hell of a lot of trouble aboard ship and off."

Lawrence stood stiffly erect, eyes too bright and pointed. "My apologies for placing an embarrassing question, Lieutenant. However, suh, when the time is right, I hope to have the honor of repeating the question."

He bowed and turned away.

The elder Jarvis fell all over himself making amends. His son was, he vowed, hotheaded at times. "But, suh, he cools quick as fresh butter in a no'ther."

The lieutenant from Maryland was exceedingly upset. "Sure," he replied to Adam's entreaties, "I'll forget it. I meant no insult. None at all." However, he continued to brood over the awkward situation he had most unwittingly brought about. The young planter was astonishingly quick-tempered.

James was taking on a bourbon when he felt the admiring gaze of a small woman of extraordinary attractiveness. She was clad in a crimson gown. He observed with rising interest that she had hair the color of a raven's wing, a complexion as white as alabaster, and a figure likely to attract men for years to come. At his request, Adam brought them together.

Miss Faustine Beaumont, down from Selma, lifted a pair of dark friendly eyes. "We've heard so many nice things about you, Lieutenant Hillyer," she began. "Even your gallantry is up for notice."

Surprised, James stammered, "Gallantry? Why, I—I don't know what I've done to deserve that."

"Now wasn't it you who rescued a marine from a heavy sea off the China coast last year?"

"Oh, that?" he replied with becoming modesty. "I just happened to be at the rail when the lad went over the side. It's worth a wager that Adam was forced to think hard to dig up that one."

"We've found our Adam most sincere." Her hand touched James's arm. "And usually correct in his judgment of people."

He nodded, watching her small red mouth part in a smile. "I understand, sir, that you're very senior on the promotion list. So you see, dear Lieutenant, we know more about you than you think."

James liked her low, throaty drawl and that almost imagined edge of accent congruous to her French name. Her gracious smile pleased him as much as her deeply penetrating glance, which slid demurely away just when something conveyed seemed snatched out of his grasp.

As they talked of this and that, he found himself believing that this lovely young woman was not one to act on impulse; rather, she seemed to plan carefully her every word and gesture. She looked to be at least twenty-five, perhaps older. He was a poor judge of such things.

Once her eyes leaped into sharp focus, causing James to follow her gaze until it came to rest on Adria. Then he could not help feeling the existence of sudden enmity between the two women. When Lawrence Jarvis escorted Adam's sister to the dance floor, Faustine sheathed her black eyes and favored James with a smile that was both possessive and demanding.

3

As Monsieur Perrone's orchestra brought the dance to an end, Adria whirled and sent her eyes searching the crowd of merrymakers.

"What's wrong, honey? You haven't said a doggone word since——"

"Please, Lawrence, I could do with a glass of champagne."

Rid of her ardent suitor, Adria moved hurriedly across the floor. Presently she engaged the couple next to Lieutenant Hillyer and raised her voice in welcome. Sure enough, James looked her way, and she dropped her lashes and lifted them quickly. But Faustine had missed nothing of the byplay. Now she was placing a gloved arm in the lieutenant's; rather, thought Adria, she was slithering it home and shrugging white shoulders in a deliberate gesture intended to draw his attention to the daring low cut of her gown.

There followed a melting look of adoration accompanied by cooing sounds as Faustine steered him toward an exit.

Adria glared. The devil with such purring affectation! Of course it wasn't the lieutenant's fault. He didn't know that cuddly Faustine Beaumont was out of necessity trying to make a good catch. Her merchant father had gone broke and committed suicide late in 'fifty-nine. But what was the Navy coming to when one of its trusted officers surrendered under a first barrage of guile?

Demoting gullible James Hillyer far down her list, Adria turned a devastating smile on young Dr. Bolton, who immediately deserted his middle-aged wife for promising conquest over champagne. Lawrence claimed her soon after, and she left the doctor speculating beyond reasonable bounds. Perhaps she should blush with shame, though in her pulsed a passionate eagerness to taunt anyone wearing pants.

Then dear, ever observant Adam was at her side. "I saw it all, Adria. You're downright bold."

"Direct is the word," she corrected icily. "But you're no saint yourself. Look, Adam, do me a favor just this once."

"Faustine?" He looked almost pleased.

"Show her the gardens or fields in the starlight." She kissed him on the cheek. "You're a dear!"

Watching him moving across the floor, she could not help reiterating, "You're a dear." Adam was. She admired her brother, almost worshiped him. He had bearing and charm. Never had she seen him at a loss for composure. To be sure, she did not condone Adam's adventures in love-making, however shockingly interesting some few had been; so she had heard. Of course he did not suspect his little sister of being even remotely acquainted with incidents of his private life, particularly a most recent affair with a Creole beauty in New Orleans. But with gossip as thick as syrup in winter, it was not difficult to learn a little here and there.

Bother! Lawrence haunted her like a shadow. "Where is my champagne?" she demanded.

"Where were you? Honest, Adria, if I didn't know better, I'd swear you were trying to dodge me."

"How could you! But I've promised the next dance to Adam's guest. Say you don't mind, sweet."

Under her smile, he melted; until he saw the look she was giving the naval officer from Baltimore. Stifling an oath, he stalked to the door and on into the cool air of the porch.

The blood flowed warm into Adria's bosom when she felt the enchanted blue eyes of Lieutenant Hillyer taking in her face and figure again. How inordinately happy she was when he tucked her arm in his and escorted her into a minuet; with no word spoken between them to dispel the things they were saying to each other in silence. He seemed so large and handsome in blue, heavy gold buttons shining, with his every step gracefully, perfectly, timed to the music. The dance ended all too soon.

"I'm selfish," he said. "If I could have one wish, it would be for every dance with you, Temple."

Temple? Annoyed, she looked away. So Adam had done it. What else had he told this man? "But I'm sure you are promised to Miss Beaumont," she said, withdrawing her hand from his. "She dances divinely, don't you think, Lieutenant Hillyer?"

"I thought you were going to call me James."

"Did I say that, really? Father warned me not to mix champagne and brandy. But I do the strangest things, which I'm sure Adam has already told you."

He looked incredulous. "You! You—mixed brandy with——? Perhaps you'd enjoy a breath of fresh air, Temple."

"Yes. Yes, indeed. Would you mind?"

"You'll need a wrap."

"No. Now what else has my dear brother said about me? Heavens to Betsy, I hope he didn't tell you I was a widow! Oh, I shouldn't have said that."

"Widow!" he exclaimed, freezing to a standstill, gloved hand tightening on the doorknob.

"Don't look so shocked, sir. My father arrived at the end of the ceremony and horsewhipped poor Hilary—he was the overseer's boy. That was the last I saw of him." Her wistful eyes slowly dropped.

She enjoyed the horrified frown in a face suddenly gone white and faintly tinged with green. She would give him something to carry back to traitorous Adam, all right. Or was he the type of fellow who carried his disappointments in silence? In any case, he made it evident that she had taken the wind out of his sails.

When the chill wind of the porch sent a shudder through her, he gallantly removed his coat, saying, "There, Temple. I can't have you exposed to the weather. No, no, I'm used to it. Really I am."

If he called her Temple once more, she would scream, or do something equally as disgraceful. And he was thinking, "My God, I never imagined this!" even as he smiled and made every effort to appear comfortably warm. Then he sneezed, and she laughed.

"I'm sorry, James. I don't mix drinks, and I've never been married. I confess I did it because you called me Temple. You see, I don't like Temple. I'm Adria. Only Adria."

James seldom acted on impulse, though seldom if ever had he met any girl as tremendously stimulating as this one. In the instant he raised her chin with a finger and tipped his head to her. The brief touch of his lips to her cheek sent his head spinning as though a tropic wave were cresting through every fiber of his body.

She stood very still, large eyes wide and luminous with flickering amber lights. Then her red lips parted in a breathless whisper. "You shouldn't have, James."

He told himself over and over that he must gain self-possession. She was Adam's sister. He had no right. She had given him no reason. But she had! Every reason! She could not have aroused him more had she caressed his cheeks with fingers of fire and raised her quivering lips to his.

His arms trembled as they crushed the yielding softness of her body to him. He pressed his mouth fiercely against hers, and they stood there blind to the world about them one long moment. Then she was pushing him away, saying:

"How could I—what must you think of me, James?" She leaned against the wall for support, the slim fingers of one hand covering her open mouth. She whirled and put her back to him. "Whatever possessed me?"

"Temple—er—Adria!" He had gone contrite, though his hands seemed unaware of the emotion as they clutched at her shoulders. "I'm sorry, Adria." Then he was saying, "But I'm not! I'm glad!"

Slowly she turned her head, then her body. "Glad?" she said curiously, in such a way that he was bracing himself for her wrath when her arms reached with amazing swiftness for his neck.

"So am I glad, James. Now kiss me again before I change my mind."

4

It seemed they had no sooner entered the ballroom than the orchestra stopped playing in the middle of a reel. Still breathless and trying to hide the flush of her cheeks, Adria accepted a glass of champagne and raised it to her lips. She did not drink, for her father was stepping to the dais. Dear Lord above! He was asking for the attention of his guests. Heaven help her and her dear mother if he had drunk too much.

The room seemed so very quiet that Adria was sure the bubbles in her glass broke noisily. Tense, she subconsciously pressed a hand to her bosom to stop the hammering inside her.

"Ladies and gentlemen," he was saying. He appeared sober enough, though Adria could not be sure. "Ladies and gentlemen, as your host tonight, I consider it my duty and privilege to acquaint you with important news just received in Mobile by telegraph.

"Today South Carolina exercised its right of secession and withdrew from the Union."

Adria's eyes closed as a great sigh of relief escaped her. "Thank heavens it's nothing worse."

The corners of her mouth were primly tucked in as she directed a smile up at James. To her surprise, a deep V formed between his eyes; his gaze seemed alternately sharp and troubled. The orchestra began the reel music as though nothing had interrupted the festivities at Bay Oaks, though there was no dancing whatever. Pursing her lips, Adria pondered the significance of secession, a most uninteresting and much discussed subject these days. Particularly since the party opposed to slavery had won a victory in the national election of November 1860. They called themselves Republicans. Southerners called them Black Republicans.

Adria studied the faces of the guests. Mrs. Thompson retained her gay expression, while Mrs. Clayborn, a distant relative from Mississippi, appeared somewhat upset. Further observation was interrupted when a state official from Montgomery halted the inappropriate music and proposed a toast to the "brave and honorable Governor Pickens of South C'lina."

"Louder," cried Dr. Bolton. "So President Buchanan can hear it! I'd hate to be in his shoes tonight."

"He's lucky, Doc—goin' out of office in March. By that time old Abe Lincoln will find half the states gone."

As the demonstration continued, with fervent toasts to the cotton-and-magnolia Southland punctuated by popping corks, gentlemen offered excuses to their ladies and drifted toward the library. The exodus was fast depleting the ballroom of males when Adria raised her glass, excitement bright in her expression.

"James, you're neglecting me most noticeably."

"Oh! Why, forgive me, Adria." He offered a gold-striped sleeve. "The news staggered me momentarily. It has a warlike ring."

Taking his arm, she smiled right through Faustine Beaumont. "I do declare, James," she breathed exultantly, "war is the last thing those money-worshiping abolitionists want. I believe a little wine might restore you."

Erasmus soon bowed before them. "It bubbles nice, Miss Adria, chile," he said, holding the tray of tall-stemmed glasses. "Y' knows, I'se believin' almos' yo' wuz right 'bout that holly tree not bringin' bad luck to a house befo' Christmas Eve. Things is uncommon lucky tonight. Yes'm, hit sholy is."

Adria became suddenly aware of James's interest in something or someone to his left, and followed his sharpened gaze. He was looking at the holly tree.

An indefinable uneasiness gripped her, though she fought it off and slipped her arm into his. A comforting warmth spread from her fingertips through her as a hand slid over navy blue and into his.

## 3.    Plantation Moon

### 1

THE GREEN AND WHITE CUTLER CARRIAGE rolled away from the lights of Mobile and on into the crisp January night. The rhythmic clop-clopping of the four horses, the groaning of coach joints and muffled rattle of wheels were broken only by humming sounds from Abel up on the high seat. Oblivious to the occupants of the carriage, the slave fondly touched the silk hat on his head, raised the muffler higher about his neck, and launched forth into a song:

> *Geese in de pond and ducks in de ocean,*
> *Ho—dee—ink—tum—diddle—ah—dee—day;*
> *Devil's in de women when dey takes a notion——*

Mammy Rose stuck her head out the window. "You dere, Abel! Miss Adria say fo' hebbens sake sing somethin' else. Hear me?"

"Is I deef?"

Inside the coach Mammy looked at Adria, then at James. "Dat nigger gittin' too big fo' his britches. Him in a silk hat. Humph!"

James chuckled. "Maybe we're spoiling him."

"You can say dat again, Lootenant. Traipsin' round ebber night. Mah honey chile gwine shrivel to skin and bones the way she carry on. Chris'mus, New Year, in between. And den some mo'. Dis heah hack go back 'n' foth to Mobile so much it pick its way 'thout no driver."

Adria drew the lap robe about her waist and watched the moon-bathed trees go past the window. Mammy spoke the truth, she admitted in dreamy silence. But the wonderful days were slipping away all too soon. January was more than a week old. She had counted every hour, hoping to prolong James's stay by virtually commanding time to stand still.

"New dresses," Mammy Rose grumbled. "Alluz got to hab new ones. Dozens already, but got to hab mo'. Aunt Fay, Bay Oaks's dressmaker won't do. Downright 'stravagant."

"Haven't I told you a chaperon should remain silent?"

Mammy Rose got in a retort before squirming into a more comfortable position.

Adria shrugged off a sense of guilt as she recalled the demands she had made on her mother and grumpy Miss Sally Drexel amid the whirl of holiday parties and dances. Often she left them gasping or shaking their heads in despair of her. And Lawrence! How he scowled, vowing he should chase the Marylander all the way to the Pensacola Navy Yard. She was glad Adam kept him occupied by following after the hounds and embroiling him in talk about the silly business of South Carolina's seizing Fort Moultrie from the Federals and threatening to drive the United States forces from Fort Sumter, property of the seceded state. It seemed so foreign and distant, as was the added excitement in Louisiana, Mississippi, Florida, and Alabama, all warming with debates over secession. James was showing concern. Even now he seemed lost in serious thought.

"Where is your mind, sir?" she asked.

"Oh." He started. "Just thinking. I suppose Adam told you we received orders to report to Pensacola on the twelfth."

"Why, no!" She stared incredulously. "But your leave was for thirty days."

He sighed hopelessly. "I know. However, with the naval base at

Pensacola and Florida hot under the collar, all furloughs are cancelled."

Adria sat back in an effort to absorb the shock. The very idea of Florida doing this to her. She was fast getting out of sorts with the neighboring states. And her father was cheering them on, praising the senator from Mississippi, Jefferson Davis, as the greatest leader of Southern constitutionalists in the defense of states' rights.

"What a terrible mess men make of politics," she said.

Adria supposed nothing could be perfect. Always, just when everything seemed in harmony with her wishes, something had to happen. First Faustine. And now this. However, the lady from Selma posed the major problem. Faustine became competitive on the night of the ball. Then next day she trapped James for a steamboat ride down to Fort Gaines and back. Following that miserable day, in which jealousy almost consumed Adria, a party of ladies and gentlemen on horseback went out to drive partridges into nets spread for them, Faustine with James again, she with Lawrence. Couples fanned out for the drive, though when next they assembled, James and Faustine were missing. They were down at the cypress brake on the river when she came upon them and eavesdropped without any compunction whatever. Unladylike, to be sure, but she watched and listened. They were seated on a log, and Faustine was tracing imaginary designs on James's sleeve with her riding crop, saying:

"You must tell me more about the Chinese, Lieutenant."

James's grin was broad. "I must admit I've never met anyone who appreciated my account of a trying cruise quite so much."

Faustine's eyes flickered sidewise under an almost feline play of her lashes, which seemed to hold him in delighted fascination. "Some people are gifted storytellers. Now Adam would try to cover the entire voyage with a few impatient words. Odd, you two, bosom friends and yet so different in many ways." She paused. "How long have you known each other?"

"Since that first uneasy day we entered Annapolis. Have scarcely been separated since. Somehow we've managed to call the same wardroom home afloat. And we plan to keep it that way."

"Suppose Alabama secedes and Maryland doesn't—what then?"

"Ho!" James stood, touched a finger to her nose, and wrinkled his brow. "That head of yours is too pretty to bother with such nonsense."

For a long moment Faustine's gaze remained fixed on him. Then she arose and tripped on a limb—purposely, Adria thought—and fell toward him. Quick as a flash she was in his arms, staring wide-eyed up into his face, cherry-red lips parted in simulated fright. Adria remembered how her own heart stood still as neither made an effort to break that pose for breathless seconds in which James colored and seemed about to tip his head to her waiting mouth. Perhaps he would have done just that had she not startled them out of their wits by driving her horse toward them at a full gallop and loosing a cry: "Partridge!" Then, reining up sharply, she added, as Faustine's black eyes flashed daggers by the dozen, "Pretty partridge."

Then, at Mrs. Le Flore's afternoon tea, Faustine went beyond monopolizing James, actually she fluttered over him with such possessiveness that Amy Wardlaw was heard to ask if the handsome lieutenant was affianced to her. And poor gullible James! Why, he purred like a cat in a cream jar.

That was yesterday. James sat beside her now. She pursed her lips lest a threatening secret smile break into the open. Several days earlier she had volunteered to convey Louise Thurmond's invitation for tonight to Faustine in person. Somehow she just hadn't gotten around to it, and now the dance at Moss Side was over. "What a dreadful oversight," she would say to both parties.

Adria wished to snuggle close to James's uniform, though she didn't dare; and Mammy Rose's head nodding drowsily despite her effort to stay awake had nothing to do with it. She had refused to so much as allow his arm about her since the night of the ball. Furthermore, she had responded to his perplexed inquiries with sincere assertions that she had been drunk on excitement that night and would forever chastise herself for such unbecoming conduct. In her own heart Adria believed that any relation founded on make-believe or insincerity could never survive. Therefore, with an almost child-like faith that correct behavior would win over Faustine's guile and constant blandishments, she told herself she was content to keep James's conquest of her on a higher plane than their first meeting.

Fingering the brooch at her bosom, Adria frowned in thought. Only a few short days remained. Then he would leave her. For the first time in her life she was seriously, desperately, in love.

The coach lurched around the bend leading to the old ferry and threw her against James. His arm went instantly about her shoulders and in his eyes burned a light that held her suspended, unable to move or think, for long moments in which he seemed about to kiss her.

Then he removed his arm and, avoiding her glance, gazed at the bluff overlooking the river. There in the pale fall of moonlight the white columns of Bay Oaks shone through the trees like tiny phosphorescent needles.

James remarked on the beauty of the nightscape before whispering in her ear, "I must talk to you alone. Tonight."

Adria's eyes seemed to dance with excitement, though she managed to keep them fixed on the bluff. Her nod of assent barely preceded Mammy Rose's coming awake with a start.

"As far back as I can remember we gathered flowers from that bluff," Adria said dreamily. "You should see the coral honeysuckle and yellow jasmine in bloom. The perfume carries upriver and boatmen love to anchor there in the springtime."

James heard her words and voice, though in half detachment. The arrival of orders evoked into being sharp pangs of regret, and more. Perhaps he had stayed too long. At first it had seemed a gay holiday adventure, a lark, another conquest or two, events to smile back on over an ocean wave, memories absorbed by routine and forgotten with the piping of the watch. But orders had come, and with them the discovery that he was in love.

She was saying ever so softly, "The old house was on the bluff. Along the walk under the crape myrtle Father asked Mother to marry him."

Under the robe James's hand closed over Adria's and she could feel the throbbing of his pulse, as he no doubt felt hers. She breathed a contented sigh and rested her head on the back of the seat, satisfied to watch his face and sit near him. Being in love was a strain on a lady, but how wonderful it was. How very, very wonderful.

2

As the gates opened, Mammy Rose came alive. "Ebber candle in de house lit up and sebben hosses in de yard. At nigh on to midnight! What's folks comin' to?"

"Probably Adam's deer club," Adria said.

"Which ain't killed nothin' bigger'n a whisky bottle."

Abel placed the iron ladder at the carriage door, helped the couple alight, then drove off with Mammy. Feeling herself being propelled toward the shadow cast by a thick oak trunk, Adria looked up inquiringly.

"Why, James, whatever is on your mind at this late hour?"

Halting on the lee side of the oak, he replied, "Something very important to me." His gaze lifted to myriad stars dimmed by a bright half-moon. "As important, I think, as everything up there." His head bent slowly downward and he kicked up dirt. "Or this."

He dared to look at her then, almost defensively, so tightly drawn were the lines of his mouth and eyes. "I hope I'm not presuming too much. Just looking at you, feeling the way I do. Well, I'm doing just what I dreaded—stammering around. But you see——"

Words failed him then, and in the silence between them neither moved nor broke the glance that bound them together. Upper branches of the old oak whipped gently as the wind whistled a shrill tune and blew on down the bay. Sounds of laughter from inside the house rose and died away, leaving them to each other, the wind, and the heavens.

Adria listened to the pounding of her heart. Then he was taking her hand in both of his, holding it as he would a delicate Dresden doll. Something of his innate tenderness became known to her then. It seemed to flow from his fingers to surge through her, stronger than currents of passion or desire, a thing real and lasting.

"I've tried all day to convince myself that I don't love you, Adria."

She listened and ventured nothing. It must come from him, all of it.

"You see, the orders to separate us suddenly threw a new light on everything. Perspectives changed, and I could no longer make myself believe it was possible to leave here with just pleasant memories of a wonderful visit and the good times in your company. I knew my heart would be left behind, for I love you, Adria."

Her eyes closed slowly. Lowering her head, she tried to conceal the happiness flooding her. Pray the Lord, she could restrain herself a little longer. Not looking up at him, she managed to ask if he was sure.

"Very sure."

Her glance raised anxiously.

"Before I speak more of the things in my heart, let me say I've been taught that honesty and consideration are on a par with regard. Therefore, I want you to know I'm dedicated to the Navy. It's what I want in the way of a career. Much of my time will be spent at sea, my wife residing in New York or Baltimore, perhaps, wherever the fleet bases.

"Nor is that all. A man goes the way his state goes. I'm not at all sure about Maryland."

A troubled frown crowded her brow. "You mean if Maryland went Yankee you'd be on their side?"

"If it came to that I'd have no choice." He winced. "And you know what would be expected of my wife."

With lower lip drawn between her teeth, Adria looked away in troubled thought. Quickly her glance returned to him. "Had you planned to be that honest with Father?"

"Naturally."

Poor James, she was thinking, so full of honor and integrity that he would walk into a lion's den a Sir Galahad and emerge with fine armor torn to shreds.

"You have a great deal to learn about Father."

He frowned. "I'd as soon face a firing squad at sunrise."

She brightened. "Oh well, this secession fever will soon cool, as it did back in 'fifty-one." Following his unconvincing "I suppose so," she said, "Is something more troubling you, James?"

"The most important thing of all. Do you love me?"

In her eyes he detected a gentle scolding. With mouth trembling into a half-smile, she said, "Yes, I love you. Oh, James, I thought you'd never get around to it."

How long they remained in each other's arms neither knew nor cared. They wished only that this might last forever. Then Adria stepped back, flushed, eyes alternately drowsy and vibrant. "My darling Adria." He drew her to him again, only to caress her forehead and eyes.

"Every man's future is uncertain," he said in low, trembling tones. "Even the times are most uneasy. Promise that nothing, even war, can separate us."

"Must you talk of war now?"

"Forgive me. My own dear Adria!" he whispered.

She treated him to a slow, adoring smile, which he memorized to carry with him during the lonely days away from her. "I have every confidence in you. And loving you as I do, trouble, war, even Father, can't keep us apart."

Then, eyes glowing, she drew his face down to hers. Moments later she disengaged herself hurriedly. "Have mercy, James dear!" Catching her breath, afraid to venture a glance in his direction, she turned toward the house.

He fell into step beside her. "I can hardly wait to talk to your father."

"Oh no!" came her urgent protest. "James, don't you dare approach him until I say the word."

A shudder ran through her, and she was wondering if the north wind was wholly responsible.

# 4.  January 11, 1861

1

DURING THE NIGHT a determined Gulf wind swept the cold air higher and by morning a cover of clouds moved sluggishly inland. As the day warmed, mist turned into slow rain. With hunting and riding dates automatically canceled, Bay Oaks settled down to what appeared to be the first quiet day in weeks.

Joseph Cutler read the paper with mixed emotions, which he made known by various sounds of pleasure and disgust. Adria brought hot coffee, refilled his cup before placing a pillow at his back, and only smiled in response to his "Why so infernal attentive?" Twice Adam intercepted James's uneasy glance at Adria, and twice drew the stakes to his side of the table.

"Keep this up, Admiral Co-Co, and I'll clean you in no time."

Poised with silver coffeepot in hand, Adria darted her brother a glance. "Why do you call James Co-Co, Adam?"

Adam suppressed a laugh. "Ask him."

James's face went crimson. The officers would never allow him to forget an error off a South Sea island. Stripped to the skin, he had gone out to get what he thought was a bobbing coconut. It turned out to be an island girl, stark naked. "I wouldn't dare tell it, Adria, and that fool brother of yours always makes capital of the fact."

"Oh?" Adria cocked her head curiously, thinking it must be something very awful. With a flippant shrug of her shoulders, she turned to Joseph again. "Poor Papa. I'm the only one who ever thinks of his comfort. Coffee, kind sir?"

Slowly Joseph put down the newspaper and lowered his reading glasses to red silk waistcoat without once removing his intent gaze from her face. "Next you'll be placing a Havana in my mouth, already lit up. Out with it. What do you want this time?"

"Goodness' sakes alive, you have been neglected! Why, you bark under the slightest attention due you."

"Your mother's words. Have you no originality?"

She gave his nose a playful tweak. "Maybe you'd like some steaming coffee down your grouchy neck."

Adam laughed. "Let him have it, Adria. He'd jump from here to Fort Sumter."

"And drive every damn Federal soldier into the sea," Joseph retorted.

Just then overseer Paul Angleton from the Clarke County plantation entered, beaming. "This is the kind of soaking the ground needs. Hope it lasts a week." His long, weather-wrinkled face broke into a grin as Adria declared he was the cruelest man in all Alabama to wish for weather that spoiled her fun.

"Thank yo' ma'am," he drawled. "It's good to know yo're still yo' right peart, healthy self. Martha had me pack a dozen jars of jelly over. Don't reckon I need say what kind."

"Red haw!" Adria cried. "As only Miss Martha can make it. How can I thank you?"

"Seems you have already." Taking a chair, the overseer faced Joseph. "The new forge for the blacksmith shop is at the landing. Cap'n Sherrod skiffed it up from his schooner himself, along with a case of cordials for you, suh."

"Cordials? The man's damn thoughtful, Paul." He added, "For all his reputation. Adam, invite the captain to join us."

Adria said in shocked tones, "That man? Father!"

"Never let it be said Joseph Cutler is——"

"Lacking in hospitality." The interruption came from the doorway, drawing every glance to a pair of flashing blue eyes in a brown face. "Captain Sherrod at your service."

Adria knew he had heard her. Never more embarrassed, she was wishing to suddenly drop through the floor out of sight. She had seen him before, but at a distance. Up close, he was positively handsome, though in a wicked sort of way. Perhaps, she thought, the shocking things she had heard about him influenced this observation. But his eyes seemed penetrating. And the smile illuminating his face was shaped in a downward curve that did little to annul former impressions.

"Your servants were kind enough to direct me here, Mr. Cutler."

The men got to their feet and Joseph said, "Come in, Captain, and join us. My daughter Adria, Captain Sherrod, and Lieutenant James Hillyer. You know Adam, of course."

Introductions acknowledged, Adam invited the schoonerman to sit in the game.

"Not interested, Lieutenant. The dons of Havana relieved me of all but jibs'ls and spanker."

"The *Gulf Wind* would have made it without them," Adam ventured.

"She's a queen, all right," Sherrod replied, eying Adria's figure with such boldness that she colored and dropped her glance. "That she is."

With the bearing of a king, he seated himself and responded to an invitation for refreshments by taking brandy. Which, Adria noticed out of the corner of an eye, he gulped without a single wince. The next he politely sipped, talking all the while with an ease born of confidence and experience.

Resentful of his coming and feeling uncomfortable in his presence, Adria was rising to excuse herself when he said, "I suppose you've heard the news. Mississippi has seceded."

"The hell you say!" from Joseph.

James's hand paused in mid-air and the card dropped unnoticed to the table. As his glance found Adria's, a pained look shone in his eyes.

Sherrod said, "And they're saying it's only a matter of time until Florida goes."

Adria felt herself grow cold all over. She arose, and the schooner-man stood and bowed and, under the cloak of courtesy, gave her another disrobing stare. She walked to a window in the library and watched the rain coming down from a leaden sky.

Then James was standing beside her in troubled thought. Almost in detachment, he said, "Your father seems very pleased with what appears to be a grave situation." His hand fell to hers then. "Adria darling, no matter what happens, remember our pledge."

"Of course," she said in a preoccupied manner. Before he could say more, she exclaimed, "Now is the time to corner Father, while he's in a good humor! Why, James, I'm half a mind to cheer Mississippi and Florida myself."

"Adria!" His voice was stern. "Good heavens, you don't know what you're saying."

2

Alone in his room that night, James glanced anxiously at his watch. It was half past eleven. He moved to the door, which was cracked just enough to admit shreds of the heated conversation from downstairs. Twice Joseph Cutler's voice had thundered, "Infatuation!" Now he was addressing Adam, asking why the devil and Tom Walker he hadn't nipped this romance in the bud. James was unable to catch Adam's reply, suddenly cut short by Joseph's clearly audible snort and, "A Marylander, of all people, Adria!"

James blew out his cheeks, dabbed at beads of perspiration on his face, and closed the door. All hope of Adria's success, so strong earlier that evening, was dwindling now. She had bid him wait until she called his name. That was to be the sign of victory. He paced the floor, pausing to listen or glance at his watch. It was nearing midnight when he cautiously opened the door. When no sound reached his ears, he thought perhaps Adria was wearing her father down.

Curious, James went downstairs. He came upon Adam, who studied him in silence before saying, "You two handed me a surprise, Jim. Suppose I was blind not to see it." Aware that his friend and sister's suitor was riding out the suspense in marked pain, Adam assured James that he could think of no one he would rather welcome into the family.

"But despite my stand, Father raised all sorts of objections. Adria's living up North, Maryland's position politically and, not the least, your own." He arose to leave, adding, "So it's up to you, Jim. Sleep on it and gird yourself for battle. Good luck."

James tossed the problem back and forth half the night before falling into troubled sleep.

Morning broke clear and warmer. Joseph departed for Mobile early and Adam left shortly after breakfast for a ride over the lower plantation. Several ladies from Montgomery came to spend the day with Adria and her mother, and later Faustine and her sister Elvy of Mobile, in response to a prior invitation by Annabel, arrived for an overnight visit. Following Joseph's return later in the day, Adria advised James that her father would grant him an audience that evening.

Well and good, thought James. There should be some reward for the longest and loneliest day on record. When toward sunset several members of Adam's deer club arrived with wives and sweethearts, he was wondering if the day would never end. The guests had come to partake of a fat deer the group had killed. The meat had been dried in strips and all were eager to taste the venison steaks Annabel had promised to broil in rich butter.

There was much to talk about, for the day had provided no end of excitement. First the state of Florida had withdrawn from the Union to become a "sovereign and independent nation." Next, and cause for alarm among the more serious thinkers, was news flashed by telegraph from Charleston.

A United States ship bringing supplies and reinforcements to the troops at Fort Sumter had been fired upon by South Carolinians as it entered Charleston Harbor.

With this report, James slowly lowered his wineglass. The deep frown creasing his brow went unnoticed by all save one person. Faustine smiled and invited him to join her for a breath of fresh air. He accepted willingly, anxiously, and walked out into the peaceful quiet of the evening with her arm in his.

In the moonlight she seemed ravishingly white and her dark hair flashed tiny sword points of blue light. She was saying:

"I simply had to get away from all that talk about Florida and trouble in Charleston. Pity poor Elvy, her husband Harold an old-time Whig and not at all in sympathy with the secession spirit. He's not alone, believe me. They're having a hot session up at the Montgomery convention called by Governor Moore. But enough of such unpleasantness."

James breathed a heavy sigh. "I'm glad to find someone who is not carried away with all this secession business. Why, you'd think the destruction of the Union was some kind of lark!"

Faustine's eyes lifted in brief study of him before narrowing with some suppressed excitement. "Really, you're quite inspiring, Lieutenant. Meeting a man who remains calm in these uncertain times is like finding a haven in a storm." Her hand tightened at his sleeve. "We need men like you, men who resort to reason instead of impulse."

James smiled. This lovely woman was full of surprises; pleasant ones, by Jove. Since few women looked for the deeper qualities of a man's mind, he was fortunate indeed to enjoy the company of one so understanding. Why, she was turning up much in him he had heretofore overlooked.

With face averted, she said in soft, low tones, "Did you ever experience a desire to just walk and walk on a night like this?"

Looking up at the southern stars, he replied, "Why, yes."

"Then shall we—say down to the boat landing and back?"

He made a slight grimace. "Do you think we should? They'll miss us and——"

"Continue discussing states' rights and politics. Forget them. You've had a trying day. It's written in your face."

"Maybe you're right," he said, half convinced.

"Of course I am. This is what you need." Commanding his attention with a smile parting the red cupid's bow of her mouth, she told him he was the type of man who so generously devoted himself to pleasing other people that he crowded his real self into the background.

"I am?" Puzzled, he rubbed an ear.

"And modest! I sometimes wonder if sweet, young Adria knows how kind you really are." Under his quizzical stare, she said, "Oh, don't misunderstand me. I love Adria as I would a little sister."

"To be sure," seemed a tactful reply. Perhaps Adria was somewhat young and impulsive. Then all at once he became aware that Faustine was leading him step by step down the shell path toward the river. He was astonished to find himself bending to her will like a tired branch in the wind, and what's more, saying not a word in defense of Adria.

Faustine gave him little time to rally his thoughts. She adroitly turned the topic of conversation, and before he caught up with her she was asking questions regarding his life aboard a cruiser. Then, pointedly, What actually dominated the mind of a man at sea on such a night as this—home, the land, one's future, or what? Gradually he opened up and for the first time in years spilled unannounced secrets of his private mind. He admitted a burning ambition to go high in the naval service, to fostering a desire to revolutionize warfare at sea, as Horatio Nelson had done a little more than a half century earlier. She seemed unduly attentive, almost fascinated, as he talked of the increased power of guns and projectiles as against the small improvement in line-of-battle ships.

"I had no idea there were guns like the—what did you call it?"

"Dahlgren," he replied. "Invented by Commander Dahlgren, and mounted aboard his ship the *Experiment*. Why, his smooth bore gun can sink a wooden frigate in a single broadside."

"Too bad ships can't be built of iron," she said.

He stopped still and looked at her, amazed. "But they can, Faustine. And you see it, don't you? Armored ships that sit low in the water, no sails whatever to be blown off. Steam-propelled."

Under his burst of enthusiasm, he caught himself with hands gripping her China-doll shoulders. "I—good Lord!—was carried away. I'm terribly sorry."

"For dreaming of rendering a service to humanity? Think of the lives your kind of ship would save. No, you must not be too modest. Think it, talk it, make it come true, James!"

"It is not my idea, really. However, I'm one of the few who have voiced a desire to command such a vessel if ever one is built. Of course, it's farfetched, but I've sketched a plan."

"Wonderful!" Her hands reached for his, and in her upturned face eyes grown large made demands on him. "I told you this was what you needed, James dear."

He could only stare at her. Yes, she had told him this, made a pleasing fact of it. This he could not deny, any more than he could admit to having ever met another woman of her physical charm who exhibited such genuine interest in things pertaining to his career. A sense of guilt accompanied the admission, to be sure, but Adria was in fact not endowed with Faustine's mental capacity for understanding a man in his entirety. He supposed she would in time.

Odd the way moonbeams highlighted Faustine's moist lips. Rather fascinating, like fairies at play. Or imps, for what thoughts that small wine-red mouth of hers put into his head! And her warm body was so close to his that he could feel the rise and fall of her restless bosom. He must control himself, must not think of her at all.

She was saying he would need encouragement in the days ahead. "Someone who will never allow you to forget for a moment the great work before you. Someone not only to share that secret, but leave no stone unturned to make it a dream come true. Oh, how I would love to help you!"

"Faustine! I——"

"Say it, James!" Her hands worked convulsively at his sleeves, then moved slowly up to his shoulders. She was pressing her body against his uniform and his arms were encircling her.

A groan escaped him, and he took a backward step.

Faustine stared into his ravaged face. "James! Are you ill?"

Stunned, he groped for words. He could not tell her how frightened he had become upon suddenly finding himself in a surprisingly awkward position. He tried to smile, to go at it calmly. Failing, he simply blurted out the truth. "Faustine, I've asked Adria to marry me."

She stared incredulously. "Adria? You?" Slowly she lowered her head and drew a hand across her brow. "You, with all your plans and ambition? But what am I saying."

Breathing a deep sigh, she forced a smile.

"Forgive me for such a display at a time when congratulations are in order, James. It came as quite a surprise."

"Yes," he replied, trying to contain his feeling of relief. With trouble on the mend, he indulged in a wry smile. "It might be a bit early for congratulations," he said. "I haven't received Mr. Cutler's permission yet. Supposed to see him tonight."

Faustine's black brows joined, then lifted instantly. "Dear me, you'll surely need luck there. But of course he'll show every courtesy to Adam's guest." Almost in detachment, she added, "Despite the fact that Joseph Cutler makes no secret of wanting Lawrence Jarvis for a son-in-law. Or," she went on, seemingly unaware of his change of expression from curiosity to growing apprehension, "that you are not the hotheaded, Yankee-hating type of Southerner he likes to have around.

"Oh, I hope all this doesn't sound discouraging. Why, I wouldn't for the world think of robbing you of a moment's happiness."

She looked up into his face and moved so close her nearness and a scent of perfume proved rather disquieting. "I wish you luck, worlds of it," she said.

As though prompted by sudden impulse, Faustine pressed her palms to his cheeks and drew his face down in friendly manner. Her lips touched his, lingered a mere moment. "My congratulations, James."

There was no calming his rearoused emotions, for rushing through him like a hot gale was an overwhelming desire to return that sample kiss with burning fire. His arms went about her, and he was drawing her roughly, blindly, to him. Her startled face drew back and he was kissing her throat. "James!" How far away it sounded. Then all the tenseness departed and she yielded up her hungry mouth.

A gull screamed out over the water and the far-off cry of a bobcat quivered in the night air. All at once he was staring at her pliant, crimson lips, then into veiled eyes. A new fire was kindling under those heavy lashes, flaming up strong now. Faint whispering sounds reached his ears and he felt her hand go rigid at the base of his neck.

The spinning of his head suddenly ceased. Like the sudden clash of cymbals in his brain, he remembered Adria.

How he broke away from her, he did not rightly know. But he was suddenly free and moving hurriedly toward the house.

3

James tried in vain to calm the tumult raging inside him. Unable to appear before Adria's father with any degree of composure, he went directly to his room and spent long hours berating himself for having ever become involved with Faustine. Perhaps he had been a fool to leave her. She stimulated him to no end. Never could he recall her equal, any more than he could remember having run away from a woman before in his life.

It was almost noon when he went downstairs and blamed his late appearance on a terrible headache. He voiced regret that Joseph had waited for him, and concealed his pleasure upon learning that Faustine and her sister Elvy had returned to Mobile. Joseph and Adam had driven them in, Adria said. Her father was no doubt waiting anxiously for some word from Montgomery regarding the legislature's vote on secession.

Secession seemed the least of James's troubles now. Staring at the wax-green leaves of a magnolia tree just beyond the window, he half listened to Adria's plans for the afternoon. Scattered bits of last night's conversation crowded his mind. Faustine's encouragement. "Think of the lives your kind of ship would save. Think it, talk it . . ." she had said. What would Adria say?

Minutes later he led into an explanation of his interest in iron ships, warming somewhat until, at length, he asked Adria if she might be proud to be the wife of the first commander of an armored cruiser.

Adria lifted her delicately arched brow. "Should I?" she replied. "It sounds rather silly to me."

The student of naval warfare stiffened. A moment more and he wasn't at all offended. It didn't seem to matter in the least, though for the life of him he couldn't understand why. Unless it was because Faustine had simply bewitched him.

By late afternoon James seemed his cheerful self. Thanks to Adria's company up the Mobile River road, he had managed to isolate unpleasant memories of the night before. Following a long embrace in the shelter of young pines, he could not help comparing Adria's kiss to Faustine's. The result was quite satisfying. Vitality and sincerity were far more desirable than experience and guile. And yet Faustine would not be easy to forget.

They were turning off the road for Bay Oaks when distant blasts of steamboat whistles and guns popping reached upriver. Like New Year's Eve or Mardi Gras, Adria observed. The bedlam continued as they rode on up the bluff and through the gates, now gleaming in coppery brilliance under the setting sun. Neither remarked on the reason for the demonstration. James frowned thoughtfully until Adria's fingers closed over his.

"I can hardly bear to think of your going," she said. "This time tomorrow you'll be gone, James. Please, dear," she implored urgently, "talk up to Papa tonight. Don't give up, and don't cross him on politics."

Adam and his jubilant father arrived shortly after nightfall with the news: Alabama had seceded. The Cutler plantation was no longer in the United States of America.

Adam continued to stare in silence from the glass in his hand to the blue uniform he wore. Often his glance swept around to James and held for long moments. Nor did he so much as break the repose of his face when Adria remarked, "I suppose we should feel odd, living in a foreign country."

Joseph laughed exultantly. Stretching his legs before a small fire in the hearth, he glanced from calm Annabel to Adria before lifting his glass. "To economic freedom," he said with fiery zeal. "I reckon the Yankee Republicans are beginning to feel the sting of the Southern wasp. Four states less for Abe Lincoln. And by thunder, wait, just wait! The whole South will follow. Already the New Englanders are calling us Rebels. Let them. We're doing what we should have done back when the Missouri Compromise and Dred Scott case——"

"Please, Joseph," Annabel said. "Just because you believe the Federal Government has no right to deny a territory admission to the Union because of slave or non-slave sentiment, or to deny a state the right to secede, or a dozen and one——"

"Madam, I contend that the South is faced with an uncompromising political machine under Lincoln that will make our stay in the Union untenable."

Adria laughed and sank into a chair near James. "Might as well let him unwind, Mother."

Undaunted, Joseph continued. "And to think that a number of street fights followed the news in Mobile. It's hard to imagine Southerners favoring the United States." His eyes fell on James. "Don't you agree, Lieutenant Hillyer?"

"Perhaps I'm too uninformed on the subject," James said evasively.

"It's high time to inform yourself," Joseph rebuked harshly.

James's drink tasted flat of a sudden. His reply had not been one to favor a man in quest of the planter's daughter. Adria's quick glance conveyed as much.

Then Joseph's eyes fell inquiringly on his son, lingered there. "Well, Adam, what are you going to do?"

Adam did not move a muscle, just stood stiffly by the mantel with glass in hand staring across the room. He said finally, with no change of expression, "I'm going to pour another drink."

He left the room a little later. Annabel watched him go and soon followed. Then Adria walked to the door, where she caught James's eye and threw him a kiss.

The time had arrived. Resolutely summoning his courage, James cleared his throat rather noisily and broached the subject of marriage. Twice he stammered and more often he was aware of a trembling of his voice. A devilish ordeal, he swore silently when his plea was finished.

Not once did Joseph Cutler look up at him. In the strained silence the owner of Bay Oaks lit up a cheroot and puffed up a cloud of smoke about his head. "Young man," he began pleasantly enough, "the very fact that you have won my daughter's heart coupled with another point in your favor, Adam's regard for you—these things, plus the good name of Hillyer beyond even your part of the country —would justify my hearty welcome to join our family." He coughed, adding, "In normal times, of course."

Rising, Joseph walked to the mantel, very carefully placed the cheroot in a corner of his mouth, and trained a pair of steady eyes on the guest and suitor. "Despite my fondest wishes for Adria to marry into the Jarvis family, I would give you both my blessing, after, mind you, I learned to my satisfaction that the attraction between you was not infatuation.

"I'm speaking of normal times, Lieutenant."

"Yes, sir," tensely.

"And I'll bend backward to do it even now, sir, provided"—Joseph lifted a finger—"you can satisfy my curiosity regarding a problem in geography and political sentiment."

It was inevitable, James admitted to himself as Joseph continued with, "Otherwise, what assurance have I that my daughter will not become the wife of a man opposed to our interests?"

"Sir," the younger man said, "I can only remind you that my sentiments are governed, as yours, by my state. I'm from Maryland and proud of it."

"Very commendable, to be sure. But you'll agree, Lieutenant Hillyer, that predicting the way your state will lean is about as dependable as my naming the weather for Easter Sunday here and now. Suppose Maryland takes sides with the North?"

"Well, as I see it, neither side wants trouble. Admitting that legislative debate has failed so far, I still can't imagine matters getting so far out of hand as to provoke a shooting war."

Joseph replied thoughtfully, "We don't want violence. Nor, sir, does the rational element of the North. The New York *Tribune* expressed this view by asserting that the North cannot conquer the South and that the South, if it so wishes, should be allowed to depart in peace. And we are departing after every effort to stay in the Union."

James's dubious expression prompted the other to say, "The facts bear out my statement, Lieutenant. When, in 1820, Missouri was admitted into the Union, the North and South entered into a compromise which provided that slavery should not be extended to any of the territories north of the parallel 36°, 30', despite the fact that all territories were the common properties of all the states. Which meant that slaveholders had no right to migrate and form their way above that line. The South, which twice fought England side by side with the North, accepted that compromise, which openly discriminated against us. You must admit discrimination and Southern tolerance."

A nod of agreement was forced from James, who for the first time realized that Joseph Cutler was not merely a rabid secessionist at heart, but an informed thinker.

Joseph said next, "When the Kansas-Nebraska bill was passed in 1854, the unjust compromise was repealed as being inconsistent with the principles of non-intervention as recognized by legislation of 1850. Nothing could have been more just. The South rejoiced when equal rights were restored.

"You know the rest, the rise of the Republican Party last year, the plank of its platform, that slavery should thereafter be excluded *from all territories*. You know of the overwhelming victory of this party, of the South's efforts to compromise after the election, even to a partial abandonment of our rights. This measure failed. Therefore, for the first time in the history of our country the Federal Government which was established to bind the states together in peace becomes an agent of oppression to one group. It denies the co-equality of the South and, therefore, has failed of its purpose.

"And we are departing from the Union because we have been

driven out. Perhaps we can make better terms out than in, young man."

"Let us hope so," James said convincingly. "What amazes me is the fact that the situation could get so far out of hand."

"Not when you realize that the question is to decide the balance of power between two sections, politically, economically. Already we are vassals of a sort. Southern exports support the Federal Government to a large degree, while Northern tariffs prohibit our buying even horseshoes from our biggest customer, England."

"I had never thought of it in that light," James replied, wondering how he could turn the subject back to Adria and himself.

"That's why we can trade better out of the Union," Joseph said. "Let the North miss our money for a while. We'll make our own terms then. Don't you agree?"

"It sounds reasonable, I'm sure."

Adria's father frowned. "The only thing left for the Yankees would be the use of force to bring us back into the Union. Already the North is saying the Constitution gives us no right to secede. Do you believe that, Lieutenant?"

"Well, yes and no. I mean——"

"Young man, I find you damned hard to pin down. Now answer this, yes or no, do you believe the Federal Government has the right to coerce the seceded states?"

"I don't know, sir. Frankly, I don't."

"Then, by God, sir, you don't know whether you're a Yankee or a Southerner." Suddenly aware that the lieutenant was a guest in his house, Joseph Cutler sought to mend his manners. Walking to James and placing a hand on his shoulder, he said in kinder tones, "I suggest we postpone this discussion until you've established your nationality, so to speak.

"Now, sir, shall we stir up a drink and sit down to a friendly game of cards?"

"But, Mr. Cutler, I——"

James was packing when, around eleven, Adam knocked at his door. Both wore long faces and no word was spoken between them as the Alabaman sprawled in a chair and tapped the edge of a folded sheet of paper against his knee.

"Sorry, Jim," broke the silence. "Sorry it had to be this way. But you'll have to admit that under the circumstances the old man couldn't do otherwise."

"I don't question that, Adam," James said, folding a shirt. "I'd probably feel the same if I were in his shoes. But it doesn't make me any happier."

Adam's face took on a semblance of a smile. "Damned if you don't look as though you'd been ordered back to the China Sea." The attempt at humor fell flat. Seriously he said, "Adria thought you could have stretched a point, Jim. I knew you wouldn't. Glad you didn't, if it means anything to you."

"Sure. Sure," came the gruff reply. "But let's put an end to this wake. We leave early in the morning for Pensacola"—a violence of feeling entered his voice—"where I hope to hell the old battle wagon is so anxious to sail she's flying the cornet at the fore."

"Well, I've got news for you," Adam said quietly. "The United States garrison in Pensacola has evacuated Fort Barrancas and moved to Fort Pickens. That's not all. Colonel Lomax of Alabama plans to take the Pensacola Navy Yard tomorrow."

James stared in speechless wonder. The socks in his hand fell to the floor unnoticed. Somehow or other he could not reconcile all that was happening in his mind. The widening breach between people of a kind, acts of aggression that might strike a spark to the tinder and set off a blaze that would not go out—impossible things, but they were real.

The Marylander was suddenly afraid of many things, not the least among them the gathering storm that might separate him from his closest friend and shipmate.

"You, Adam," he said falteringly, "you're not—not letting all this influence you?" There was no reply. "Is that what your father meant when he asked what you were going to do?"

With the other's slow nod, James asked anxiously, "What are you going to do, Adam?"

"Just wait," came the patient reply.

5.    Severance

1

ON A WARM AFTERNOON IN LATE FEBRUARY, Adria stood on the upstairs rear gallery gazing over the gardens ablaze with color. Banks of pink and flame azaleas flanked the brick walkways, lined the terraces, and circled the arbors and central fountain. Carefully tended beds bordered in small white and yellow flowers framed the vivid green stalks and colorful heads of tulips. Above the maze of bursting blossoms trees of crimson and white camellias vied with a blanket of lavender cascading down from the old oak midway between the carriage house and domestic quarters.

"If James could only see Bay Oaks now," she said pensively. "Acres and acres of flowers and I can't so much as send him one single blossom."

Adria realized with a strange sense of bewilderment that early spring had given blossom to another kind of flower. A new nation had recently come into being up at Montgomery. Since James's departure, the states of Louisiana, Georgia, and Texas had withdrawn from the Union. Seven strong, they had banded together and formed the Confederate States of America. On the ninth of February the ex-senator from Mississippi and former Secretary of War of the United States, hero of Buena Vista in 1847, had been elected President of the Confederacy. On the eighteenth Adria had seen Jefferson Davis, a friend of her father, inaugurated at the Alabama State Capitol in Montgomery. Although he inspired confidence because of his untiring efforts for conciliation up to January 21, his last day in office, Adria found it difficult to reconcile a man not six weeks out of the United States Senate to the President of the new Republic. But for that matter, she lacked the comprehension to understand and keep pace with all the exuberance and excitement and proud, warlike boasting attending the birth of the Confederacy.

Perhaps it was because she felt instinctively the presence of some threat to her romance with James. Certainly the situation promised to involve James as well as Adam. Her father had said as much. Already, such prominent Alabamans as Commander Raphael Semmes had given up posts in Washington and cast their fortunes with the homeland.

And songs were being sung about the fighting South. Her father, Erasmus, and even Abel, were constantly singing "The Bonnie Blue Flag," written by a traveling showman when Mississippians created the flag by that name in anticipation of their state's exit from the Union. For every state that followed a new verse was added. And Joseph Cutler knew them all.

"It will be our national hymn," he said after Montgomery rang with it. Crowds sang it there, Adria recalled. How they had cheered the second stanza:

> *As long as the old Union was faithful to her trust,*
> *Like friends and like brothers kind were we and just.*
> *But now when Northern treachery attempts our rights to mar,*
> *We hoist on high the Bonnie Blue Flag that bears a Single Star.*

Each state waved its own flag, and even communities flung aloft their own banners. The Bonnie Blue Flag was merely one of hundreds. Adria smiled at the memory of her father's fervent outburst upon reading the Confederate Government's advertisement in the newspaper asking for flag designs to be submitted in order that a standard emblem might be selected and adopted for the Confederate States. "Annabel! Adria! We're going to design that flag. Get your sewing kit and material." He gave up the idea in favor of helping organize a company of volunteer riflemen.

What's more, there was in evidence much enthusiasm concerning a national uniform. Adria's parents told of dear Mrs. Napoleon Lockett of Marion, Alabama, who was urging a Prussian artist residing in Marion to design a uniform. Furthermore, it was rumored that this Mr. Nicola Marschall had sketched designs after the Austrian pattern, showing soldiers dressed in striking uniforms of gray, with green trimmings, the green denoting the branch of service.

Adria was imagining James in such dress when from the upper-hall doors someone cried, "Miss Adri! Oh, Miss Adri."

Whirling, she saw impish Claribel, Mammy Rose's eleven-year-old niece.

"Is yo' all heah, Miss Adri?"

"Looking straight at me, you ask that?"

"Yes'm, cause it ain't me wants to know. Mistuh Law'ence Jarvis ask it. Got him a brand-new buggy, and he whistlin' lak they never was no navy man to Bay Oaks a-courtin' yo'all."

Adria suppressed a caustic reply lest Claribel go directly to Lawrence and blab it. "Tell Mr. Jarvis I'll join him in the parlor shortly."

Bother! She drew a deep breath and, on sudden impulse, flung open the french doors from the gallery to the room occupied by James during his visit. Why, she didn't know, unless the gesture was in defiance of something she could neither shape nor control.

Standing there, she shifted her glance from the pair of pink and white Sèvres vases on the mantel to the prayer pad at the side of the great tester bed. She could almost feel James's presence in the room.

Being in love affected her strangely, she mused. Separation from James left her utterly defenseless and perplexed. Memories buoyed her, often falsely, for they would surface and leave her lonelier than before. Love seemed a tenuous and mystical thing, sometimes touched with infinite sadness. But of one thing she was sure: love, to use Adam's expression, played the merry devil with one's behavior.

As with Lawrence, for example. He irritated her when she needed company most. Only yesterday she had turned a dazzling smile upon him simply to cover a feeling of resentment that came over her because he was not James Hillyer. And for all his claim to worldly wisdom, he could not hide the fact that he was flattered by the passionate intensity of her gaze. It was downright mean of her to tease Lawrence in this manner, though little imps prompted her.

Only James could put the imps to rout.

She recalled the morning of his departure, January twelfth. She stood in the rear twin parlor facing the mantel and saw him in the mirror as he paused under the arched doorway and just stared at her. Outside Adam said, "Say your adieu, mister. I'll be waiting in the hall." Wincing, James looked away, then back to her, this time with eyes misting up a small storm of rebellion at the thing called duty that demanded his leave-taking. She shared his feeling, only more so, because she was a woman, and tried her best to retain her composure even as her anguish welled up to trembling lips.

She remembered it all vaguely, so great was the flood of her emotions at the time. She faced him and called his name, and he rushed to her. In his grasp, she clung to him, her heart beating hard against him.

He spoke in broken phrases, calling her his own darling sweet Adria as he touched her cheeks and eyes and hair with his lips. "If only your father knew how much I love you."

"Or how much I love you, James," she whispered.

"Then tell him of our love every hour of every day."

She heard the clatter of the carriage at the front of the house. Adam cleared his throat louder than usual and said, "In a minute, Father," and James tilted her head back and held her eyes with his until it seemed they were eternally fused together. Then he kissed her mouth, lightly, briefly, and took a backward step. Making a wry face, he squared his shoulders.

"Nothing can come between us, Adria. Remember that."

"Nothing. Nothing," she breathed.

"I love you, Adria," he said.

"I—love you——" She stood as in a trance, wondering why he was moving away from her.

Then he was gone.

She stood there a long time. The room had not changed. The same gold cornices and brocatels graced the tall windows; the same Victorian pieces sat still and silent on the Aubusson carpet; the bell pull hung motionless, and the garnitures held their prim expressions—all as before his going. Only she felt a change. Too sudden and real, it descended upon her, a girl who had known social success, gaiety and luxury, and only small discouragements and precious little of the primitive basis of things.

Adria shook her head savagely, turned from James's room to look down on the gardens again.

"January twelfth," she said almost unbelievingly.

The flowers mocked her. It was nearly March now.

From the upper hall Mammy Rose called out, "Honey chile, Mistuh Law'ence ain't gwine wait fo'ever on yo'all. Now git on downstairs 'fo' he lose all de patience he done got lef'."

Adria walked slowly toward the hall. She supposed Mammy Rose was right. But she did not look forward to Lawrence's lengthy discussion of the widening breach between the North and South, which he would of course make evident by relating all the fresh happenings from Fort Sumter to Washington. Whatever was the world coming to, with tempers flaring and men drilling and oiling guns? Worse, what was happening to her when her own father remained stubbornly deaf to her entreaties regarding the lieutenant from Maryland?

At the staircase, she paused and said with eyes closed, "James dear, please hurry and convince Father that you are a Southerner."

## 2

On this day there was no drearier place in America than Baltimore. A chill wind was blowing down from the upper reaches of the Chesapeake and heavy clouds were beginning to dump a wet ballast over the city. Already, Fort McHenry seemed a dim gray hulk swathed in a blanket of mist.

As the horizon closed in from the Patapsco River to the Northwest Harbor, James Hillyer lowered the window and sank to a chair before an escritoire. He frowned over the half page he had written to Joseph Cutler before shaking his head hopelessly. It was no use. The sly fox of Bay Oaks wasn't interested in half measures, so there was small hope for reward in angling with such bait.

" 'While, sir,' " he read aloud, " 'I believe the South is justified in presenting an attitude of independence in an endeavor to force legislation in Congress of a democratic nature in keeping with the principles laid down in the Constitution of the United States, I cannot, as a citizen of the State of Maryland, sincerely and honorably renounce the flag which I serve ahead of a formal declaration by the Government of Maryland. To do so at this time, as you must agree——'

"Tripe!" James snorted. "Wordy, irrelevant. Fuel for Joseph Cutler's wrath."

He breathed a despairing sigh. *"To force legislation in Congress—* I wrote that? Why I'm a good three months behind the time."

Indeed, for this was a season when the South was sharpening swords instead of plowshares. Therefore, the letter was void of useful content. For all the good it would do, it could be addressed to the Queen of England, or his own parent, for that matter.

He winced. Should his own father, "Old Navy" Hillyer, read any portion of the letter, the flames of anger would figuratively issue red as a dragon's breath from his weather-wrinkled face. In the first place, the Navy came ahead of all else but the flag. *The one flag,* his father had said not two weeks in the past; and in Adam's presence. "You can't divide the Navy, Son, because you cannot split tradition in two. It's a part of the flag, which no man or group of men can tear down the middle and carry half of it South."

James got up and stalked across the room.

Beset from all sides, his love for Adria and her father's single requirement on the one hand, his own father's unyielding convictions on the other, James found himself caught between wind and water.

"Just how the hell does one go about changing his loyalties and affections?" he blurted angrily.

The door opened suddenly. "How was that?" Adam said, smothering a chuckle.

"Nothing. Nothing at all." James reddened to the roots of his sand-colored hair.

Adam walked to a table and lifted a Bristol glass wine decanter.

Pouring, without so much as a glance at James, he said, "There must be an internal change in one first of all, my dear Co-Co. Maybe you're trying to have your cake and eat it. The Navy versus Adria. Isn't the question simply this: Are you a Southerner or aren't you?"

"Sure! It's damned easy for you, with Alabama taking a side. A great help you are."

"Have I ever tried to proselyte you?" Adam demanded.

"No. But why don't you? Maybe I could reach a decision."

"And blame me if it's the wrong one? Not on your life, Jim. But who is the letter for, Adria or Father?"

"Your father. Read it and see if you agree that it should go by the board, as the others."

Adam sat down, sipped wine, and grinned. "A dozen times you write him and a dozen times you destroy the letters. I'd send them, regardless, just to show the old boy I meant business. Instead, you're letting him pipe weather and wind and fag your rope ends."

"Holy sailor!" James said incredulously. "Wasn't it you who told me not to send the first half dozen?"

Adam stroked a mustache and looked up sheepishly. "Maybe I thought you'd find yourself sooner or later if you kept on writing." He sent his cap sailing toward James's head, and laughed loud as the other ducked. "By the way, has any message come for me?"

"A perfumed envelope, by any chance? No."

"Hand it over, Jim." Adam's hand was extended.

"I don't know anything about a girl named Nancy of Crafton Hill down in Anne Arundel County."

"Tell it to the Marines. Now give."

"Else?" A mischievous grin spread over James's face.

"After I finish with you, I'll write Adria all about your double life. I could mention Faustine and she would believe it. Might even tell Father you're Abe Lincoln's first cousin."

Adam was shedding his coat and James was bracing himself for the tussle ahead when suddenly both turned curiously to the window. What sounded like a lively brawl on the sidewalk below was soon verified as just that.

Quickly Adam flung the window open. The lurid profanity of a gang of waterfront hoodlums mingled with shouts for help from a trio of cavalrymen caught afoot in the wrong quarter. A huge bearded man was pounding away at a young soldier's head with a barrel stave and crying with sadistic glee:

"Sing 'Dixie,' ye blue-bellied, nigger-lovin' bastards, before we chase the lot of ye across the Susquehanna."

"Harder, Tomkins!" yelled one of his companions. "Make him sing a hurrah for Jeff Davis and secession."

The three Yankees were soon pressed against the wall. Cornered, they waded into the gang with fists flying and voices crying for the police. The largest took a bone-cracking blow on the forehead and sank to the pavement. A second bluejacket had gone down when a pair of sailors well along in their cups came upon the scene. Pausing to eye the excitement, they soon realized their mistake.

"Look, lads! The Yankees come by land and sea! At 'em! Cram their anchors down their gullets!"

Above them, unnoticed, Adam nudged James. "Well, Admiral, do we come to the aid of the Navy?"

"Aye, aye, sir!" James sang out, reaching for a weapon. As Adam seized a heavy glass foot warmer, James said, "I'm the gunnery officer. Let me have it while you pipe to quarters."

He broke it in two on the sill and carefully aimed the larger half at the aggressor called Tomkins. A direct hit was scored. The hoodlum's knees buckled. As he fell face down, his backers looked up at the pair of naval officers.

"Good God! The bloody bluecoats'll be droppin' out of the sky next!" shouted a ragged wharfmonger.

"After 'em! They're cornered, lads." So saying, the speaker flung his cudgel with such speed and accuracy that both Adam and James were hard put to get out of the way. It struck the glass and sent a rain of jagged slivers over the room.

Adam dabbed at a trickle of blood on his chin. "Hell, they're coming, Jim! Barricade the door."

"The stairway is better. Grab a chair."

"Chair? By damn, we might as well do this up shipshape and Bristol." Grinning wickedly, Adam pointed to a heavy carved chest.

"Aye." James arched his brow. "Together we should swing it hard down the stairs. But somebody might get hurt."

"Really!" Adam scoffed. "Had you rather be hanged for a lamb or a wolf?"

Without further preamble, each hoisted an end of the chest and hurried the cumbersome thing down the hallway. As they lowered it at the top of the stairs and caught their breath, a half dozen ruffians rushed up after them.

"Heave sailor!" Adam cried, bending to the task.

"Ho!" James grunted, coming up with his share of the weight.

Back and forth they swung the chest. "One, ho! Two, ho!" they said in unison.

The attackers paused halfway up the stairway. "The bloody thing'll murder us," one cried. "Over the rail, me bullies! We'll take 'em after they drop it."

"Three—go!"

The chest sailed a good six feet before crashing like thunder end over end down the staircase. With full retreat of the ruffians blocked by latecomers crowding the steps, the lot of them pushed and rolled into a yelling, tangled mass of humanity seeking escape from a charging teakwood monster. The stair rail splintered and gave way under the weight of numbers, though the chest on a straight course grazed a noggin here and knocked the breath from a stomach there. Howls of pain rose from those who caught the chest in full.

When it was over, the gang that represented "Secessia" (as the Confederacy was called), for the sake of villainy and looting, had lost its desire for further combat. Broken arms, legs, and collarbones numbered five, and three men lay unconscious. The innkeeper arrived with three policemen before a single one of the culprits could escape.

James looked pleased. Standing with hands on hips at the top of the stairs, he said, "After such sport, I could do with a couple of bourbons."

Adam leaned against the wall in an attitude of indifference. "Shall we continue where we left off before this interruption?" he asked quietly. "Or will you surrender the letter?"

"Two letters, Adam. One was in a blue envelope. From Montgomery."

Adam's eyes thinned to narrow slits. "At last," he said, suddenly coming alive.

They entered the room crunching glass under boots and James produced two envelopes. "My orders came this morning," he said. With no reply, he added, "I leave tomorrow for Norfolk and the Gosport Navy Yard."

"Just as well," Adam replied absently, breaking the paper seal on the letter dispatched from the capital of the Confederacy. "The rioting here is getting out of hand, almost. It won't ease any when the crowds start pouring through for Abe Lincoln's inauguration. Rumor has old General Winfield Scott planning to parade the Army, rifles and field guns loaded, to assure Republican Abe a safe March fourth."

"A show of force, eh?"

"Which might backfire on the new President."

"Maybe," James reflected. "But what would you do?"

"I?" Adam said, ripping the envelope. "I'm about to find out."

Leaning forward, elbows on knees, eyes sharp, Adam read the letter.

NAVY DEPARTMENT
*Confederate States of America*
*Montgomery, Alabama*

February 20, 1861

My dear Mr. Cutler:

Shortly after resigning my commission in the United States Navy, I compiled a list of officers in whom I have the utmost confidence in the uncertain days ahead when true-born Southerners may be forced to show their valor in freeing our beloved Southland from the Northern yoke of oppression. Among the names submitted to Mr. Conrad, Chairman of the Committee on Naval Affairs, Congress of the Confederate States, was your own.

Today, finding your name approved, I, your former commander and friend, urge your quick consideration of our need for the services of such men as yourself. In event that you should desire to share in the noble effort of creating a Navy dedicated to the glory and defense of the new Republic, please repair at once to Montgomery, where we may have the honor of welcoming a son of Alabama into our busy midst.

Respectfully & c,
JOSIAH TATTNALL
*Captain, C.S.N.*

P.S. Since writing the above, I have learned that another Alabaman and true patriot of the Cause, Commander Raphael Semmes, former Secretary of the Lighthouse Board in Washington, will be on a "tour of inspection" in Baltimore shortly. Perhaps it will be possible that two gentlemen of Mobile may exchange greetings before he continues north on official business.

Without a word, Adam extended the letter to James and moved to the broken window. Gazing blankly at masts half hidden by swirling mist and snow, he was relieved to know that he was burdened by no decision hanging in the balance. He knew his course, knew its risk, its consequences. Only the parting with the past and present troubled him. He had served the Flag, as the Cutlers and Temples before him, though unlike his forefathers, it had fallen his lot to serve in a time of peace. A flag was more than a mortal, and therefore harder to bid adieu, because of its long hold on one's allegiance. But there was small regret now that the color of the bunting represented Republicanism and absolute monarchy. Gone was the emblem of good faith between the North and the South.

So far, Adam realized, he had waited with amazing patience and calm. But now he wished for a flag to wave. Imagine, he said to himself, no national flag! The Confederacy was that young.

He turned a glance on James, who sat in troubled thought staring at the letter, and felt for the first time the price he must pay for parting with stanch and true friends.

"Adam"—James grimaced unduly—"I hope you consider this from every angle."

"I have. My name will be stricken from the list. Lieutenant Cutler, U.S.N., will be no more."

"Correct," James said significantly. "You'd lose your seniority and right to claim old-age half pay. Really, you would be cut adrift."

"I'm from Alabama," Adam said proudly. "And I hear the piping of my watch down in Montgomery."

"But—Adam! You're throwing career to the winds."

"Then so is Semmes, who had more to lose than I. So are Captains Tattnall, Rousseau, and Ingraham. There will be more, dozens and dozens more. As you know, the majority of officers in the service are from the South."

"Um-m. You're right, though all the seamen are from the North. So are all the ships-of-war. Just what will the Confederate Navy use for service afloat?"

"Ships," Adam declared readily. "We'll buy, build, beg, borrow, and steal them. And you can lay to that. And the government of Mr. Davis won't be long in building a navy. Why? Because we have a coast many times the length of the North's. In event of war we'd have the ports of Charleston, Savannah, Pensacola, Mobile, New Orleans, and Galveston to keep open.

"Furthermore, when Virginia secedes, as she surely must, the South will take over the Gosport Navy Yard."

"Just like that, eh?" James scoffed. "You make the wine taste flat, Rebel Cutler."

"I'm serious."

"So your mind is made up." James looked painfully incredulous. "Actually, do you mean it, Adam?"

"Your time may come, Jim Hillyer. In fact, I know a certain

party who is pleading with you to do it now. First we would go by train to Montgomery." He paused. "Then Mobile, Jim."

James's expression underwent a swift change. His anger flared and surfaced as he came to his feet and ran both hands through his hair and down his neck before dropping them at his side almost hopelessly. And then his manner suggested uncertainty, that and a compelling urge to follow the dictates of his heart.

He glared at Adam. "Dammit all, why punish me?"

"Punish you my eye. You're doing it to yourself. As long as your state remains in the Union, you'll go on doing it, unless you follow the example of another Marylander who adopted Alabama as his home state."

James looked up curiously.

"He was born in Charles County, Maryland. You've heard of Raphael Semmes of Mobile, Jim." Lifting his palms, Adam said, "There's your precedent and pattern. Adria and my whole family will welcome you to Alabama."

Walking to the window, Adam felt a little embarrassed at having allowed for a moment the ardent zeal of a proselyter to surface. As if to mend the break in his reserve, he said hastily, "Not that I like the cut of your jib, sailor. It's just that I've been stuck with you for years."

Expecting a vigorous reply of "Go to hell!" Adam felt almost offended when James said, "I didn't know 'Old Beeswax' Semmes was from Maryland."

Adam thought of the ties that bound his closest friend. Strong as ropes of steel were the inculcations of family and tradition. Upon closer examination, Adam realized that a Hillyer's bonds were forged from a refined metal no different from a Cutler's, that neither hell nor high water could force from James a decision that was incompatible with duty and honor as prescribed by lifelong influences. So what on the surface looked to be weakness and indecision were in reality strength and loyalty. But often one's virtues were a source of unhappiness.

James said hotly, "Damn that open window!"

"Aye." Adam smiled. "Before morning it'll freeze certain unmentionables off a brass monkey." Then he sat down and worded a most important letter to the Honorable Isaac Toucey, Secretary of the United States Navy:

Sir:

I respectfully tender the resignation of the commission which I have the honor to hold as a Lieutenant in the Navy of the United States. In severing my connection with the Service, I request that my commission be terminated at your earliest convenience.

I have the honor to be respectfully your obedient servant.

"Done," Adam said, affixing his signature and rank. "Now I must send a telegram to old Tatt in Montgomery."

"So you've cut the knot," James said wearily.

Adam looked up and replied calmly enough, "I've cut the knot."

## 6.    March Winds

### 1

NEXT DAY the sun shone in determined manner, though the wind continued to shift northwesterly with a promise of more winter. Icicles dripped from warehouse roofs and the long yards of ships in harbor furl, and sailors and civilians alike swore that the weather appeared every bit as uncertain as national politics.

Adam heartily agreed. Without looking at James, who waited out the last minute before boarding the Norfolk packet, he said to cover his true feelings, "The sooner I put the Monumental City under my stern the better."

"Right," said the other, dreading their parting handclasp. "Baltimore is unlucky enough to be caught in a squeeze between Rebel and Yankee sympathizers."

"Geographically, politically," Adam replied, striking a match. Lighting his cheroot, he said, simply to keep the conversation going, "Maybe Mr. Lincoln knows what he's talking about. In his speeches as he travels toward Washington, he assures the country that there is no crisis other than an artificial one."

"We can only hope he's right." James frowned, shifting his gaze from the pier to the ship's gangway.

"Sounds odd, coming from him, especially after the Confederacy has been formed," Adam said meditatively.

"It does, at that."

A silence gathered, tension mounted.

"However," Adam went on, "it's rumored that such able politicians as Seward, whom Lincoln has chosen for his Secretary of State, believe that war can be avoided. I've heard that Seward favors evacuating Fort Sumter of Federal troops as a precaution against hostilities."

James nodded thoughtfully. Suddenly he looked at Adam. "The way we're talking weather and jerking fuses from powder kegs, we might as well be counting the hairs in an admiral's beard."

Adam said wryly, "It was getting downright comical, wasn't it, Co-Co?" He stuck out a hand. "Good luck, Jim. May we meet over champagne and under the same flag."

"Dammit all!" James growled, taking Adam's hand in his. "Lieutenants aboard the same old battle wagon again. That's the way it's got to be."

"Even with all your faults, I'd be willing to give it another try."

"Faults? You're perfect, I suppose. Snored in my ear from Newport News to Singapore. A fine midshipman you were, cutting my hammock that time in Sydney Harbor just as the captain walked by."

"Melbourne, Jim. Besides, I won't ever admit it."

"Any more than you'll admit to stealing that pretty Eurasian girl from me in Bombay. Had me thrown in the brig for something I didn't do. Remember?"

Adam checked a grin. "They're taking in the lines, Jim."

So they were. Up on the quarter-deck the captain's lobster-red face was making all sorts of threatening expressions as he bellowed for all hands and damned this and that.

Still grasping right hands, each avoided the other's direct glance. James said, "When you write home, tell Adria to bear with me. If you don't mind, put in a good word for a fellow, will you?"

Adam nodded. James had his sympathy, for he was as much in love as he was confused. Poor Jim, unable to make the choice that would place Adria squarely in his arms for good. But who was he to criticize? Love had never fastened its claws into Adam Cutler. There had been women in his life. There were women now, like Nancy, though he entertained no ideas of casting aside a bouquet for a single flower. With Jim, it was just the opposite. So it was with Adria.

"Just don't disappoint her, Jim. She has never been in love before."

A look of alarm flashed in the other's eyes. "But suppose——" He broke off and stared dispiritedly at the worn planks of the pier.

Adam said, "Sorry I mentioned it." Brightening suddenly, he placed a hand on James's shoulder. Meeting the other's bewildered glance, he said, "I'll let you in on a secret. I've been betting two to one with myself that you won't take the Norfolk packet."

James was too astonished to protest or argue his point. His jaw hung slack. When he finally recovered, he looked hurt, as though Adam had slapped him. Presently his eyes began to snap ominously.

"I'm afraid I must," he said caustically. As it was his nature to cool as suddenly as he flared, James added contritely, "Forgive me, Adam. I know how you feel."

"If you do, grab your things before the engineer shoots steam into the whistle. Hell, for once take a chance, Jim!"

"I can't. Not now, Adam."

James turned away. He stalked up the gangway, which the captain ordered taken in immediately, and looked at Adam. Forcing a weak grin, he said:

"Don't get involved with too many perfumed envelopes."

The attempt at cheerfulness fell flat.

Sounding above the on-decks bedlam was a hiss of steam. The single stack belched black smoke that streamed due southeast. The water churned under the round paddle-wheel cover on which was painted in gold, *CALEDONIA*, and beneath, Baltimore Steam Packet. Adam knew her speed, faults, and groans and vibrations by heart, even the deep-throated growl of her whistle, now sounding deafeningly. Often in the past he and James had stood her decks and shared her staterooms.

Right now she was gruffly demanding full right to the harbor road. She was under way, slipping between tall-masted ships in harbor stow, her paddle beating the water into a frenzy of foam to the delight of caterwauling gulls.

Aboard and moving away from Adam was James Hillyer, with whom he had sailed arm and arm over the years and over the seas. They were sailing divergent courses now. And where they would meet again and under what circumstances no man in these uncertain days would venture a guess.

Adam snugged deeper into the heavy serge greatcoat of navy blue and turned to face the howling wind. He could use a hot toddy now. Ahead, a teamster was calling another a "South Carolina fire-eating secessionist."

Adam looked out over the harbor. The Norfolk packet was lost in the traffic. He decided he could do with a second toddy also. "One for Co-Co," he said.

2

In a mood that matched the dismal change in the weather since James's departure a few hours earlier, Adam returned to his room and fell to work gathering up his belongings as though his very life depended on a hasty exit. He was thinking that first thing tomorrow he could probably discard the uniform of the United States Navy for the best civilian dress available on short notice when an urgent rapping at the door was followed by:

"Telegram for Adam S. Cutler, Esquire."

He stood out a moment of puzzled wonder before moving to the door, where he signed for the telegram and rewarded the messenger with a coin.

"Now what?" he said, turning the envelope over and considering its content with a pessimism unusual to his nature. Trouble or sickness at home, he decided, which he would prepare for by warming himself with spirits more potent than the money-grubbing barman poured into a toddy. Uncorking a bottle, he thanked his stars that he would soon be off for Alabama. And the devil with Nancy Eskridge, who was nothing short of a tease—the kind of woman who enjoyed filling a man with hot thoughts before whirling away exhilarated by another coquettish achievement. Given a few more days here, he might change the picture.

Odd thing, he had learned little of Nancy's background. There was a hint of things untold in guarded conversations about her. He know only that she was a niece of the owner of Crafton Hill, that she had suddenly left Florida about a year back to make her home in the old dignified mansion. Other than these things, he knew only that she kept the men jumping about.

"Adam Cutler included," he said, ripping open the envelope. Then he sat down and read:

Washington, March 1, 1861

Sir:

Upon learning that you have disembarrassed yourself of your Federal commission, I beg leave to request your consideration of duties connected with our Department which I am constrained to impose upon you and which I shall explain in person on or around March fourth. Should it be your pleasure to accept without further explanation at this time, please engage suite of rooms on Charles Street and advise.

R. SEMMES

ADAM S. CUTLER, Esq., Baltimore, Md.

Adam's brows joined as he read the message again. Questions he could not answer popped into mind: What was Semmes doing in Washington, what could he possibly have in mind for an ex-lieutenant without a commission in the Confederate Navy, and what would the mysterious imposition require of him, and where, and for how long?

"And why a suite of rooms on fashionable Charles Street?" he asked with mounting curiosity.

Up came his eyebrows as, like an imp, Nancy scattered his thoughts. Perhaps she might prove more responsive in the privacy of an elegant setting. The devil with such transient ideas! Semmes had a reputation for pushing things through almost to the point of autocracy. A man might not like "Old Beeswax," Joseph Cutler had once said, but he could not fail to respect the Mobile lawyer who had during the Mexican War superintended the landing of General Scott's troops at Vera Cruz. Therefore, the old boy had a purpose in mind for the suite, and it did not include golden-headed Nancy.

Realizing that Semmes could not have chosen a more inappropriate time for obtaining such quarters, due to the expected overflow of crowds anxious to see Mr. Lincoln's inauguration in Washington on March fourth, and which would fill every hotel in Baltimore at outlandish prices, Adam decided to waste no time.

Late that evening he managed to secure a suite in one of the finest hotels, though not without considerable difficulty and expense. Tired and out of sorts from the ordeal of lengthened persuasion and waiting, he was shown to rooms overlooking famous Charles Street, where wealthy and fashionable Baltimoreans promenaded afternoons.

Upon entering the parlor, he suddenly forgot his desire to toss the hosteler into the street. "Um-m," he said, pleasantly surprised. "Seems I've chanced upon the bridal suite."

The parlor was a spacious room, with pale blue velour draperies and walls papered with scenic views of old New Castle, Delaware. The furnishings were made up of fine pieces of hand-carved walnut and upholstered in brocade. An ornate chandelier was piped with gas, thanks to the enterprising Gas Light Company, said to be the only one of its kind in America. Amazing indeed; why, the more important streets were illuminated with gas. A pair of statues, one of which reminded Adam of a similar marble piece at Bay Oaks, which his father called the "bearded Greek," were placed in diagonal corners.

His humor on the mend, Adam said, "The quarters seem shipshape and cozy enough for business or champagne and petticoats."

Early next day Adam received notice from Washington that his resignation from the United States Navy had been accepted. After dispatching a telegram to Semmes in Washington, he spent most of the morning in the shop of a tailor and emerged in better fitting attire than he had expected. Except for alteration of a burgundy-colored velvet house coat and a supply of fine muslin shirts, which were to be delivered by tomorrow evening, he was outfitted in fair style from top hat to shoes. True, the high astrakhan collar was devilishly uncomfortable, and the gold-headed cane seemed a nuisance of the first water, but despite these minor irritations he was quite pleased with the mirrored image of Adam Cutler, Esquire.

That afternoon he notified several friends in and around Baltimore of his new address, among them Miss Eskridge of Crafton Hill Plantation, penned a letter to Adria, another to James, laid in a supply of wines and liquors, and dined in style that evening at an inn famous for Eastern Shore dinners. While eating, he remembered a remark made by an officer on his first day at Annapolis. "The Chesapeake is famous for oysters, diamond-back terrapins and naval officers." A lad was supposed to find the moral lesson therein.

The day following brought sunshine and melting icicles, though the afternoon promenade through Monument Square and the length of Charles Street failed to materialize. There was no room for the fashionable on sidewalks now crowded with civilians of every class and color. Rumbling through the streets were horsecars filled with Northern soldiers on the way to the inauguration in Washington. The bluecoats remained silent but tense as Secessionists hurled insults, and often cobblestones, at them. Mobs formed and were soon dispersed by overworked police only to reassemble. The Baltimore & Ohio Railroad kept its extra trains running for Washington, dumping more regiments and curiosity seekers into Baltimore. It was a great day for the Rip-Raps, a lawless gang claiming sympathy for the South, and who did much to hurt the Cause. To the hoodlums, a riot was merely an excuse for pillage and more.

A tradesman standing near Adam in the lobby ventured a remark. "This town's a likely spot for hostilities any moment. If there's war between the North and South, it'll probably start here." Fingering a cheroot, he added, "Damn if I ever saw people so tense and jumpy. You from the North?"

"Mobile."

"Secesh, eh?"

"Just biased, sir." Adam smiled and departed.

Minutes later he received a telegram: Commander Semmes would arrive around seven that evening.

At a quarter to seven Adam was placing a bottle, water, and ice on the table of his private dining room. The knocker sounded of a sudden, rather impatiently, he thought, for a man of Semmes's dignity. Nevertheless, he hurried to the door and flung it open.

"Nancy!" he exclaimed, barring her entrance.

For the merest instant the young woman met his stern gaze with a look of utter disbelief. Then she laughed lightly, twisting her lithe body past him, and hurriedly shut the door. Leaning against it, she breathed a sigh of relief.

"Heavens, I was followed here!"

"Look here, Nancy," he began ominously, "you can't stay here. Not now."

"Fiddle-faddle! Would you like dear Edgar to see me leaving here? Just because I'm pledged to marry him come May, he thinks he owns me." She sent him a melting glance, and literally cooed, "You don't want him to own me yet, do you, Blackie?"

"Right now, yes," he declared frostily.

"My, but you look different out of a uniform. When did you do it?" She was studying him intently from head to toe. "Maybe I'll get used to it in a moment."

She was undeniably lovely, he admitted. Though she was dressed for the raw weather, thick wool failed to hide in full a figure as nicely rounded and well proportioned as any man could desire. However indiscreet and untimely her visit, he could not deny the bewitching power of her lively green eyes or the taunting curve of her full red mouth. But she amazed him by her contradictory behavior. He had rushed her and got nowhere. Then all of a sudden here she was in his room without chaperon and with a most seductive look on her face.

He said, keeping a tight grip on his patience, "Whatever kind of game you're playing with your fiancé, take it elsewhere."

"Please, darling," she coaxed, "I simply had to see you."

He wondered, though the circumstances gave him no time to

dwell upon it. In a dead-serious tone of voice he said, "You've got to go, Nancy. Now."

"Why, Adam! I've never seen you like this. I do believe you're out of your mind." As he advanced menacingly, she backed a step. "Adam!" she exclaimed, eyes growing wide with incredulity.

Grasping her shoulders, he whirled her around to face the door. "Sorry as the very devil, but I'm expecting Commander Semmes any moment now."

Suddenly she twisted free, ducked under his arms, and struck an attitude of outraged insult. With lips and eyes narrowing into thin lines, she thrust her head forward and cried defiantly, "Touch me and I'll scream so they can hear me on Federal Hill!"

A toss of her head played havoc with the maze of yellow ringlets and set her hat askew. Under different circumstances Adam would have flung back his head and laughed. But anger flared strong within him as he considered the irreparable damage she could inflict on his unborn career within the space of seconds. Semmes would take one look at her and—he didn't want to think of it.

Thoroughly exasperated, Adam was thinking of raising the tangle of petticoats and braving the flailing of arms and long silk-stockinged legs to give her the spanking she deserved. On second thought, he decided he would sooner tackle a panther barehanded.

He was spared further conjecture, for just then the knocker advised that a patient, well-bred visitor was paying call.

"Edgar! I just know it's he!" Nancy's expression was no longer militant, but one of terror. Her mouth opened wide and a slim hand lifted to cover it. "I think I'm going to faint."

Adam took the step separating them and shook her roughly. "Through that door! Hear me? And if you so much as breathe out loud, I'll——"

She broke and ran. When the swish of petticoats fell away behind the bedroom door, Adam swore a silent oath and prepared to meet his guest.

3

A moment later he stood facing Commander Semmes. Having expected a meeting with the rather quiet citizen of Mobile with whom he had occasionally exchanged greetings in the city or at Bay Oaks, Adam was momentarily nonplused by a feeling that he was in the presence of some venerable lord of a quarter-deck. The feeling persisted even though the smile on the tight, severe mouth was friendly enough, and the clear gray eyes, as sharply penetrating as Adam had ever seen, seemed to denote pleasure.

Twisting the tip of one of his black mustaches, Semmes bowed stiffly. These waxed pointed spikes had earned him the sobriquet of "Old Beeswax" among men of the naval service. The small beard between his nether lip and chin seemed largely responsible for the stern set of his countenance.

Adam's greeting was falsely hearty. Nancy seemed to hang like an anvil suspended by a hair above his head, though he went through the necessary motions of host without revealing his uneasiness. They were no sooner seated and past formalities than Semmes tugged at the collar of his sack suit and leveled his eyes like a pointed finger at Adam.

"When I learned that you had shed that false uniform, I wrote Joseph Cutler of my plan to use you. Now I must beg your indulgence while I acquaint you with a few facts."

Smiling, Adam lifted a hand to indicate refreshments.

"I suppose Captain Tattnall informed you of President Davis's decision regarding the rule of accepting all officers from the Old Navy without increase of rank."

"No," Adam said curiously.

"The rule is a good one," Semmes told him, "since it will not tempt any officer to join us for the sake of immediate promotion. The Confederate Navy desires no self-seekers. We are all on equal footing in the race for honors."

"So I am Lieutenant Cutler."

"You are merely *Esquire*. When your mission is completed here, you will be given the rank you held in the Federal Navy. But hold your protest in check—I have seen to it that you will not be penalized by arriving late to a navy of few if any ships. I guarantee you service afloat."

"Thank you, Commander."

Semmes talked on slowly, in a deep, pleasant drawl.

"Now, Mr. Davis, our President, is sending me North to secure materials of war and mechanics skilled in the manufacture and use of ordnance."

Adam showed surprise.

"Despite the fact that we have captured all but a few forts and arsenals within our limits," Semmes said, with eyes burning brighter by the moment, "the South has not enough percussion caps to fight one single battle."

Adam's face screwed up into a knot. "Actually, sir!"

"No treasury, no credit, nor a single gunboat to support the appointment of our friend the Honorable Stephen R. Mallory to the post of Secretary of the Navy, Confederate States of America."

Under the spell of this zealot and his startling revelations, Adam forgot Nancy. So Mallory was at the helm. Odd how the news of his appointment seemed dwarfed by his very need. Adam could not remove his eyes from the high forehead and iron-gray hair of the man seated across from him. Semmes talked on, often bitterly, always determinedly . . .

There were only two navy yards in the South, one at Norfolk, Virginia, which state had not seceded. The other was the Pensacola Yard, fitted out solely for repair and shelter. There was but one plant in the South that could supply large-caliber guns; that, too, was in Virginia.

"In the eyes of the world the existence of the Confederacy, while recognized as a revolutionary body, is not acknowledged as a government of stability. Hence, we are given to understand, its credit is not established.

"But," he thundered, "we are not dismayed!"

Completely bewildered, Adam said on the spur of the moment, "By God, I am!"

Semmes laughed. There was a ripple of relaxed tension, however brief.

Inclining his head, Semmes paused. Some strange light flickered in his eyes and burst like sheet lightning across his stern features. Madness or imagination, it was suddenly gone, and he was saying, "Are your services at my command, sir?"

"In any capacity," Adam replied directly.

"Then, knowing our needs, you will remain here and enlist mechanics, secure ammunition, as listed here"—he produced a paper—"examine arsenals, and scour the Chesapeake for the types of vessels we must have without delay."

So saying, he gave Adam the name of the Confederate purchasing agent for the Baltimore area. Surveying the room and the parlor, he said, "Let us hope that, while I am in New York and New England, these walls may witness many transactions in favor of our noble cause."

Adam was given little time to reflect on his first assignment in the service of the Confederate Government. Semmes had no sooner gathered his papers than he reappraised Adam with a look that was meditatively steady if not cautious. A moment later he seemed reassured, for he launched into a subject that had little if any bearing on the mission that brought him here.

In view of his experience, it seemed that he had been besieged with questions having to do with the naval policy of the South in event the young Republic was suddenly plunged into war. His reply to responsible parties had been in the form of a suggestion based on careful study of existing conditions. He advocated an "irregular" naval force.

Adam asked what he meant by "irregular."

"First," Semmes said, rising and moving to the fireplace, "let us examine the situation and look at the North's most formidable weapon. A commercial marine second only to that of England's. So it is at Yankee shipping that we should aim our blows. Why? In order to cut off that chief source of wealth which would equip great armies and ships-of-war bent on destroying us."

Adam tried to contain his astonishment with a remark. "Why, I never so much as gave it a thought, sir." But he was thinking of it now, and the idea stirred his imagination. To effect a commercial blockade of the North would strangle the Yankee war effort. But how could it be done?

Of a sudden, Semmes dropped considerably in Adam's estimation. Perhaps the commander had dreamed too violently for his own good.

"Sir," Adam said with polite caution, "wouldn't such an ambitious undertaking require first the destruction of the United States Navy?"

"No," came the quick reply. "Remember I spoke of an irregular naval force." Twirling one of his mustaches, he said in a soft voice that belied the excitement in his face, "I mean armed ships, called privateers."

"Privateers?" Adam frowned at the glass in his hand as though he had suddenly discovered a bug in it.

In Semmes's eyes appeared a touch of humor. "You are thinking that this type of warfare will degenerate into piracy. But under sufficient legal restraints this abuse could hardly flourish."

"Privateers," Adam pondered aloud. He saw it all now, from the point of necessity in the event of hostilities to the point of legalizing ships of prey. However, all he saw failed to wholly satisfy him, for there was still something about Semmes, rather than his scheme, which subordinated the whole thing.

Adam was searching for the missing element that fanned his zeal into a flame when Semmes cocked his head in startled manner and gazed at something over Adam's shoulder.

"I could have sworn I saw that door open and shut, Adam," he said crisply. "Are you sure we are alone?"

Under the intent gaze of his superior, Adam said, "Alone?" Never more alert in himself, he sent his mind racing ahead to Semmes's reaction to either a bald lie or the bold truth. Either way, he saw repercussions ahead. But he had to gamble on the possibility that Semmes had caught a glimpse of Nancy.

"We are not alone, sir," he replied with no loss of composure. As Semmes stiffened and glared, Adam said, "It so happens that a lady arrived unexpectedly just before you came."

Adam met the other's steely glance without wavering, though he felt himself grow cold. It was as though he were an offending officer awaiting his superior's decision to break him. It amounted to just that.

Semmes narrowly and covertly surveyed both Adam and the closed door. "I suppose I must appear dubious. But I know a Cutler would never betray a fair lady or a cause."

"Thank you, sir," Adam replied, bowing slightly. "I regret the circumstances more than you realize, Commander Semmes. In the lady's behalf, I must assure you that her reason for coming here was for protection. You see," he lied, "a group of ruffians who pretend to be Southern sympathizers seized her carriage."

"The damn Rip-Raps!" Semmes said vehemently. "Then I must be off so you can attend to her needs."

At the door, he smiled. "I'm counting on you, Adam."

Adam closed the door and breathed a great sigh of relief. "Damn!" he said. "One foot in a whirlpool, I was caught between the devil and the deep."

Then suddenly he was staring at Nancy. She was poised in the doorway with head cocked in an attitude of inquiry. He wanted to storm out at her, and then he wanted to sit down and laugh. As he stood a moment irresolute, she ran to him and threw her arms about his neck.

"Adam," she said, "when I opened the door for a peep, that horrible old man looked me straight in the eye."

Adam scarcely noticed her as she turned the key in the lock, then drew his face down to hers; he was too busy thanking his lucky stars that he had gambled rightly this once, for, no mistake about it, Semmes had with one simple question placed his very future in the balance.

Then Nancy's warm, pliant mouth pressed against his and she was kissing him with a passionate eagerness that scattered all thoughts of hazards, war, and privateers.

## 7.    And April Showers

### 1

FROM THE PATH LEADING TO THE BLUFF, the proud columns of Bay Oaks gleamed a dazzling white in the April sunshine. Until the walkway curved to parallel the river, no obstruction marred the narrow flower-lined strip other than a few limbs of ancient oaks festooned with Spanish moss. But once the cleared swath turned north to intersect the carriage road several hundred yards ahead, the mansion was suddenly screened off by an orderly Gulf-coast wilderness.

Lawrence Jarvis chose the privacy of this setting that afternoon to press his courtship of Adria. But he had no sooner drawn her into his arms than she broke away, a little flushed by anger, which she tried to conceal by reminding him that she had not come here to listen to his proposal but to watch for Adam.

"I do declare, Lawrence, you choose the strangest times to make love," she said with noticeable vexation.

"Do I now? Any time is a good time, I'd say," he replied hotly. "Just because Adam is coming home, you work yourself into a nervous fit. I——"

"Temper, temper," she teased. "Remember what I said. Next time you fly into a tantrum I won't see you for two whole weeks."

With eyes narrowly fixed upon her, Lawrence stood stiffly erect with broad planter's hat in hand. Eying him covertly, Adria was forced to admit that she rather enjoyed the faithful, houndlike devotion of this most eligible and handsome Alabaman. But it ended there. She supposed she demanded masculine attention as much as one's body demanded food. Otherwise she would have long ago sent him traipsing back up the Tombigbee for good.

"Sometimes I think you keep me dangling just for the fun of it." His very coolness bespoke a seething anger at work inside him. "Or is it because I'm handy and your Yankee sailor isn't?"

"La, la, la!" She masked her derision in a sidewise glance and smile before putting her back to him in a swirl of full petticoats. "If I were a man and thought that, I'd leave and never come back."

His eyes on the huge bow at her slim waist, Lawrence considered the challenge in silence. He was not blind to the disparity between her words and engaging smile, though he was not sure which actually governed her humor. Should he parry the quip or depart in righteous anger? He did neither; instead, he swung his cane viciously and knocked the head off a flower.

"Feel better?" she asked, facing him.

"A right smart better, ma'am," he replied crisply.

"Good." Taking his arm again, she said, "Next time you feel like kissing me, I'll just lead you to a daisy bed." She added hastily, "Look at that dark cloud rolling over the bay."

"One of these days, Adria, I'm going to forget I'm a gentleman. And when I do, you'll think a swamp bear is totin' you up a bee tree."

"How romantic, Lawrence dear! Now be a sweet boy and don't tax my patience further."

"*Your* patience!" Shaking his head hopelessly, he looked down at the swirling eddies below them.

From the point of the bluff, the river stretched wide and muddy, with only one boat breaking its swollen surface. The deep-rutted road was empty.

"Adam said he would arrive today," Adria said anxiously. "Did I tell you he is now a lieutenant in the Confederate Navy?"

"Mr. Joseph did. He said also he'd like to send word to your Yankee that I helped in the capture of the sloop *Isabella* on the twentieth of March. There's one load of provisions that won't leave Mobile for the Federals hanging on at Pensacola."

"Lieutenant Hillyer is no doubt as patriotic as any Southerner," she said. "You wait and see."

"He's waiting, not I. He knows our Navy has few ships, and it's first come first served if he gets a berth. I'd say he doesn't want one."

Adria drew her lower lip between her teeth and said nothing.

James did seem confused. Of course he loved her, but—— She bit her lip. Oh well, he was justified in waiting for his state to secede. Hadn't Adam and others done just that? The letters from Norfolk came regularly. There was no mistaking his love or loneliness. His parting with Adam had left him sad. And now, the way things were in Washington, Maryland must soon cast loose from the North. Adam in his last letter from Baltimore had said as much. Excerpts from his message flashed across her memory:

. . . My work here has borne fruit. Skilled mechanics and such ordnance as was available are already on their way to New Orleans. But our needs loom larger as tension mounts here and in Washington. Virginia seems to be waiting for just one overt act or statement from the cautious Lincoln administration. This state is the key to naval stores. God speed her decision in our favor. . . . Commander Semmes has purchased and contracted for great amounts of powder, batteries of light artillery, and other munitions. Oddly enough, he writes that the Northern people were not only willing but anxious to contract with him until the Federal Government grew more watchful. . . . If only our Confederate agents in Washington can remain a little longer we can add to our meager supplies. But if Mr. Lincoln refuses to follow Seward's policy of conciliation and sends supply ships to Fort Sumter (it is rumored here that Lincoln is about to do this), our agents will depart and Fort Sumter will be taken from the Federals. God only knows what will follow. . . .

A hasty postscript told of his preparations to return here:

I have just received a telegram from Commander Semmes advising that he is leaving New York on a Savannah steamer, flying the Federal flag at the peak, the Confederate flag at the fore. He urges me to be in Montgomery by April sixth. Adria, James requests, by letter, I send you his love.

Adria stared up the road, impatiently now. Adam seemed, was in fact, the only real connecting link she had with James.

She hummed the song that was taking the South by storm, "Dixie's Land," if only to console herself. My, but it stirred something in one.

*To live and die in Dixie——*

If only James would return and sing it with her, it would sound even more wonderful. Then she was forcing him out of her mind.

"Lawrence, Adam wrote from Montgomery that he would arrive here today."

Pointing his cane to the sky, Lawrence said, "That storm is going to get here first. It's boilin' in fast."

"Bother! It'll blow over. Besides, I can beat it to the house."

"Can you?" he demanded, tilting her head up.

"I've been wet before," she scoffed.

"So you have." Bending his tall figure in a sweeping bow, he said, "Which prompts the gentleman to bid his stubborn lady adieu and go after the carriage."

Watching him stride off in a hurry, she said, "Good riddance," and forgot him in favor of James; rather, James's promise that buoyed her in moments of despair, that stood as a refuge in a world of madness—"Nothing can come between us, Adria."

A cold drop of rain struck her neck. As others fell, heavy and large, she glanced up into the gray-blue bosom of the advancing storm cloud. She was looking about for shelter when a gust of wind broke the humid stillness and blew moss into horizontal streamers. The next warning came in a ragged stab of lightning that darted to the ground with a flash of unreal light. As though it had struck an arsenal within arm's length of her, there followed an earsplitting clap of thunder. It seemed to jar the very universe and tear the boiling clouds asunder, for immediately the rain began to fall in wind-lashed sheets.

Adria ran for the lee shelter of a live oak tree, though she was drenched to the skin long before reaching it. The wind was blowing stronger now, and moss and small branches were sailing through the rain as though on wings. Another bolt of lightning ripped a hole in the torrent to explode in thunder between her and the river. She could smell the scorched air as an old oak was split in half not fifty yards away.

Frightened as never before, Adria ran. After minutes of stumbling and slogging through mud, she reached the road and cried, "Lawrence!" to the top of her voice. Angry, water streaming down her face, she put her back to the wind in a run for the carriage gate. Suddenly she heard a clatter and sloshing of wheels and hoofs behind her. As she turned to see a carriage and horses, someone thundered forth:

"Belay, you damned nag! Seems we've got a passenger!"

"Adam!" she cried, leaning on the wind.

But the man who leaped from the carriage was not Adam. He was scooping her up in his arms when she cried out in surprise, "Captain Sherrod!"

"At your service, ma'am," he said above the noise of the elements.

"Put me down! At once, sir!" she commanded in loud, outraged tones.

His reply was a devilish smile.

She remembered his disrobing stare several months earlier with a shudder of revulsion, and demanded once again that he let her go. And again he resorted to silence, with only a flashing of blue eyes in his deeply tanned face advising that he was even aware of her presence.

"You just wait until my father hears of this!" she flung at him, squirming to free herself.

He was no more than a step from the carriage when a jagged tongue of lightning and a clap of thunder, almost in unison and terrifyingly near, caused her to throw her arms about his neck and hide her face against his sea coat.

"Lord in heaven!" she cried, trembling with fear.

A moment later she opened frightened eyes. Upon finding herself alive and safe, she gave vent to her temper again. "Captain Sherrod, let me go! This very instant!"

"As soon as I place you in the carriage."

"I wouldn't get in that carriage if my life depended on it. Put me down! Oh—you . . . !"

"Very well," he said, laughing lightly. "You can't get any wetter, ma'am."

Abruptly he tipped his head and covered her mouth with his.

For an instant of shock and disbelief Adria remained inert. In the next she was fighting and twisting her head in a frantic effort to escape his kiss. But there was no yielding in Randall Sherrod. He held her to him until the firmness of her mouth dissolved and resistance was drawn from her. What Adria felt was no change in her regard for this terrible man but in the whirl of conflicting emotions a strange fire sweeping her loose from her conventional roots.

Then she was suddenly standing on her own two feet in the downpour of rain, with trembling hands covering her face and no memory of how she succeeded in breaking away from him. Perhaps he had let her go. It didn't matter. The damage was done. Her next feeling was that of a stinging sensation in her palm as it struck his face.

Whirling, she ran toward the carriage gate as fast as she could go, oblivious to storm and mud as her incredulous mind tried in vain to reconcile such a shameless embrace as she had never expected to enjoy to the chaste woman of short minutes earlier.

Ahead, she saw Lawrence turning the horses and carriage toward the gate, while from behind, the sounds of Captain Sherrod's laughter reached her ears on the wet wind.

2

Completely unnerved and soaking-wet, Adria rushed past her mother and gasping Mammy Rose for the privacy of her room. In her wake tiny pools marked her path through the hall and up the staircase. As though stricken dumb, she was unable to reply to their maze of questions when they burst into her room close on her heels. She could only sob and choke on incoherent sounds that formed in her throat.

"Lawdy me! Git offen dat bed in dem wet clothes!" Mammy scolded, removing her wet garments.

"Adria, what on earth? Didn't you see the cloud, or have I reared a daughter who doesn't know to come in out of the rain?"

"Git me some towels, Miss Annabel. Don't jest stand there. This chile done half drown, and if she ain't, she gwine shake up a dretful chill."

Completely nude, Adria got to her feet and stared blankly at the wall while the slave and her mother rubbed her dry. Mammy's "Even a chicken know to git outen de rain" went unheard. Adria wanted to cry, run away, find the rakehell Sherrod and claw his face, all at once. Helpless to do anything but remember what had happened, she felt a wave of panic and shivered all over. Suddenly she sneezed. Somehow the spell was broken and all trembling ceased.

"Mother," she said, "that man picked me up and kissed me."

Annabel slowly removed the towel from her daughter's thigh and looked up. "Who, Adria?"

"Captain Sherrod."

"Plumb delirium! Talkin' outen yo' head." Suddenly Mammy Rose raised her head. "What's dat yo' say, chile?"

"Quiet, Mammy," Annabel said, studying Adria's face with more concern than she realized. "Why did he, Adria?"

"I was running toward the house when he came along. He picked me up bodily, and when I fought him he kissed me."

"Teasingly, I'm sure, Adria. Some people just don't believe you've grown up. Besides, you shouldn't have fought him when he was offering shelter."

"Shelter my eye! Why, I'd sooner get into a carriage with a cotton-mouth moccasin. Just wait until Father and Adam hear of it. Or Lawrence."

Annabel sat down and looked at Adria. There was something in even the way she held her hands in her lap that calmed one. Only she and Adam were gifted with that quiet patience and reserve, Adria admitted in detached thought.

"Adria," her mother said, "I must warn you not to mention this to the men. It could cause nothing but——"

"Trubble, dat's what!" Mammy said. "Don' want no blood gushin' roun' heah. Dat debbil man from de ocean, he——"

"Adria, you know your father and Lawrence. If you don't, I do. They would no doubt wish to settle the affair with a duel. Regardless of who got hurt, you would be a subject for Mobile gossips. So I'll do the talking to this Captain Sherrod myself."

Adria gasped. "You mean he came on to the house? Actually?"

Mammy Rose hurried to the window. Drawing the curtain aside, she said, "Somebody come. Must be him." Rolling her eyes, she added despairingly, "May de good Lawd be linament wid de wicked."

At the door, Annabel surveyed Adria with open suspicion before saying, "Furthermore, if your father and Lawrence learn of this, they'll use it to rush your engagement and marriage—for your protection, my dear."

When Adria's expression assured her that the men would never know, Annabel went downstairs and drew Sherrod to the back porch under the pretext of making a purchase through him of a certain object in Havana. When he was comfortably seated, she proceeded to lecture him in quiet but stern manner.

Whatever his precepts of integrity, honor, and gentility, he should know that such effrontery could never be countenanced by decent people; furthermore, he should direct his attentions to women whose sensibilities were not so easily disturbed; and furthermore, since it was evident that he had offended both her daughter and herself, he should, under penalty of what she might do next time, avoid Adria in the future, and transact his business with Mr. Cutler in Mobile.

Rising, she said politely, "Now, Captain, you may escort me to the parlor."

"Indeed, ma'am." He bowed and extended an elbow. "If your daughter possessed your mature charm and composure along with the beauty you have given her, I'd challenge you to do your worst."

Remembering his unperturbed, if not mocking, expression throughout the lecture, she was wondering if he was not challenging her now.

"Now would you, sir?" she said.

"To blow the gaff, I would."

Despite her feeling of indignation, Annabel could not suppress a smile, nor could she bring herself around to admitting an actual dislike for this bold adventurer who made sport of her threats with such easy grace. But the very fact that he in a way disarmed her made her more determined that Adria should never again be brought under his influence.

"So, ma'am," Sherrod was saying, "now that you've done with moralizing, spare me a moment to fetch something from the coach." He returned shortly with a parcel and proceeded to unwrap it.

"I picked this up in a shop down in Havana," he said, spreading yards of white lace from Annabel's shoulder to the parlor entrance. "Unless the old trader played me for a sucker, it's genuine *point de Venise à réseau*. Please accept it with the compliments of Captain Sherrod, ma'am."

Annabel's eyes shone with delight as she ran her fingers over the delicate needle-point lace.

Joseph appeared with a gruff question. "See here, Captain Sherrod, are you turning my house into a bazaar?"

"Joseph, isn't it a wonderful present?" Looking up, Annabel said, "Captain, how can I ever thank you?"

Sherrod met her glance with his best smile. "Don't try. It's the least I can do for as fair a lady as ever trod Alabama soil."

Annabel's eyes fell under his intent gaze. For a moment she was wondering if the doors of Bay Oaks would be closed to this man in the future. Then she forgot all but the exquisite lace in her hands.

3

It was nearly three in the morning when an insistent hammering of the big brass knocker penetrated every corner of the house. Muttering, Joseph made his way to the balcony just as the visitor cried out impatiently:

"Open up, you Alabama Rebels! The Confederate Navy has arrived!"

"Adam!"

Adria leaped out of bed. Snatching up a robe in the dark, she raced downstairs and flung the door open. Her arms flew about his neck before he could move a step. "Liar!" she cried. "Said you were coming yesterday. Why didn't you?"

"By ship and banner pompano, what a welcome!"

As Adam entered, Joseph appeared holding a candle high. With a broad smile breaking across his sleep-heavy face, he jerked at the bell cord to the servants' quarters as though the house were on fire. Oblivious to Adria's questions—they were coming sixty to the minute—Adam swooped down on his mother at the newel post and lifted her bodily into his arms.

"Oh! Adam, you'll drop me!" she cried. Looking at Adria, she said, "We don't like this sort of thing, do we?"

Adria looked daggers at her mother. "For a few yards of fine lace we Cutler women will suffer most anything."

Annabel burst into laughter that wouldn't stop. Nor would she tell Joseph or Adam what was so funny. But her mirth was so infectious that soon even Adria could not sustain a vindictive expression.

While Mammy Rose fried chicken, Erasmus beamed and hovered about Adam, who sipped brandy and told of his trip home, as well as his stay in the capital city of the Confederacy.

"The air is tense in Montgomery," he said solemnly. "In fact——"

"Did you see James before you left Baltimore?"

Adam looked at Adria, who sat cross-legged on the floor between him and Joseph. "No. But I heard from him on the sixth, I believe. Tell you about it later."

"You were saying," Joseph prompted.

"Adam," said Annabel, "have you lost weight? Or is it that suit you're wearing?"

"Probably the suit, Mother," Adria replied. "Funny, every regiment has a uniform. Why doesn't the Navy?"

"What about Montgomery?" Joseph asked, frowning.

Adria pointed to a large flag, with seven white stars circled in a field of blue, completed by one white horizontal bar between two of red. "How do you like our banner, Adam? It was adopted on March fourth."

Joseph slammed a fist hard against the arm of his chair. "Thunderation! By all that's holy, this place is a magpie roost! Quiet, everybody, while Adam talks." As though the sudden hush rebuked him, he added a polite "If you please."

Adam began anew. "As you probably know, when the Confederate commissioners learned that Mr. Lincoln had ordered supply ships from New York to Fort Sumter, they broke off negotiations. Anyhow, soon after I arrived in Montgomery, Mr. Davis called a cabinet meeting to decide whether or not to open fire on Sumter. The ice was getting thin."

"And, glory be, it'll get thinner," Joseph said excitedly.

"How right you are," Adam replied gravely. "I wish Mr. Davis's hotheaded advisers hadn't been so hasty. We need time to arm."

"For what? The North won't fight, Son. Afraid to."

Adam's brows lifted. "Look here, old boy," he said, grinning, "you're letting the Rebel in you do your reasoning. We have over five thousand troops waiting for the order to fire on the fort. And despite the fact that Federal Major Anderson offered to surrender within three days if not provisioned by his government, I understand the order will be to fire."

"Good."

Adam said soberly, "If we do, it means war."

Annabel flashed Adam a sharp glance, but said nothing.

"War?" Adria looked astonished, then troubled.

"Then let it come," Joseph said, rising. "If we don't dictate peace terms in Washington by June, I'll eat a barbecued bobcat for breakfast."

Erasmus thought this very funny. Shaking with laughter, he spilled brandy on Adam's hand. "Sorry, suh! Got me a case o' giggles. Bobcat, he say."

Adam smiled grimly. "Yes. He said bobcat." Frowning, he turned to Adria and drew an envelope from a pocket. "Jim sent it to you through me. Must be mighty important."

Adria opened the envelope only after she was curled up in her own bed. Eyes bright with anticipation, she read:

My darling Adria—
As I write this, I am sorely tempted to leave Gosport in all haste for Mobile.

"Oh, James," she implored, "why don't you?" Wondering if he was leading up to just that, she read avidly:

But I sincerely believe that my future and yours are best served by my remaining in the service, since I am convinced that the war threat will dissipate and stanch loyalties cannot but meet with proper reward. Please think as I do, darling, regardless of influences brought to bear on you. Remember that we are very much in love.

*With this and only this sweet thought in mind,* my dear Adria, please consider the urgent request I set down here—

With or without the consent of your parents, come to me, Adria. Leave by train or ship for Norfolk, where we can be married.

There was more, much more. He poured out his lonely heart to her and he argued convincingly. His convictions became her own. A crisis would be averted, and despite all evidence to the contrary, Fort Sumter would not be fired upon. There would be no war, and James, faithful to a trust and a flag, would be rewarded with an improvement in rank. But all this was neither here nor there. She loved him. How very much she loved him.

Sudden excitement quickened Adria's pulses and trembling fingers lifted to the divide of her breasts. "Dare I go?" she breathed aloud. As some inner voice answered, she stared in round-eyed astonishment at the flickering candle, as though the flame prompted her decision.

"I'm going," she said, leaping out of bed to do her packing in secret. "I'll tell Adam after breakfast and let him do the explaining later."

Outside her window the dawn was coming up fast. Pausing with an armful of petticoats, Adria gazed over the lush grounds at dripping branches and flower stems. What would Norfolk be like? Or would it matter, with James so near? Nothing would matter!

She turned away from the window with a song of gladness in her heart and began piling dresses, hats, and slippers atop the bed.

At around half past eight Adria sat at the breakfast table sipping a third cup of coffee and wishing her mother would leave her alone with Adam. Instead, Annabel remarked rather curiously on Adria's sudden fondness for coffee. Then Adam pushed his chair back. He was dabbing a napkin at his mouth when Adria's significant glance arrested him.

A minute later Annabel left for the kitchen and Adria hurriedly placed James's letter before Adam. Watching him anxiously, she saw his brows join in a frown that deepened by the moment.

"Jim's crazier than a yellow-billed loon," he said without looking up. Then he was staring at her. "Adria, why did you show me this?"

"Because I'm going to him. Today."

Adam laughed. "Just a minute. Please. I won't ask if you've forgotten who you are, when you lost your mind, or if you know what this would do to Mother and Father. All I ask is this—think it over a day or so."

"Adam, I didn't come to you for advice. All I want is your help after I'm gone. Just make Mother and Father understand, that's all."

He was drumming the table with his fingers and fast assuming an attitude of exasperation when she jumped to her feet. "Oh, you!" she exclaimed. "I won't listen to you. I simply won't!"

"Then there's little use talking to you," he said resignedly. "So go ahead and make the mistake of your life."

"Mistake? We love each other, Adam. I thought you would help."

"I'm very anxious to help you, Adria."

She eyed him dubiously.

"You won't like it." He sat with fingertips touching, his narrow glance fixed on a spoiled child used to having her way. He didn't wish to hurt her, but she was his sister. He said the rest.

"I'll be blunt and tell you that I don't believe James will reach a decision his father doesn't make for him; that he'll probably stay in the Federal Navy even if there is war, and you'll have to live with the fact."

"I don't believe you," Adria said, though she was lacking in conviction.

"Don't. Just the same, imagine how you'd feel, a Southerner in a Northern camp. So maybe you would be wise to tell James to come after you himself. However"—Adam made a pretense of gravity—"he probably wouldn't do that."

"Why wouldn't he?" she asked.

"On account of what you don't believe about him. But it's your question. Suppose *you* answer it."

With that, he left her standing in troubled thought.

After long moments of indecision, Adria wandered into the parlor. Adam was cruel, she kept telling herself in an attempt to put down rising doubt. But he had planted well, for despite her faithful defense of James she was beginning to wonder. The heart and the mind were painfully at odds.

Suddenly, defiantly, she spun about and raced into the hall and on up the stairs. "I'm going! I'm going! And nothing can stop me!"

Within the hour, she managed to leave the house undetected by any member of the household. Seated in a phaeton, she turned her head for a final glimpse of Bay Oaks as the road sloped for the river. As a feeling of nostalgia assailed her, she compressed her lips and stared straight ahead again.

"I'll think of James, and only James," she said to herself, opening her reticule. The money she had taken from her father's drawer should be enough for passage to Norfolk. Oh, he would be furious at finding her gone. But she wouldn't think of that either. Just James.

Abel brought his song to an abrupt end. "Look yonder, miss," he said. "Ain't dat Mistuh Adam waitin fo' de ferry?"

Adria looked ahead. Sure enough, Adam sat atop a white horse in lazy fashion. Engaged in conversation with a river boatman, he looked up as the Cutler vehicle approached.

Adria braced herself for an argument before the greased wheels rolled to a stop. A moment later she sat stiffly, pretending to ignore Adam, who merely nodded before resuming his conversation. She overhead something about General Beauregard and a flag of truce from the boatman, who was timing the episode to an hour or so before dawn. Then he was telling of conflicting reports as to which fired first, the Mount Pleasant Battery or Fort Johnson.

"They say it began at four-thirty sharp, Adam. The time don't matter. It's that first shot we're gonna remember, praise the Lord and Jeff Davis!"

"Right," Adam said thoughtfully.

Adria listened with curiosity increasing by leaps and bounds. As the ferry approached, Adam flung a farewell warning to the other —to hoist his flag and oil his gun—and very casually tied his horse to the back of the phaeton. Climbing up alongside Abel, he said:

"Let me drive this hack for once, Uncle."

Adria leaned forward. "Adam, what were you and the boatman talking about?"

"Oh, that," he replied, waving at the ferryman. "War, I guess. Our batteries began shelling Fort Sumter this morning."

Adria uttered a little cry of protest. "But—but James said the war threat . . ." Her words ran out, and she sank back against the cushion as though she were watching the Confederate guns at Charleston taking deliberate aim at her dreams of happiness. They thundered forth at the behest of some remorseless destiny that she could not fully understand, but only guess at vaguely beyond a knowledge that it was bent on cheating her of something very dear.

"War," she said, not wishing to believe it, but believing just the same. Perhaps it would jar James out of his state of incertitude. But suppose it did not. Her troubled mind moved in great circles, always returning to the same starting point—the outbreak of war. Today, tomorrow, flags flying, the Stars and Stripes, the Stars and Bars, men and women rallying to the colors, excitement, fervent words and wishes and prayers mingling with rash words and boastful remarks—

these things, if the prelude to war formed a pattern for the near future, would mark the beginning of a struggle without James at her side.

"Declare yourself, darling," she urged in silence.

Adam was saying, "Where to, Adria?" There was no reply, and he turned in time to see her cover her face with shaking hands.

"I don't know, Adam. I—I just don't know."

Without a word, Adam turned the phaeton about and drove slowly toward Bay Oaks.

BOOK TWO

# The Proud Banner

## 8.  The Jubilant South

1

ADAM was sure his father would burst a blood vessel unless his mirth subsided. Already his red face was taking on a purplish hue, and Annabel was urgently demanding that they leave crowded Dauphin Street before the angry officer resorted to profanity.

The open carriage had drawn to a halt near Bienville Square, where recruits were being drilled. Despite the nervousness of the horses, which was causing Abel more concern by the moment, Joseph refused to budge until the sergeant convinced a bewildered private that the drillmaster's word was law. "Left wheel" was followed by "Right, oblique, march," and, "Right face," and a thunderous "Halt!" for a "polite" word with the misfit. "So you're tired!" he said. "I'm a mind to put you on immortality, friend. Corporal, take this man out and drill him like billy hell!"

The Stars and Bars stood out from rooftops and balconies, waved from the maze of steamers, packets, and banana boats, the fifth flag to fly over the city founded by Jean Baptiste le Moyne Sieur de Bienville. Reminiscent of Mardi Gras days, Dauphin, Royal, Government, Water, St. Francis, and Conti Streets were crowded with people of every walk of life, all united in celebrating the fall of Fort Sumter less than a short excited week in the past. Under the flush of victory, the city seemed to be dancing to a new and fascinating rhythm. It was seen and heard and felt. It was everywhere.

Annabel said in amazement, "Why, Mobile has gone stark mad!"

As the corporal marched the unhappy private off on the double, Joseph said, "Adam and I will get out at the Battle House while you go after Faustine and Elvy."

After exhorting Abel to drive with care, the men alighted in front of the hotel. "Seems we have a little time on our hands," Adam said, looking at his watch. "The *Southern Republic* hasn't steamed in from Montgomery."

Joseph didn't mind waiting for Commander Semmes. A young

merchant was shaking his hand and replying to a question. "Sure, Mr. Cutler, but for the present brown jeans will have to do for our uniforms. What do you mean they're not as pretty as the Forty-Second's?"

"Danny, they're beautiful." Joseph laughed. "Any merchant who lays down his daybook and ledger to form a company and drill night and day has my vote. But look who's coming."

A seaman was weaving down the street, singing to the top of his unsteady voice, "Oh, the Confed'rate flag's me battle rag—fer one more drink I'd fight, I think. Oh-ooo——" He broke off suddenly. "If it ain't Cap'n Sherr'd I'll swaller a squid wi' fo'teen laigs! They say ye was flyin' the Federal flag on the old *Gulf Wind*. Did ye?"

"Aye. So I could enter Havana, Tommy boy. They didn't know what the hell the Stars and Bars were down there."

"They'll learn, the goddamn Spanishers——"

Inside the Battle House, the air hung thick with tobacco smoke. Voices in a score of conversations blended into a steady drone. Closer, snatches of talk about this and that reached Adam's ears: "And after a forty-hour siege our guns didn't kill a damned Federal at Sumter! Amazing, you say? The devil, suh, we need target practice." On their left, Joseph was listening to a florid-faced merchant in a heat over news from the North. "Certainly Abe Lincoln's call for seventy-five thousand volunteers don't bother me none! Didn't President Davis ask for a hundred thousand? And he'll get them. It's the damn talk up North. Stephen Douglas a-rilin' the folks at mass meetings, and Bell and Everett Whigs taking Lincoln's side, and Washington calling former Secretary of Navy Toucey a traitor for scattering the Federal Navy all over the world. I believe, gentlemen——"

"Three cheers for Virginia! Everybody!" The roar that followed was deafening. Adam was hoarse from yelling before the demonstration ended. Virginia's secession ranked with the surrender of Fort Sumter in importance.

Adam counted seven different uniforms, representing as many companies. Lawrence stood near his father in a brilliant gray costume trimmed with red, denoting—Adam wasn't sure—artillery, 2nd Alabama Volunteers. A fourth corporal. And there stood Captain Cleveland of Company I listening to a paunchy cotton broker.

"Captain," he said, waving a hand, "the world is our oyster. With cotton on our side, the war won't last a year even if the North decides to fight. Back in 'fifty-eight I heard Senator Hammond of South

C'lina say in a speech in the Senate, 'Would any sane nation make war on cotton? Without firing a gun, without drawing a sword, should they make war on us we could bring the whole world to our feet.' He said, 'What would happen if no cotton was furnished for three years? England would topple headlong and carry the whole civilized world with her, save the South. No, you dare not make war on cotton.' "

A group of older men cornered Joseph in a discussion of ways and means of supporting the Confederate Treasury, leaving Adam free to check on the latest wire dispatches from all parts of the country. As he made his way through the crowd, his attention was drawn to an announcement regarding the change of names of several Mobile streets. Whether they had been or were about to be renamed, he could not make out in the bedlam of excitement, but the citizens were severing all Northern connections. Appropriately, Massachusetts Street should become Charleston. Other changes were: Vermont to Texas; New Hampshire to Augusta; New York to Elmira; Maine to Palmetto; Pennsylvania to Montgomery.

As Adam's brow lifted and a grin of appreciation lit up his face, a friend slapped him hard across the back and suggested a drink to the future. "I'm on my way up to Talladega, Adam, to drill Rebel troops."

"Peace be on your ashes, Alex. If you don't make it, I'll see that you're embalmed with bay water."

"Make it blackstrap molasses and I'll rest better." Turning suddenly, Alex cried, "Hey, look over there! Seems trouble is on the make!" He left to investigate and returned a few minutes later.

"Adam, young Jarvis and Captain Sherrod are exchanging hot words over there. Maybe you can pour a little oil on the water."

Upon learning that Lawrence had spoken his opinion of any man who ran supplies to Federals holding Fort Pickens at Pensacola, that Randall Sherrod had laughed in his face in reply, Adam elbowed his way through the crowd and stood between them.

"Lawrence," he said placatingly, "if General Bragg with an army of well over two thousand men in Pensacola can't stop the traffic, how can you?" To Sherrod he said, "I don't believe you're guilty. But I do believe both of you would eat each other up or die in the attempt. Suppose you save your guts for Abe Lincoln's bluecoats."

A ripple of laughter broke the tension. Sherrod executed a bow in the pink of courtesy and amazed the crowd with a magnanimous gesture: He would buy drinks for every loyal Southerner in the house. Unable to refuse, Lawrence stiffly said he would match the other's generosity. Soon schoonerman's and planter's money flowed like the Mobile on a rampage.

Lost in the merry gathering, his ears ringing with vainglorious boasts, ribald laughter, and heated arguments over the military prowess of such men as Bragg, Beauregard, Jefferson Davis, Cobb of Georgia, and among others, Lee of Virginia, who had not as yet committed himself, Adam glanced at his watch. He was pushing his way toward the hotel entrance when a hand clapped him vigorously on the shoulder.

"Lieutenant Cutler, I confine you to the brig!"

Adam turned quickly. "Chapman!" Beaming, he grasped the other's hand. "As big, black-eyed, and devilish-looking as ever. Beard and all."

Stout Lieutenant Chapman possessed the brightest eyes and smile of all the naval men Adam had ever known. Although he and Adam had shared little time afloat, both were Alabamans. Chapman was saying:

"Lucky dog, you. Here I am taking hasty leave of my wife for New Orleans, and you, dammit, aren't even hooked."

"That's only the half of it," countered Adam. "But what about New Orleans?"

"Wait! What's this, Adam?"

Both trained eager eyes on the public announcer who stood atop a desk yelling to the top of his voice, "Gentlemen! I repeat——" He paused for quiet. "I repeat. Your attention please. A wire. The 6th Massachusetts Regiment, on its way to Washington, is now being mobbed and stoned in Baltimore!"

When the cheering subsided, the announcer waved another telegram. "Hear! Hear this!" he cried. "Mr. Abe Lincoln has declared a blockade of the Atlantic coast south of the Chesapeake. That's the laugh of the day, gentlemen."

"Blockade, he says," shouted a bull-throated sailor. "First thing ye know, he'll be taking in our Gulf. Yah!"

Men threw back their heads and roared. Adam and Chapman joined them, laughed louder at the jokes: "What with, Abe, mermaids or sharks? Oh, Mister Lincoln, please don't do that to us!" The noise drowned out the next message, though Adam caught enough to learn that the New York 7th was marching down Broadway.

When the clamor and excitement died down somewhat, Chapman

advised that he had been detailed to report to Commander Semmes
for duty in New Orleans, where a ship awaited them.

"The *Sumter*, Adam. Heard of her? No? As you know, Mr. Mallory
approved Semmes's idea of warring on Yankee commerce and ap-
pointed a board of naval officers in New Orleans. These men have
worked day and night in an effort to secure light, fast steamers to
turn loose on the enemy's commercial marine. Seems the board
could find nothing entirely satisfactory. However, Semmes over-
ruled the decision on one craft, the *Habana*, which the Navy Department has renamed *Sumter*, for obvious reasons. So I'm aboard
of Semmes to help ready her for sea."

"And you called me a lucky dog, Chapman?"

"Mean you're left out of it? Really?" A deep gruff laugh followed.
"We heard you were in Baltimore on special duty. Didn't swallow
your anchor there, did you?"

"I'm beginning to wonder," Adam said curiously, thinking of
Semmes and Nancy on that night in Baltimore. "That laugh of yours
—just what prompted it?"

Chapman was having fun. "So there was a woman! Adam, you
really get around."

"The devil with you! I'm waiting here for Beeswax Semmes also,"
Adam said, producing the wire from Montgomery.

Then Chapman was reciting the names of other officers chosen to
help refit and sail the *Sumter*.

Adam listened and forced a grin to cover the disappointment
sweeping through him. Semmes had promised him service afloat,
and he had been fool enough to think it would be under the zealot
whom all believed would be the first to raise the Stars and Bars at
sea.

2

The drive to Bay Oaks resolved itself into a loquacious duel, with
Joseph vying for supremacy over Annabel and Elvy. As events of
the day clashed with fashions and refined gossip, Faustine's silence
appeared studied as compared to Adam's complete indifference to
everything that went on about him.

Faustine recalled Adam's perfunctory greeting upon seeing her
for the first time since mid-January. Pursing her mouth, she drew
in her unfocused gaze from the verdant woodland and let it fall
quizzically on his profile. She was wondering if he had actually

been aware of her. It was odd, she thought, that a man and woman could have been thrown together as much as she and Adam without exciting any spark to stand out sharp in memory. Rather, their association had seemed more like that of cousins.

Faustine's eyes narrowed in examination of Adam's half-averted face. Even as she replied to a question from her sister, she pondered the strength of character indicated by his jaw and chin. "Heavens, no, Elvy. You should know I'm not the type who can wear heavy laces and ornaments."

Adam turned his head slowly and looked at her, or through her. She wondered.

Joseph said with vast exasperation, "If the weapons of war were silks and lace, we'd have our victory before June." Folding hands over the head of his cane, he looked at Adam. "Well, any time you care to open up, I'll be listening."

"Um-m. I've been thinking—about the reward a man gets for doing his best on a job he doesn't like to begin with. He gets promoted to the same job again."

Joseph turned to Abel. "Really makes sense, doesn't it?"

Abel chuckled, and Adam said, "Commander Semmes wanted me aboard the *Sumter,* but Mr. Mallory told him that due to my accomplishments in Baltimore they were considering me for the same work in England."

Joseph nudged him. "Go on."

"I reminded the commander that he had promised me service afloat. Seems I'll get it, that is until Mr. Mallory sees fit to exile me to Liverpool. Up in Montgomery they're juggling me like a ball, thinking of placing me aboard the Georgia steamer *Savannah* on coast defense to relieve Lieutenant John M. Kell.

"So Kell can board the *Sumter.*"

Faustine was listening avidly to Adam's every word. His changing tones of voice and the expressions crossing his face seemed of greater importance than all he was saying, for she seemed to feel without any awareness of searching him that one's strength and weaknesses were revealed by little things.

"The alternative," Adam went on, "is to make a strong bid for what I want."

Faustine asked, with seeming constraint, "What do you want, Adam?"

He sent her a quick glance. "A job under Rousseau, the commanding naval officer at New Orleans."

Faustine met his direct gaze without wavering. "In order that by some stroke of luck you can sail with Commander Semmes?"

"Why, yes," Adam replied, smiling his sudden appreciation of her.

Under his scrutiny, she demurely lowered her eyes, then lifted them quickly, as though she had discovered in him some disturbing quality that had hitherto escaped her. Slowly the intensity of his glance faded into a semblance of a frown and he looked thoughtfully at the road ahead.

Faustine covered her pleasure of the moment by asking of Adria. Upon learning that Adria was entertaining young ladies from an upriver plantation, she made a cautious inquiry about James Hillyer.

"Adria hears from him regularly," Annabel smiled.

Joseph literally snorted, "Maryland!"

Adam intervened before his father could muster suitable words to express himself. "Jim will come through. Depend on him."

"I do hope so—for dear Adria's sake," Faustine replied in sincere tones.

Annabel's hand fell gently atop Faustine's. "Bless you, dear."

Faustine thought of the almost sisterly devotion that had bound her deceased mother and Annabel from childhood, but with an awareness that such a relationship between Adria and herself was impossible. Of course, Annabel knew little or nothing of the strong undercurrent of resentment of one for the other. It was better that kind, thoughtful Annabel should remain uninformed.

Faustine caught a glimpse of Bay Oaks in the distance. Through a screen of live oaks the white columns were tinted in soft shades of pink by the low sun. A lovely sight, she admitted. How very desirable—for what it was, for all it represented. She could see in memory its crystal chandeliers, silver doorknobs, the rosewood furniture, marble mantels, great mirrors—splendor. And stretching quietly under the Alabama sun were vast acres of land. Rich land, up in Clarke County.

At Bay Oaks, Adria had stolen James Hillyer from her. Adria, a spoiled child, had ripped her plans apart and scattered them to the winds. Denied her were the things the Hillyer name would have made possible. But worse, she had learned to care for James more than she realized. And only to lose him to a rich girl who owned ten dresses to her one, who had only to beckon for slaves by the score to humor her slightest wish.

The tightness about Faustine's small mouth fell gradually away as she thought of the future. Adria would marry away from all this, while Adam would bring his wife, the next mistress of Bay Oaks, home to live.

Faustine's delicate eyebrows arched gracefully and her gaze shifted slowly from the big plantation home to Adam.

## 9.   The Crescent City

1

WEARY AND OUT OF SORTS, Adam paused before the door of his Royal Street apartment and dabbed at beads of perspiration on his forehead with a thoroughly wet handkerchief. It was unusually warm for early May, even considering that this was low, humid New Orleans. And a damn sight hotter, he reflected, being cooped up in the Texas of a steamboat most all afternoon with pigheaded carpenters and fitters. Besides, he doubted if they would ever succeed in converting the raised river hulk into a gunboat. And what with the Louisiana State Navy competing like some foreign body with the Confederate States Navy for steel, mechanics, ordnance, even scrapped propellers, Commander Rousseau would be lucky to commission a single fighting craft into service against the enemy.

"Luck is a lord," he muttered, fitting a key into the lock. But he had reason to be thankful, he supposed. Tomorrow he would steam up to Natchez aboard a former luxury stern-wheeler to inspect a craft. Probably another derelict, with gingerbread gleaming topside and a bottom you could stick a thumb through.

Entering the dimly lit room, he felt the sudden coolness of the interior and stood for a moment relishing his rank extravagance. One did not occupy the entire second floor of an old Creole mansion on a lieutenant's pay. No, *mon cher cousin*, one didn't. The soft sea-green walls, crystal sconces, Bacchus urns of porcelain and furnishings of the Directoire period, a prized Verney cabinet, a pier mirror, the hand-carved four-poster, the grilled balcony, a courtyard and fountain surrounded by roses, camellias, banana trees, and purple bougainvillaea—these things, by the grace of Cutler cotton—made New Orleans tenable to dozens of Confederate naval officers.

While he was shedding his coat, Adam's attention was drawn to an envelope on the mantel where Ti-Coo, the old mulattress, had a habit of placing mail and magnolias. She would, of course, expect him to buy *gris-gris,* the most feared of Voodoo charms, with which one invited harm to the enemy. And he would humor her, as usual. Aye, for Ti-Coo had no peer in the science or art of preparing gumbo.

Adam sat down, slapped at a mosquito on his cheek, and extracted from the envelope a letter written in his mother's fine hand. Stretching tired legs, he read:

May 14, 1861

Dearest Adam:

As I have spent the entire night at the slave hospital trying to save Uncle Ralph's youngest boy Ray from pneumonia, I am too tired to write my best. It is very hot today, the wind being from inland, and we hear that the ice boats from the north will cease coming.

Adam, I know you have enough worries, but I most anxiously request your help with Adria. As you know, she wrote to James Hillyer, demanding that he resign from the Federal Navy. Thinking that he would do so, due to the fact that Baltimore has been in the hands of Secessionists for several weeks, I was not prepared for what followed. He wrote a sweet letter in reply, really poured his heart out, poor boy, but it all amounted to his refusal to comply with her wishes. Hurt, angry, and weary of Joseph's stand against her "enemy suitor," Adria created quite a scene last evening. For once she got the better of Joseph, and I do believe he might have consented to her marrying the devil himself had she not turned her fury on James. She made a vow that she would marry Lawrence before he marches off to war, if only to spite James.

Lawrence dropped in this morning and, to my everlasting surprise, left here beaming. Prepare yourself, Adam—for Adria is serious. She and Lawrence are engaged to be married. The date set is Sunday, June twenty-third.

While I would naturally be pleased to have Lawrence for a son-in-law, I am horrified at the possibility of his coming into our family out of sheer spite. This marriage must not take place, since it can only be an unhappy one. So, Adam, I implore you, do something! Advise Adria, tell Lawrence the truth. Write him: Fourth Corporal, Suggsville Grays, 2nd Alabama Volunteers, Fort Morgan. Better still, if at all possible, come home.

All my love,
Mother.

P.S. Of course, Joseph sends his love. Uncle Ralph's little boy is going to live, praise God. The stand of cotton is good. And, I almost forgot to tell you, Faustine left on the sixth for New Orleans. She has been engaged to tutor a Creole's young daughters—can't recall his name, but he lives on Toulouse Street.

Adam lowered the letter and sat staring in troubled thought at the gold brocatels across the room. Poor Adria. She was all mixed up. And who wouldn't be? Suddenly angry at James, he walked to the window overlooking the courtyard and opened the shutters. The blast of heat from outdoors caused him to close them hurriedly.

He was pouring brandy when old Ti-Coo slipped into the room and stood with scrawny hands folded at her waist.

"M'sieu is trouble. He ver' distress."

Adam frowned. "I'll need more than a charm this time, Ti-Coo."

"*Non! Non! Non!*" White teeth flashed against pale lips and her yellow face wrinkled in a cryptic smile as she gave him a small bag of brick dust. "*Misérable fille* mus' 'ave strong charm. She make marriage. *Mon Dieu!* You make marriage!"

"I? Make marriage?" Adam's face wrinkled under an amused smile. "Oh no, Ti-Coo." Then he was thinking that a year ago he would have said this war was impossible. And less than a month ago he had laughed loud at Lincoln's declaration of blockade of the Atlantic coast. Then on the twenty-seventh of April, by an amended proclamation, old Abe extended the blockade to the Rio Grande—thirty-six hundred miles of seacoast. In this era of madness anything could happen—

Except marriage for Adam Cutler.

Placing a coin in the wrinkled hand of the mulattress, he further tickled her vanity by asking for her strongest magic to ward off such a calamity. When she had shuffled off, he sat down and pored over the letter again.

"What a mess!" He got up, rammed a fist into a palm, and walked back and forth for a minute or two. "Dammit all, I believe Adria would actually go through with it."

Perhaps he should have asked for duty in Mobile Bay instead of clinging to Semmes's coattail. He recalled the trip upriver to Montgomery and his visit with Secretary of Navy Mallory, which could not have been better timed. The capital city of the Confederacy buzzed with excitement, and elated Mr. Secretary's cherubic countenance beamed upon a mere lieutenant as he sat with hands folded at his prominent abdomen one moment and fingered whiskers running from ear to ear under plump chin and jowls the next. He was jubilant for good reason . . .

On the night of April twentieth the Federals evacuated the Gosport Navy Yard after scuttling and burning four line-of-battle ships, *Delaware, Columbus, New York, Pennsylvania,* the great *Merrimac,* pride of the fleet, and a number of frigates. The torch was applied to buildings of the yard, though Confederates saved for their navy an estimated ten millions of dollars' worth of armor plate, heavy ordnance, chain and assorted arms, as well as the dry dock. Hundreds of heavy modern cannon, including famous Dahlgrens, now belonged to the Confederacy, and the screw frigate *Merrimac,* after burning to the water line, was saved.

Adam remembered that in the minutes before Mr. Mallory signed the official order of his transfer to New Orleans he could not but wonder at James Hillyer's part in the cowardly Union destruction of Gosport.

And now, frowning at his mother's letter, he said aloud, "That alone should have forced James's decision." He added grimly, "But what can you expect when even Adria failed to move him?"

Small wonder then, Adria's fury. He found it not at all difficult to picture her with mouth drawn into a tight line, eyes flashing fire, petticoats swirling as she paced, panther-like, with hands alternately on hips and locked behind her. In love, she was demanding her right to love, nothing more. By thunder, if he knew Adria, and he thought he did, she would actually marry Lawrence if James ignored her threat. Adria gambled like a man. Which, he thought unhappily, was more to be regretted than admired.

However, Adam admitted, the whole thing boiled down to a simple, pointed fact: he had to do something to stop it.

Procrastination was not one of Adam's faults. He tiredly arose and, after fanning his zeal with a couple of brandies, spent the next hour in writing three strongly worded letters. The first, to Adria, was an ultimatum; the second, to Lawrence, carried a terse appeal to a Southerner's sense of chivalry; the last, to James, was in effect an expression of amazement concerning their political differences coupled with a warning of his sister's hardheadedness.

"There," he said with relief, affixing seals. "Out of three charges, two at least should hit the mark."

His glance dropped to the postscript of Annabel's letter, and he stood rubbing at his chin contemplatively. "Um-m," he said. "Toulouse Street. Tutor." Nothing extraordinary about that, since many Creole children grew up unable to speak a word of English. The oddity was Faustine, whom he could hardly reconcile to the word tutor.

Suddenly fresh in his memory was the spark she had struck to his imagination on the ride home from Mobile several weeks in the past. Strangely he had paid no attention to her small figure until she said something about being unable to wear heavy lace and ornaments. Rather odd, after all the years he had known her, that all of a sudden he should discover she had nice curves and a certain depth of expression in her eyes.

"Toulouse Street," he said with a lift of his brow.

Then he shrugged it off. His evening was promised to a Mademoiselle Légère of Iberville Street. He would probably spend it sitting over tiny cups of black coffee listening to Maman chatter. However, by the law of averages, the mother should fail to appear one evening.

"Perhaps this is it," he said hopefully.

2

Due to the absence of Confederate Commissioner Rousseau from the city, the letter from Mr. Mallory concerning Adam Cutler, Lieutenant C.S.N., was passed on to Commander Semmes, because, as a sentence expressed it, "I believe his influence properly brought to bear on Lieutenant Cutler will gain us a volunteer particularly adapted to the service in mind."

Unaware of why the commander sent for him, but hoping that a permanent home in the *Sumter's* wardroom would result, Adam made his way to the river for a crossing to Algiers, where the vessel's refitment was in progress.

While waiting for the ferryboat, he counted only one vessel in motion on the Mississippi. The transition from peace to war had robbed the formerly busy port of its commerce. Idle ships lined the banks. Brigs and barks sat with yards and cordage as still as bird roosts. River boats were tied up by the dozen, their twin stacks gathering rust where a month ago they had belched smoke in order to turn paddle wheels in the transport of cotton.

"Cotton!" Adam exclaimed under his breath. What had happened to the chief Southern crop and item of export was at least controversial, since the South was divided in its opinion of what President Davis called a strategy to "cotton-starve" England until they were ready to send ships-of-war to the aid of the South. Whatever the outcome of this "king cotton diplomacy," the dismal and undisputed fact remained that sheds, warehouses, and stretching levees were piled high with white bales which nobody would buy.

Adam was inclined to agree with his father, perhaps because the shoe happened to pinch. Joseph declared, "Mr. Davis had better get the cotton out now before the damn Federals jump from token to real blockade." As though to excuse the compliment, he unwittingly paid the United States Navy, he added, "Just in case."

There was a rumor, so openly talked about of late it might be well founded on fact, that the Union Navy would seal the mouth of the Mississippi on the twenty-fifth of May, a mere two weeks in the future.

Despite this threat, Adam could not wholly discount the wisdom of withholding cotton from Europe. Quietly ignoring the loud howls from sea captains and stevedores, prosperous cotton brokers spoke optimistically of Mr. Davis's embargo on cotton shipment, declaring that the President meant to pay for the war by waiting until the price of cotton shot "higher than a cat's back" before selling to England. They said, "Figure what the two million bales on hand will fetch at say fifty cents a pound."

Other than the air of business depression hanging over the river front, New Orleans had changed little. Rather, where commerce left off, preparation for war took over. Adam admitted that he would never cease to wonder how a people who made pleasure a business could almost overnight turn the grim business of war into pleasure. But the Orleannais were very demonstrative in their show of patriotism. Almost every coat and bosom sported a tiny Confederate flag. The approach of a company of soldiers drew a gay crowd along the banquettes and, to the joy of marching men, romantic ladies on the balconies to shower them with blossoms and kisses flung by fair hands. Adam dwelled on the possibility that the ladies crowded the lacy iron galleries to compare the uniform of this group with that one. Each newly organized outfit adopted a different and, if at all possible, fancier and more colorful attire than its rivals. The private regiments of the Creoles outdid them all; it was nothing out of the usual to see gaily caparisoned hussars and lancers of another day tramping the narrow streets at drill. One company had spent twenty thousand dollars on uniforms and seven hundred and fifty for its flag.

Any event was an excuse for celebration. One of the largest followed the news that the State of Arkansas had adopted an ordinance of secession on the sixth of May. Again on the seventh, when Tennessee entered into a military agreement with the Confederacy.

But this was New Orleans. The statement of fact admitted with mild surprise a city of gay, passionate, polylingual people on a bend in the Mississippi in a setting of hot sun, rain, mosquitoes, Creoles, quadroons, chaste and scarlet ladies. A den of iniquity, a heaven. Over champagne or coffee black as a raven's wing, a native merely lifted a shoulder and said, "*Mon ami,* this is New Orleans."

And so it was, Adam agreed, boarding the ferryboat.

Watching the muddy water churning in the boat's wake, he thought of his meeting with Faustine earlier in the week. It had been quite accidental, and not a block from his place on Royal Street. Holding her hand was a small girl of about seven in ruffles and flounces, whom Faustine introduced as Celeste, daughter of Monsieur Estève Decloux, part owner of a mercantile establishment in the Vieux Carré. "*Bon jour, m'sieu.*" The child spoke up proudly. "Or good morning, sir. Coozan Faustine teach me to say." Adam bowed low and held Celeste's hand. "*Bon jour,* my pretty one. Now tell your tutor that m'sieu the Confederate thinks her most beautiful in the *couleur de rose.*"

Beaming under adult attention, the child relayed the message in French and hastily translated Faustine's reply. "Coozan say m'sieu mos' 'andsome in—what you say—Confed'rate—gray. But she not tell m'sieu we walk pas' your house many time."

Faustine playfully scolded. Coloring slightly, she said, "I admit it, Adam. Often I grow lonely for Mobile."

He strolled with them toward Toulouse Street. They talked of Bay Oaks, Adria and James, a dozen and one other things and, at last, about his work in New Orleans. Before the Decloux house, he refused her invitation to come in because of a prior engagement, but promised to visit them in the near future. Faustine extended a small hand and he held it, liking the touch as well as the interest in her eyes. Before he knew it, he was asking her and Celeste to dinner.

The boat was touching in at Algiers. He put Faustine out of his mind and thought of Semmes and the *Sumter.*

Alighting from the ferryboat, he paused in survey of the small former packet ship that had run regularly to Havana and back. Now on the construction dock, she was to be the first warship of the Confederacy. Amid the noises of saws, hammers, and the banging of metal on a deck littered with sawdust and seemingly disordered stacks of lumber, coils of hemp, pitch buckets, and no end of equipment, sweat-soaked men braved the midafternoon heat without grumbling.

"They don't seem to be making much headway," Adam said, thinking of his visit a few days earlier. Everyone agreed that Semmes had taken on a man-sized job. The dismantled packet of 437 tons' burden, 184 feet long, beam 30 feet, had presented the determined commander with upper cabins to be removed as well as top-hamper. She would, according to the plans, sail barkentine-rigged, with a single steam-driven propeller, a collapsible smoke-stack, which, lowered, would enhance the handling of her lower canvas.

Commander Semmes saw Adam then. Dressed in the lightest civilian clothes and wearing a wide-brimmed, somewhat battered leghorn straw to protect his head from the merciless sun, he invited Adam on deck.

"Mr. Cutler, I can see you're wondering if we'll ever put her to sea." With Adam's "I am that, sir," Semmes took his arm and began prowling the deck. "The guns which Commander Harry Sinclair of the Norfolk Yard dispatched by rail cars have not arrived. I'm send-ing a lieutenant in search of them. He'll find them, I'll wager, on some siding totally forgotten in favor of other freight. But that is only one of my problems.

"Everything has to be manufactured, from kids and cans to gun carriages. Deck beams must be strengthened to support the battery, to consist of an 8-inch-shell gun and four light 32-pounders, in broadside. And to do one thing I must wait on another, over and over, day after day.

"Leeds and Company Foundry are casting my shot and a former customhouse employee is constructing out of railroad iron the slide and circle for my pivot gun."

Pausing with a hand on the stump of a mast, he said, "You know, Lieutenant Cutler, this is my first experience at this sort of thing. Believe me, I miss the workshops and skilled mechanics of the old navy yards. But——"

Grinning, mopping sweat from his face, he said, "I'll even the score with the Federal tyrants once I get to sea."

Adam met his flashing glance. "I'm still hoping for the chance to help you do it, sir."

"You could have taken the *Savannah* and done it ahead of me."

"True, but I predict a short success for her. Also, if you'll pardon me, I said, '*help you*,' sir." Adam smiled engagingly.

"You'd like to take temporary berth aboard the *Star of the West*." He referred to a Yankee transport steamer which a band of Texans had captured at Indianola and given to the Navy for a receiving ship.

"So would a dozen and thirteen officers without a ship. As you know, sixteen captains, thirty-one commanders, seventy-six lieutenants, together with one hundred and eleven regular and acting midshipmen, have resigned from the United States Navy up to now. To make room for these officers, our service was increased by the Amendatory Act of April twenty-first to include——"

He broke off suddenly. "Am I convincing you of anything, Mr. Cutler?"

"No, sir. No offense, sir."

A fitter appeared with a request for the measurements of the copper tanks for the magazine. "See Mr. Kell, my executive. He's below aft."

Leading Adam to the bows, Semmes stared across the river. "On the ninth, Secretary Mallory, having reached the conclusion that our resources are not sufficient to complete a navy adequate to the defense of the South, commissioned James D. Bulloch to go to England to have constructed there ships suitable to our needs."

Adam cocked an eyebrow at him. "Is this a true condition, sir; are we lacking in resources?"

"We are," Semmes replied with emphasis.

"And yet Mr. Davis publicly states that we don't need a navy because Great Britain will send warships to engage the Federals in battle within two months."

"Yes, I know." Semmes looked thoughtful. "However, the President and his Cabinet are taking no chances. But back to Captain Bulloch. As you must realize, he will require the services of a few trusted and dependable men. I hope you are beginning to understand."

"I am, sir," Adam replied, more wretchedly than he knew. First he had refused command of the *Savannah*, now a commissioned privateer on Atlantic duty. Should he fail to accept this, the second offer from Mr. Mallory, he might find himself a member of that unenvied group of naval officers stationed at forts and on obscure river boats simply because there was no ship for them.

"Mr. Mallory," Semmes was saying, "believes you ably qualified to serve the South in England. It should prove a most interesting adventure."

"Are those my orders, sir?"

"No. Mr. Secretary desires the services of volunteer Cutler."

"Then, begging your understanding, sir, I request that he be notified of my decision to decline his most generous offer in favor of service aboard a ship-of-war."

Semmes trained a sharp eye on Adam. "You are quite a gambler, Mr. Cutler." A friendly expression suddenly relieved the stern set of his countenance. "At mess last evening Lieutenants Kell, Stribling, Evans, and Chapman predicted your reply almost verbatim. Confidentially, they are conspiring against me in your favor. Perhaps it stems from their fresh memories of the fine champagne served in the comfort of your Royal Street house."

"Perhaps." Adam's hint of a smile remained tightly controlled.

"I'll think about it," Semmes contemplated aloud. "I might find a place. But don't build your hopes too high."

"Naturally, sir," Adam replied, wondering just how close one could place a saucer of cream to a cat's whiskers without exciting the cat.

## 10.    *Ruse de Coquette*

NEW ORLEANS was looking about for something to celebrate when the news was flashed from the head of the passes that the U.S.S. *Brooklyn,* a screw sloop-of-war built in 1858, was riding anchor in Pass à l'Outre. As soon as it became generally known that the Federal blockade was real and not a mere dream of Mr. Lincoln and his Secretary of Navy, Gideon Welles, demonstrative New Orleans waved its flags and marched its troops to put an end to pessimism and fear of the future.

Below Adam's window a troop of gaily uniformed Creoles marched before a cheering crowd. The street rang rooftop high with the "Marseillaise." Odd, he thought, how these people responded to a show. Almost with childlike credulity, they seemed to believe that the trooping of the colors would banish the Federal obstacle at the mouth of the Mississippi. Now were he able to think like the New Orleannais, he would say, "Pouf!" and like that, the U.S.S. *Powhatan* would vanish from her position outside Mobile Bay, where she had been stationed since the twenty-sixth. Then he would go merrily on his way.

But he was acutely aware of the slow, tight squeeze of the blockade. Like some sluggish giant girding for battle, the Union Navy was coming alive, even as those giants of land, the armies of the North and South, were gathering and creeping ponderously toward mortal combat.

Closing the shutters, he turned to a mirror, adjusted his sword belt, and examined the well-dressed image of Lieutenant Cutler, who would pay call on Miss Faustine Beaumont again this evening. Five nights in a row, he reflected. Looking forward to the sixth, and realizing that he had an hour to kill, he left the house and sauntered toward the river.

Adam was unable to put a finger on any specific attraction Faustine held for him. Often he thought it some lurking quality behind her deep, quiet eyes or hidden in the sultry curve of her exquisite red mouth, the arch of her brow, the soft lines of her white throat and bosom. Again it emanated from something said that hinted more of things untold, a vitality and strength of passion, perhaps. The trite, poetic comparison of a woman to a stream—which placidly mirrors azure sky and shimmering trees above swift currents in her hidden depths—seemed a fitting one. Faustine reminded him of many things.

She was desirable. She was the other side, the pretty side, of insurmountable naval problems, frustrations and gloomy pictures of *Brooklyns* and blockade by day. And where the worries of the day left off, the challenge of night began. Faustine parried subtle thrusts with subtlety, gave a small kiss but withheld her true self. At times he could not help thinking that she was carefully guiding their relationship through a period of transition, as it were, from the old Alabama friendship to a possible New Orleans adventure. Which, he admitted, was wise. He could scarcely expect a passionate kiss from lips that a moment before spoke of Annabel as a second mother. Nor was he an impatient schoolboy in such heat that he flamed at the sight of her.

Adam forgot her instantly as he was nearly caught up in a small throng moving fast toward the river. While side-stepping to keep from being run down, he heard one of the group cry out, "You dere, Dago Joe, de schooner she come wid ice! Yes, she de *Golf Wind,* I tell you!"

*Gulf Wind?* Adam quickened his step and soon verified the impossible. There sat the handsome fore-and-aft-rigged schooner with something new on her cluttered deck, a single smokestack. From her bows hung a crudely lettered sign: ICE. Adam could understand this, though the question in his mind was the one everybody else was asking, and he spoke it to her captain.

"How the devil did you get past the damned Federal?"

Sherrod stood buccaneer style, arms folded across his wide chest, feet planted apart, a hard downslanted smile on his face. "Customers ahead of curiosity seekers, gentlemen. I've got ice for sale." Turning to his sweating ebony-black crew in knee-length dungarees, he said, "No ice on deck until the buying crowd arrives, lads."

A moment later he moved to the rail. "Mail for you, Lieutenant." Passing a couple of letters, he told of the *Powhatan's* presence outside Mobile Bay.

"So I heard," Adam replied. "But I'm as curious as any man here, Sherrod."

"About the *Brooklyn?* I simply ran the Southwest Pass in the night."

A strapping sailor in the uniform of the Louisiana State Navy thrust his beet-red face forward. "That ain't the story you told first, Cap'n. Said you talked yerself past Cap'n Poor of the *Brooklyn.* And they're sayin' you sent the Federal in chase of a Morgan ship from Texas, which was caught. That how you did it, Cap'n?"

A guffaw sounded over Adam's shoulder. "Not even the owls fly that pass at night."

Sherrod extended his cigar case to Adam, not removing his eyes from the offending pair of doubters. But behind his cool glance Adam detected a patient menace that reminded him of a brandished marlinespike. "Gentlemen," he said, with crowd-pleasing humor, "I've heard it's better to be lucky than smart. I congratulate you on your luck." Lifting his brow, he added, "Thus far."

The uniformed man backed off, though the other, a typical waterfront tough, squared his shoulders and thrust out a barrel-bellied front. "Like the so-called Confederate Navy, Captain," he said belligerently, "you blow up a fine wind and dodge a scrap."

Adam whirled instantly. His hand lashed out, and a resounding slap of his palm against the bully's cheek was followed by another with the back of his hand. Before the other could gather his wits, Adam grasped his coat lapels and sent him reeling head first toward the *Gulf Wind's* solid rail. The ship failed to give and a second later his limp body splashed into the river.

"Nice and gentle," Sherrod observed. "A pity he has friends." So saying, he gave Adam a helping hand aboard. In response to his cry of "All hands!" five grinning Negroes sprang to the rail with black arms rippling like oiled threats as they toyed with lengths of chain and tarred rope.

The murderous weapons in the hands of blacks, who made it evident that they were anxious to split scalps and faces, soon convinced the river toughs of the futility of attack. When they slunk off, Sherrod turned to Adam, saying:

"Care to see how much profit I can make on frozen blocks of Yankee water?"

"Hardly. But how did you come by it?"

"Off Mobile. The bark *Sharon's* captain was damned anxious to get rid of his cargo when he saw the *Powhatan*. If I don't pay for this schooner, steam auxiliary and all, before midnight, I'll join your navy."

"You could do worse," Adam said, still wondering how Sherrod ran past the *Brooklyn*.

"Worse?" Sherrod scoffed openly. "So a fifteen-hundred-dollar-a-year lieutenant tells me. But maybe you're merely waiting orders at twelve hundred pay."

Adam tensed. The temptation to handle Sherrod as he had the ruffian was hard to put down. But some inner caution intermixed with puzzlement intervened, and he stalked off the ship without a word in reply.

Before he reached the house of Estève Decloux on Toulouse Street, Adam was forced to admit that Randall Sherrod was a strange rascal, for he discovered that the schoonerman had detailed two of his blacks to follow and protect him in event of trouble.

It was half past one in the morning when Adam returned to his house. A glance at his face in the mirror presented a pair of stormy eyes which he failed to appreciate in the least as he considered the reason for his wretched mood.

A wrathful "Damn that Creole Decloux!" served to break the tension, though only for a moment. He was asking himself if the affair aboard the *Gulf Wind* had any bearing on subsequent events of the night, knowing as he did so that he was dodging the real issue, which was Faustine.

On the other hand, he could be imagining a great deal. It was baffling in a way.

He dashed off a bourbon, his seventh, eighth, or ninth since late dinner; it didn't matter, he was stone-sober. Out of his memory, Faustine appeared in a gown the color of a midnight sky. He recalled the tight bodice that accented the curves of her bosom and waist, the yards and yards of the skirt under a delicate mask of azure blue lace. About her soft white neck she wore a velvet band the color of her dress; and for ornament, a single white jasmine at the divide of her breasts; nothing more.

A slave served refreshments and, later, dinner in the courtyard. Then Decloux and his daughters, Celeste and Aurelie, returned from the theater. There followed an exciting account of the play by the children and a romp through the hibiscus and banana trees of the small enclosure. They sipped black coffee while the daughters sang "Listen to the Mocking-Bird" in English until their black mammy led them protesting off to bed.

Adam frowned, poured bourbon, and forgot to drink it.

This dark-skinned Creole who employed Faustine as tutor for his lovely girls! He, with those fine dark eyes, striking figure, and polished dignity. What sort of man was this widower? According to Faustine, he had lost a considerable sum through land speculation in Texas. With business in a slump, he entertained ideas of recouping his losses in Matamoros, Mexico, should the Federal blockade tighten. *Mon Dieu*, yes! There one could make a quick fortune selling supplies to the South!

Some people had a twisted sense of patriotism, Adam reflected. Like Sherrod, who seemed to have dedicated himself to serving the South with needed supplies, but under the expansive influence of the almighty dollar.

But that was irrelevant. The adoring and possessive glances Decloux bestowed upon Faustine soon provoked Adam's curiosity, and more, for she was by no means blind to his open regard of her. Often her eyes dropped under his intent gaze and she made conversation to cover either what was between them or something ahead, which he suggested in eloquent silence.

Sitting there, a witness to the puzzling byplay, Adam's imagination began to run away with him. He checked it, however, by reminding himself that he wasn't in love with Faustine. He desired her, but not in marriage. So if Decloux happened to win her first, well, that was that. And so he convinced himself of this, until it was time to go.

The Creole arose, bowed, extended Adam a cordial invitation to return, all in manner so polite and engagingly French that one was inclined to believe him sincere. When Decloux left him alone with Faustine, curiosity and doubt returned strong in Adam. At the front door, he was bidding her a cool, and in his own mind, a final, adieu when she said in low, almost fearful tones:

"Oh, Adam, I wish he hadn't joined us."

Surprised, he asked, "Just what goes on here, Faustine—between you two?" As her glance slid sway, he said, "Forget that I asked it," and turned to go.

"Wait! Adam——" The sudden pressure of her small hand on his restrained him. Without looking up, she said, "Perhaps we shouldn't see each other again."

He brought her eyes up, sharp, with a crisp, "Just what I was thinking."

A wondrous though surprising smile of elation played across her face for the merest instant. "Oh," she said in troubled afterthought, which held him rooted there in a state of puzzlement. "I suppose I mistook your meaning, Adam."

"For what?" he demanded.

"Nothing!" she said angrily, turning her back.

He drew her to him, almost roughly, and held her in his arms for a moment's study of the look of surprise on her face. "You mean to tell me——?"

Fingers soft as velvet covered his lips. "I mean to tell you nothing you don't already know, Adam Cutler."

Then all pretense fell away. Her cherry-red lips parted and her eyes darted about his face as though she saw in him the pattern for masculine vitality. Her hand quivered at his cheek then slid softly about his neck.

Adam remembered the giddy sensation of floating off into space, his sudden recklessness, and the flood of passion surging through both of them in the long, fiery kiss that followed. They kissed again, and once more, then stood staring into each other's eyes. Hers were enormous, demanding, as she pressed herself to him and clung tightly to his neck.

"Adam! Ah, Adam!" she panted endearingly.

Then to his voiced questions, she whispered, "Yes, darling! But I wouldn't dare go to your place."

"Why? Afraid of Decloux?"

"Because I'm afraid of tomorrow." A pause followed. "It seems I've learned to care more for you than I really should!"

Adam remembered the drink he had poured and downed it in a single gulp. He looked at his watch: ten minutes to two. It made little difference, for damn little sleep was in store for him on this night. The raw liquor seemed as ice water against the hot tidal wave that continued to surge through him. While in conflict, the thought of her eager, passionate kisses seemed to pinpoint the memory of the glances between her and Decloux. Desire versus suspicion, one over the other.

By thunder, he seemed caught between wind and water without a helm. Why, absurd as it was, a sane observer might actually think Adam Cutler was suffering the torments of jealousy.

## 11.   The Marylander

### 1

THIRD ASSISTANT SURGEON FRANCIS MARTIN, U.S.N., looked up from crude shelves of assorted medicines and bandages in the temporary hospital, thrown together not a week back in what had been the customhouse, and raised his bass voice with a weary "Next patient."

Under his breath, he cursed the luck that had placed him, an aspiring surgeon of the fleet, ashore in Alexandria, Virginia, to administer to the naval heroes who had done nothing greater than present him with cases of itch, vermin, dripping noses, and a maze of similar ailments.

The Potomac flotilla was a "damn sorry" outfit—they said it even in Washington. Except for the U.S.S. *Pawnee,* fifteen guns, which had witnessed the fall of Fort Sumter, and which under Commander

Rowan, in co-operation with a regiment of Zouaves, had taken Alexandria on May twenty-fourth, there was not a large vessel on the river to combat the hidden Confederate shore batteries.

Martin placed the lid on a jar of ointment, tugged at his Dundreary whiskers, which lent him years above his twenty-seven, and glared at the door as it opened.

"It's me, butcher boy."

Martin suppressed a grin. "So I see. Come to have the dressing removed. You know"—he sighed heavily—"I long for a nice gangrenous leg to sever." Falling to work, he said absently, "Heard from Adam recently?" Seeing James wince, he said, "Didn't hurt you, did I?"

"No. But Adam's letter did. Burned me a damn sight worse than the Gosport Navy Yard fire."

"Which you're finally getting over. But you'll have a scar on that arm the rest of your life. Now what did our Rebel friend have to say?"

"Plenty!"

Martin gave him a wry look and smile. "About his sister—what's her name?"

"Adria," James said pensively. "And I had it coming, Francis. Dammit all, I've got to do something about it, and soon, or——"

"Hold it, sailor! If I'm to play father confessor to a political hermaphrodite again, we'll do it in my quarters. There should be about a quarter of a bottle left."

He gave James a key. "Wait for me there. The Navy Department wouldn't like it if I quit plucking eyebrows and blowing noses this time of day."

James said, "Ready to release me for duty? Captain Samuel du Pont wants me at the Washington Navy Yard."

Martin examined James critically. "You're losing too much weight. I can hold up that release, maybe get you a leave so you can go home and fatten up."

"Thanks. That would please Father, but all I'd get is more 'Star-Spangled Banner' and Old Navy. Got to make up my own mind this time."

Two hours later the pair of old friends sat before Martin's window watching the Potomac in the sunset. They had literally squeezed the bottle dry over talk of everything from General Scott's old age to McClellan's and McDowell's growing armies that would oppose Confederate Generals Johnston's and Beauregard's forces.

They had talked of the South, of the blockade, of Secretary of Navy Gideon Welles's farfetched plan—nothing was secret any more—to bottle up the Southern ports, then cut the Confederacy in two by taking the Mississippi River. With feet propped at the window sill, they discussed the uneasiness in the Navy Department that stemmed from the February report by a House committee which revealed the shocking news that the Navy had so deteriorated under Buchanan's administration that only two vessels of the entire fleet were capable of defending the Atlantic coast.

"We're obsolete," Martin admitted. "Atop that, of the 322 officers who resigned to join the Confederate Navy, 243 were officers of the line. You'll probably raise the figure by one, James."

"I didn't say that."

"No." A wry expression crossed the surgeon's face. "You didn't. Neither did you say you resented Butler's occupation of Baltimore on May thirteenth that ended Secessionist control of the city, or that you approved Maryland's imprisonment in the Union, or that you disapproved our state's stand against coercing the seceded states.

"Or," he went on, "that you're head over heels in love with a Mobile beauty. Hell, Jim, some things show all over a man. Sorry the whisky is all gone. After a day of what I've been through . . ." His voice trailed off.

James broke the gathering silence. "I've been thinking about the South's chances. Since Queen Victoria issued her Proclamation of Neutrality, forbidding the subjects of Great Britain to break our blockade, which blows Mr. Davis's cotton-screw to hell, isn't it apparent that England intends to stay out of the fight? Which brings me to say Mr. Welles's plan of blockade will eventually meet with success."

"What the devil! Won't the war be fought on land? Johnny Reb has us on the hip when it comes to fighting. Besides, don't ever predict what England will do. She could be mobilizing her Navy. After all, which is likely to be her best customer? The South? Correct, my boy."

James turned up his palms, smiled resignedly. "Have it your way. But England spent millions of pounds freeing her slaves back in 'thirty-three. So is she likely to support slavery now?"

"Prattle! Seems the ancient control of business over government is something you don't understand."

"Perhaps. But back to fundamentals. I honestly believe the golden age of the South is gone, its aristocracy regressing. Despite the Rebel spirit and successes at Fort Sumter and Gosport, I believe the Confederacy is doomed."

The tired assistant surgeon shook his head sadly. Suddenly he burst out laughing. His mirth subsiding, he said, "Jim, we're sitting here, each championing the other's true sentiments like a pair of fools."

James said crisply, "I meant every word I said."

"Sure you did. You spoke your mind, all right. Now speak your heart. Where do your sympathies lie?"

Slowly James pointed south.

"That's what I knew all along. Now where is your sweetheart? South. Then what the devil are you waiting for? No, let me tell *you*— believing that the sovereignty of the state is the foundation of civil liberty, you're waiting on Maryland. I know of no better way to lose your girl."

James said dejectedly, "Maybe I've already lost her. She hasn't answered my last letter."

"You know how the mails are," Martin said. "If you head for Washington, perhaps on north, her reply might have to catch up with you at sea."

With that, he blew out his cheeks, combed the whiskers of his right cheek with long fingers a minute or so, then placed a hand on James's shoulder. "Look, Jim, I don't mean to pry, but I can't help saying what's on my mind." He got up and moved to a chest, where he stretched his legs and leaned back facing James, who eyed him curiously.

"The way you seem to be balancing the strength of the North and South, weighing this against that, back and forth, back and forth, it would appear that you're trying to pick the winner and let a decision of the mind govern your true sentiments."

James sat out a moment of bewildered silence. "No," he said thoughtfully. "I don't think that's it. Not exactly. Perhaps I am groping about for something to give me a push in the proper direction, but I'm not trying to get under the winning flag."

"Then what is it? Take me, for instance. I know where I stand. I don't wish to see the Union dissolved, and I'm against slavery. Our friend Adam has taken an opposite stand. Just how do you feel about these things?"

James's hands dropped limp, and his expression seemed pained. He said at last, almost hopelessly, "I don't know."

2

James glanced at his watch and looked up the tracks of the Orange and Alexandria Railroad. Another troop train cast its light down the rails. At this rate, he admitted impatiently, the train for Washington, already two hours late, might not depart from the Alexandria station before the war ended.

As the train rolled in and ground to a noisy stop, soldiers poured out of the old coaches crying, "Make way for Schenck's Brigade!" and, "Here we are, General McDowell, ready to chase the cotton-picking Rebels all the way to Richmond!" Then the cry became general: "On to Richmond!"

Odd, James thought in detachment, that the Confederacy should move its capital from Montgomery to Richmond, within a hundred miles of Washington. It was nothing short of a display of confidence.

"Hey, you, sailor, why ain't you on a ship?" a gangling, bearded militiaman yelled. "I've heard we don't have a navy."

He passed on, but others came, laughing, cursing, talking of this or that, jeering, groaning under knapsacks and gear. Some were silent, others seemed afraid or stunned, and not a few were bent on mischief. "Say, Mr. Lootenant o' the Navy, which way is Mr. Jefferson Davis's house from here?"

James grinned. "About two points of the compass west of due south—general."

"Thanks, admiral. Where you from?"

"Maryland."

"Well, I'll be! That's the damn state that's half Secesh. Look, Joe, here's something you ain't seen, I'll bet, a Federal from Maryland."

James tensed all over. He might have had the opportunity to battle singlehanded the whole brigade had not a sergeant prodded them on.

When the tramp of marching feet fell away in the direction of McDowell's camp, James was suddenly alerted by the monotonous cry of a messenger: "Lieutenant James Hillyer. Lieutenant Hillyer, please."

"Here! Over here, boy!"

The lad ambled up and extended a letter. "From Surgeon Martin, sir. Said I'd find ye here. 'Tis a threatenin' night out, don't ye think, sir? Likely to start rainin' most any minute. I said to the surgeon, 'Sir, if I get soaked——' "

"Here," James said, dropping a coin in his hand.

Staring at the envelope, he hurried to the light cast by the station lantern. "From Adria!" he said, tingling all over.

Porters, recruits, and artillerymen brushed past unheeded as he opened the envelope and stared at a single sheet of paper. Oblivious to all about him, he read:

> Bay Oaks, Mobile
> May 13, 1861

Dear James:

As I recall, it was you who proposed marriage in January and caused me to believe your endearing words sincere. But was it James Hillyer who said, "Promise that nothing, even war, can separate us"? And after Captain Sherrod told of Mississippi's ordinance of secession, was it really you who said, "Adria darling, no matter what happens, remember our pledge"? And in parting, "Nothing can come between us." So gentle in manner. So strong in deed!

I beg you, sir, forgive me for having been so much in love with you that I was forced to embarrass myself by demanding *sans gêne* your resignation from the tyrannical Federal Navy, to which you are so devoted. But I was a child who placed my heart in your care. I wanted you to bring it to me and tenderly guard it always. But, alas, that was not intended, and it behooves me to live with the fact. However, I shall not do so in the manner you might impose upon me, but as the wife of an honorable Southern gentleman, Corporal Lawrence Jarvis, to whom I shall be joined in marriage at Bay Oaks on the evening of Sunday, June twenty-third.

Be pleased, sir, to accept my warm and earnest wishes for your every success and happiness, and believe me most sincerely yours,

> Adria.

James groped for something to lean against and, finding nothing, sat down in the station doorway. There he stared out of eyes grown large with shock, unaware that his lips were drawn back over dry teeth in an expression of severe pain.

"Something wrong, sir?" a trainman asked, bending over him. There was no reply and he repeated the question.

"Yes. Everything."

"If you're going to Washington, better board the train, sir."

"Yes. Of course," James said, rising. Staring straight ahead out of unfocused eyes, he walked toward the nearest coach.

## 12. The Prize Master

1

EARLY ON THE EVENTFUL DAY OF JUNE THE THIRD, jolly Lieutenant Robert T. Chapman of the C.S. *Sumter* rapped at a door on Royal Street. Upon entering, he flashed an appraising eye over the fine furnishings before training his energetic smile on the host, now pouring morning coffee.

"They're coming from the bayous and villages to see the *Sumter* commissioned into service today, brother lieutenant. By steamboat, railroad, and pirogue."

"Rub it in. But sit down first," Adam demanded. As the other slumped into a sofa and accepted a cup of the potent brew, Adam took a seat opposite him. "You have neither John McIntosh Kell's whiskers nor his finesse. Now just what brings you here?"

"News, most of it good," Chapman drawled. "Of course, you know that the fast Federal steamers *Niagara* and *Minnesota* have joined the *Brooklyn* down at the passes."

"Yes, and I'm aware that Leeds and Company delivered the *Sumter's* tanks on May thirty-first, that the ammunition and arms from Baton Rouge, which you went up to see about on the twentieth, arrived on the thirtieth. Also, the crew is due to board the ship, today, Monday, June third."

"You're as well informed as your coffee is terrible. Tell me more," Chapman said, touching his short beard tenderly.

"You tell me." Expecting the mischievously inclined Alabaman to carry on for some time, Adam was caught unawares by what he said next:

"Too bad you don't own a dress uniform such as the *Sumter's* officers will break out today."

"And if I do?"

Chapman arose, placed his hand on Adam's shoulder. "Brace yourself." With jet-black eyes twinkling, he said, "I'm afraid you'd stand a good chance of wearing it."

So saying, he brought his most devilish expression to bear on Adam, then handed over a note from Commander Semmes.

Adam's face beamed, and for good reason. Semmes had found a place for him. "Lieutenant Cutler, Prize Master!" he exclaimed joyously.

Minutes later Adam appeared in a brand-new long-skirted coat of steel gray with two bars on the collar, the Austrian knot in gold braid on the sleeve. Clad in the double-breasted coat over blue-striped gray trousers, he drew expressions of sincere admiration from Robert T. Chapman.

"Anticipating something like this, I had the same tailor that made yours do it," Adam said.

With a sweeping bow, Chapman struck a pose and spoke in lofty tones. "With dress sword at his belt and white gloves on his hand, he'll trod the quarter-deck once more——" There he lost his art, and both laughed.

The day had an auspicious beginning. At long last Lieutenant Adam S. Cutler was assured a berth aboard the first Confederate States man-of-war dedicated to the deep stream. In the hours that followed, the *Sumter* was formally commissioned into service.

The ceremony aboard the spotless decks touched Adam deeply. It was Old Navy with something new added. Perhaps the ingredient was one of mixed joy, solemnity, and thankfulness, as his mother once said, that comes with one's first-born. It was indeed a deep and profound feeling that enveloped him when Commander Semmes came on deck and, later, when the Confederate commissioners accepted the vessel into the service of the Navy from the refitting firm and, in turn, delivered the cruiser's commission to her master, who read it as though inspired. But something more tugged at Adam's emotions. Never would he forget the stimulating effect of the presentation of arms as the Marines honored Richmond's Commissioner Rousseau, the trill of the boatswain's pipe, the hoisting of the commission pennant to the maintop. Then the colors. Bent to a halyard, the ensign, the proud Stars and Bars of the Confederacy, rose slowly to the signal gaff and unfurled gloriously, its every graceful motion stirring his soul with the poetry of adventure.

He was proudly a part of all this, of all it stood for. He stood in the midst of the officers of the *Sumter* unmindful as they of the blistering heat over the Mississippi. The speeches could last all day and still he would not complain. Mr. Monroe, Mayor of New Orleans, held the rapt attention of all on board as well as the great crowd assembled for the occasion.

Amid rousing cheers, the crowd broke and the officers of the *Sumter* welcomed the new member of the wardroom into their midst. First the zealot Semmes, with a trace of a tear in his eye, then the Georgian Kell, who edged in a word of advice following his sincere words of welcome—"Since we'll be a week or ten days here, Adam, you may wish to keep your Royal Street house." He was followed by Chapman, and the youngest lieutenant, Evans, and handsome Third Lieutenant Stribling.

As a fitting climax to a memorable day, Mayor Monroe honored the officers of the *Sumter* that evening in lavish style. The great and near great gathered and raised glasses in toast after toast to the flag, the Cause, the health, and success of the men who would soon challenge the hirelings of autocracy on the high seas. While immaculately attired slaves refilled glasses with the finest of champagnes, the buzz of conversation increased with talk of war. What would England do; wasn't there an oversupply of cotton in the British Isles; could Beauregard take Washington, with Johnston's help, of course; how would the great Semmes get to sea, by ruse, or with guns raking the Federals' decks?

Adam parried a number of questions with polite shrugs and easy grace, backed out of others, and surveyed the gorgeous evening dresses, actually rivaling the flowers in Mr. Monroe's parlor.

He had just bowed away from a Galveston newspaperman and citizens from Houston when his glance collided with Faustine's. For all the excitement of the day, her unabashed regard of him made his blood tingle. By any standard, she had no peer this fine evening. Small, shapely, mature, she seemed more radiant than ever in a low-cut gown of crimson. Perhaps the neckline was a trifle on the daring side. In any case, it caused him more than idle speculation as he observed the attention she was receiving from officers of the New Orleans Foreign Legion. Frowning his displeasure, Adam looked toward Commander Semmes, now protesting mildly to a group of prominent New Orleannais who were evidently exhorting him to address the merrymakers.

An arm as white and soft as an egret's plume slid into the gray folds of Adam's sleeve. Faustine's dark eyes lifted and held his as her mouth curved into a teasing smile. "Thanks for bringing me, *mon cher*. It gives me an opportunity to appraise a few other men of note."

"And to what end and purpose, mam'selle?"

"You're conceited already." Her unhurried survey of his uniform and face uncovered the secrets of her mind.

In that tumultuous moment he wished above all else to crush her to him. With the next, he was thankful for a timely distraction that allowed his blood to cool.

Raphael Semmes stood. A hush fell over the room. Poised, as though keenly aware of the effect of silence, the *Sumter's* commander stared beyond the faces turned on him, gray eyes wide with distant vision. With no change in his expression, he snapped an order:

"Mr. Kell, bring me the unstained flag behind you."

When the executive of the *Sumter* presented him with the Stars and Bars from over the mantel, he touched it to his lips and draped it, tenderly, over the back of his chair.

Adam's pulses quickened. He wondered why. He asked what it was about Raphael Semmes that stirred a man. One and all seemed to know and feel that destiny had placed a finger on this great man, who was now saying:

"Fair ladies and noble gentlemen of the South, I shall quote from the proclamation of President Lincoln of the Federal States of April fifteenth, in which he called out seventy-five thousand troops to avenge the disaster of Fort Sumter:

" '*And I hereby proclaim, and declare, that, if any person, under the pretended authority of said States, or under any other pretense, shall molest a vessel of the United States, or the persons, or cargo on board of her, such persons will be held amenable to the laws of the United States, for the prevention, and punishment of piracy.*'

"Under the pretended authority!" Semmes scoffed. "Piracy!" he mocked, before reading the reply of the Confederate States of the sixth of May wherein President Davis issued a proclamation which legalized privateering.

"Let us examine the sly little game the Northern government has been playing. Mr. Lincoln and his Secretary of State have failed to convince the governments of Europe that this war is but an insurrection of no importance. Blockade in universally recognized as an act of war, so there cannot be a blockade without war. Then how can there be war without at least two belligerents? Therefore, the Federal Government refutes by deed its own statement of falsehood, to the apparent disgust of foreign powers, who admit the existence of war. So war becomes an accepted fact because it can be nothing else. England's declaration of neutrality between the combatants proves the South is a combatant—and not, as Mr. Lincoln would have it, a pirate."

The explanation of this fighting lawyer seemed timely indeed, thought Adam. The South was in need of a logical interpretation of facts.

Again Semmes paused and, this time, searched the faces of his officers. "Piracy," he said once more. "Gentlemen of the cruiser *Sumter*," he addressed them, holding the flag aloft, "has destiny called upon you to sail under an outlawed banner?"

"No! Never!" Adam shouted with the others.

When the cries of protest and the cheers of everyone at long last subsided, the *Sumter's* officers walked forward and stood in impressive salute of the Stars and Bars.

2

Under the spell of the chauvinist and drunk on excitement, Adam handed Faustine into a carriage, gave the driver his Royal Street address, and took his place beside her. He had no sooner placed an arm about her shoulder than he noticed that she appeared lost in serious contemplation. He wanted her gay and exuberant, in a mood to match his own feeling.

He was thinking that a little wine in the privacy of his rooms, which she had never seen, might calm him and buoy her; place them on an even keel, so to speak. After all, this fine day would not join the past for another hour.

"Adam," she said, almost hesitantly, "you had better take me home. Without chaperon, I——"

He laughed in her ear, whispered, "Afraid?"

She replied with cool assurance, "I have nothing to fear other than the loss of my good name. Which," she added frostily, "seems of little concern to you."

"Hm-m." Adam's brow lifted. "I stand reproved, madam," he said jauntily. "Evidently your dressmaker and I are equally at fault."

A slim hand rose protectively to her bosom. As she treated him to a sharp glance, he very gently lifted her fingers and touched his lips to the palm of her hand. Softly he said, *"N'est-ce pas, ma chère?"*

"I shall try to be more discreet," she said, instantly withdrawing her hand.

"To protect your good name," he reminded complacently.

"Adam, do you mean to imply something?" she demanded.

"Of course not, Faustine. What's wrong with you?"

"My feelings are easily disturbed, I suppose." She relaxed against his shoulder. "Particularly by someone I admire and"—under his prompting, she said—"think more of than I really should."

Suddenly she asked, "When are you sailing?"

"Not before the tenth, so Kell advised."

"So soon?" Her hand tightened at his sleeve.

"Where to, Faustine? Toulouse or Royal?"

After a moment of silent debate, she said, "Toulouse."

Adam raised his voice to the driver, then sat back and gave himself up to sober reflection. Somehow he was not quite convinced of Faustine's total honesty. He had given her no reason to believe that he entertained any serious hope for a lasting romance between them. What began as a mere transient infatuation remained exactly that, despite the green-eyed devils provoked into being when he thought of her living in the same house with attentive and admiring Decloux. Little by little, by a word here and glance there, she let him know that their relationship transcended infatuation. Where he felt, as he did now, that given the opportunity he might succeed in possessing her, she, on the other hand, carefully parried his every move, avoiding any private meeting with him.

As though, he told himself for the tenth time, she was holding out for a ring on her finger. For which, he could hardly censure her; if she was sincere in her affection, of course. But was Faustine sincere? Often he had asked that question, usually in the wake of some remark she had innocently dropped regarding Bay Oaks or an object of art there. Once, only a few nights before, she had asked which was the larger, the Cutler or Jarvis plantation. Almost in businesslike manner. But he could be, probably was, imagining more than was real.

She was very quiet. He looked at her and saw in the dim light a handkerchief touching her eye. Suddenly contrite, for he had not intended offending her, he said, "I'm not ready to call it a day. Shall we stop at some café for a glass of champagne?"

Her voice was proof of a brave attempt to mask her emotions. "With chilled Bordeaux and Madeira at the house?"

"I can do better than trade smiles *à la Creole* with your suave employer on this night."

"He won't be there." Hastily she added, "Only Tante Mimi, the housekeeper. The girls left this afternoon with Grand'mère and

Grand-père Decloux for Baton Rouge, where they will remain until their father finds a house in Matamoros."

"So he put the uniform aside," Adam said, as though he had predicted as much. "But what about you?"

"I have no desire to go to Mexico, if that's what you mean. At least, I told Mr. Decloux this—before I learned that you were sailing aboard the *Sumter.*"

"I see," he replied thoughtfully.

The carriage was stopping at her house when she said, "And just when I refuse the luxuries of peaceful Mexico, perhaps France, you have to leave me."

Under the scrutiny of his eyes, she smiled, as if she teased, or wished to hide her regard for him. But her expression seemed forced, and he was thinking again that she was all for self. The impression held, and he said:

"On second thought, Faustine, I've had a hard day. I'll see you to the door."

"No, Adam!" Her eyes were even more demanding. Her hand slipped softly into his. "Don't go, yet," she implored. With less urgency, she said, "Mimi is too deaf to hear a cork pop."

He could not sustain his most recent opinion of her. Smiling broadly, he helped her to alight, saying, "Then dear Mimi might not hear the second cork."

A crystal sconce reflected the glow of a single candle over the Decloux parlor. It highlighted gold and silver threads of the sofa, the gilt of wide frames enclosing soft browns and greens of French pastoral scenes, and the play of excitement in Faustine's eyes. A sudden movement, a twist of her body, sent the mellow light sweeping across the high curve of her breasts in a crimson streak. In an instant it was gone, except for the place it occupied in Adam's photographic mind.

He was gazing at her intently, thinking that she might have been done in oil by candlelight with the brush of some old master who knew and appreciated subdued tones, out of which a single stroke of color presented a pose and beauty of maturity hidden to the eye. It was a moment of magic he would long remember, a moment he could not allow suddenly to evanesce.

For she had teased him on, by fleeting contact and warm mouth pressed to his when circumstances annulled all danger. He wanted to feel the warmth of her under his hands as he clutched her fiercely to him.

Nor was Faustine blind to all that surfaced in his glance. She stood as though rooted to the floor a few steps from him, her eyes taking him in with unconcealed fascination. The blood rushing to her bosom swept away all uncertainty and restiveness, as a gale of wind dissolves streamers of fog. Aroused, unable to put down or hide the importunate desire threatening to consume her, she whirled and said breathlessly:

"The wine! I forgot——"

She did not rush from the parlor as planned but turned slowly, her mind racing with an idea that reconciled her governing emotion to her material interest.

"Adam! My darling——" Her voice was tremulous and low.

She had freed herself. A soft, exultant sound escaped her.

For a fleeting second he stared at her, doubt strong in him. Before her look of torture, doubt vanished. He whispered, "Faustine——"

His voice broke under the burning pain now possessing him completely.

He took her in his arms, watched her eyes grow large, saw her lips writhe apart. Then he kissed her in the manner she demanded and responded to again and again. Roughly he held her to him, and felt her quivering under his kisses. Gasping for air, she threw back her head and arched her throat to his lips. For the merest instant her melting glance met his, and he saw in her complete surrender.

"Marry me, dearest—tonight!" she demanded.

"There's no time for the kind of wedding I have in mind, Faustine," he said in a voice heavy with passion.

"Then take me, Adam—my darling!" she begged. "Now! Mimi went with them." And running through her mind as her hand guided his to her swelling breast was a comforting thought: "Tomorrow he will marry me. Failing that, I shall one day present his child and mine to the Cutlers of Bay Oaks."

But tonight she was his. And the longing she felt pushing fast through her veins was not to be denied.

A delicious murmur escaped her as he picked her up and carried her across the parlor to a French sofa made for a queen.

The candle flickered and the quiet scenes adorning the walls remained as still as before.

13.     Boston Adventure

1

THE MIDSHIPMAN FROM NEW JERSEY gazed absently through a dirty window of the railroad coach at the New England scenery under a midday sun.

"You always hear the worst about the side you're on." Darting a glance at his superior, he said, "Isn't that so, sir?"

Lieutenant Hillyer nodded agreement. His ashen face, the red-headed middy observed, had not broken with a smile since their departure from the Washington Navy Yard on the ninth of June. He supposed a week in the base hospital with dysentery and fever did that to a man.

"Yes, sir"—he addressed the middy from Troy, New York—"we were too close to it to realize that the Rebels nearly had Washington back in late April. Why, they had the capital cut off by railroad and not even a telegraph wire was open for days."

"Right, Benjie. And where the lieutenant and I were, the Virginia batteries were blockading the Potomac." He chuckled. "Even though Mr. Lincoln declared a blockade of the South, the Rebs were the first in the field with it."

"I never thought of that. Say, we should be in Boston soon." He looked at James. "Any idea of how long we'll be in this port, sir?"

"Not the slightest."

James withheld the rest. "Furthermore, I don't give a damn." Nor was he curious as to why Captain Samuel Francis du Pont of the Navy, a member of the board commissioned to draw plans for some undisclosed offensive, had selected him for duty in Boston. There had been a hint of his boarding at a later date the *Wabash*, and something about a squadron under the command of Flag Officer Stringham. The *Wabash* was talked up as the pride of the fleet. Perhaps she was, he thought dispiritedly.

The train rocked on, jostling him about. At times the motion made him dizzy, then again sick. The week in the hospital after leaving Alexandria had just about done him in. Sleepless nights, just lying there, staring at nothing and thinking. Too much thinking had sent him there in the first place. Many were the times he had clamped his teeth together and wished he had never seen nor heard of Mobile. But he had.

He would never cease to wonder at the power of a tossed coin. Back in early November. If he won, they would spend the holidays in Maryland. But Adam won. They went to Mobile. He fell in love. The war came.

He made a wry grimace, shifted his position, and closed his eyes. If he could only sleep. The damned wheels kept up a ceaseless rhythm; over and over, reciting, "The twenty-third of June, the twenty-third of June." Somewhere in the coach a baby squealed, and one of his group laughed at something. The train slowed, jerked forward. And he was recalling again the face of Lawrence Jarvis.

"Me?" The lad from Troy laughed. "I don't hold any grudge against the Southerners. I'd a helluva——"

James closed his ears to the desultory conversation, only to hear in memory his father saying, "Son, I hold no grudge against the people of the South." But he had said more: "My allegiance is to the flag I served, the same as my father served. Never let anything, trouble, friends, personal desire, or gain cause you to dishonor that flag." How did a man reply to that, to his own father?

With desertion? He shuddered and at the same time thrilled to the thought. It was a way out. He continued to entertain the idea of boarding a merchantman to Havana and thence to Mobile. It could be done. It was a ray of hope. The only one, since he had been unable to telegraph any message to Adria from either Washington or New York. If he could only stop her marriage.

"Twelve days to do it," he said in silence.

Better to ride South and get across the lines than risk a slow sail. With luck, he should see the gates of Bay Oaks within a week.

A tradesman's voice boomed from the far end of the coach. "Wait until the Rebels meet the 54th Regiment from Boston. I hear it's going to be all Negroes."

James opened his eyes and glared at the man. The very thought of a battle between the races caused one to think of slaughter. New Englanders possessed a queer sense of humor. Now the man was laughing, and his companion, a prosperous-looking man with three chins, was gloating over a fact: England had enough cotton to last for two years; the proof, his firm had contracted for a shipload to be sent from Liverpool to Boston in July.

New England, he mused. Her people had taken the cradle of liberty and made of it a bejeweled bed of oppression.

"Lieutenant, sir, an officer in the coach aft said the U.S.S. *Powhatan* is blockading Mobile. That was my ship, sir! Paddle-wheeler, twenty-four-hundred tons."

The lieutenant showed interest, the lad observed. But he looked as though he didn't approve. Odd, he would say. Very odd.

Late that afternoon James stood where he and his father had disembarked from the ship *Alice* when he was only nine. What a great day that had been, walking India Wharf and repeatedly slowing his parent while he paused to examine this ship or that from jib boom to fantail. "The water is the life for me!" he remembered saying. "That's the boy," came the reply from proud Captain Hillyer, U.S.N. "Now come along, and I'll show you where Captain Kidd the pirate was examined before they threw him in prison."

It all came back to James, causing his eyes to grow misty. Why did boys have to grow up? A fool question, he admitted, moving on up past the famous clipper ship wharves to the busy foot of Commercial Street.

No longer responsible for the dozen midshipmen, whom he had literally dumped across the Charles River into the navy yard, he was free to pursue his course for the evening. It was planned and, though his behavior would shock his father to the roots, he intended to follow through this time. It would hurt his family, himself, but he could think of no way to make it easier for all concerned.

Worming his way through throngs of sailors, riggers, armorers, hawkers, soldiers, and assorted crews arriving from and departing for booming East Boston, Lieutenant Hillyer in navy uniform entered a tavern and ordered a bottle of liquor sent to his table in the back corner of a dimly lit room.

He began drinking, deliberately. Although he did not relish the taste, he desired the numbing effect. First he would be able to forget the incident aboard the train that afternoon. He had allowed his imagination to run wild with pictures of Adria in Jarvis's intimate embrace. He cringed inwardly at the memory of it. There he stood in the coach with every eye upon him. He had leaped up and shouted, "No! No!"

He drank in order to shelve Adria in some corner of his brain, so that his wits, under the sharpening influence of drink, might serve his purpose. He intended finding a southbound clipper in need of a deck hand or paying passenger in the short hours before the brass at the navy yard began asking questions regarding the whereabouts of Lieutenant Hillyer.

For a while he enjoyed himself immensely. Everyone had a good word for an officer of the Navy. Good-natured ribbing ensued and, surprisingly, he gave as good as he received. Only once did he think of Adria. Remotely then. He drank guardedly, munched tidbits, all with a keen sense of balancing energy expended with energy imbibed, to sustain that fine sense of exuberance wherein every man is friend. After an hour of it, he began to drink heavily.

Then a young lady appeared across the table from him. Where she came from, he did not know. He realized only that she was gay, carefree, and rather pretty, that her low, throaty voice fascinated him. He had no sooner caused to be placed before her the best wine in the house than she raised a glass. Thin scarlet lips curved merrily as she burst forth in purposely stilted tones with a ditty that pleased him greatly:

> *Oh sailor, sir, think not of war*
> *In terms of slow disaster;*
> *You were born to love, to hate and die*
> *And war will do it faster.*

Throwing back her head, she laughed. James was in a mood to appreciate the burlesque and spontaneity of this strange person. She was just the tonic he needed.

"Encore!" he demanded, refilling her glass.

Her green, amber-flecked eyes seemed to tease and challenge in the same expression. A speculative light flickered in them and quickly evanesced. Then, as saucy and bold as you please, she obliged him with:

> *Oh sailor, sir, weep ye not*
> *For me so pure and chaste;*
> *Before the call to arms is done*
> *I'll lay an army waste.*

Leaning toward her, he said, "By Stars and Bars, I believe you would!"

He was surveying her red-brown hair, done in a maze of carefully tousled ringlets, wondering as he did so if he approved her coiffure. Completely sober, he might think it a bit theatrical. But never less critical, he gave her the benefit of doubt, until the worn lace and braid about her neck caught his attention. He quickly put down the thought that she might be a Cyprian on a nightly excursion in favor of a more appealing opinion that this lovely woman had been sorely neglected, perhaps mistreated, by the unappreciative Yankees.

"Blockade or navy yard?" she asked inoffensively.

Before he could reply, a huge merchant seaman ambled by their table and drew her soberest glance. Then he was gone. James studied her narrowly a moment before dismissing the incident with a laugh.

One drink followed another and the conversation's play swung between outward celebration and realities. She had her story, nothing sensational: a part in a small show brought her here from Albany; she was out of work. What was his story? James sighed heavily. The Lord only knew how much he needed someone to talk to. He told her all, from Adria to coming here, omitting only his plan to desert the service and take a ship out of Boston.

She proved attentive and sympathetic. Her hand fell over his. "What will you do?" she asked.

James thought about it, wishing he had kept it all to himself. He had drunk himself into the doldrums.

Unhappily he said, "I don't know." Gulping down his drink, he went on. "When I came here I thought I had the answer. Hell or high water couldn't keep me from her. And," forlornly, "I wish that was all that was stopping me now."

Her laugh jerked his glance upward. "Easy as you go, sailor." She smiled. "I can't imagine war at its worst keeping me from the man I loved."

"Yes you can. I believe you'd feel the same as I if it involved something you were afraid to tamper with—honor."

"Honor?"

He thought she held a look of amusement in check.

"Yes. But what is honor?" A pause lengthened into seconds. "If it robs a man of the things dear to him—even of life?

"And what is life if it robs one of honor? That is the question, Miss er——"

"Georgia. Georgia Stoddard."

## 2

James opened his eyes and closed them quickly. The light of day seemed to strike his aching head like a blow from a shipwright's adz. But he had seen enough to realize that he was in a strange bed somewhere near the harbor. The assorted noises of commerce and building made the fact painfully evident.

Braving another look, cautiously lest the glare jerk a groan from him, he brought his curious glance into focus. A small, poorly furnished room was all he saw. Slowly his head turned.

Sitting on the side of the bed, clad in only a filmy robe, a girl was polishing her fingernails. The pink of her skin and the curves of her body showed clearly through the silken mask of pale green. Suddenly she looked at him and smiled, rather accusingly, he thought.

"So you finally decided to wake up," she said.

"I beg your pardon, Miss——"

"Stoddard. Georgia. Remember?"

"Of course. Of course," he replied lamely. Given a minute or so, it would all come back to him. Somewhere down the line he had lost his anchor, but for the life of him he couldn't recall where, unless——

The tavern, of course! Gradually the picture re-formed, something about one's being born to love and die, and war had a bearing on it. Made it faster, that was it. Quite appropriate, come to think of it. He had bought her wine. An actress out of work, she had listened to his story. "Honor," he had said. Then they had come here.

His eyes grew wide. Under his intense gaze she gave her mouth a curious twist and, on impulse, threw back the gossamer robe. "Remember, Lieutenant James?"

He did. Nor could he take his eyes off her uncovered pointed breasts.

How willingly she had given herself to him. The memory of her hoarse wordless sounds and the excited motions of her fingers as they twined in his hair returned. He was sensuously aware of her unquenchable physicality, of the sudden awakening of his tired body.

He was asking questions of himself—who was she, and what did she want, and had she robbed him?—when Georgia's eyes grew heavy. With a slight cooing sound, she squirmed close. Then, taking his cheeks in both her palms, she gazed at his mouth a moment before slowly pressing hers to it.

James awoke to a banging on the door. As he sat bolt upright and stared at the darkness, he wondered where the day had gone.

"Georgia, who the devil is it?"

There was no reply. Aware that he was alone, he slowly stretched out once more. Whoever it was could go away, and the sooner the better.

The visitor did not depart, however. Instead, he lunged at the door and sent it flying back on its hinges. James's angered protests gave way to "Who are you?" when the glare of a lantern blinded him to all but a dim shape advancing toward him in menacing silence. The lantern bearer paused at the foot of James's bed and addressed an order to someone outside the room.

"It's him, Turk. Come on in and close the door."

James leaped from the bed and gave them to know he was Lieutenant Hillyer of the United States Navy. "What's the meaning of this?" he cried angrily. "What do you want here?"

"Grab him, Turk. We'll see who he thinks he is this time tomorrow."

James made a dive for the larger man. His fist crashed into a jaw that seemed as solid as iron, sending the intruder staggering backward. The lantern fell to the floor as he tried to retain his balance, and James was quick to grab it up and fling it through the window. Quickly he swung around just as the one called Turk brought a short club into play, though his fist barely grazed the ruffian's neck. The bar fell hard across James's biceps, causing him a howl of pain. Off guard, he was unaware that the larger of the pair was closing noiselessly in from behind him.

In another second an arm tightened about James's neck like a vise. Struggle as he might, there was no release from it. Nor was he able to so much as move his head out of the way when his assailant said:

"Let him have it, Turk."

He seemed to be floating through space on the bosom of a cloud. Slowly the exquisite sensation of total peace departed and he was vaguely aware of the terrible height of his billowy carpet. Then an acute sense of danger, of falling, seized him and he was clutching for support. The undulant sea was suddenly at his back, rocking him.

James's eyelids fluttered open. He lay still a long minute trying to make out the horizontal planks a few feet above him. Raising both hands to his bursting head, he rolled over on his side and stared, dumfounded, at a binnacle lamp, a mess table, and the varied gear of men before the mast. He knew what the inside of a forecastle looked like.

"A merchantman!" he said. Incredible. He could not believe this. Why should he be here; and who but the enemy, if he could honestly call any devoted Southerner that, could be possessed with enough effrontery to dishonor the uniform of the United States Navy by berthing an officer of the service in a lowly forecastle bunk?

The question sent his glance to the clothes he wore, and the answer struck his brain like a blow on the head. He stared in disbelief at the faded blue stripes of a deck hand's shirt and dungarees fresh from the slop chest. He wore these weather-and-work garments, and not the blue of the Navy.

In short, James Hillyer, Lieutenant, U.S.N., had been neatly impressed aboard a merchantman.

He put down the myriad questions assailing his mind, slid out of the bunk, and made his way unsteadily on deck, where he stood taking in the scene of ship and ocean. The blue sea rolled gently, its broad surface dotted with white-topped wavelets, and the little bark —she was that, and none too old—gave to the scend of the waves in a harmony of rhythm that caused men to sing of the open sea. The wind blew invigoratingly across deck and hummed through the rigging. Blocks creaked lazily. And fluttering in the breeze was a flag, the Stars and Stripes.

James's forehead wrinkled into a frown and he ran a hand nervously through his sand-colored hair.

"Impressed!" he said audibly. "Why? Now is it possible that——?"

How she had fascinated him. Her voice and laughter, and——

> *You were born to love, to hate and die*
> *And war will do it faster.*

A sailor approached, and James said, "What ship is this?"
"The *Golden Rocket,* matey. Bound for Cuba."

## 14.     Up Anchor

### 1

BY THE MIDDLE OF JUNE the strain of waiting was beginning to tell on Commander Semmes and his officers. Two weeks after the C.S. *Sumter* had been formally commissioned into service, past trial runs up the Mississippi and the maze of vexing problems that arose in readying her for sea, the word came that she would sail on the eighteenth.

Upon receiving the message, Prize Master Cutler, C.S.N., rubbed the tip of his nose with a forefinger and said thoughtfully, "Day after tomorrow."

Glancing at his watch, he saw the time was close to six in the afternoon. A deep frown creased his brow as he walked slowly toward the window overlooking the courtyard. Wide banana fronds swayed lazily in the faint breeze, a miniature jungle of emerald green masked by shadows of deeper green and mauve. Banks of flowers bloomed profusely, sending their perfume up to a window. But Adam had no eye for the beauty and splendor on parade. His gaze was fixed on a curled, unopened banana leaf that pointed like a lance toward the sky. He realized vaguely that it stood for something in the scheme of the universe. Sever it and it must bleed and wither. Another shoot would appear, and the wound of amputation would be forgotten.

That was physical.

Without turning his head, he said to the silent old mulattress who busied herself tidying up the room, "You know, Ti-Coo, I thought I could hardly wait for the order to sail. Now that it has come"—he raised a shoulder—"I'm not so sure."

"*Oui.* Ti-Coo know, m'sieu. She mos' distress."

"Because I'm leaving?" he said absently.

"*Non.* Becoz the charm. *Enfin,* against the heart—*enfants perdus!* You make marriage!"

Ordinarily Adam would have replied with a light laugh. Even now he discounted her prophecy by 100 per cent. However—and the fact raised his brows—he had been unable to put Faustine out of his thoughts as he had the others. Strangely, she clung to the fore of his mind and got in the way of all else. Why? He had taken her in fair conquest, had breathed no promises, made no vows. He recalled no sequence of love-making on his part. Her passion had equaled his and their descent into the maddening whirlpool had been together.

He had lain with many women whose physical zeal far exceeded Faustine Beaumont's. An English widow in Singapore, Nancy Eskridge, the Légère girl—now there were three for you—eager, smooth as checkered silk, and endowed with boundless vitality.

No redeeming vows. Gracious adieus, memories. Nothing more.

With Faustine it was different, the difference being lodged in

Adam S. Cutler! Rather perplexing, to put it mildly. He was oddly bedeviled.

"Ti-Coo, pour me a spot of brandy." She obliged. "Have one for yourself. But tell me, first off, what are the symptoms of love?"

For a moment she stared into his eyes, her expression inscrutable. Then without any word whatever, she began her pantomime. How she used her eyes, mouth, hands, and shoulders—she must have been a great one in her day, he decided—to express first infatuation, then adoration, followed by bliss and contentment, next a storm, jealousy, perhaps, quivering anger and, at last, utter desolation.

Bowing before him, she stole a glimpse into his face. "That is the *grande passion,* m'sieu."

Adam turned abruptly and left the house.

At about the same time, Faustine left her room and stood with her back to the closed door in serious thought. Mere moments had elapsed since she paused before her mirror for a touch of perfume to her ears and hasty but critical study of her image. The cool white dress, with low neckline and the ruffles of a flowing skirt bordered in crimson edging, did nothing to detract from her face or figure.

Slowly dark eyelashes lifted and her speculative glance slid to a closed door behind which Estève Decloux was no doubt dressing, as was his habit, for his usual visit to the courtyard. There he would partake of iced refreshments and watch his daughters romp glee-fully until it was dark. He almost made a ceremony of twilight over New Orleans.

Today Celeste and Aurelie, the little darlings, would be else-where. Faustine's small bright mouth took on a cunning twist as she removed her hand from the silver doorknob and sauntered toward the stairway. She hoped Mimi would not allow them to run wild through Cousin Josephine's house. Maman Marchand worried so about her precious things; and, heavens alive, so would anyone lucky enough to own her collection of Sèvres and Meissen, not to mention the wealth of French bisque and Waterford crystal. Only last week poor Aurelie had broken two sillabub cups presented to Josephine by a friend from Natchez.

It had not been difficult to plant the idea of a visit in their little minds. How she adored them.

Pausing at the foot of the stairs, she gazed at a sofa. Despite her great sacrifice a few weeks earlier nothing was definite. Her own physical enjoyment was both revolting and irrelevant; what mattered was her failure to land the prized catch. Then only this morning she heard that the *Sumter* would reach for the passes within a few days.

All of which pointed to a salient fact: Adam had not the slightest intention of taking her for a wife.

Her gaze dropped only to lift slowly and follow the stair railing to the second floor. Within a week, Estève, whom she had kept at arm's length, would depart with his daughters for Mexico. She must, therefore, shorten her arms a trifle this evening. Indeed, she must.

It was quite warm. He might prefer gin and water over light wine. It was quicker.

His voice startled her. "Celeste! Aurelie! Come!"

Quietly Faustine slipped into the courtyard and stood before a rosebush heavy with red buds. With her back to the grilled doorway, it occurred to her that the buds were the color of blood. She greeted the discovery with a tight smile as he entered the courtyard.

"Mademoiselle Beaumont, where are my kittens?"

Closing her eyes, tensing herself, Faustine deliberately pricked a delicate forefinger with a rose thorn. "Oh!" she exclaimed, jerking her hand away. "That horrid thorn!"

She faced Decloux with the finger in the grip of her other hand and a frown of pain on her face.

In the brief interval before he strode anxiously toward her, Faustine examined him from head to toe. He wore the brilliantly decorated uniform of the company of hussars which he officered. Minus dolman and shako, he appeared in full dress for his final meeting with his group. And how handsome, she thought, with short boots polished a glistening black beneath baggy white trousers, ornamented by gold braid scrolls down the front and a belted coatee of crimson and Turkish blue.

As he held her hand and tenderly wiped tiny drops of blood with a silk handkerchief, Faustine felt a small twinge of conscience. The concern of this kind and gullible Creole was genuine. Little did he suspect that she, with innocent eyes lifting adoringly to his face, was cunningly at work on him.

"Ah, *chère mam'selle,* this is mos' regrettable."

There was no reply, only lengthened silence and its compelling effect as her glance held steadily to his face.

"*Mon Dieu,* such lovely hands! So slender——" His statement ended there and the handkerchief was forgotten as his eyes took on an expression of pinched curiosity and slowly turned to meet hers.

Faustine's glance remained deep and unwavering for a few breathless moments. Then long-lashed eyelids dropped and her chin quivered ever so slightly. The almost imperceptible pressure of her fingers over his preceded the hesitant withdrawal of her hand. Slowly she put her back to him.

It was a fleeting contact of touch and glance, though he was warmly aware of having stirred her emotions. His heart beat fast and he could feel the blood mounting to his neck and face. A French gentleman whose code of honor was valued above his life's blood, he had seldom allowed his growing regard for this lovely woman to surface, and never by word expression. But something of the kind had risen in her, had made itself evident. Thus, he told himself, he was free to make an honorable advance.

He stepped in front of her and tilted her chin upward. "*Ma chère,*" he began in a whisper. There he paused, for her eyes and face were suddenly stricken, as though she were on the verge of tears. He did not wish to offend her.

Then she uttered a strangled cry of "Estève! Ah—Estève!" and swayed toward him as if she were about to faint. She clung to him and her lips crushed to his, and she was thinking, exultantly, that it had happened with amazing swiftness.

Adam pulled the bell cord at the Decloux house and waited, thinking it was odd that he had left his house for the river and wound up here. Worse, that on the way he had come to the startling conclusion that he, Adam Cutler, was in love. Gone was his immunity to the fairer sex. He, who prided himself on the impregnability of his bachelor's armor, had been pierced through and through. What had happened to him demanded some justification, however, and he came up with a few lame excuses:

He owed Faustine something, some security, if only to satisfy his own sense of duty and honor. Yes, that was it. But marriage?

The door opened and an aged Negress admitted him with, "*Bon soir,* M'sieu Cutler." She leveled a bony finger at the courtyard. "No announce need fo' m'sieu."

Adam strode down the hall, opened the door to the exterior, and took a single step forward. As though paralyzed, he stood with mouth open, eyes wide and staring, unable to move or speak.

Faustine, if he could believe his eyes, was locked in embrace with Decloux.

He could and did believe it. As he clamped his jaws shut and spun on his heel, he heard her urgent cry. It reached his ears almost a scream:

"Adam!"

It sounded again, closer, as he reached the street. As he stalked on, blind with shock and rage, she ran in front of him and threw herself in his path. He brushed her aside and continued up the street, deaf to her cries of "Wait! Listen to me, Adam! Please! Please!"

He paused only when she clutched at his hand and fell to her knees on the banquette, where she pleaded with him to listen only a moment. He had never seen such a terrified expression on a woman's face, nor had he ever imagined that calm, poised Faustine would ever cry out in voice pinched and strangled in utter abasement.

A small crowd was gathering. A carriage stopped and the driver's neck craned forward.

"Adam! God as my witness, I'll kill myself if you don't listen!"

Glaring down at her, he said icily, "That's a damn good idea."

On sudden impulse, he jerked her to her feet and swept her toward the carriage. "Royal Street," he barked, shoving her roughly into the seat.

At her side, he sat stiffly, too angry to speak, too furious to remain silent. The muscles of his jaws rippled and his breathing was labored, as though he were pushing the vehicle.

Faustine remained inert, staring out of shocked eyes first at the driver then Adam. Something she could not understand was happening to her. Rather, it had come over her at the sight of Adam's grim face as he stood in the courtyard. Never had she wanted to hold on to anything so much as Adam. Never was she more ashamed of herself. But the latter fell away under the urgency of the former, and she was praying to heaven that he would relent.

Her prayers seemed to go unanswered. In his parlor, he poured a huge amount of liquor, drank it down, and burst the glass into a million pieces against the mantel. His eyes were pinpoints as they regarded her, and under his strong and menacing attention, she sat on the sofa trembling all over. It was not fear of him, but fear of losing him. Nor did she cringe when he stepped to within a foot of her and said:

"I'm going to take you as I would the commonest whore in New Orleans." He paused, hands working into and out of fists. "Say something!" he roared angrily.

"There is nothing you would believe. Go ahead. You can't hurt me any more."

He slapped her, as he would a man, and stared at the heavy red print of his hand on her white face. "On second thought, I'd rather have the blackest wench on the levee."

Her fingers touched her cheek tenderly, affectionately. He had not hurt her, she realized; instead, he had sent a thrill tingling through her, a sense of awakening to his masculine vitality—but more, an awareness that his angered passion was but a manifestation of his love. With its fury spent, he would be amenable to reason.

But she underestimated the storm raging inside him. He grew calm and icy-cold under it. She didn't know how to deal with this turn of affairs and she grew afraid. All confidence had drained out of her when he quietly advised that he would see her home.

"So it is final," she said, half to herself.

"Definitely," he replied with maddening complacency. "My apologies for striking you, Faustine. I regret it, sincerely."

She rose with amazing swiftness and came close to him. "Regret?" Her lips curled with scorn. "That for once you lost your dignity? But what else! What a blind fool you are, Adam Cutler. You seek no explanation, none whatever. For loving you I am branded in your narrow, self-centered mind as a woman any man can have for the asking."

"You were no virgin," he said incisively.

It was too cruel and unexpected. But if there was to be no quarter, she would ask none.

"That, sir, is debatable. But not to the uninformed." She took a backward step and resorted to contemptuous study of him. It was apparent that he was in doubt on that score. She continued:

"Being in love with you did something to me. The war hastened it, as it does all things, to a rotten finish. It caused me to respond to a farewell kiss from a man who has been kind to me and considerate in all things."

She paused, and he considered the direct matter-of-factness of her voice as much as all she said.

Adam's brow rose. "Caused you to *respond*, you say? I can vouch for that."

"Of course you can!" caustically. "Even as I can honestly vouch for the fact that I have done no wrong with any man but you.

"But don't you believe that! Not you!" she hastened to say. "Remain as you are, Mr. Cutler of Bay Oaks, skeptical, wholly mistrusting, but dignified and lordly in your condemnation of a truly *bad* person. Even in your lonely hours at sea, don't allow compassion to enter your heart, for in a moment of weakness you might humble yourself long enough to pray that your baby and mine is not born with the print of your hand on its tiny face."

This staggered Adam. He had naturally heard of such things, had seen birthmarks. The horrible thought was simultaneous with the shock of learning that there would be a baby. Nor did it occur to him to doubt her as his vast astonishment evanesced under a strong surge of regret for his treatment of her.

"Faustine!" he said falteringly, taking a step toward her.

"Don't you come near me!" Her voice was recklessly bitter. "You can push even me too far." As he came on, she struck a belligerent pose. "Take another step and I'll—I'll fight you, Adam."

He took the step separating them, and she fought with all her strength until he pinned her arms at her sides. Spent, she stared wide-eyed up at him a second or two, then gave in to tears.

"Oh Adam, Adam!" she cried in desperation.

As his mouth touched hers, she drew her face back from him. "Why hurt me again?" she asked weakly.

His lips caressed her cheeks and eyes, and he was whispering something in her ear. Slowly her eyes closed and she murmured, "My own darling Adam!" even as under her breath she cried triumphantly, "I've won! I've won!"

2

Two days later the C.S. *Sumter* dropped down to the barracks for her powder. That night she ran on under a moon nearing its full to Mississippi anchorage between Forts Jackson and St. Philip. Of her officers and crew, numbering more than a hundred in all, there was perhaps only one man who was not dominated by the excitement of embarkation and the big question which only the short future could resolve—could the first Confederate cruiser make her way safely to sea past the U.S.S. *Brooklyn*, stationed near the head of the passes?

That man, Prize Master Cutler, stood on deck with a hand on a 32-pounder gazing up at the moon. He was very much in love, and he was thinking that his letter home should by now be moving through Mississippi Sound toward Mobile Bay. It was perhaps the shortest message he had ever written to his parents; but, without doubt, the most important of his entire life.

## 15.    A Bridal Bouquet

1

JOSEPH had just crumpled the Mobile paper and flung it across the room. His stormy eyes darted from Annabel to Adria and back again.

"I swear, ma'am"—he addressed his wife—"I'd find more peace in the army camps of Virginia! One minute there's to be a wedding, the next there isn't. Frankly, if it wasn't for the embarrassment of it, I'd call the whole damn thing off once and for all."

Moving to the doorway, he turned. "I'm going up where the cotton grows, if only to get out of this damned house until the arguing is done with."

"Joseph!" Annabel said sternly. "You'll do nothing of the kind. The Clarke County plantation is in good hands. Bay Oaks could use the calm Mr. Cutler I once knew." Her hand touched Adria's. "Quiet, Adria. Let him talk of uncertainty, tell us that guests are invited and all that. Heavens, I wish Adam were here."

Joseph loosed a muffled snort. "I told you, Annabel, not to drag all this before Adam in the first place. This war is going to be short enough as it is, and if he and Raphael Semmes don't hurry to sea they'll miss any part of it."

"War! War!" Adria cried, exasperated. "That's all you can talk about!"

"That's all I know around here," he retorted. Stroking a mustache, he peered at his daughter. "Actually, Adria, I believe you could singlehanded wear down the Federal Army and take Washington."

"Enough, Joseph. Now can you sit down and calmly discuss the situation? Adria has decided definitely not to go through with it, so we must get word to all invited, regardless of our own embarrassment."

Joseph's hands fell resignedly against his thighs. "Three days before the wedding. And I've got to be the one who faces Leland Jarvis of Brierlane."

As he ambled wearily to a chair, Erasmus brought mail. Joseph opened a letter. "Beat this for a proposition, will you. That scoundrel Sherrod, offering me a *golden opportunity*. For five thousand dollars I can buy ten shares in a steamer to run the Federal blockade. A long war, he says. Rot!

"But look here, a letter from Adam!"

"Open it," Adria demanded impatiently.

Joseph did. His face, as he read it, grew pale. Unconsciously he rose. "Annabel," he said, "better sit down. Brace yourself, honey."

"Is he hurt?" Adria leaped to her feet and snatched the letter from his hand. Then she and Annabel read:

New Orleans
June 17, 1861

Dear Mother, Father, and Adria:

You will no doubt be every bit as surprised as pleased to learn that today in a quiet ceremony on Toulouse Street, Faustine became my wife. Since the *Sumter* embarks tomorrow for the mouth of the Mississippi, I am sending my bride to Bay Oaks for the welcome I know you will give her. Until I can see you all again, I entrust her to your loving care. In haste, I am

Devotedly,
Adam.

Annabel pressed a calming hand to her bosom. "My Adam—married!" she said, staring at Joseph.

As Joseph ordered Erasmus to fetch bourbon, and to be quick about it, Adria shook her head with disbelief. "Surely not," she said in prayerful tones. "Not to that woman!"

"Adria!"

"Mother, it's simply, utterly impossible."

"Adria. Control yourself."

"But read this! Good God a'mighty, he's sending her here! Entrusting that scheming creature to *our loving care!*"

"She's a fine girl." Joseph spoke up. "I've always said so, haven't I, Annabel?"

"Yes. Of course. She's a wonderful girl. But to think—my son is married. I do believe I'm about to cry, Joseph."

"Cry, the devil! Be calm, woman!"

Erasmus came running with bottle and glass. Nervously he uncorked it and poured.

"More!" Joseph thundered. "You'd think the blockade had me conserving liquor." He gulped it down. "Erasmus, you heard. Adam's married."

Staring straight ahead, he sank into a chair. "Adam married," he said. "My boy, it's quite a shock."

"Are you all right, Joseph?" Annabel rushed to him.

"Quite. Quite, thank you."

"But you're white as a ghost."

"At least I'm calm about it. Hell, every man gets married. To a woman. Now don't go getting upset again, Annabel. Erasmus! Now where the devil did that nigger go?"

Adria's face burned red as she began to pace the length of the room to the swish-swish of taffeta petticoats. "I can just see dear Miss Beaumont's cat-eyed possessiveness as she alights from the carriage. Mrs. Adam Cutler, queen of all she sees. 'My darlin' Adria,' she will coo. 'Oh, I love dear Adam so very much.' And all the time she's thinking, 'Adria, Bay Oaks is as much mine as yours, thanks to Adam.' But I won't tolerate it."

She stood still, then stamped her foot. "I won't! I won't!"

"Please, Adria," Annabel said firmly. "You will remember Faustine is Adam's wife and treat her as such."

Adria lifted an eyebrow and pursed her lips. "Yes, Mother." Her expression said otherwise as she turned toward the hall. "But I'll do it from a distance. I've decided to marry Lawrence and live at Brier-lane."

She left them staring at one another. Joseph spread his hands wide in a gesture of despair. "*Now* she's going to marry him!"

Annabel gazed moodily from the floor to Adam's letter. "Joseph," she said, "I don't think a small glass of wine just now could do me harm."

Adria left the house and walked angrily down the flagged walk. She moved on, between the columned two-storied kitchen and matching servants' quarters, to a parterre of roses.

"Adam, you crazy fool man," she said between quivering lips, "can't you see she'll bring you nothing but unhappiness?"

She studied the roses, scarcely seeing them, then for some reason looked back toward the house. She felt a little mean, for just when her dear parents were in need of consolation she had launched into another storm. But maybe, she thought, it was just what they needed to take their minds off the horrible thing Adam had done to them.

"Poor, poor Adam." Anger had fled and left her wanting to cry. Then she recalled her last statement before flinging herself in a rage out of the room.

Marry Lawrence! She had said that.

It had rained gently that morning and the damp air was heavy with scents of blossoming roses, honeysuckle, and jasmine. Up in the moss-laden oak a mockingbird sang its heart out and, like animated splashes of vermilion against the purple bougainvillaea, a pair of cardinals flitted nervously before separating for a contest in full-throated melody.

Somehow these things were not the same to her. A year earlier the melodious songs and the perfume of the gardens had filled her with an indefinable ecstasy. Her blood had tingled with surging life. And now everything had changed. Much had happened, to the nation, to her. War, her first love, the unbelievable failure of that romance, her own impetuosity. She had been, was now, lacking the emotional stability one needed most in time of stress.

But how could events have taken such an awful twist? In love with James still, she was to marry Lawrence three days from now. Despising Faustine, she would be forced to welcome her brother's wife. Small wonder the birds had lost their voices and the flowers their exotic scents.

All this angered her. Feeling the blood rushing up to her bosom and neck again, she bit her lip and forced herself to remain calm despite the fact that refusing herself even an outburst of temper greatly vexed her.

She walked on, pausing before a plaster statue of a boy. His hand pointed toward distant trees, toward the north and Brierlane, the home of Lawrence. A hummingbird drinking nectar from a flower was suddenly gone, like happiness and hope. If she could only run away, perhaps to Aunt Eugenia in Galveston, and start all over. But the boy of plaster looked serenely beyond his pointing finger as if to say, "Duty lies in that direction."

"James," she implored in trembling tones, "please don't let this happen to us." James was far away and unheeding. Suddenly she despised him. "I hate you! Hate you!"

She had hated him yesterday, and the day before that. It was a part of love, a sign of frustration; it only proved a fact . . .

Slow at first, swifter now, matching the tempo of war, a giant whirlpool was spinning her about, drawing her closer and closer to the vortex. And there was nothing, not a thing, she could do about it.

It frightened her. Her brows drew together and she was gazing at the trees, then the sky, and at last the house.

Perhaps the realization of total defeat was worse than defeat itself. She wondered about it. She had had no experience in bearing up under troubles. How did one go about getting used to wretchedness?

She gathered up her skirts preparatory to running as fast as possible away from the garden, from herself. Then she forced calmness by telling herself that she was no longer a child but a woman, that to run from trouble merely increased her fears as it lessened her ability to cope with either. But the reward for strength proved small indeed. The small plaster arm continued to point unwaveringly, and near the house Abel and a few helpers were stringing lines for the lanterns that would illuminate the gardens—

At Sunday evening's gay wedding party.

2

Sunday came, for there was nothing one could do to prevent it. At around ten that evening Adria managed to lose Lawrence and work her way through the crowded hall of Bay Oaks to the stairs. How she accomplished it she did not know. Everything had happened with such amazing swiftness that her confused mind failed to keep pace with events.

As she reached the second floor and ran toward her room, Mammy Rose came puffing up the back stairs. "Git back down dere where yo' belongs, chile! All dem well-wishin' folks gwine say yo' ain't got no manners or 'preciation."

"Not you, Mammy! Please! I couldn't stand another minute of it."

"Careful wid dat weddin' dress!" Mammy cried, opening the door. As Adria entered her room and dropped into a slipper chair as though in a daze, the fat Negress commenced waiting on her. "Purty! Chile, I nebber seen the likes o' yo' in dazzlin' white satin a-movin' down de stairs on Mistuh Joseph's arm. And Miss Clay a-playin' dat march, and Miss Annabel a-standin' wid a prayer on her lips. Drink dis water, honey."

"Get me a glass of brandy." Adria seemed to be talking out of a dream. "A big glass, Mammy—from Father's room."

A moment alone, Adria drew as deep a breath as her tight dress would allow and stared confused at the wall. It all seemed so far away, as though it had happened to someone else. White candles all over the place, ladies in their finest dresses, Leland Jarvis beaming, Lawrence tall and handsome. Then her father had stepped back, disappeared, like the hummingbird in the garden, and Lawrence stood at her side. Before them the minister of Mobile's Government

Street Presbyterian Church moved his lips and spoke a jumble of words. She and Lawrence responded. Her heart, she recalled, had turned to ice. Almost she had said her vows to James.

Mammy Rose returned. "Dis here stuff pow'ful, honey. Go easy on it."

"Mammy, I waited tense, like a silly child, thinking, hoping, that James would arrive in time to stop the wedding."

"Hush up! Joshin' yo' ole mammy, dat's what. But yo' ain't no chile. Nossuh, a look at mah baby prove dat. Um-m-m! Mistuh Law-'ence done got hisself a purty woman, fines' in all Alabamy!"

Adria darted her an unpleasant glance.

"All them toasts drunk to yo'all in champagne and all de kissin'! Jest lissen at 'em now—scrapin' and shufflin' to de Virginia reel! De Virginia backstep and Geo'gia turn-down, dey done wore out. Yo' look mighty purty dancin' wid yo' husban'. Miss Faustine, she sholy cut a fine caper. Ain't missed a dance. Not a dance!"

"Probably never will," snapped Adria. "By timing her arrival from New Orleans on my wedding day, she almost stole the show."

"She sholy did when folks learn she Mistuh Adam's wife. Dat sea cap'n what done insult yo'all once, he kiss her so she won't soon fo'-git."

Adria looked shocked. "Sherrod? Was he invited here?"

Mammy Rose laughed. "Wait'll yo' see what he done brung fo' a weddin' present."

"He can take it back where he got it. And you can stop packing my clothes. I told Lawrence I wasn't about to go to the Battle House with him."

"Did, huh?" Plump hands came to rest on wide hips. "Honey, lissen to me. Don't nobody love yo' mo'n Mammy Rose. Nobody, not even Miss Annabel. 'Cause she couldn't. Who held on yo' little hand and let yo' toddle all over dat garden; who sing yo' to sleep when yo' didn't weigh fo'teen pounds drippin' wet; who brung yo' up fo' to be a lady? Is I fail? Done plumb mis'able fail?"

"Oh, Mammy—please!" Adria rose only to sit down again and stare at long fingers interlaced in her lap.

"All right, baby, I say dis and no mo'. Yo' ain't no chile now. A wife, dat's what. On de Holy Bible yo' vow was took. Mistuh Law-'ence yo' husband. He got a right, cause he take mah baby in holy wedlock. Remember dat.

"Now git on down to yo' guests. Dis minute!"

Adria lifted a pleading pair of eyes that threatened to melt her old

Negro mammy's heart. A minute later she walked dispiritedly out into the hall.

Alone, Mammy Rose dabbed her eyes dry with the hem of her skirt and continued packing Adria's bag.

Warmed by brandy, Adria brightened as she joined the crowd of merrymakers. She smiled and curtsied under the compliment of an aged banker and his wife, moved on under the admiring eyes of Lawrence's friends from up in Marengo County to the double parlor and graciously accepted a tall-stemmed glass of champagne from no less a person than handsome, stern-countenanced Brigadier-General Braxton Bragg, who touched glasses with Governor Andrew Moore of Alabama to her happiness.

Suddenly gay, she gave the martinet a smile. "General, sir, may Federal blue continue to fade at your approach." Eyes beaming over the brim of her glass, she drank and, to the delight of the notables, broke the delicate glass against the back of a rosewood chair.

Moments later a handsome captain in gray placed the train of her gown over her arm and led her to the ballroom floor, where, she realized with a catch of hurt, she had last danced in the arms of James.

He said above the music, "It is indeed regrettable, Mrs. Jarvis, that Lawrence must be called away so soon. We are all——" He paused, amazed, when she frowned inquiringly. "You didn't know?" he said contritely.

She didn't know, but before the orchestra brought the dance to a rousing climax, she learned that Lawrence had weeks earlier asked for service in Virginia. He was ordered to depart next morning, on the day after his wedding, for Tennessee.

"I'm truly sorry, ma'am," the officer said with genuine regret. "I thought you knew."

"I know now." She smiled, much happier than her embarrassed informer would ever know.

Suddenly the second orchestra, playing outside near the back porch, struck up "Dixie's Land." Cheers drowned the music for long seconds as everyone who could crowd the flagstones danced and shouted.

As Adria moved into the square of light, a young Mobile merchant stopped the music long enough to cry out, "For the queen of all Dixie, Mrs. Lawrence Jarvis! Play 'Dixie,' boys!"

How she thrilled to the compliment, then the stirring music. Erasmus bowed with a tray of wine, his face beaming. "Dat gen'leman sholy spoke de truf, Miss Adria."

With a hundred pairs of eyes upon her, Adria accepted a glass and lifted it to all. As she drank, her glance fell on Faustine and Captain Randall Sherrod, and she was thinking that Adam's bride of a few days could easily be mistaken for the schoonerman's property. This would never do.

She was moving toward them when two young gentlemen in crisp new uniforms stepped before her and bowed.

"Miss Adria," said the taller one, "you're the most beautiful creature I ever set eyes on. Tom here, Lieutenant Harrisson, ma'am, bet me twenty dollars I couldn't dance with the bride. I never refuse a bet."

"Why, Jerry Clark! Even in school you used to bet you could do things for me. Shame on you. And you too, Tom. Now you two just cancel that wager at once and I'll oblige you both."

Swirling to the music in Clark's arms, she forgot Faustine and Sherrod for the moment. Her partner was wishing her happiness and expressing his envy of Lawrence.

"Don't ever forget, Miss Adria, that I was in love with you." Wincing, he added bravely, "Don't reckon I ever quit loving you."

"Flatterer!" She smiled up at him accusingly.

"It's the God's truth, ma'am."

"Bless you, Jerry. Then take this to Virginia with you." She gave him a light kiss on the cheek just as the music stopped.

Following a dance with Lieutenant Harrisson, she returned to the porch and looked toward Adam's wife.

Under Adria's intent scrutiny Faustine removed Sherrod's hand from her shoulders and came toward her sister-in-law just as Lawrence appeared on the scene with several ladies from Linden and Demopolis. As pleasant conversations followed, Adria felt Faustine's critical eye on every stitch of her wedding gown, her hair and face. Then Mrs. Adam Cutler was saying:

"There wasn't time for us to have a big wedding. Not with Adam sailing down to meet the Federal cruiser *Brooklyn*. But you ladies must return to Bay Oaks. Adam exacted one promise of me. 'Be gay,' he said. 'Entertain. It's good for our morale.' So we must be brave, mustn't we, Adria?"

"Indeed we must, dear Faustine," Adria said, trying not to drip honey where it could be noticed.

"Poor Adria." Faustine smiled at Mrs. Porter of Linden. "Why,

Lawrence won't be able to carry her across the threshold of Brier-
lane. He leaves at dawn."

"So," Adria responded quickly, "I shall remain here." Under her
breath she said, "If only to show you a thing or two, Faustine Beaumont."

Adria looked up at Lawrence. She tried to smile, but failed, for
never in her life had she seen such hunger and impatient longing
in a man. Frightened, she looked away and her glance collided with
Faustine's before the latter could wipe the wise, exultant expression
from her face.

3

Adria thought she was surely going to die when at ten to one her
mother breathed a heavy sigh and left the room. She paused for a
horrified glance at her figure, so shockingly revealed under a filmy
pink night rail, then rushed to the bed. There she drew a sheet up
to her neck and leaned back against the pillows to await the dreaded
moment.

The next person to open the door would be her husband.

Lawrence had argued and pleaded with her to go to the Battle
House, where a small party had been arranged by his friends from
Fort Morgan. Joseph and her mother had sided with him, and even
Faustine had spoken in his behalf when Lawrence swore she would
surely make a laughingstock of him. But here she was. Despite the
wine she had drunk and the sweet definitions of marriage her mother
had tenderly poured into her ears, she remained sober and afraid.
Terribly afraid.

A timid rap on the door caused her eyes to grow wide. Her voice
froze in her throat. Then the door opened slowly, and Lawrence
entered.

He stood before the closed door a long time in silence, his eyes
searching, asking, wondering, as though he too were more apprehensive than elated. He shook his head at last, savagely, and raised
a decanter and glass and poured with hands quivering.

"Drink it," he said, moving to her.

She refused. He gulped it down and winced before placing brandy
and glass on a stand.

"I love you, Adria," he said, bending to her.

She sat still and tense, her mouth a tight line above the sheet she
clutched at her chin, her eyes enormous and fixed on him. Her heart

seemed to stand still and her breathing was quick and labored as she prayed that he would go away at once. It was too late to ask herself why she had placed her foot in this trap, but she did ask. Unable to bear up under the strain of his very nearness, she closed her eyes, unaware that he mistook this for a sign of wordless surrender.

His arms went suddenly about her and he was pressing her to him, kissing her eyes, cheeks, lips, and throat. She gasped for air and struggled against the weight of his arms and face. Her muffled cries seemed to puzzle him, for he stood back from her with an utterly confounded expression twisting his countenance.

"Don't! Don't touch me, Lawrence Jarvis!"

Unable to reconcile his views regarding marriage to such a reception, Lawrence gaped at her in speechless wonder. Recovering his wits, he said, "For God's sake, Adria, we have only a few hours together."

"Lower your voice," she demanded. "Someone will hear you."

Boiling mad, he put his back to her, then whirled with a question. "Why did you marry me?"

"I—I don't know," she stammered.

"You don't?" he said, amazed. Baffled, he walked to the door and back again, jaw muscles working furiously, eyes darting from her to the floor. "Look, honey." His hands lifted as he groped for words. "You love me. Of course you do—else you wouldn't have married me. Perhaps I frightened you."

A wide smile wreathed his face. "Of course. That's it. I'm sorry, honey. Why you're the prettiest, sweetest thing in all the South, the whole world. I'm proud, darlin'. Why, just knowing you love me when I take aim at a damn Federal up in Tennessee is all I'll need to see me through. Just give me the memory of your love to take with me, Adria."

Meeting with the same startled look, he said with diminishing confidence, "A man is supposed to have the love of his wife, Adria. We promised that much in our vows."

Adria bit her lip. A tear rolled down her cheek. "I'm upset, Lawrence. I do believe I'm going to have a chill."

"You're just downright scared, honey."

She nodded, and he hastened to reassure her. "Now don't you fret, honey baby. Why, you'll think you're a Dresden doll in my hands."

Adria studied him closely. He meant to be kind. Marriage made certain demands which exempted no woman, not even her own fastidious self. She supposed that when all avenues of escape were closed, one could only ask for kindness.

A faint smile of resignation crossed her face.

"My darlin' Adria!" he said, moving to her.

He lifted her from the bed tenderly and felt the trembling of her body under the cotton sheet she still clutched about her throat. As he brushed her forehead with his lips, he cautioned himself— "Easy, easy"—for she was at once both sensitive thoroughbred and fragile blossom. Ah, he would be gentle with her.

Lawrence reckoned without the coverlet, which hid all but her face until he in his elation swung her away from the four-poster. She was suddenly uncovered and he was standing as though frozen, unable to take his eyes off her.

A glimpse of white thighs beneath the transparent night rail sent the blood pounding at his temples. Then as she squirmed in an effort to hide her semi-nude figure from his raptured gaze, her gown fell open, exposing magnificent breasts.

The change in Lawrence was quick and startling. He could not suppress the longing he felt pushing through his veins. He did not try. The heaviness of his passion was revealed to Adria, who felt all gentleness depart under the pressure of his extreme desires.

Her one thought was escape. She succeeded in freeing herself, then ran to the door, flung it open and, without looking back, rushed for the stairs. Frantic, yet aware in the turmoil of her mind that her mother would only lecture and return her to Lawrence, she raced down into the dark hall and on outside the house.

She was soon pounding at a door inside the servants' quarters. Presently it opened and the whites of the slavewoman's eyes shone in the candlelight. "Chile! Lawd God in hebben! What yo' doin' heah half nekkid dis time o' night?"

Adria flung her arms about the Negress and sobbed, "Oh Mammy, I'm so scared! That brute from up the Tombigbee tried to rape me!"

Early next morning Adria came awake to find Mammy Rose shaking her. As events of the night flashed through her mind, she recalled having come to the servants' quarters, where her one dear friend in all the world had given up her bed and stroked her forehead and hair until sleep came. And now it was morning.

"Git up. Now. Yo' husban' am fixin' to leave fo' Tennessee. Git on de clothes I brung yo'. He waitin' wid de family to say good-by."

"No! I won't face him or the family, Mammy."

"Don' blame yo' none. Dey is truly plumb genuine embarrassed, lak yo' is. But yo' is gwine face 'em. And right now quick."

Sitting up in bed, Adria said defiantly, "Who says I must?"

"Me. Just a pore ole black nigger what realize she still got a chile on her hands. Dat's who!"

Adria entered the house a little later and forced herself toward the parlor. Her heart beat wildly and the blood crept up to her neck and on to diffuse her face with color. As she paused in the doorway, a cold silence greeted her. Lawrence and her father rose, while her mother and Faustine looked at her out of expressionless faces. All condemned her without any word. Only Lawrence looked haggard and injured.

She had come upon them with guilt and contriteness in control of her emotions. But such a reception quickly dispelled these feelings. A small wave of resentment buoyed her, gave her the assurance she needed.

"A good morning to you, dear Lawrence." She smiled and moved toward him with hands extended.

Momentarily overcome by her cheery greeting, he smiled and muttered a lame " 'Morning, Adria."

Suddenly himself again, he stiffened and said, "I regret my haste, but the company has been waiting at the river for almost an hour."

So saying, he kissed Annabel's cheek, Faustine's hand, and took Joseph's hand in his. Returning to Adria, he eyed her critically a moment, pecked her on the forehead, all the while doing his utmost to hide the deep pain surging up stronger by the moment. He knew in his own heart he loved her more than she might ever realize and, standing there with her hands in his, he tried in silence to convey his feelings to her.

Joseph could no longer hold his temper in check. He growled something about a woman sending a man off to war with a memory of his bride's spending her wedding night in the "nigger house" and stalked out of the parlor.

Adria felt a sharp pang of regret. In a measure it was overlaid with selfishness, for she knew that once the story got around, as it probably would, there would be no end of talk about her cruel and unpatriotic treatment of a gallant Southerner off to war in defense of her, home, and honor. In due time she might be snubbed socially. Yet something deeper stirred within her; she pitied Lawrence, almost loved him, if only because of what she had done to him.

She was seriously thinking of throwing her arms about him and kissing him as she should have done hours earlier, when he said:

"I must go." Looking deep into her eyes, he added, "God bless you, Adria. I love you."

As she stood there bereft of tongue, he bowed low, straightened, and walked away from her.

Adria moved to a window and watched him climb into an army wagon. A few minutes later Lawrence disappeared under the bluff that led to the river, and she could not help wondering if she would ever see him again. How would she feel if he became a casualty of war? She didn't wish to think about it. She wouldn't.

Instead, she would walk in the dew-sprinkled gardens of Bay Oaks and breathe the fresh morning air. Nor would she so much as glance at the horrid plaster statue of the boy who pointed—just pointed.

## 16.  The C.S. *Sumter*

ON A BRIGHT SUNDAY MORNING the trim little steamer of five hundred tons' burden swung lazily to her anchor as the muddy Mississippi flowed indifferently past to meet the waters of the Gulf of Mexico. The *Sumter's* every yard, mast, and spar gleamed, as did her single smokestack amidships. She sat the water long and sleek, with bowsprit and jib boom reaching far out in fine clipper fashion, her tall masts rigged barkentine style, square sails on the fore and main. From her main-truck a long pennant curled gracefully in the gentle south wind, while aft, the Stars and Bars of the Confederacy rippled undulantly.

Nothing broke the peace of the hot summer morning. A pelican flapped sluggishly over a grove of moss-laden trees and across the river egrets flew in a dazzling white formation down toward the Southwest Pass.

On board, the officer of the deck made the ship ready for the

Sunday services, while below, the lord of the afterguard was engaged in writing a letter to the Secretary of the Navy. Pausing, he read his opening sentences:

> C.S. Steamer *Sumter,* Head of the Passes
> June 30, 1861

Sir—

I have the honor to inform the department that I am still at my anchors at the "Head of the Passes"—the enemy closely investing both of the practical outlets. At Pass à l'Outre there are three ships, the *Brooklyn,* and another propeller, and a large side-wheel steamer; and at the Southwest Pass there is the *Powhatan,* lying within half a mile of the bar, and not stirring an inch from her anchors, night or day. I am only surprised that the *Brooklyn* does not come up to this anchorage, which she might easily do . . .

Raphael Semmes mopped perspiration from his face and neck, and adjusted the cloth under his forearm lest a drop of sweat mar the letter to Mr. Mallory.

" 'Which she might easily do . . .' " he read aloud.

Indeed, she might, he reflected. For more than ten days he had sweated and conned the river and dreamed up ways in which he might get his ship to sea. There were problems, there was peril in an even chase. The *Brooklyn* had the speed of him. She was reportedly good for thirteen knots against his maximum of ten under full steam and sail. His propeller under sail alone was a drag, and since he shipped only eight days of coal, he must conserve fuel. But he would use all, even oars if they would help, to get to sea, to fulfill his mission:

"To burn, sink, and destroy the enemy's commerce in the shortest time," he said with grim resolve.

Nothing should deter him, he vowed, staring out of the port. How he had pushed his men, almost without mercy—gun drills, boat drills, over and over! This green crew would learn to protect the ship and inflict damage on the enemy. God's will, they would.

Twisting a pointed mustache, he decided to pray. On his knees, he asked for guidance and an opportunity to serve his country. Slowly he rose and, calmer now, picked up his pen.

While he was completing the letter, the steamer *Empire Parish,* sent down with provisions from New Orleans by Commander Rousseau, returned from a scout of Pass à l'Outre at top speed, cast off a boat, and hailed the *Sumter.*

"The *Brooklyn* has gone off in chase of a sail!"

The barkentine literally came alive. The officer of the deck, eyes burning bright, crisply ordered Lieutenant Cutler to inform the captain, then shouted a command that put an end to Sunday muster. As the crew hastened to stow their bags, Mr. Semmes appeared on deck, having just called on Chief Engineer and Marine Officer Miles Freeman to get up steam. Quickly boats were run up and swinging booms taken alongside. When steam began to hiss, the order sounded to "walk the capstan round in double-quick." Up came the anchor in record time, and then the long-awaited cry that pointed the graceful bows into the four-knot current. Gently, beautifully, she rode out on the cushions of the Father of Waters and slid downstream. Her propeller turned now, and the grin on the quartermaster's face as he "hellumed" her out was wide and eager.

In all the excitement of getting a way under her, the pilot towed up by the *Empire Parish* went unnoticed. First to observe his state of nervousness was Adam, who immediately brought it to the attention of Commander Semmes. Whereupon, the captain questioned him and learned to his dismay and anger that the oysterman was a Southwest bar pilot and knew nothing of the other passes.

"Mr. Kell, this man has deceived us," Semmes declared vehemently. "Mr. Cutler, hoist the Jack at the fore!" As Adam leaped to the order, a signal for a pilot, the commander said, "Not that it will help us, but as a matter of course. Seems I'll have to run l'Outre Pass by my lighthouse inspector's memory."

Short minutes later the foretop cried the deck, "The *Brooklyn,* sir!" The "Where away?" revealed that she had chased to westward some seven miles and not out of sight, but had lost herself from the *Empire Parish* behind a delta spur. That, however, was of the past. The present brought home with terrific impact the gravity of the situation.

Both ships stood about the same distance from the bar. The *Brooklyn,* said an officer who had sailed of her from Tampico to Pensacola short months before, could do fourteen knots, to which Semmes countered, "We hold the advantage of a four-knot current." In the silence there was not one of the officers who failed to compare fire power. The enemy could gun them under.

The situation resolved itself into a gamble for all or nothing. Defeat could ring on a dirgeful wind from New Orleans to Richmond, reduce Confederate naval prestige and hopes to a pitiful state. But the sea ahead did not belong to men who excused cowardice with prudent logic. So there was no talk of turning back, and had there been, the fluttering petticoats and handkerchiefs, from first the balcony of the pilothouse and next the lighthouse wharf as the Confederate swept gallantly past, would have caused the entire crew to shout, "Carry on!"

Near the lighthouse a pilot caught a towline and came grinning aboard to stand at the horse block, the leadsman's platform, beside the commander.

"She lays down a pretty wake, sir." Mr. Kell smiled through his beard. "How close is the enemy now?"

"Not more than four miles distant," came the reply. "But we're not making top speed. Mr. Chapman, I'll trust you to heave the log."

Adam ventured a guess. "We're flirting with the reach of Captain Poor's guns."

"With nothing to spare," Semmes admitted anxiously, lowering his telescope.

No sail fluttered to the wind as yet, though officers and crew realized that once the bar of Pass à l'Outre lay under the stern, the order to loose canvas in the wind would send men scampering aloft. Even now Boatswain Benjamin Mecaskey eyed the foreyard and topgallants with a "hurry-up-sail" look on his beet-red face. Surgeon Galt tugged at his portside mustache and frowned thoughtfully at Gunner Thomas Cuddy, who fondly patted the big pivot gun amidships. The "fine little fellow" could hurl shot more than one mile, and rather accurately after ten hot days of drill.

Lieutenant Chapman reported a speed of nine and one half knots, and drew a crisp order to heave again. "Outrageous!" Semmes barked. "With a four-knot current sweeping us along."

When Chapman verified his report, Semmes directed Midshipman Armstrong to have Mr. Freeman report immediately to the quarterdeck.

In the meantime the pilot reported on a hazard around the bend, now coming into view. A Bremen ship lay grounded on the bar, with kedge run out and warp attached and run across the passageway. Alarm showed on deck, for there was barely room to pass.

Adam stiffened and grew tense all over as they neared the German with engine thumping at full speed. Now they were squeezing through. Just barely room—or was there that necessary inch? Ah, she made it. The sighs of relief on deck turned to cheers of thanks, and the Bremen's crew were shouting good luck in their tongue.

Adam and Lieutenant Evans were engaged in having the pilot's boat brought around to the side. The cruiser slowed an instant, and the pilot, turning loose of Semmes's hand after the latter's warm expressions of gratitude, dropped from the horse block and cried:

"Now, Captain, you are all clear. Give her hell and let her go!"

Glowering, sweat-caked, and coal-blackened, Engineer Freeman was reporting foam in the boilers as a result of getting steam up in too great a hurry. "When this subsides, sir, we may be able to add half a knot more."

"We'll need it!" cried Lieutenant Kell. "The *Brooklyn* is breaking out sail!"

Whirling, Adam narrowed his gaze on the enemy, now closer by a good half mile. If she kept this up, her guns would soon bark. He knew her armament, realized what a few direct hits would do to the little commerce destroyer. Now she was belching black smoke from her funnel.

"She's bracing sharp up on the starboard tack!" Lieutenant Evans called out. "With amazing speed, if I may say so."

"My compliments, Mr. Evans," Semmes replied. "We can trim sail as expertly as she, as you'll soon learn." Thereupon, he cried for sail and ordered the *Sumter's* yards braced just a little sharper than his adversary's. As the topmen scrambled aloft, he turned to Adam.

"Mr. Cutler, how does she lie on my weather quarter?"

"A couple of points, I'd say. Which, dammit all, gives her slightly the weather gauge of us, sir."

"Correct. But are you blind to our advantages?"

"No, sir. We have larger fore-and-aft sails, stays'ls, trys'ls and a devilish fine spanker—that is, if——" Adam's brow rose and dropped in a speculative frown.

Semmes's stern features broke in a sharp smile. His telescope came up as he said, "Indeed, that *if* you so gallantly suggest is the risk I shall run, Mr. Cutler. We'll hold our wind so closely that the *Brooklyn* may be forced to furl her sails."

"Despite the fact that the maneuver will place you athwart the *Brooklyn's* bows and allow her to work within close gunshot of you, sir?"

"Have you a better suggestion?"

Adam looked at the cloud to windward. "None, sir, though I'll be praying that rain squall bears down between us and the enemy."

Lieutenant Kell, who had heard the conversation, said in his Georgia voice, "And I'll join you in that humble petition, Mr. Cutler.

Aye, for the waters of the Mexican Gulf were never so invitingly blue before."

A look at the decks presented gunners stripped to the waist waving the squall in. All guns lay waiting with tarpaulins cast off, tompions removed, and powder and shot handily near. Loaders, spring and compression crews stood by for battle, which, if such developed, would be the first engagement of the war at sea.

Adam studied the gun crew in detachment, then with interest. They continued to coax the squall to leeward. They wanted the odds in their favor.

"And who the hell doesn't?" he said to himself, turning an anxious eye on the Federal cruiser.

Soon the wind-lashed cloud reached for the surface and lay a slanting, silver-sheeted screen between the vessels, overtook the *Sumter,* and heeled her far over to port as it drenched decks and men. Quartermaster and mate strained at the wheel as the wind bore down like a howling demon, reeling the masts in arcs and pushing up vicious seas. Shot rolled across deck, banging hard against stanchions, causing men to leap about and look lively for their safety.

Then, as suddenly as it had torn in, the rain squall departed in a hiss to leeward. Visibility returned and with it quick anxiety, for the U.S.S. *Brooklyn* roared closer to the *Sumter,* yards squared and broad bows flaring as she rocked on the waves, with the Stars and Stripes whipping from under the lee of her spanker.

She was not a pretty picture to the grave-faced, water-soaked men of the Confederates' quarter-deck. Semmes's eyes were mere pinpoints as he sent the paymaster his compliments with an order to fetch up the ship's papers and public pay chest, conclusive proof that he was preparing for the worst; or, said the expressions on the faces of Lieutenants Chapman and Evans, the inevitable.

Though it was sound, sensible Kell, now gripping the weather rail with one hand and wet beard with the other, who said, "She'll greet us with her bow chaser in another minute."

The statement evoked no argument among these men of the Old Navy, who recognized opportunity when they saw it, be it theirs or the enemy's. It was in this case armed bow Federal versus unarmed stern Confederate, with distance between the ships diminished to an extent that should provoke a tentative blast by the pursuer. Nor was it a matter requiring an instant's decision on the part of Captain Poor, since a full half hour elapsed with neither ship making any appreciable gain. As the freshening wind held, it soon became apparent that the *Sumter's* ability to point closer to the weather was causing the blockader to fall more to leeward.

Semmes spoke up with mixed elation and hope. "We're eating her out of the wind."

"A little more! Just a little more!" Kell urged. "Move on, Federal tyrant, into our wake!"

Miles Freeman rushed on deck to inform them that the foaming of his boilers had subsided. This gave the propeller a few extra turns a minute. Then the tautness of the quarter-deck enveloped him also. He saw the *Brooklyn* sailing into a trap. Unless they braced her up sharper on the full and by, she could not avoid the long bouncing wake of the little *Sumter*.

A few minutes later Captain Poor's reach for fame was suddenly reversed into a certain bid for censure by his government. His ship struck the *Sumter's* wake and he could do nothing but let fly the *Brooklyn's* sheets and halyards. This he did. Amid cheers from the *Sumter's* decks and yards, he clewed up and furled from courses to royals.

Toward midafternoon the *Brooklyn* gave up the chase, and the first cruiser commissioned into service by the Confederacy heeled to the winds and dipped to the heave of the welcome blue sea with all the grace and joy of a bird suddenly free of a cage.

That evening Lieutenant Cutler joined the officers of the wardroom, who had invited their commander to a glass of wine as they relived the bark's escape. All were weary from the strain of gaining an offing under such trying circumstances and at the same time buoyed to a high pitch by the success of their bold adventure.

When the ceremony ended, Adam went on deck and leaned against the rail. As he looked out over the waters that mirrored the starlit heavens, his thoughts turned to home. The *Empire Parish* had brought a letter that morning from Faustine. A smile of longing and contentment formed on his face as he recalled their glorious hours together. Slowly it faded and he was thinking of Adria's marriage to Lawrence, of her behavior on their wedding night as described by Faustine.

On the surface Adria was inexcusably at fault. But Adam looked beyond the deed to the cause, James Hillyer, who, unwittingly or not, had shaped this unhappy state of affairs. Adam could not put down a feeling of growing resentment. It baffled him in a way, since it was directed at a man who hung in the balance between former close friend and future enemy upon the high seas; and barring the latter, if one could, the loyalty of brother to sister was not easily put aside.

The voices of Semmes and Kell reached Adam's ears as the pair came on deck. James and Bay Oaks were forgotten as the commander said:

"The Secretary of the Navy assigned me no cruising ground, Mr. Kell. Since we sail *carte blanche,* I intend to swoop down on enemy shipping under Cuba without delay."

Observing a moment of silence, Kell said, " 'To sink, burn, and destroy.' "

"Aye. Everything that flies hate's polluted rag!"

Something of Semmes's feeling possessed Adam as he recalled the verse written about the American flag by a prominent South Carolinian. Often, when moved by patriotism to the Southern cause, Semmes spoke these lines with amazing fervor:

> *Tear down that flaunting lie*
> *Half-mast the starry flag*
> *Insult no sunny sky*
> *With hate's polluted rag.*

Adam could not wholly subscribe to such bitter hatred of the flag he and his forefathers had served; the break was too shockingly defined. But he felt himself leaning more and more in that direction. Perhaps a deck under his feet, the return to action, emphasized his increasing animosity toward the "Black Republicans," who stained the Stars and Stripes with a tyrant's lies.

In any case, he was impatient to do his part in sending fast to the bottom of the sea, by shot, torch, or auger, any craft flying the banner of the North.

## 17.    The Doomed Ship

1

ON THIS CLOUDY AFTERNOON OF JULY 3, 1861, the Maine bark *Golden Rocket*, seeking in ballast a cargo of Cuban sugar, ran before a freshening east wind between the south coast of Cuba and the Isle of Pines.

As some sea was on, the captain of the bark stared ahead in the direction of the Cayos de San Felipe, tugged at his stubby chin whiskers, and glanced at the man who only two days before had been elected to fill the office of his ill second mate.

"Mr. Hillyer." His voice was crisply New England. "Ye'll do well to keep one eye inboard and the other aloft." Almost in the same breath he ordered the helmsman to make four bells, two o'clock.

"Aye, sir," the new mate responded in manner so nautically decorous that the master eyed him sharply a moment, as if he were pondering again the impressed sailor's claim to a lieutenancy in the Federal Navy.

James turned his gaze from the verdant line of Cuban coast and distant blue peaks up to the main royal and forward down to the jib sheets. She was trimmed for the breeze and tack. Unless the wind veered, the yards would call for but one brace around before they put Cape Corrientes broad on the starboard beam. But as for doubling the cape before sunset, the Old Man had made a landsman's forecast.

The trim little ship, nearly new, of about seven hundred tons, dipped and rose to the waves like a thoroughbred. She shipped a fine crew and good officers. A few years earlier in his life James would have welcomed this adventure despite the humiliating circumstances attending his acquaintance with the Maine merchantman.

His first day aboard would forever be vividly etched in his memory. Almost unbearable shock and remorse following his drunken orgy had gradually given way to stunned indifference as he scrubbed decks and scampered aloft to loose and furl sail. He knew enough about captains of the sea to bide his time in registering a complaint. Other than heavy weather that first day out, the Old Man, a respectful name sailors gave a captain regardless of his age, had watched the new sailor to see if he could hand, reef, and steer. Deck hand Hillyer had qualified, had spent the day asking himself which it would be, loyalty to or escape from the United States Navy. From Havana to Mobile was just under six hundred miles, but could he arrive in time to stop a wedding?

The captain jerked James's mind back to the present as he boomed forth: "Foretop ahoy! What flag does the vessel ahead fly?"

James looked toward the cays, at the sail, then up into the fore. The lookout replied, "As near as I can make out, Spanish, sir!"

Blocks creaked, the wind aft sang through the rigging, the water swished at the sides. James thought again of the voyage down, of his continued state of indecision as day after day passed, with the Old Man finally breaking out a terse compliment: "As I don't like a hand to grow barnacles, Hillyer, I'll advise that I like the way ye battle the watch."

Then the day came when the U.S.S. *San Jacinto,* presumably of the Charleston blockade patrol, spoke the *Golden Rocket* far out to sea. He was acutely aware that here was his opportunity to identify himself, for he knew every plank, spar, and gun aboard the cruiser. But he watched the screw steamer belch smoke from her single funnel and reach for the western horizon. Only after she had dropped all but smoke under the edge of the sea did he tell the bark's captain who he was. Meeting with a narrow dubious look and "Why the devil didn't ye speak up?" James said, "Could be I didn't wish to, sir. Or I might say I didn't want to see your voyage interrupted." To which the other replied with Yankee forthrightness, "Then we shall see in due time if ye speak the truth as to who ye be. If 'tis so, I'll make proper amends."

When the bark turned southeast for the Bahamas and the Westward Passage around Cuba, James gave up hope of reaching Mobile before the wedding date. Never could he forget the nights of tranquil seas and pearl-blue heavens, the moon painting the water in silver and throwing shadows of masts, yards, and cordage to deck in sharp outline; and Adria filling his heart. The thought of his sweetheart in another's arms dulled the moon points over the sea. Married to someone else! No, it could not be! A violence of feeling, of jealousy, hurt, and unendurable longing assailed him. Better were he dead, with her the wife of Jarvis, with a war he might never condone threatening his future.

The world had gone mad, mad!

But the will to live remained strong in him. The sea had a way of dealing with mortals and their troubles. She imparted to one some of her enduring patience. Watching the roll of the unhurried waves, the dawn breaking over a wine-dark expanse of water, the sparkle of the restless prairie under morning and evening sun, a man could not but feel the presence of something greater than himself.

James squinted his eyes for another look at the Spaniard threading the cays. The Old Man said he was going below, and the chief mate ambled across the quarter-deck, as forward of the main the off-watch crew raised their voices in an old whaling song:

*They send you to New Bedford, that famous whaling port*
*And give you some land sharks to board and fit you out.*
*They send you to a boardinghouse, there for a time to dwell—*
*The thieves they there are thicker than the other side of hell.*

The foretop cried the deck, startling James, who was thinking of Adria, "Sail ho!" The "Where away?" placed the sail two points off the port bow. By the looks of her, a barkentine. Told to trim a sharp eye, the lookout reported at five-minute intervals.

She shipped a funnel amidships, and now it issued smoke; she was hoisting red English colors; now she was speaking the ship ahead; the Spaniard was taking in sail, coming around into the wind's eye; now she was hove to, and the Englishman was sending a boat across the narrow expanse of water.

"Enough!" barked the chief officer disinterestedly. "Helmsman, strike the bell one."

As the half hour sounded aboard ship, the captain came on deck, with a hand at his paunchy middle. Upon learning the ship ahead was British, he yawned sleepily and sent the cook an order to prepare for his supper the boiled pudding he had been unable to enjoy Sunday on account of indigestion. The cook responded with, "Aye, aye, sir. Duff for the cap'n's table."

The *Golden Rocket* ran fast toward the ships hove to in the stream. By six bells, three o'clock, the sails of both were not two miles distant. The red and yellow colors of Spain were soon on the move again and the English ship was coming on rapidly.

Suddenly she fired a shot in their direction.

James ran to the rail and gripped it. Then the captain cried in alarm, "For God's sake, show the fool our colors!"

The American flag had no sooner flattened in the breeze from the Maine bark's mizzen gaff than the oncoming stranger lowered the English colors and hoisted another flag at her peak.

James's mouth fell open and his eyes widened with astonishment. As a yell broke loose from the other ship and beat its way to windward, he managed to gasp:

"The Stars and Bars of the Confederacy!"

2

Before ordering an 8-inch gun fired in warning, Semmes said, "She has New England written all over her." He could not entirely hide his elation as he addressed the crew and officers lining the *Sumter's* rail. "This looks like our first prize of war."

Adam said on the spur of the moment, "Sir, I hope you're aware of how anxious your first prize master is to deal with her."

The guns had been readied and crews stripped for action, the first time since their escape from the *Brooklyn* a few days earlier. Twenty marines under First Lieutenant of Marines Howell appeared as anxious to engage the enemy after days of sham drills as the gunners. Although the clarion call was not forthcoming, for a shot across the water proved the merchantman unarmed and unresisting, the occasion proved as joyously exciting to these men as to the officers. Their mingled cheers and catcalls rang loud as a boat was lowered for the boarding party under the command of Lieutenant Cutler, whom Semmes was now giving instructions:

"Examine her papers carefully. If she proves to be a legal prize of war, seize her at once in the name of the Confederate States of America."

Adam, at the stern sheets, alternately watched hard-muscled sailors bend smartly to the oars against choppy, rising seas and stared calmly at the Yankee bark. He caught himself wishing that so pretty a vessel might be protected by a Certificate of Neutrality, which, while it would not save her from capture and adjudication, would spare a fine ship from total destruction.

If she were spared, it would no doubt fall his lot to sail her to a neutral port. But what port? England had closed her ports to prizes of either belligerent. But what was the disposition of the Queen of

Spain, in whose waters they sailed? "In Spanish waters!" Adam said, assuring himself that the prize lay well outside the marine league, a distance of three miles, as prescribed by international law—because a cannon ball could not be hurled farther to sea from a shore battery.

However pretty the Yankee bark, any fond wish of saving her was offset by something else. Fresh in Adam's memory, and a source of anger to every true Southerner, was the report that the crew of the Confederate privateer *Savannah*, captured by the U.S. brig *Bainbridge*, were charged with and would stand trial in New York for piracy on the high seas, in keeping with Lincoln's April fifteenth proclamation.

Adam glared at the ship and speculated on the time it would require for flames to consume her freshly tarred masts.

Adam had hardly set foot on deck before the captain demanded the cause of this outrage. He was aware that these waters had once belonged to pirates, but he thought those days were of the past. Politely, but firmly, Adam announced his mission. His marines at attention lent unspoken authority, causing the Maine captain to lead the way to his ship's papers without further complaint.

A puzzled frown accompanied Adam below; there was something strangely familiar about the bewhiskered second mate. Almost, he seemed a twin of Jim Hillyer, which was of course impossible.

He was further annoyed to find the ship minus any cargo, though the fact that she was as Yankee as Semmes had expected, minus any neutral connection, was a source of satisfaction to him, for she was a legitimate prize.

The two mates entered the cabin just as Adam took possession of the ship's papers and said, "I must inform you that this vessel is hereby declared a prize of war and is now the seized property of the Confederate States cruiser *Sumter*. Captain, you will accompany me to my vessel."

The officers appeared stunned, minus tongues. The mate whose resemblance to James was nothing short of amazing, even under beard and sailor's faded getup, stared incredulously.

Adam was turning to depart when the second mate grinned broadly and caught his arm.

"Look, Adam. It's me, Jim! We're harmless, not a ship-of-war. Even though I was impressed aboard in Boston, there's not a better man alive than the captain here."

Adam held a tight face. His first impulse was to throw his arms about Jim and say, "Admiral Co-Co. You didn't fool me for a minute." But beyond the necessity of presenting a stern dignity of office in the execution of his duties, a wave of mixed anger and disgust assailed him. Thinking of James's hesitancy and indecision in both war and love, he said crisply:

"Mr. Hillyer, I believe you would prove less disappointing to me in Federal blue."

James was too pleased at seeing Adam to consider the insult. "Haven't got the mate to the uniform you're wearing, eh, Adam?"

There were ready answers to that question, though Adam made his way to the deck without further comment, posted marines, and took immediate leave with the *Golden Rocket's* master and papers.

On board the *Sumter*, Adam presented the papers to Commander Semmes and tersely stated the facts. Semmes, in steel-gray uniform, smiled graciously at the captured bark's master, who blew out his whiskered cheeks and said unhappily:

"A clap of thunder in a cloudless sky could not have surprised me more than the appearance of a Confederate flag in these waters."

Adam saw in Semmes's narrowed eyes that "hate's polluted rag" look, heard him say with icy politeness, "My duty is a painful one, to destroy so noble a ship as yours, but I must discharge it without vain regrets; as for yourself, sir, you will only have to do as many thousands have done before you, submit to the fortunes of war. Yourself and your crew will be well treated on board my ship."

The formality of capture and pronounced judgment ended there. The merchantman's master accepted the death sentence of his loved ship with controlled amazement and grief. One man's tragedy was soon forgotten as men leaped to orders. Boats were dispatched to the *Golden Rocket* to remove her crew and all available provisions. All that afternoon boats plied back and forth between the ships, and soon after darkness set in, the *Golden Rocket's* crew, stores of paints, sails, and cordage were on board the *Sumter*, while under Adam's direction the bark's cabin, main hold, and paint and oil locker were littered with charts and dry dunnage. Coal oil lamps were placed handily about. Since the decks were of pine, calked with old-fashioned oakum and paid with pitch, Adam entertained little doubt as to the blaze she would make.

By ten o'clock the wind had died to a whisper, and the overcast sky held its curtain between brilliant tropic stars and smooth sea. Only a few hundred yards from the *Sumter*, the captive ship in a night as black as ink was but a dim, ghostly shape.

Officers and crews of both vessels lined the Confederate's port rail as the boat carrying Lieutenant Cutler on a mission of destruction was swallowed up by total darkness. Only the diminishing sounds of oars in the locks broke the heavy silence of sea and deck.

James Hillyer stared into the pall and felt the weight of silence. It was like death in a way, he thought; rather, like the expectancy of doom, since it was electric, packed with dread suspense. Again it seemed as final as a burial, for Adam had told him late in the day of Adria's marriage.

In the brief conversation on the *Sumter's* deck they had recaptured something of their former relationship; not in full, as James wished, but in part. Each had listened to the other's story, sympathetically, attentively. Adam married! To Faustine! Well—"You can push me over with a feather," James had admitted. Then, timidly, a sense of guilt rushing over him, he had asked about Adria. Adam had seemed to ice over before saying, "She married Lawrence Jarvis."

And James recalled his feeling of utter misery. He had wanted to die.

"Your fault," Adam said. "She waited, and still she waited."

Silence. Even a man at fault tried to hide his hurt.

There was no end to silence. The oars could no longer be heard, which meant Adam, the sergeant of marines, and the steersman were boarding the *Rocket*.

Confused, without a mind of his own, wounded deeply and minus any will to bolster him in the depths of trouble, James screwed his face into a grimace of self-despair. The Lord only knew what would happen to him unless he got a hold on himself. He was asking all sorts of questions—how far down the ladder could a man slip; where was the strength of manhood he once possessed?—when out of the pitch-black night a tongue of flame licked suddenly skyward.

James could only stare in horrified fascination as the main hatch vomited fire as from a legendary dragon's mouth. Masts, yards, sails, and cordage were painted in fiery reds and crimsons. A burst of flame issued from the forecastle as varnishes and oils ignited. Then, aft, the third blaze burst through the smoke in a mighty hiss.

"She burns," one of the *Sumter's* officers said, and a stifled cry sounded ahead of, "My God, that's my ship!" from the doomed bark's captain.

James tore his eyes off the burning ship to stare, dumfounded, at the Confederate officer. Odd, this thing, he was thinking. Something cryptic and eerie about it. Only once before had he witnessed planned destruction, at Gosport, by the Federals, and then he had stared in shame. But this was armed ship over harmless merchantman.

Slowly his glance slid back to the fire. Now painted in bold outline was the boat returning the torchbearers, the chief of whom was Adam. Perhaps he was dreaming, for the Adam he had known could never have done this. The flames now licking wildly, greedily up the ship's masts said Adam had done this thing. And the hush, the awful quiet aboard the *Sumter* made him think of a gloating sea serpent lying atop the still sea in surfeited calm.

Why? Why burn the gallant little ship? The question formed in his throat, though he choked it back.

The easy sea mirrored lighted sky and fiery furnace in all their dancing colors. The indraught, like a monster's breath, fanned new flames up out of the holds and cabins, sent them reaching ever upward to devour shrouds and sails and envelop booms and yards. The roaring increased and beat against James's ears like the rasping of a giant bellows.

Before Adam's boat touched the *Sumter's* side, forked tongues of brilliant yellows and reds shot out of wallowing smoke clouds to the topmast heads and on to topgallants, darting out and up for the royals and trucks. Cordage against the black background was traced by pencils of fire until, snapping, ignited threads writhed and twisted like serpents. A sail parted and rose in the heat aflame, leaving in its wake showers of sparks before settling down, a glowing char upon the sea.

Somewhere in the lost world of deck about James, Adam was receiving the heaped congratulations of commander and officers. Then utter silence fell over the ship once more, and he felt a faint awareness of Adam's presence near him. It seemed, all of it, a ghastly nightmare, even as he stared again at the sea of rapt, gray-and-gold-clad arsonists lining the *Sumter's* rail. The stern, craggy features of "Beeswax" Semmes, with pointed mustaches lighted in red, seemed the devil's own.

"Why this, Adam? Why didn't you run her to port instead of committing this crime?" James tried to keep his voice calm.

Adam and a score of others glanced sharply at the unkempt, sandy-bearded prisoner who had the temerity to ask this, to say now, "It's vandalism without precedent!"

No one bothered to answer the question or charge.

The mizzenmast, a pointing stick of fire, was slowly leaning, falling. Crashing, she went by the board, her hissing sounds reminding James of a red-hot horseshoe suddenly plunged into a blacksmith's bucket. Then the foremast toppled, leaving only the great mainmast lifting an incandescent finger to the sky. Slowly it, too, tottered and reeled and splashed into the sea.

Something slow and formless had been building up in James Hillyer. He did not try to define it, for he had been wholly unaware of self, of past and future, since the first light had shone aboard the *Golden Rocket.* The present was like that of every second before it since the fire began, only now inner rebellion had reached the bursting point. He did not know that his former dejection had faded under the flow of hot blood sweeping through him like a gale of vengeance. But something advised him that he had at last found himself. Perhaps it came when his voice lifted loud and clear to break the silence of deck with:

"This is a goddamn outrage against civilization!"

Semmes roared: "Who speaks so?"

Before James could shout any reply, a hand flicked out and stung his face with a resounding slap.

The hand belonged to Adam.

For a moment they stared with unbelief at each other, and another moment of defiance, in which both saw what neither a few months earlier would have believed, that bosom friends since their first days at Annapolis had in the space of seconds become mortal enemies. One a gray wolf of the sea, the other a ragged, cornered lion determined to wear avenging Federal blue; men separated by war, by one of war's deliberate acts of destruction, which was in a dreadful and profound sense novel to all, since it was the *Sumter's* first prize.

Adam's voice was cool and relentless as he said, "Sir, I suggest we clap this man in irons."

Semmes agreed, since the safety of ship and men were threatened, and in a flash James was surrounded by marines.

As they hustled him below, the Marylander felt like a new man. He exulted in the realization that he had after days and weeks of vacillation found something to live for or something to die for.

Aye! For God as his witness, he would never know peace until the Confederate pirate was driven from the seas.

On deck, under the garish light of the flambeau, the commander ordered the boats run up and steam raised in the boilers. Then the *Sumter* was under way.

In the distance the *Golden Rocket* of Bangor, Maine, was settling by the head. Dying flames cast a final red glow on clouds of steam boiling up as the little bark struggled in her death throes. Then suddenly there was not even a spark of fire upon the sea; nothing but total darkness where light had been.

## 18.    Doña Antonina

### 1

THE NEXT DAY BEING THE FOURTH OF JULY, a holiday the *Sumter's* officers considered as much the South's as the North's, Commander Semmes was invited to dine in the wardroom. He expressed his regrets and advised that the customary extra ration of grog for the crew should not be served, since "The Declaration of Independence proved to be a specious mask under which our loving brethren of the North contrived to draw us into a co-partnership with them, that they might be the better enabled in the end to devour us."

The weather continued cloudy that morning, with occasional rain squalls racing on the wings of the trade wind across the blue sea. Toward noon two brigs were sighted and Semmes ventured an opinion that the Fourth would be celebrated in proper fashion before noon. His prediction came true, with minutes to spare. A blank cartridge caused two ships to run up the American flag and back their topsails.

The *Cuba* and the *Machias* were laden with molasses and sugar for English ports and could not therefore be burned. Prize crews were placed aboard them and the flotilla got under way for the port of Cienfuegos. Later in the day the *Cuba* suddenly made sail and away, and all aboard the commerce destroyer realized that the prize crew had been overpowered.

Watching her with an avenger's eye, Semmes said, "A bird has flown, but there will be others flying the false banner of liberty."

So saying, he turned to Adam and asked if he had looked in upon his friend that day. "Mr. Cutler, I must remind you that war does not annul charity."

Semmes's treatment of the *Golden Rocket's* crew was fresh in the memory of all aboard. He had placed them on equal rations with the *Sumter's* men and had given them freedom of the deck; had subscribed to the wardroom's idea of raising a purse for the unfortunate captain to supply him with necessities upon landing.

"Mr. Cutler, if I ever rate a line in history, I would have it said that Raphael Semmes derived as much pleasure in treating the enemy's sailors humanely as he got out of burning their vessels."

The point was not lost on Adam, though he could only ponder the other's show of benevolence toward a man who had robbed his only sister of life's happiness. But some reply was expected.

"Sir, I hope the pattern you have so kindly drawn is not lost on a man who has yet to reconcile in his own mind war and charity."

Semmes was a most discerning man, Adam learned. "Perhaps you meant a personal war, Mr. Cutler."

A wry smile crossed Adam's face. Then he asked for James Hillyer's release from the lazaret.

Several minutes later a sergeant of marines saluted the quarterdeck. "Commander, sir, the prisoner wishes me to deliver a message." With the order to proceed, he said with pained hesitation, "These are his words, sir: 'Tell the pirate and his buccaneer lieutenant from Mobile I'm enjoying every goddamn minute of my misery and prefer ship's rats to their company.'"

As Semmes's face burned red with anger, Adam decided it was better to evaluate the commander's abounding charitableness of the moment with a sober expression on his face.

As for James—well, he was to be congratulated for taking a stand; even the convictions of a Federal were better than none at all.

On the next afternoon the foretop cried two of sail in the southeast laboring for an offing. In a matter of hours the *Sumter* added to her prizes two American merchantmen laden with sugar, cargoes documented as Spanish property, the *Ben Dunning* of Maine and the *Albert Adams* of Boston. The decks of the Confederate rang with jubilation. Five prizes in as many days! Not even Semmes had expected the "clover to be this high."

The bright tropic sun of the sixth had no sooner revealed a blackgreen coast spilling down to a sheeted emerald sea than a streamer of smoke drew the deck's attention to three ships in tow with American colors set. The Yankees were working out, clinging desperately to the land wind, hoping to gain an offing before the sea breeze came in. But all lay inside the marine league.

Semmes chuckled. To the officer of the deck he said, "In order not to frighten them, Mr. Chapman, cockbill your yards a trifle and bend on a Spanish merchant flag. We'll let our Northern friends think we're a common merchantman."

Next, he ordered the Spanish jack at the fore, a signal for a pilot.

As the ships left the tow and crowded all sail before the weak wind, the tug steamed for the *Sumter*. The pilot, upon learning that the captain of the craft he thought was Spanish intended to capture and return to port the ships he had just towed out, asked how that could be. "They are *Americanos del Norte,* bound to Boston and *la Nueva York.*"

"And we are *Confederados,*" Semmes advised. "We have *la guerra* with those *Americanos del Norte.*"

The astute Semmes allowed the trio a seaward reach of almost twice the marine league before crowding sail and pushing steam in chase.

Within a few hours the *Sumter* headed for the white fort of Cienfuegos with six prizes, the last three the barks *West Wind* and *Louisa Kilham,* of Rhode Island and Massachusetts respectively, and the brigantine *Naiad* of New York, all heavy with sugar for neutrals.

Under the fort, the decks came alive when two musket balls whistled through the rigging. The *Sumter's* anchor splashed, and the *Comandante* sent a messenger to determine what country the strange flag represented. Later he said, "I think perhaps she might be *pirata.*" He detained the ship until a messenger returned from the Governor of the town with permission for the *Confederados* to enter.

The *Sumter* took in her anchor and steamed ahead to the official jetty amid cheers from a British ship and a small crowd ashore who cried, "*Viva los Confederados!*"

Semmes assembled his officers and read a lengthy message addressed to the Governor of Cienfuegos. "If I seem to be overdoing it, gentlemen, please realize I am actually writing to the Queen of Spain. Every word will be telegraphed to the Captain-General in Havana."

Other than outlining the South's side of the struggle, her ports closed by blockade, he named his prizes and their nationality and appealed to His Excellency the Governor to hold the prizes for judicial proceedings in the prize courts of the Confederate States.

"This is more than a social call," he advised his officers. "We are in dire need of coal. Also the diplomatic courtship of the Governor must proceed in all haste, since a belligerent's time in port is limited, and since the U.S. consul here will waste no time in telegraphing Havana to hasten a fast Federal ship-of-war to effect our capture.

"Now you will draw lots to see who will act as my ambassador and purchasing agent."

The result of the drawing jerked an amiable snort from Lieutenant Chapman. "Mr. Cutler! Must all honor fall to the black-eyed devil we took aboard out of the pity of our hearts?"

Soon "Lord Adam, Prince of Luck," dressed in his finest gray uniform, braid, shoulder straps, and sword glittering, descended the ladder to the captain's gig with his midshipman aide and took off for the town.

2

At the boat landing a group of citizens in immaculate white linens greeted the handsome Confederate lieutenant and hustled him off to a private club. While one amiable don escorted the midshipman to the Governor's palace with Semmes's letter, Señor Don Mariano Dias called upon his Spanish friends, in company with an English merchant and a Dutch trader, to toast in champagne first the captain of the *Sumter,* the ship herself, then Señor *el Teniente* Cutler. They begged the privilege of serving him, and in response to his request for coal, provisions, and a case or two of Bordeaux and Cette, Don Mariano said enthusiastically:

"*Caramba!* It is done." Turning to his secretary, he said, "My dear Juanillo, the finest chickens, produce, wines, and flowers. Now be off, and see to it that our friends the *Confederados* are not robbed."

Lifting a mustachio above a brimming glass, he drank his dismissal of business and a return to convivialities.

"Señor, I have never seen our town so excited. Someone said the *Comandante* had fired upon your ship. Another said your ship she fire back at the fort. *Jesucristo!* I do not wait for the war, but proceed to gather my friends and get drunk at the same time. Only I never get drunk."

Adam was wishing he could say the same as, under his breath, he cautioned himself, "Easy as you go. Easy."

With the passing hours from noon to a golden sunset over the crystal bay, evidence of Adam's industry and Don Mariano's zeal reached the *Sumter* by the boatload. Squawking chickens, piles of peppers, from the dark red *chile ancho* to the green *chile jalapeno*, oranges, limes, muskmelons, watermelons, apricots, plantains, pineapples, and a maze of other edibles kept the crew gasping in surprised delight. As the cornucopia of the tropics continued to spill itself aboard, Lieutenant Chapman vowed that Adam was getting gloriously drunk. Sampling a mouth-burning red *chilpotle,* he cried with pain:

"He's drinking with a vengeance!"

While in another section of Cienfuegos the recently freed crew of the *Golden Rocket* sat in front of the U.S. consul's house staring in bewilderment from a throng of curious citizens to the door behind which their captain and second mate sat in conference.

The purse raised by the *Sumter's* officers fresh in his pocket, the master of the burned *Rocket* signed a statement charging Raphael Semmes and his officers with brutal treatment of himself and crew. The consul admitted that Northern newspapers would make much of this report. Then he looked at James.

"So you're a lieutenant in the United States Navy, Mr. Hillyer. Now do you wish to add to the captain's account of maltreatment of the crew?"

"I do not, sir," came the emphatic reply. "You and I know what Semmes is up to. That's the issue here. If he can influence the Governor into opening this port to his prizes, the American flag will not be safe in West Indian waters."

This rekindled the consul's rage. Also, it shaped a fresh estimate in his mind of the zealous naval officer, whom he mentally pictured in better dress at the Governor's palace. Indeed, this outspoken ally might do much toward outmaneuvering the Confederate officer who had surrounded himself with men of local prominence.

A thorough man, the U.S. consul.

The Governor was seated at an ornate iron table in his patio overlooking red roofs and a bay as blue as the Caribbean itself when his personal secretary appeared to announce the arrival of the American consul and a naval officer. The latter, suggested the secretary, was meticulously dressed in linen and had the bearing of an *hombre* of authority; perhaps he was the emissary extraordinary sent here by the United States Secretary of Navy.

The Governor's brows lifted. Shifting his corpulent body in the chair, he frowned at a glass, intent on a ray of late sunlight burning a ruby sheen through the wine. As sparkling and red, he reflected, as the small mouth of Doña Antonina, young wife of his senile friend Don Alejandro.

A question—had the Captain-General in Havana acknowledged his long telegram regarding the Confederate ship?—drew a reply of "No, Your Excellency."

The Governor breathed a heavy sigh and looked down on the *Sumter* at anchor. How tiny she seemed, like a toy model. He had placed coal at her disposal to be rid of her and an embarrassing situation, had directed the town's elite to entertain the Confederate officer at the club.

"*El Teniente* Cutler. Send him my greetings, and regrets that I cannot reply to his superior until it is my pleasure to quote instructions from Habana." He waved a pale brown hand impatiently. "So forth and so forth. You fix it."

"Yes, Your Excellency. And the señores who wish to see you?"

"*Diablo!*" The Governor's plump face discarded one expression after another until it assumed a curious fixed look. "Keep them waiting. No, send them in. This naval man could be *el señor extraordinario*. But they will gain nothing until I get some light on this affair from Doña——" He broke off, adding hastily, "From Don Alejandro."

Standing stiffly before Adam, the Governor's aide concluded with, ". . . until it is my pleasure to quote instructions from His Most Illustrious Excellency the Captain-General at Habana. Meanwhile, consider yourself and all aboard the gallant steamer *Sumter* the honored guests of the town."

Adam felt the sobering effect of the message. Even so, he could not but admire the neat Spanish art of brushing one off with politeness.

Don Mariano came to his rescue with an assuring laugh. "Ah, there is cause for rejoicing. You just wait and see, *amigo*. In no time at all your prizes will be condemned and you will be in need of a prize agent.

"But look here! By *Dios*, we are invited to a celebration in your honor! At the fine house of Don Alejandro Francisco de la Tosta, where you will spend the night, of course." He winked an eye, suggesting a juicy secret before whispering one that invited attention to the fact that he was quite a gay blade himself.

"Don Alejandro can be depended upon to wobble off on his cane to bed before the clock strikes nine. But not lovely Doña Antonina, who is young enough to be his daughter. Ah, señor! She will show you the merry time."

Before the cathedral bells tolled the hour of midnight, Adam learned that Don Mariano had spoken the truth.

Under bright Spanish stars, glittering like jeweled pins in a canopy of deep blue, the hilltop patio of wealthy Don Alejandro became a setting for lavish entertainment. Everyone who was anyone at all in Cienfuegos and environs was in attendance, so Adam learned; with the exception of the American consul, who sent his regrets. Ladies with flashing black eyes and cherry-red smiles extended lovely and dainty hands to be kissed by the honored señor. Often Adam would find his admiring gaze at a gorgeous mantilla and tortoise-shell comb suddenly fixed on the half-averted face of the wearer as she darted him a flirtatious glance over the curve of her lace fan.

The finest of vintages of Old Spain flowed freely into tall-stemmed glasses, sparkled like a sudden light in a señorita's eyes before the drop of a lash, and disappeared amid a hundred toasts to beauty, virtue, courage, to Don this and Doña that and, of course, to *el Teniente* Cutler.

More and more, as chilled wines and liqueurs continued to flow as from an inexhaustible fountain, Adam's attention was drawn to the Doña Antonina. She was everywhere, greeting this guest or directing a liveried servant to serve that one; then she was gently scolding or complimenting friends of both sexes, giving instructions to the orchestra of violins, guitars, and shotted gourds, which swished out a rhythm enchantingly West Indian and Spanish.

Small of figure, she reminded Adam of Faustine. Her skin was equally white and her hair seemed so black that the starpoints animating it shone in blue. Though it was her face that held Adam's firm attention; because, he supposed, she used it to convey a hundred expressions: sudden alertness to something, an instant's thoughtfulness under a hint of a frown, a moment of jealousy, in which she looked positively cruel, a hint of weariness, a smile or a sulk, a flicking glance at a servant, an exposed look of passionate desire. But she knew how to host a party.

"A woman of amazing energy," he said to Don Mariano.

Don Alejandro, pale of face, thin and stooped, had long since said his good night and departed on the arm of the *mayordomo*. Poor fellow, he seemed afraid of the slow pace of the future as compared to the fast tempo of the past, said Don Mariano, brushing the ashes from his panatela. "Two mistresses and a young wife are too much for a man of fifty-five. Don't you think so, señor?"

Adam cocked an eyebrow at his companion. "And the Doña—she knows?"

Mariano shrugged. "But of course. She was brought up to exhibit the utmost in Christian charity. You see, señor, her marriage was arranged shortly after her birth."

The Doña drew Adam into a dance. "I have waited with much excitement for this opportunity." She smiled up at him, not like Faustine or American women, but with eyes as sharp as a scalpel. *"Pues sí!"* she added. "Life is a fast thing. One is young, then one finds a friendship, and next one is married. There is a moment of passion, a vow to God, then death."

He observed that she was less serious and more matter-of-fact. She had too much energy. Her eyes, high-bridged nose, and jet-black eyebrows made her appear as eager as a hawk. She demanded, impatiently, he thought; every moment she demanded something to feed upon. He was thinking that the sweet-scented woman in his arms perhaps thought on impulse and acted accordingly when she paused in the dance.

"Señor Cutler!" She laughed merrily. "You do not dance well to our music."

He was opening his mouth with an apology when she said, "But it does not matter, handsome man, for you do something else—you send little devils running up and down my thighs!"

Feeling the blood stirring in his veins, Adam whirled her into the dance. Avoiding her glances of amusement and inquiry, he made a resolve to declare by letter on this very night his undying fidelity to Faustine.

A minute or so later the Doña's attention was drawn to a uniformed man. Disengaging herself, she walked toward him and accepted a sealed envelope. It was very odd, thought Adam, for the man was none other than the Governor's aide.

3

Adam was shown to a large room furnished with great pieces of native mahogany. Through the open, barred window perfume from the garden below rose heavy and sweet now that the breeze from the sea had died to a whisper.

He was standing at the window trying to catch up with the fast day just ended when Doña Antonina appeared in the doorway with brandy and apologies for the absence of refreshments in the room of a guest. Although his head buzzed from the twelve-hour spree and the very sight of another alcoholic beverage sickened him, he told her that this was just what he needed.

"Then pour for us, señor." She took a chair and watched him with rather ambiguous attentiveness as he served her, with undisguised interest as they sipped and looked at each other. "You're married," she said. "And recently."

"In New Orleans, less than a month ago. But how did you guess?"

A laugh followed. "It is written all over you, *Teniente*. That young idealism is to be envied."

Adam grinned, took a seat. "I am many years your senior, and yet you talk as though I were a mere boy."

"Perhaps. At twelve I was married to Don Alejandro. At thirteen I was a mother. And when I am your age, I shall be old." Her eyes narrowed demandingly. "More brandy, señor."

As he stood to obey, she said, half gay, half bitter, "The circumstances would seem unique enough in themselves to justify sympathy from an *Americano*. But what is a custom is not a bid for pity, *amigo mio*. Rather," she continued as he paused to stare at her, "let us say that I am sick of old men and fat men who smell of pepper and black *cigarros*."

Adam nodded. He was beginning to understand. Somewhat apprehensive, he sat down and made a bid for the initiative, saying, "I shall never forget how you and the don honored me in Cienfuegos. Never have I been more royally entertained."

"Thank the Governor, who requested it."

She seemed to take pleasure in his surprise and subsequent perplexity.

"Incidentally, señor, not an hour ago His Excellency sent to my house copies of the American consul's telegrams to the Captain-General in Habana. The consul demanded that you and all aboard your ship be arrested and thrown into prison on charges of piracy."

Adam leaned toward her, his face tight with concern.

"There is also a *Teniente* Hillyer who is working against you. His wire to the *hombre* in command of the Habana squadron of his country condemns the *Confederados*. See the wire for yourself. He calls you arsonists and pirates."

"James!" Adam said furiously, reading copies of the messages.

"Damn their souls, they insist on calling us pirates even after England and France have recognized us as legal belligerents!"

Stabbing a paper with a forefinger, he cried out angrily, "That man was my best friend six months back!"

Doña Antonina lifted fine eyebrows and a milk-white shoulder in a shrug. Touching her full bosom with slender fingers, she said, "The cup of bitterness is engraved with every mortal's name."

"True." Adam bowed, begging her to excuse his outburst.

"Perhaps I can help you." She smiled tentatively. "Your enemy sought to prevent delivery of coal to your vessel—in vain. But I must advise that he succeeded on one score. A fast *Americano* sloop-of-war should arrive here by midnight."

Adam thanked her for her generosity. Curious, he said, "Should I convey the appreciation of my commander to His Excellency for his kind services?"

"To me, señor. His Excellency is not aware that I have acquainted you with these secrets."

Adam could not hide the frown creasing his brow any more than he could bluntly resort to inquiry concerning the Governor's reason for giving her such information. So he maintained a discreet silence.

"I thought you would ask a question," she said, eying him with suppressed amusement. "Since you are a prudent man, and I admire such a virtue, I shall relieve your anxiety by saying that often His Excellency consults with my husband the don before reaching any decision. In this instance he is wondering which of the parties, you or our friend the U.S. consul, he should favor in his dispatches to the Captain-General of Cuba."

"And your husband the don advised?" Adam placed directly.

She rose, took a handkerchief of Spanish lace from the divide of her bosom, and breathed its perfume. Her intent, hungry glance did not waver from his face.

"Señor, I am the don's mind."

She walked to him and drew his face down to hers. Then she placed her mouth to his, clung to him, as his mind raced this way and that for some release from her trap before the surging desire for her consumed him. But all the while he was drawing his arms tight about her, even as he realized with a wave of anger that neither she nor the ruler of a remote Cuban town could in any way influence the decision of the Spanish Queen.

As her lips slid away, he felt the trembling of her young body against his, read the torment in her face as she appealed to him.

"*Por el amor de Dios,* señor, have me now!" Her cry was low and hoarse, breaking off with, "My wonderful pirate."

Then proud Doña Antonina threw back her head and ripped the silk and lace from her shoulders. He took a quick backward step. The burning pain he had felt a moment before turned suddenly into disgust as he stared at her uncovered breasts as though they were the first he had ever seen.

Her lust was like ice water thrown in his face. He turned quickly and strode out of the room and out of the house.

## 19.    Satin and Iron

### 1

ON A HOT, HUMID AFTERNOON IN LATE JULY a man dressed in crumpled white linen stared out over the harbor of Havana. Alternately mopping sweat from face and neck and running the other hand through his sandy hair, he was unaware of the scrutiny of a seaman on the forward deck of a long gray schooner.

As he drew in his gaze from the old Paseo and turned it on the watchtower of the Castillo de la Real Fuerza, the schoonerman hailed him.

"Lieutenant Hillyer, I believe."

James spun about, it came so unexpectedly, and eyed the man narrowly.

"Or is it ex-lieutenant?" scoffed the other.

"Could be, sir." James winced at the reminder. He awaited transportation to the Washington Navy Yard for a naval hearing and possible court-martial. Perhaps his efforts in Cienfuegos and later Havana toward effecting the release of the *Sumter's* prizes by the Captain-General of Cuba on the nineteenth would stand in his favor. In any case, he had served his country well and had helped bring the criminal activities of pirates Semmes and Cutler to naught in Spanish waters.

"You don't remember me, Mr. Hillyer. Of course, I can't blame you, for you could hardly take your eyes off Adria that day."

James's face lightened. "Sure now, you're Captain—Sherill—er——"

"Sherrod. But what brings you to Havana in civilian whites?"

Loneliness greased James's tongue. Soon he was telling of impressment aboard the *Golden Rocket*—which drew a chuckle from Sherrod—of the burning of the ship at sea, and then of his zealous work which, he said modestly, might have helped in freeing six American merchantmen.

Sherrod smiled through the story, his amusement unmasked. "Now there's a yarn to set Mobile on her ears," he said. "So the *Sumter* raised sail and away."

"Aye," James replied mournfully. Then he glanced sharply at the other. "But aren't you a Southerner?"

"I find it exceedingly profitable, Lieutenant."

"I thought our blockade had Mobile bottled up."

Sherrod suppressed a downward grin, proffered a leather cigar case. "Have a panatela." A moment's pause was followed by, "Come aboard the *Gulf Wind* for a drink, sailor. Ice and gin or bourbon."

In the cozy cabin Sherrod served refreshments, sat down, and eyed his guest curiously. "Maybe you'd like to sail with me to Mobile."

"It's a little late for that."

Sherrod looked up from the glass on the small table between them. "Care to send her a gift?"

James's features turned suddenly hard. "Just tell her my story. That's my gift to her."

Randall Sherrod blew a curtain of smoke, flicked ashes from his black cigar in thoughtful manner. "Jarvis departed for Tennessee the morning after the wedding," he said. "Left mad as hell, according to rumor."

James lowered the glass he was lifting to his mouth. His curiosity mounted as the schoonerman got up and fished out of a chest a worn satin slipper and a paper. Placing the former on the polished table, Sherrod read aloud:

" 'Please fetch four pairs of finest slippers of same size and pattern. Joseph Cutler.' Adria's slipper, Lieutenant."

As James studied the slipper with mixed resentment and dreaminess, he heard Sherrod say, "It's the fancy goods that bring the prices. And a hold full of salt makes it a fair wind."

"Salt?" James asked in detachment.

"Six months back it was eighty cents a bushel. I'll get a dollar and a quarter, that is, for what I care to sell. Twice that for all in storage come fall. Care to get rich, Lieutenant?"

Meeting with no reply, the blockade-runner replenished drinks and sat back with a glint of sardonic humor in his sea-burned face.

"Yes siree, in Mobile they refer to Lawrence Jarvis as the 'virgin's husband.' They'll tell you that if he has a child by Adria it will have to be an immaculate conception."

He laughed openly at James's startled expression.

"Aye, they're tossing her virginity around like a politician's promise. And there's a reason for it.

"You see," he went on, "the word got around that Adria ran out of her room in a pink and ribboned nightgown as thin as you please and spent her wedding night in the servants' quarters."

James's mouth hung open. To Sherrod's pleasure, he sat in a state of shock.

"Help yourself to whisky, Lieutenant."

"Thanks. I could do with another."

Sherrod pretended ignorance of the unmistakable trembling about James's mouth and eyes. "Oh well, people will talk." Toying absently with the slipper, he said, "So you've decided to champion the Northern cause. Just because a Rebel friend of yours puts the torch to your ship."

"Not exactly. The incident just happened to convince me of something."

"Now, Lieutenant, are you sure it was a ship on fire that did it?"

"What are you getting at?" James demanded.

"Adria." Sherrod's hint of a smile was mocking. "Now suppose you'd been able to desert the Union Navy and reach Mobile before the wedding, would a burning Yankee have bothered you?"

James's forehead wrinkled in perplexity as he tried to place an estimate on the other. He said presently, "Seems you go out of your way to call a man a liar, Captain."

"Maybe I like to see a man honest. Take me, for example, I don't believe the South can win either. But she'll put up a damned good scrap. So I'll serve the South as long as there's profit in it. But back to you and Adria. I'd lay ten to one, British pound sterling, that right now you'd go Rebel for her."

"You'd lose. I'm not the least interested in her, Captain Sherrod."

"No? You know, Mr. Hillyer, Adria is a damn handsome woman. And Jarvis was a fool. Now if it had been me, I'll guarantee I'd have spanked her pretty bottom and made an eager woman out of her before morning."

James was on his feet instantly. "Why, you low-down, dirty——!" In his rage, words failed him. Hunched forward, he swung an arm with all the strength he possessed. His fist met nothing but air, for the schoonerman had slipped from his chair with the quickness of a cat. When James gained his balance, Sherrod stood with drink in hand grinning insolently.

"Perhaps you'd like to go to Mobile after all, Lieutenant."

James growled out an oath from low in his throat, picked up the slipper, and rushed out of the *Gulf Wind's* cabin.

2

On that same afternoon, seven hundred miles south-southeast of Havana as the gull flies, the captured fore-and-aft schooner *Abby Bradford* of New York put to sea from the town of Puerto Cabello, Venezuela.

Standing the deck of the prize taken only the day before, Prize Master Cutler looked longingly toward his home afloat for almost a month before reading again the paper that might forever separate him from the adventures of the *Sumter*. The letter of instructions was dated July 26, 1861, and read as follows:

You will take charge of the prize schooner *Abby Bradford*, and proceed with her, to New Orleans—making the land to the westward of the passes of the Mississippi, endeavoring to run into Barataria Bay. . . . Upon your arrival, you will proceed to the city of New Orleans, in person, and report yourself to Commodore Rousseau, for orders. You will take especial care of the accompanying package of papers, as they are the papers of the captured schooner, and you will deliver them, with seals unbroken, to the judge of the prize court, Judge Moise. You will batten down your hatches, and see that no part of the cargo is touched. . . .

Adam folded the letter, felt of his belt, under which he carried a most important sealed letter from Semmes to Secretary of Navy Mallory.

"Guard this message, Mr. Cutler." The parting rang fresh in Adam's memory. It stemmed from yesterday's entry into Puerto Cabello, a letter from Semmes to the Governor, a reply, which strained of its politeness, meant, "Take your prize and get out of this port at once." It's effect on "Beeswax" Semmes was as expected, though it provoked him into fresh and interesting comparisons, which never failed to excite the admiration of his officers—"The South American chieftain is *as mild a mannered man as ever cut a throat.*" If he quoted a line from a poet, he did so aptly. He blamed the Governor's decision on the American consul, "who," he said, "represents not only those grand moral ideas that characterize our Northern people, but Sand's sarsaparilla and Smith's wooden clocks. He is, *par excellence,* the big dog of the village." Then today:

"Mr. Cutler, I can't spare you, but neither can I do without your services on this mission."

Looking northwest, thinking of the two thousand miles he must sail in that direction, Adam took into consideration the trade winds, possible hurricane weather, for the season was at hand, and pondered the schooner's ability to show her heels to a Federal screw sloop-of-war.

She was a trim little sailer, with clean lines, a clipper bow, tall masts, good timber, new sails, and a dead rise in her bottom that promised sailing at a fast clip over the blue Caribbean. He would use her; now that he was on his way, he would send her home with mainsail and foresail boomed out, one to port, one to starboard, wing and wing.

The sooner he made the land of Louisiana the quicker he would reach Mobile and Faustine.

The *Abby Bradford* made a quartering wind out of the trade once she put Puerto Cabello under the stern and the long coast on her left safely off the port beam. The bold outline of the shore under the tropic sun bled inland from black and dazzling greens to the blue of height and distance. As the hours passed, shadows deepened to eastward in a riot of purple hues. To westward, by contrast, slopes and crags of the Venezuelan jungles shone far off in garish yellow and emerald. Shadows were flung far out to sea, their shades deepening. Then suddenly the swift change from day to night wiped out the land.

With her bows pointing toward Curaçao, the prize ship bounced on into the quick night.

Ideal sea breezes, an expanse of blue ocean and bright clear skies by day, starlit heavens by night, favored the schooner all the way up to the Yucatán Channel. There a couple of vicious squalls struck in one day. Beyond the westernmost tip of Cuba, which Adam kept far to windward, bad weather was making itself felt. The air came in puffs, mere cat's-paws, and then the sea lay flat and glassy as a hellish storm absorbed all energy of the elements. Soon it would hurl that energy back across the Mexican Gulf in a gale of fury.

Slanting northwest, hoping to avoid the storm, Adam drove *Little Abby,* as the crew named her, up to the Tropic of Cancer, caught himself a fair blow, and walked the imaginary line due west.

The storm took its time in building up. Then, as though its hungry eye had dwelt upon the schooner, it shaped a crazy whirling course to the northwest. Adam watched the horizon aft, the falling barometer, and heaving swells with rising trepidation. He wondered what gave the monster direction, or if it ran like a mad dog of the sea, aimless in its destruction, and he hoped fervently the thing would steer another course.

He battened down, set all sail to the advance winds that came rolling over the horizon, winged her out, and ran like a scared fox. Rain and rising seas followed. The wind blew through the rigging in a banshee's wail, screeching louder by the hour; now out of the north, proving that he was on the fringe of a counterclockwise circle. Putting the wind on his port quarter, he doubled south, sailing by guess and prayer, hoping the cyclone was moving north.

Two days later the *Abby Bradford,* salt-caked, battered, her decks a shambles, sighted the northern Yucatán coast in a sea dotted with coconuts. Adam and his weary crew spent a day in patching her up, then set a course for the Mississippi, some six hundred miles north.

The seas headed over, the trades blew as before after catching their breath again, and the schooner made a fair wind of it up to the flat Louisiana coast, which seemed to slide up over the horizon, a long thin smudge of gray on the edge of the water late one afternoon.

Alerting the lookout, fixing his position as due west of the opening of the Southwest Pass, Adam hastened to put some distance between him and any Federal steamer lurking in the swampy inlets. Recalling Semmes's advice, "Don't sail too close to the passes," Adam ran in the direction of Galveston, planning to double back for Barataria Bay next morning.

The slate-gray false dawn was reaching across the littoral waters in a deathly hush that presaged a day of calm when from the foretop rang a cry of alarm: "Steamer off the starboard bow!" The lookout did not wait for the "Where away?" but yelled forth, "Not a mile off!"

Adam leaped for deck, half dressed, shouting to the top of his voice, "Run her for the swamps!"

The cook met him on deck, spat lustily over the side, and asked, "What with, sir? We ain't a wind to our name."

Not a breath of air stirred.

The steamer came on. Eying her anxiously, Adam was hoping the luck that enabled him to survive a hurricane would come to his aid here and now. However, the day coming up fast over the sea soon verified his fears. She was the U.S.S. *Minnesota*. The jig was up.

Adam faced a new experience and debated on how to deal with it. Capture by the enemy was a serious thing. Three courses lay before him, the first of which was to lower a boat and row for the bayous. Instantly discarding the idea as sheer folly, he considered playing the part of an ignorant schoonerman. The remaining choice was surrender, for there was no time for anything else. With the decision to do this, he resolved to face the Yankee proudly.

He went below, changed into his best uniform, and concealed Semmes's letter to Mr. Mallory in the cleft of his buttocks. Then he calmly returned to deck.

The big *Minnesota* steamed close before speaking the schooner and lowering a gig. Adam studied her, recalling that she was a screw steamer of 3,307 tons, forty-three guns, one of which was a 10-inch monster. Watching the smoke lifting straight up from her engine stack forward of amidships, he instructed the crew as follows:

"You know nothing about the *Sumter* except that you sailed of her. Understand? Stick to your story and you'll be released." To himself, "I hope."

"But, sir," the midshipman said, "they charged the *Savannah's* crew with piracy. How do you know they won't hang us?"

"I don't. Now if you so desire you can swim for it and take your chances with the bull alligators."

The boarding officer returned Adam to the deck of the Union warship, where the Yankee captain, officers, and crew stared in astonishment at the Confederate naval uniform, which by its very splendor and color violated marine traditions. Aware that even the stern-visaged, cold-eyed Captain Van Brunt was impressed, Adam came close to enjoying the moments at stiff attention as he said proudly:

"Lieutenant Cutler, Confederate States Navy, sir."

A quarter hour later Adam found himself below surrounded by enemy officers who for ten minutes had proceeded to question him. The captain was saying:

"Again, Mr. Cutler, what is the *Sumter's* course?"

Adam remained unruffled. "Only Commander Semmes can answer that, sir."

"Where did you capture the *Abby Bradford?*"

"In the Caribbean."

A chart was placed before him. "Where?"

"I don't recall, sir."

The captain's weather-wrinkled face hardened. "We can make a prisoner's stay aboard pleasant or untenable, Mr. Cutler." As Adam nodded, a lieutenant stroked a carefully cultivated mustache in an attitude of wisest contemplation before asking:

"What is the *Sumter's* speed?"

"Steam and sail, or just steam?"

The men in blue took heart, said their hopeful faces. The prisoner was, after all, amenable to reason.

"Steam only," the lieutenant replied.

"Twenty knots."

Van Brunt emitted a snort of disgust and said, "Take him away."

Adam stood and bowed stiffly. "As a prisoner of war, or is the case of the Confederate privateer *Savannah* a pattern for the treatment of prisoners by our benevolent Yankee friends?"

A quick surge of anger in Captain Van Brunt's face fell away under his careful scrutiny of the Confederate. He said pleasantly enough, "Mr. Cutler, you have been a long time at sea. Our government has decided to treat the *Savannah's* crew as prisoners of war." He paused as if debating with himself.

His expression bordered on a frown and a faint smile of humor before melting. "For reasons, sir, namely: A man named Smith of the captured Confederate privateer *Jefferson Davis* was condemned to death for piracy in Philadelphia. In response to this, your President, Mr. Davis, aware that thirteen others of the crew would meet the same fate, wrote President Lincoln that he had selected fourteen prisoners of war, of rank from general to captain, as hostages who would receive the same treatment as the crew of the Confederate."

Adam's grin was wide. "Sir, if I may ask, how did we gain a general?"

Van Brunt winced. "At Bull Run. Seems the Gray won a signal victory on the twenty-first of July."

"Thank you, Captain. You would make a fine Confederate."

"Complimentary, I suppose," came the stiff reply. "By the same token, Mr. Cutler, you might look fine in blue."

"I did sir—once," Adam said, stepping between the pair of marines who had entered to take charge of the prisoner.

With his going, the captain rubbed his face in agitated manner. "What I'd give to learn the course and speed of the pirate Semmes."

A look of cunning stole over his pinched face as he dismissed all but his senior officer with an order to take the schooner in tow to the Southwest Pass. Turning to his executive, he said:

"A proud lot these Rebels. But the proud are often boastful. However, if the damn fellows can drink like they can fight——"

The senior lieutenant was suddenly wise. He realized that the captain could hardly expand on the idea, so he said, "It might be charitable to invite the Rebel to dine in the wardroom, sir."

The brig of a man-of-war offered small hope for comfort or escape, Adam admitted as the marine sergeant ordered him to shed every last garment in a search for hidden information. It was steaming-hot below decks and the hot summer day had just begun.

Undressing, Adam protested. "You've seen enough. Besides, I was kicked in the loin by an Alabama mule, Sergeant. I'm rather sensitive."

"And I'm curious," came the reply.

Stripped naked, Adam awaited the command to turn around, though the marine just stared and finally made a remark about the mule's weakness and disposition before advising the Rebel that he could put on his clothes again. Adam thanked him and breathed a sigh of relief, for Semmes's letter to Mr. Mallory remained safe at his rump.

Through most of that hot August day Adam sweated and looked back on his mistake. Odd, the more he thought about it, that he should have sighted land some ten miles east of his charted course. The fact remained that he had done so. So he looked ahead, at days and weeks in the enemy's brig; it was either that or take an oath not to again take up arms against the North, which he would never do.

He was asleep when the cruiser dropped anchor. Shortly after her screw ceased to thump the water, a lieutenant and marine escort appeared with an invitation from the officers to dine with them that evening. Adam readily accepted.

At dusk he was escorted to the quarter-deck. The guard relaxed, and the crew stared, amazed at the manner in which the brass hobnobbed with the Rebel. Actually, one might be inclined to believe some foreign admiral was aboard. Nor did the prisoner in steel gray and gold measure up to their ideas of what a pirate should look like.

Appearing casual, though never more alert, the prisoner guest responded with ease to questions regarding the *Sumter's* escape from the *Brooklyn.*

At the officer's mess they served him with brimming glasses of champagne, then heavy sweet wine. When brandy appeared, he thought they were making it quite obvious. But it was their game and his stomach. He should soon speak thickly, perhaps boast a little. And, by the banner pompano, if he continued at such a pace it might not be play-acting. Shades of Don Mariano, the stuff was buzzing in his head already, and these lads in blue were watching him eagerly, priming him for the big kill.

Time slipped by. The hosting party listened to his account of Semmes's greatness, his treatment of prisoners, his ability to cope with any situation. But they were more interested in his program of destruction and soon were listening to the story of the burning of the *Golden Rocket.*

"Some fire, gen'lemen. Pardon, but my tongue gets fuzzy." He giggled, stopped suddenly, frowned soberly for a minute. "By God, she blazed! Roared! Snakes on fire—thass her cordage. Twistin', coilin'. Then we steamed off." He stared at the table. "Pitch-black night."

"Steamed off? How fast, Mr. Cutler?"

Adam tongued his lower lip, grinned, and weaved a forefinger. "Now, now, sir. No foolish questions."

They were generous; they gave him more wine.

"Took six prizes into port. The *Machias,* the *Ben Dunning*—or maybe it was the *Ben Adams—West Wind* and——" He tried to think, gave up. "If I didn't know better, gen'lemen, would swear I was drunk."

"Where did you sail next, Mr. Cutler?"

"Where, you say? Sure. Where? Thass the question."

"But why this destruction? Our merchant ships aren't making war on you."

"Ha!" Adam laughed. "Wait'll Commander Semmes enters Boston Harbor."

"Eh? What was that, Mr. Cutler?"

"Nothing. Talked too much."

"Have more wine, sir. So Semmes is moving up for Boston."

Looking up wonderingly, Adam shook his head. "Did I shay that? Don't you believe that, mishter. He's——"

Catching his stomach with both hands, Adam contorted his face. "Tryin' to hang on, lads. Good God!" He rose and stood looking frantically for an exit. Swaying and weaving, he rushed for the deck, a young lieutenant on his heels.

He almost fell atop the rail and forced a jet liquid stream over the side. Then he groped for support.

"Now you'll feel better," said the officer in blue.

Adam's fist came up fast and landed hard on the Federal's chin. Not waiting to learn whether the other collapsed to deck or not, Adam leaped over the rail and struck out hand over hand for the jungle of the riverbank. A cry of alarm ran the decks. It was followed by the bark of a rifle. A bullet struck close by, then another. He heard boats being lowered by the falls, saw the streaks of lantern light on the water.

Minutes later he reached the growth and slime of the swampy shore and half swam, half walked deeper into the mud and ooze, into the protecting cover of alligator grass and salt cane.

BOOK THREE

# The Edge of Fury

1

SINCE NINE THAT MORNING more than a dozen carriages had braved the chill, rainy weather to deliver members of the Wednesday Sewing Circle at the door of Bay Oaks. Both parlors were opened and logs burned in the twin fireplaces. By eleven all twenty members were present.

Near the hall door of the second parlor Adria looked up in surprise from the cotton she was carding. "Surely, Mrs. Starr, not Harry Baker. Why, he was one of the first to volunteer."

"Just the same, he's back with a furlough wound. It's high time for women to quit visiting every Tom, Dick, and Harry who uses a scratch in order to spend a few weeks at home." She leaned toward the president of the circle. "Petty, I make a motion that the gray jeans we're weaving do not go to holiday, furlough, or feather-bed soldiers."

Plain, sharp-faced Miss Petty idled her spinning wheel, asked for silence, and had Mrs. Starr repeat the motion. It was quickly passed.

With a note of exultation in her shrill voice, Miss Petty used her office to remind the group that true Southern women should rise up in protest against the evils of blockade-running also. She went on to say:

"They're responsible for the outlandish prices we're paying for things these days. And they're getting rich while people in Alabama are actually starving. At the Aid Society last week, I heard from a reliable source that a certain notorious schoonerman was in cahoots with the surgeon up in Montgomery who has charge of the exchange of government cotton for medicines. And how much quinine did he fetch from Havana? Little. But he traded public cotton for what? Salt, which we're paying over three dollars a bushel for—four times what it was last January, mind you. Robbing the government, then robbing us."

"Petty Grant! You don't say!"

"I do say, and I don't mind saying he's Captain Sherrod."

"Tut, tut!" said Eugenia Temple. "Small wonder Joseph calls this the Cut on the Bias and Gossip Club."

"Aunt Eugenia!" Adria gasped, wondering now as she did often how her mother's buxom sister could be so outspoken and still command the respect and love of everyone.

"Adria," she said, not glancing up from her loom, "when you reach fifty-five, you'll learn that a pinch of honesty is worth a pound of sham.

"Which," she continued, "prompts me to say, Petty dear, the blockade-runners aren't the cause of high prices. Back in Galveston when the blockade was announced, we flew into a panic, afraid imported articles would be scarce. So we tried to buy them up before there was a blockade or a runner. Prices jumped, naturally. They're still rising, and *we* are to blame."

"Well, you just ask the merchants, Eugenia. They'll recite instances that will actually amaze you."

"Silly girl," scoffed Eugenia. "Next time one of the pious merchants blames the blockade-runners, ask him why the price of bacon has jumped from twelve to thirty cents a pound in the last few months."

"Oh well," Adria said with a toss of her head, "it can't last much longer. Not with England aroused over the violation of her flag on the high seas. Father said the Federal Government would regret the day its warship seized our commissioners to France and England, Messrs. Slidell and Mason, from the British mailship *Trent*."

The pretty young wife of Lieutenant Chapman of the *Sumter* said spiritedly, "This Captain Wilkes of the Yankee warship *San Jacinto* will find all his popularity in the North backfiring when the British troops land in Canada. I hope he hangs."

"He was hunting the *Sumter*, so the papers said," Adria declared.

"And when the eight thousand British soldiers march down on New York, he'll think he found a hornets' nest," said another. "The Mobile *Register* and *Advertiser* said last August, at the time the British squadron was in the Gulf under Admiral Milne, that a conflict between the English and Yankee forces was expected. Thank heavens it's here."

"And the British soldiers are singing 'Dixie' to the top of their voices."

Mrs. Starr eyed Adria curiously. "In the account of the reception given Captain Wilkes and his officers in Boston while John Slidell and James Mason were imprisoned at Fort Warren, I noticed the name of a Lieutenant James Hillyer. Wasn't that the name of the young man Adam brought home for Christmas last year?"

Adria colored. Her glance fell quickly. "Yes, Mrs. Starr."

"Jumpin' Jehoshaphat! A Yankee in the house!"

"He was not a Yankee at the time," Adria advised more sharply than she realized.

Mrs. Starr nodded her head wisely, as though she were weighing this statement for its gossip value. Aware that several pairs of eyes dwelled inquiringly on Adria, she said with cutting intent, "Well, my dear Mrs. Jarvis, he's a hard-shell Federal now. The paper my husband saw told how he vowed never to rest until the pirate and arsonist Semmes was driven from the seas. Seems he was a prisoner aboard the *Sumter*."

"Poor, dear Adam. How is he, Annabel?"

Adria forgot prying Mrs. Starr and the others as events of the summer and fall crowded her mind. Fresh in memory was her own cry of hurt when a carriage came to the door that September morning with her fever-ridden brother. Watching them carry Adam upstairs, she had cried out in despair and anger against the horror and uselessness of a war that violated everything good and decent in life. And to think that she had only a few weeks before they brought Adam home cheered this very same war. . . .

That was back in July, when everyone awaited the clash of arms up in Virginia, which would put an end to hostilities. For days and weeks Joseph Cutler had fumed and fussed over the newspaper accounts of the jockeying of thousands of troops by Confederate Generals Beauregard and Johnston and Northern Generals McDowell and Patterson. At breakfast the Bay Oaks household heard, "We're outnumbered up there by twenty thousand men, but one Southerner is worth three Yankees." At noon, "The whole North is ringing with the cry of 'On to Richmond!' But we've got a cheering squad ourselves, singing louder, by thunder, 'Take Washington and clap old Abe Lincoln in irons!'" For dinner Joseph gave them his unbiased opinion of General Robert E. Lee of Virginia, who, he said, could have taken Washington in April had he not stood in awe of the flag he had once served.

Faustine had been in Selma. The watermelons were ripe, and at a lawn party at Bay Oaks on the twentieth, a quartered melon had gone for fifty cents for the soldiers' aid fund. And that same evening a Lowndes County planter had offered twenty dollars in specie to the fund for one kiss from the hostess, Mrs. Lawrence Jarvis. A Mobile cotton broker raised his bid by ten dollars, and others picked it up until a touch of Adria's lips brought at auction one hundred and ten dollars.

When the news of the Battle of Manassas Junction reached Mobile, the city became wild with joy. Bells rang, whistles blew, crowds singing "Dixie" filled the streets, and speakers talked loud and long in Bienville Square.

The Confederate troops had turned the Union soldiers into a disorganized mob that ran all the way to Washington.

For once Joseph Cutler had predicted correctly; except for one small error—the Confederate generals did not follow up their smashing victory by marching on defenseless Washington. However, as far as he was concerned, the war had been won. The South was free of the Northern yoke.

And freedom was all the South asked, the right of a state or a group of states to make laws suitable to people and conditions instead of living under a government as foreign and unsympathetic to their needs as England had been to the American colonies.

The wave of optimism that seized Joseph caught up almost everyone in the Confederacy. As a Georgian had said in February, "We are in the dawn of an era of prosperity and happiness unprecedented in the annals of nations," everybody seemed to believe that this era had been achieved at Bull Run on the twenty-first of July.

This was the war Adria had cheered. Rather, she thought now, in defense of self, she had merely celebrated a victory that belonged to her people.

Petty Grant distended her thin nostrils, sniffed the aroma from the kitchen, as though to remind the hostess that she was hungry, then settled back to prompt Eugenia into telling the story of the Federal blockade of Galveston in July. Getting nowhere on this score, she listened to the buzz of voices a minute or so before asking about Faustine.

Annabel replied, "She's upstairs. Doctor Joe said she shouldn't climb the stairs."

"She couldn't be over six months." Petty's eyebrows lifted. "However, my Sarah was large at five months."

"With twins." Annabel smiled. "I'd welcome that stork to Bay Oaks. So would Joseph."

Adria said nothing. Mrs. Starr looked up, said, "I know Faustine's sister in Selma. She didn't have twins, so I don't imagine you'll get your wish."

Petty drew a deep breath. "Faustine is such a dear, devoted wife to Adam. If he asked for twins, I just know she'd do her best. Don't you agree, Adria?"

Caught with her mouth drawn into a tight line, Adria started. She forced a smile of innocence. "Oh yes, of course."

To herself she said, "What a lie! May the Lord forgive me!" It was bad enough to be cooped up in the same house with Faustine. But telling lies for her was too much. The very thought of Adam's implicit trust in and devotion to her sent a wave of pity surging through her. How very gullible men were; how helpless was a man's own sister in affairs of her brother's heart.

With her hands tied and mouth sealed, Adria felt again all the anger and resentment that boiled up in her on that day in early August, about a month before Adam's return . . .

It was midafternoon of perhaps the hottest day of summer. Not a breath of air stirred over the bay or land and, minus the prevailing breeze off the sea, the thick outer and inner walls and high ceilings of Bay Oaks did little to ward off the humid heat.

Dressed in next to nothing, Adria lay flat of back on a quilt in her room while coal-black young Claribel, oblivious to the weather, fanned her. Adria was thinking of whatever came to mind, a party of last week, of one in the future, of this obligation and that, all drowsily. Then she seemed to be reading a letter from Lawrence. She stirred, frowned, and turned her thoughts to James. Next she was wondering if the South's victory at Manassas would hasten her husband's return home.

She hoped not, even as she wished, guiltily, that the end of the war, which she believed was at hand except for the formality of a peace treaty, might bring James. She thrilled to the thought of his coming. Oh, she would not soon forgive him, outwardly at least, but would offer just enough encouragement to keep him dangling until he was thoroughly repentant and beaten. Then she intended divorcing Lawrence.

Claribel interrupted her pleasant dream with, "How come yo'all got jest one nigger fannin', Miss Adri? Miss Faustine, she got two, and she got Liza a-rubbin' her belly wid salve, so it stretch good whilst de baby grow. Co'se, Mammy say it am a little early fo' dat."

"Mind your business, Claribel. Besides, I'm not going to have a baby."

"Iffen yo' hadn't slept wid Mammy Rose on yo'all's weddin' night, yo' might."

Adria was preparing to give the tongue-doughty girl a stern lecture when a commotion in the back yard diverted her attention.

"A ton of ice from Havana! All hands fall to before she melts!"

That Captain Sherrod again. She despised him. Furthermore, the sun could be melting the iron gates of Bay Oaks and she would still refuse his evil ice. She lay down again, though cries of delight from the slaves made sleep impossible. When all was quiet once more, the desire for rest was gone.

From the upper gallery she looked down upon her father and the schoonerman seated in the shade of live oaks. Their voices were distinctly audible, so she listened for a time. Sherrod wished to sell her father shares in a fast steamer to be used to run the blockade, though Joseph laughed and asked, "What blockade? The war is just about over." The other's reply, that the war had only begun, brought on a speech.

Just what had happened to Sherrod's mind? Why, Manassas was by far the greatest battle ever fought on American soil, and one of the decisive battles of the world. When history was recorded, people would years in the future refer to Manassas as the place where the South secured by valiant arms her independence.

After hearing him out, Sherrod said, "A thousand dollars says the war won't be over this time next year." When they had sealed the wager with a handclasp, the seaman raised a glass tinkling with ice. "To your son, Joseph. I've got news for you."

Adria listened avidly as he told of the prizes taken by the *Sumter* into the Cuban port of Cienfuegos, where they were later released.

"Adam set the torch to the first Yankee vessel burned at sea. Guess how I learned that. Well, it's a small world, for the man who told me had been a prisoner aboard the *Sumter*. Lieutenant James Hillyer."

Joseph's "The hell you say!" just about declared Adria's astonishment also. But Sherrod had only begun to uncover surprises. James Hillyer had emerged from witnessing the burning of the *Golden Rocket* a new man, one resolved to make war to the death on Confederate "pirates." He had spoken his mind on the *Sumter's* deck, and Adam had slapped him.

Adria bit her lip and stared out of troubled eyes. Unable to reconcile the enmity of brother and sweetheart in her mind, she tried not to believe it. But war did strange things. God simply turned his back on warring nations and peoples. Adam married to Faustine and she to Lawrence.

"So I asked Hillyer if he wanted to go to Mobile," Sherrod was saying. "He said it was a little late for that. But you should have seen him when I placed one of Adria's old slippers, the one you gave me for style and size, before him. He kept it, walked off the ship with it."

They laughed at a huge joke. How could they when her heart was breaking?

She turned away. In her room she flung herself across the bed and sobbed until her pain was somehow relieved. Then she was asking the good Lord in heaven to watch over poor James.

"He's weak, and confused, dear God, so please forgive him for being on the Yankees' side."

The passing minutes failed to sustain her mood of total misery, and she was slowly buoyed into that state of transition between grief and an acceptance of her troubles. Then she had a sense of being drawn to James, irresistibly, of feeling his hand in pledge of all the sweet things they had spoken of in the past. With it came a longing to feel his arms about her, his lips against her own. A moment later she colored in shame.

How she hated James then. She wanted him thoroughly punished.

Company at the front door drew Joseph inside. Since the visitors were calling on her aunt Eugenia, Adria did not go through the ordeal of dressing and tidying up; instead she got into a robe, went in search of a breath of cool air out on the upstairs gallery again. It was from this point of vantage that she saw something that held her in a state of shock and disbelief.

Almost entirely screened off from any eye at the ground level was a small arbor shaded by a growth of climbing roses. Seated on the iron bench were Faustine and Randall Sherrod. She was leaning back in his arms with her mouth to his. They remained this way for some time before drawing their faces apart and staring at each other. Then Faustine's hand slid sinuously up to his neck and he was kissing her again, and she him, fervently, passionately.

Adria could not think at first, could not adjust all she saw in her dazed mind. Suspecting Faustine of being untrue to Adam was one thing; stark proof of her unfaithfulness was something else. But it was there, revealed in loathing sordidness before her very eyes. Name of heaven, what had Adam done to deserve this?

It was awful. She didn't wish to look at it. Turning her back, she re-entered her room and put down as best she could the storm of anger tearing through her. Soon she called Claribel and told her to advise Faustine that she must see her at once.

Faustine arrived a little curious, though upon learning that the abrupt summons had nothing to do with news concerning Adam she showed her pique.

"Sit down, please," Adria said as calmly as possible. "I have something to say that won't keep."

"Heavens! It must be important to bring me panting up the stairs after a walk in the garden." With a controlled look of disdain, she took a chair and cocked her delicate head inquiringly.

Adria's direct eyes narrowed in study of her sister-in-law. "We might as well bring it into the open," she said. "The fact that we're not overly fond of each other has no bearing on what I have to say. You're my brother's wife and I've tried to treat you as such."

Faustine's mouth twisted into a smile. "Continue."

"I shall. First, allow me to correct your reason for panting. A walk in the garden wasn't the cause, Faustine. From the upper back gallery, the view of the rose arbor is excellent."

Faustine's expression was suddenly sharp and defiant. "Why—you little spy!" she exclaimed.

"No, I wasn't spying. Mother or Father could have seen you as easily as I. Where would you stand then? Don't bother to reply; just consider it while I remind you that if I didn't love Adam too much to hurt him, I'd write a letter telling him the truth about his dear, devoted wife."

"Listen to who's talking about a devoted wife." Faustine rose and walked to the door, closed it, then laughed derisively. "The bride who spent her wedding night with a nigger mammy."

Adria felt the restraint she had resolved to maintain fast departing. It was a great effort to say calmly, "Don't try to dodge the issue with slurring remarks about me."

"I make remarks? Why, child, it's on every tongue from Fort Morgan to Marengo County. In Mobile you're pointed out. 'There goes a woman who owns both a wedding ring and her virginity.' And Lawrence is the subject of a hundred raw jokes."

Adria stood aghast.

"I don't believe you. They couldn't say such things."

"No? You poor, protected child. Now let me tell you something. I've tolerated you the same as you have me. I've put up with your fine airs because I couldn't do otherwise. But this! With your wedding night behavior a burlesque for Mobile to snicker at, imagine your having the gall to question my conduct! What I did, if anything, was at least private and discreet. But you, dear, had to catch the public eye."

Adria wanted to cry, to run and beat down the gossips all at once. For some reason she believed Faustine, hated her all the more. And never, as long as she lived, would she show her face in Mobile again! Never! But this cheating woman had seized the initiative and was, guilty, making a fool of her, an innocent woman!

This fact alone was enough to revive Adria, to fan her anger into a fury beyond control. Slowly she moved toward Faustine, hands working spasmodically into small fists and out of them into talons, eyes flashing her desire to hurt and destroy.

"You horrible creature!" she cried recklessly.

"Adria!" Faustine backed a step and another, her expression no longer triumphant but apprehensive.

"So this is what my brother was fool enough to marry. Any man's woman! One who goes out of her way to lower a decent woman to her level!"

"Adria! Stay where you are! I never told anyone about your wedding night. Not a soul."

Adria moved closer, head outthrust. "I wouldn't believe you if you were on your deathbed. You're cheap, rotten! And if it wasn't for Adam's baby you're carrying—I hope it is his—I'd scratch your eyes out! But I'm warning you—don't you *ever again* forget you're Adam's wife!"

"Yes, Adria! I—I promise."

Faustine jerked the door open and ran down the hall as fast as she could.

With hands knotted at her hips, bosom heaving, Adria stared at the door for long minutes before sinking into a chair. As the tempest inside her fell away, a sense of personal hurt, no longer able to take refuge in her madness, made itself felt. It grew into a damning, unbearable thing.

She needed her mother now, but she could never speak to her

regarding Faustine's treachery. Nor would she run to Mammy Rose this time. She just wouldn't.

But she did, and the kind Negress held her to her bosom again while she unburdened her troubles. When there was nothing more to tell, her mammy told her that the world was a bad place and good place, a home for both devils and angels.

"De good peoples tries to make de bad peoples good and de bad folks tries to make de good folks bad. De Scriptures done say they is gwine be wars and pest'lence and grasshoppers and famines. Why? 'Cause de good folks is got to be tested. So, chile, put yo' trust in de good Lawd and hol' yo' head high in Mobile."

## 2

Adria looked at the cotton cards in her hand, then at Miss Petty, who was talking of Christmas, only five days from now. But she was thinking of how rapidly the summer had turned into hot fall, of how she had forced herself on Sundays to the Government Street Presbyterian Church with head proud and high, of many things. . . .

From every side she heard of the North's poor financial condition. The war was costing the Lincoln government over two million dollars a day, five times as much as the Confederacy was spending. Such a debt would soon crush the Black Republican cause, and the North's lack of cotton would bring on its economic collapse. To further prove the ruin of the enemy, weeds gathered in the streets of New York were placed on display up in Selma, Alabama. But, strangely, the war did not end.

Adam's return home in September brought the hitherto remote war to the very doors of Bay Oaks. For more than a week he lay between life and death. No one had any idea of what had happened to Adam other than the tugboat captain, who knew only that he had taken him aboard in New Orleans and hurried to Mobile by way of Mississippi Sound, as Commodore Rousseau had instructed. Faustine surprised Adria by remaining at his bedside night and day until the doctor put her to bed. Toward mid-September, Adam began to win over fever, brought on, he told them, by a night and day in the swamps following his escape from the U.S.S. *Minnesota*. When he entered New Orleans aboard a pilot boat, there was scarcely a spot on his hands or face untouched by mosquitoes. But the letter from Semmes to the Navy Secretary had gone through.

Adam was reluctant to talk about James, and Adria recalled the stubborn set of his countenance when any mention was made of him, usually by Joseph. But she would not soon forget his subtle inquiries regarding her sentiments toward the Marylander. Adam wanted her to be happy.

The feeling was mutual. To his questions concerning Faustine, she gave answers that pleased him. Odd, she thought, brother and sister pitying each other in secret. Or was it anything other than a manifestation of love for one another? She thought not.

By October, Adam was up and walking in the gardens with Faustine, his mother, or Adria. The color returned to his cheeks and he sat with the family spinning shipboard yarns. Faustine seemed happy, and Adam was happy until news of an attack by Confederate gunboats and fireboats on the Federal fleet at the head of the passes below New Orleans reached Bay Oaks. From that day on he appeared restless. Against the wishes of all, he wrote Mr. Mallory requesting immediate service afloat. Early in November he departed for Richmond and arrived there on the day the South heard that Union Flag Officer du Pont, commanding seventy ships and land forces said to number twenty thousand men, had captured the forts at Port Royal, South Carolina.

The "damn Federals" were strong by sea, though to offset their little game of blockade, the *Sumter,* pride of the South, was leading the United States Navy a merry chase. The North was feeling her sting.

Then a message reached Bay Oaks advising that Corporal Lawrence Jarvis had been wounded in a skirmish up in Tennessee. He should arrive in Montgomery within a few weeks.

This was indeed bad news. Adria remembered the sympathy her expressions of unhappiness evoked and felt ashamed, for her chief concern had not been for poor Lawrence but herself. She dreaded his coming as she might an operation.

Early in December, Adam had written from Richmond, advising that Secretary of Navy Mallory was sending him to England, where he was to work with Confederate agents North and Bulloch in speeding up delivery of the 290, a craft which he prayed they would hear much of in the months to come.

Faustine cried, and Adria thought her grief was genuine. Perhaps she had learned her lesson. Else fear of childbirth, remorse, or some maternal instinct had checked her desire for any extramarital affair; temporarily, at least. On the other hand, it was not difficult to believe that Faustine had at last fallen in love with Adam. Only time would tell.

Adria sighed.

How swiftly the days came, how slowly they departed. The long, lonely evenings rolled around regularly, each leaving her tense with expectancy, afraid that every sound was an announcement of the arrival of Lawrence. . . .

Today was the twentieth, the anniversary of her meeting with James, the glorious night of the ball. One year in the past South Carolina had seceded from the Union. However strange, these events coincided. Harbingers of happy days ahead. But this year——
Why, only yesterday Erasmus had entered the house grinning from ear to ear.

"Miss Adria, done got yo'all the purtiest holly tree in all Alabamy. Want I should put hit in de parlor?"

Poor Erasmus. He had not expected the reply she gave him: "Don't you dare bring that unlucky thing in this house before Christmas!"

## 21.    Yuletide Gift

### 1

ADRIA ran an eye down the shopping list and marked off another item. The store was crowded on this Saturday before Christmas and Abel was nowhere in sight. Cutler bundles were piled high on the counter and she was steadily adding more.

"Oh, Mr. Levy!" she called. The merchant nodded, adjusted the pencil at his ear, and hurried to Adria. "I want four yards of this red ribbon and—what pretty broadcloth! How much is it?"

The storekeeper named a price, adding, "The blockade, you know," in a manner that absolved him of all blame.

"Heavens! But not that high, surely!" She eyed the material, all the while tapping her chin with a forefinger. "Oh well, I know I shouldn't, but measure off ten yards."

Next on the list was tobacco for the slaves. She was of a mind to ask her father to buy the nasty stuff. But he was not to be found either. Among the brands of chewing and smoking tobacco were Parlor Luxury, Diadem of Old Virginia, Nelly Gray, Christian's Comfort, Southern Star, and more. It seemed very strange to her that a planter should humor his slaves with store-bought instead of field-grown. Next was a case of "Rebel" matches, though not one of five would strike. Then an umbrella for Mammy Rose, bless her heart. A looking glass for Uncle Ralph's yellow daughter Lucy, queen of the servants' quarters. And——

"Mr. Sam, did father buy the barrels of sugar for the lower plantation?"

"No, ma'am."

"We'll need two—no, three."

Someone behind Adria said, "Never mind the sugar, Sam. I've already dispatched four barrels to Bay Oaks."

Adria whirled, and the schoonerman bowed, saying, "Fresh from Havana, Miss Adria. Compliments of Captain Sherrod."

Forcing a stiff curtsy, Adria said icily, "I'm sure my father will express his gratitude, sir."

In fine shore blue and white Sherrod looked the part of the prosperous blockade-runner. But for the air of mockery about him, emphasized by the downward slant of his mouth when he smiled, he seemed every bit as handsome as bold.

"Thank you, ma'am. It will be my pleasure to serve your father and all members of his family eggnog and apple toddy in my apartment at the Battle House any afternoon between three and six. And I may say that our good Confederate Santa Claus fetched ice from the frozen north all the way to Mobile."

Adria's glance lingered on him a moment, half curious, half intent. Aware that he had coolly, expertly, reprimanded her with a gesture of welcome, she could not withhold a retort couched in a winning smile.

"Did Santa forget salt, Captain Sherrod?"

As she had intended, the reference to his salt monopoly, a source of considerable talk and grumbling in Mobile, turned the attention of shoppers within the range of her voice upon the notorious speculator.

"No, he didn't forget, Miss Adria," Sherrod replied with devilish ease. "You see, Santa doesn't own the salt supply. I do."

The expressions of shocked surprise and accompanying gasps from several of the women only served to widen the smile on Adria's face. She actually admired and liked the man in that moment. Furthermore, she was afraid the look she gave him conveyed as much. But he did not press the advantage his challenging eyes acknowledged; instead, he surveyed her from head to toe as he had done in the past and executed a sweeping bow.

She glanced at her list, but he was not that easily dismissed from mind. She watched him until he was lost in the crowd; then, under a spell of gaiety and excitement, told the kindly Jew to double her order for broadcloth.

"Nor will I quibble further over the price of that bottle of French perfume, Mr. Levy. After all, it is for my brother's wife."

Looking up, she saw Abel and her mother. "Where's Father?" she asked.

"Marse Joseph outside waitin'. He say don't see how we gwine git another single thing in dat carriage. Lawdy me, it am brimmin' full and runnin' over now."

Once in the crowded carriage, Adria tried to think of items she had forgotten, as did her mother. Both succeeded, volubly, much to Joseph's displeasure. He declared that any man who turned two women loose in a store was no saner than a planter who allowed his stock access to fields of young cotton. Soon he said, as though the shoe was beginning to pinch:

"Have you noticed how prices have risen since that damn Federal Butler closed Mississippi Sound early this month? We're cut off from New Orleans by water, Annabel. Cut off entirely."

Annabel made a slight shrug, then looked at her husband thoughtfully. "I don't understand it, Joseph. After we won at Manassas, we just seemed to quit. What happened?"

"I'll tell you what." Joseph twirled a mustache angrily. "We're minus military leadership. A crime it is, with the people crying for our troops to take Washington—actually our pickets were able to see the spires of the city—and a general like Johnston saying our troops were almost as demoralized by victory as the enemy was by defeat! And President Davis sanctioned that kind of talk."

"Joseph, you shouldn't criticize."

"The devil I shouldn't. Haven't the Federals under General McClellan pushed us out of West Virginia? And didn't they drive that misfit 'Old Granny Lee,' or 'Old Spade Lee'—'cause he likes to dig in and sit—over the mountains? And today I heard that the Federals are releasing Mason and Slidell to pacify England. Frankly, we've got one more hell of a poor government, Annabel. One that missed the boat."

He added seriously, "Damned if I don't believe Sherrod is right, after all."

"Sherrod?" Adria put in.

"He thinks we're in for a long war. Still wants me to buy shares in a fast paddle-wheel to run the blockade. Says he, 'Five thousand will get you fifty.' But looking ahead at a government-reduced cotton crop next year, that and higher prices on everything we buy, five thousand dollars is too much to gamble."

Adria said, "Didn't you gamble a lot more than that to help finance the Confederate Government, Father?"

"I did. But not for private gain. I don't approve of profit that robs my friends."

Annabel laughed. "Then it's a matter of principle with you, Joseph, instead of a business risk."

"It is no such thing, ma'am!" he declared vehemently.

Adria and her mother smiled and exchanged glances. Then Adria was relating the incident of her meeting with Sherrod in Levy's store. Her father saw no humor in it; instead, he frowned and said:

"Adria, I wish you'd stay in a lady's place in public. Now everybody who heard you will say you're a bold woman. What's more, they'll link your name with his. He has a bad reputation."

"Your father is right," Annabel said.

Adria looked contrite. "I never thought of it that way."

"There's another side to it," Joseph said. "If you'd been informed, you wouldn't have tried to embarrass him. Admitting he's wrong in speculating in salt, give him credit for distributing over fifty tons to needy families from here to Montgomery. I know that he sent ten tons upriver to Selma."

Adria's mouth fell open. "Well!" she said. "Knock me over with a broomstraw."

Minutes later she asked, "Father, how many bushels of salt are there in a ton?"

"Figuring short bushels, say fifty pounds, it would come to forty. Why do you ask?"

"At three dollars a bushel, Captain Sherrod gave away a great deal of money, didn't he?"

Joseph multiplied in silence. "By thunder, he did!"

"Which is proof he's making money."

Annabel said, "What on earth are you getting at, Adria?"

"Nothing, Mother. Nothing at all."

2

Joseph Cutler took a second look at the horse tied to the hitching block as the carriage rolled through the gates. "Why, that looks like Leland Jarvis's mare," he said.

Adria paid no heed. She was too absorbed in thought: Perhaps it would be a long war; and if so, prices would continue to soar whether or not England came to the aid of the Confederacy. Just supposing that——

The carriage rolled to a halt. Mammy Rose stood on the porch with hands on hips. "Now yo'alls go on in de house, Marse Joseph, whilst me and Miss Adria has a talk."

"Leland Jarvis inside?" Joseph asked.

"Nossuh, he ain't."

Annabel tensed, met Mammy's glance, and looked at Adria, who seemed lost in thought. "Careful, Mammy," she whispered, and moved toward the door.

Left alone with Adria, the Negress said, "Now lissen to me, honey baby. Yo' is a grown woman and done got responsibil'ties. Ain't no chile no mo'."

Adria stood with back to a round white column. "What on earth ails you, Mammy?"

"Ask yo'se'f dat. But when yo'all enters de house, remember what's embroidery on yo' pillow shams. Hit say 'I slept and dreamed dat life has beauty; I woke and found dat life has duty.' Gospel truth! Now git inside and remember all I says, fo' they's a gen'leman waitin'."

Adria felt the color drain from her face. "Who?"

"Yo' husband, dat's who."

The front door opened and Adria saw Lawrence. She groped for some support. Finding none, she closed her eyes and felt herself spinning off into total darkness.

She was lying on a sofa in the parlor when her eyes fluttered open. Her parents, Lawrence, and half the household slaves were gathered about her, and her mother and Mammy Rose were alternately placing cold towels on her forehead. She closed her eyes to think, to try to adjust herself to this horrible situation.

There was no escape this time, she realized. Either she must become his wife or demand a divorce. An annulment, perhaps. But she had to face it.

She opened her eyes.

Lawrence had lost a lot of weight. She studied him, almost with blank expression. Still tall and very handsome, but a stranger. There was anxiety, and love, the devoted kind they sang about, in his face; and pain.

She held a hand up to him. "I'm sorry, Lawrence. Just took me by surprise, I guess."

He took her hand in his and dropped to his knees beside her; rather hesitantly, she thought, as though he were trying hard to avoid a second hurt.

She had married him. Actually, she had no right to punish him for something James had done. She had made the mistake, had drawn him into it, shamefully. Mr. *Virgin* Jarvis! But what must she do?

He arose slowly. "Well, I must be on my way," he said. "To Mobile," he added, tearing his glance away from her face. "I don't seem to bring anything but trouble."

Joseph boomed out, "You'll do nothing of the kind. See here now, we're going to settle this thing——" He broke off. "Skedaddle, all you niggers."

After Erasmus had led the servants out of the parlor—excepting Mammy Rose, who said she wasn't "skedaddlin'," Adria sat up.

"Father, this is my affair. I'll settle it." She looked at Lawrence. "If you have business in Mobile, attend to it, then return." Under his hopeful look, she said, "To settle matters."

Color surged up in Lawrence's face, proving he still owned a quick temper. He was bowing out when it suddenly occurred to Adria that some of the slurring remarks about their marriage might reach his ears. Then trouble would begin. He might get hurt, though what she dreaded most was further scandal.

"Mobile can wait, I'm sure," she said, rising. Taking his arm, she guided him outside and into the privacy of the gardens.

Noticing his slight limp, she said, "Your wound, was it in the leg?"

"The calf. A Yankee bullet lodged there. But I'll soon be walking as good as before."

"Of course you will."

Nothing more was said between them until she paused by the statue of the boy, who continued to point. Her glance remained fixed on him a minute before drifting on to stately oaks in the distance.

"Lawrence, it is a little late for honesty, but I have no alternative." She forced herself through an explanation of her engagement to James and on into a confession of her love for the Marylander even on her wedding night. She did not glance up into his face, for she had no desire to see the pain and anger her words evoked in him.

She walked slowly a few steps away when he sat down on an iron bench. With her back to him, she said, "I don't think I love James now."

He said nothing.

Turning her face to him, she said, "I don't love you either, Lawrence. Not as a wife should."

His ravaged face worked its every muscle to hold in check his misery. A tear slid down his cheek, then another.

"I've hurt you deeply," she went on. "I'll be punished for it. I just know it. But I had to tell you. I'm sorry, and ashamed, very ashamed. But I feel better now."

He rose and looked at the coat of his uniform, brushed it with a hand, as though it were very important.

She walked toward the statue with a hand at her breast to still the fast beat of her heart. "What are we going to do?"

"I'm leaving for Fort Donelson on the second of January," he said, straightening to his full height. "As for you, ma'am, do whatever you damned please."

Adria jerked her face around. "Temper won't solve a thing." She added quickly, "I've learned that much."

"Then learn something else," he blurted angrily. "Since I was knee high to a duck, I've loved you. I grew up wanting you for my wife. I let you flirt and take up with other boys; let you treat me like a nigger slave. But all the time I knew I'd marry you. That was my life. You were the one star up there as far as I was concerned.

"So I did marry you! For what? You answered it. Tear a man's heart out and see what's left of him. Take a good look, Adria."

"You'll mend, all right," she retorted.

His look of utter incredulity fell away. He sighed hopelessly. "I suppose so, but I'd rather go through life with both arms and legs shot off than go on loving you the way I do."

"Loving me the way you *do?*" Adria could not believe this. "You mean you still love me after all I've told you? Actually?"

He nodded soberly. "Enough to ride down to Mobile for that diamond brooch I ordered last June."

"I hope you're not trying to buy me, Lawrence."

"Think what you like," he replied. "I've told you how I feel."

She believed him then. His air of resigned indifference made him honest.

The frown clouding her face was deep. How any mortal could continue to love that much after such treatment was beyond her understanding. She felt cheap and rotten. Then a great wave of pity engulfed her. Surely the Lord had given her enough warning. No, she could not have this man's ruin on her conscience.

Nor could she allow him to show his face in Mobile, for in his recklessly bitter mood he would invite trouble.

"Lawrence, I'd be ashamed to accept a gift from you," she said honestly. "Much less an expensive brooch. Why, every time I looked at it I'd feel guilty."

"What you do with it, ma'am, is no concern of mine."

Adria knew she must keep him away from the city. Suddenly her mind was churning with thoughts of blockade and salt, a fast paddle-wheel steamer and, "Five thousand will get you fifty," and her eyes were narrowing speculatively on her husband.

"Lawrence Jarvis, if you're that careless with your money, suppose you give it to me to invest—for us."

"For *us?*" he said, amazed but skeptical.

"Yes." She looked him in the eye. "If you still want me after all I've told you."

"If I want you? Adria, honey! I'll make you love me if it takes a lifetime!"

"It's your gamble," she said, thinking that the price of a diamond brooch invested in a fast steamer was a better risk by far.

## 22.    Black April

### 1

FAUSTINE was in a happy frame of mind. She forgot that the weather was exceptionally warm for the Gulf Plain this time of year, or that with April nearly two thirds gone reports of the disastrous battle of Shiloh were still pouring in to depress everyone.

Making an effort to suppress her mounting excitement, she entered the upstairs bedroom and sent an inquiring glance at the Negro woman who rocked a large canopied cradle of polished mahogany. Her lips formed in silence, "Asleep?" As the slave nodded her head slowly, timing the motion to that of the cradle, Faustine picked up the front of her full skirt and tiptoed to the sleeping baby.

Joseph Adam Cutler lay still, with thumb in mouth, a tiny fist flattening his nose. As if he knew someone was watching him, he started, opened his eyes an instant, and murmured protest before resuming his sleep.

Mammy Cora showed white teeth in a broad grin before whispering, "He gittin' plumb spoil'."

Faustine knew Cora spoke the truth. Annabel, Joseph, and Adria vied with one another in finding excuses to handle little Adam. No end of new dresses, tiny shoes, coverlets, and ribboned garments were showered upon the new monarch of Bay Oaks. Why, the Wednesday Sewing Circle had even fashioned for him a Confederate cap like his father's. But Joseph and Adria were by far the hardest to deal with. As often as not, the moment she turned her back one or the other would disappear with the baby and Mammy Rose would play innocent. "Yo' means dat little Confedrut done gone agin?"

He would be two months old on the fifth of May. Faustine had often counted the months of her married life on her fingers, as she knew many "dear" women had done. Eight and one half months made the other half month rather conspicuous. Just the same, she had never been happier. Despite whatever the confirmed gossips were saying or the fact that her baby resembled Adam no more than a perfect stranger, he had been, and was, the bright spot in her life.

Of late, however, she had felt a desire to circulate among people again. Annabel agreed that she had been cooped up too long for the good of herself or baby, and took her to various circle and aid societies, a musical and other gatherings, all of which were, frankly, very dull. Instead, she secretly craved gaiety and excitement, if only for a few short hours.

Then last evening something had happened to vaguely shape a course in that direction. Elvy and Harold Fisher had visited awhile after returning Adria from a bazaar in Mobile to raise money for a gunboat for the Confederacy. Adria's idea, but heavens alive, how it had caught fire! For five straight days Adria had gone from house to house in Mobile gathering up clocks, jewelry, vases, china sets, silverware, furniture, and books to be raffled off at the Gunboat Bazaar in Bienville Square. Joseph had given his two morocco-bound Audubon volumes and a case of champagne, and Annabel had parted with her childhood doll. The gunboat craze had gotten off to a fine start. And for good reason . . .

The Federal blockade was tightening like a slow screw in the hands of a gloating giant. Federal gunboats had captured Biloxi, Mississippi, on the last day of December, 1861; had aided in the capture of Forts Henry and Donelson in Tennessee, a severe Confederate defeat in February; had taken Jacksonville and San Augustine, Florida, in March, and Island No. 10 in the Mississippi early in April. Gunboats were transporting Yankee troops on the Tennessee River into upper Alabama, and a huge Federal flotilla had assembled at the mouth of the Mississippi under Flag Officer Farragut, its aim the capture of New Orleans.

Last night Harold had spoken of going to New Orleans on a matter of business. "While there's time," he said. "If the Federal fleet gets there first, I'll lose several thousand dollars."

Joseph scoffed, declared that the combined fleets of Britain and France could not win past Forts St. Philip and Jackson.

"I hope you're right, Joseph," Fisher said, unconvinced. "But I hear the forts are under heavy mortar fire."

"Suppose they are," Joseph argued. "They'll stand off the invader. Besides, we can put a few modern gunboats between the forts and New Orleans. I hear the *Louisiana* is as powerful an ironclad as the *Virginia,* the old *Merrimac,* which nearly destroyed the United States Navy at Hampton Roads on the eighth of March. Admiral Buchanan and Josiah Tattnall—Adam sailed under old Tatt, you know—revolutionized naval warfare that day. Besides, we've got steamers and rams aplenty to protect New Orleans."

"Joseph," Annabel scolded, "you vowed never to predict the outcome of a military campaign again."

"But this is different."

"So was Shiloh, dear."

A silence fell over the room as every mind seemed to pause in review of the signal defeat of General Albert Sidney Johnston's army, in which the general himself was wounded and bled to death. As Shiloh was in lower Tennessee, the loss exposed the Confederate posts on the upper Mississippi to the almost unhindered Federal advance under Generals Grant and Halleck. But the dead and wounded included many soldiers from Alabama. Lawrence had fought at Shiloh, had written about the battle from Corinth.

Joseph frowned, jerked his brows up suddenly. "I still believe New Orleans is impregnable."

Harold stroked his mutton-chop whiskers and came up with a decision to make the trip while the city remained in Confederate hands.

"I'd give anything to go," Faustine said.

"It would do you good," Elvy declared. "Don't you think so, Annabel?"

"I suppose. I hear people are in want there, however. It might not be very pleasant for Faustine."

Adria, still flushed from her success of the evening, said amiably, "Just don't you dare leave this house with the baby."

"Of course, she won't," Annabel laughed. "She needs freedom from responsibility in case she does go. But I won't sanction it, not with the Union fleet that close."

"Go how?" Joseph demanded.

"Captain Sherrod's *Gulf Wind*," Harold Fisher said.

Adria arched her brows. "Then Faustine isn't going."

Adria had been in error, Faustine admitted, looking up from her baby. All night she had dreamed of visiting gay New Orleans. How she got there didn't matter. Sherrod was merely a means to an end. If he tried to kiss her again, he would learn to his regret that she was very much in love with Adam.

She bent and placed a light kiss on little Adam's cheek. Straightening, she studied the Negress a moment. "Cora, I'm thinking seriously of taking you to New Orleans with me. Oh, my little angel will be in good hands, never you fear."

Faustine moved across the room to the bell cord, pulled it, and laughingly said, "I'm wondering if I'll be in good hands. A lady's personal maid is supposed to see nothing and remember less."

2

Randall Sherrod soon learned that a change had taken place in Faustine. Whether Adam, her baby, or both, were responsible, the fact was made evident by her polite coolness. All the way down Mobile Bay she remained in the company of her maid and brother-in-law.

The schooner captain smiled.

After successive tacks in the strong wind off the sea, the *Gulf Wind* pointed her bows toward Pas aux Herons at sundown. Fort Gaines on Dauphin Island slipped from a position broad on the port beam to fast astern as the schooner entered Federal-dominated Mississippi Sound for a run in the dark.

Sometime in the night Faustine felt the ship lurch. Almost thrown from her bunk, she sat up and listened. A shot screeched overhead and the sound of feet running the deck was followed by an order.

"Bend on a new jibs'l. We've got a race on our hands!"

Faustine dressed tremblingly and joined Harold on deck. At the wheel Sherrod eyed her, told her to lie low, that he was running between Biloxi and Ship Island, between the Federal hammer and anvil, with the gunboats *Lewis* and *Water Witch* hot on his heels. He knew the sounds of their engines, and he had a past acquaintance with the smell of their powder.

Another shot whistled close, causing Faustine to wish she had never left the safety of Bay Oaks. She wanted her baby, and Adam, as never before. Dear Adam, whose letter had arrived just before she departed for Mobile. He had received no mail from home since February. Though she had written often, Adam was unaware that he had a son.

The shot fell in the water near the ship's stern.

She was afraid. Shaking all over, she stared wildly into the night toward the spot from which the flame stabbed the darkness, then at Sherrod's face in the dim glow of the binnacle lamp. She saw in him a haven and refuge and she rushed to him with no thought of her brother-in-law.

"Careful, woman!" he urged in low tones. Then his voice split the night with, "Stand by for tacks! We're running for the deep under Cat Island!"

The schooner's head swung to port in a boil of foam, threw her decks into a list that seemed about to lay her on her beam ends. Righting herself, she gathered headway, rocking and reeling and heeling down toward the open Mexican Gulf. The shots of the pursuers faded into the distance as by skill, luck, or experience, or a combination of all three, Sherrod slipped under the island and bent a cautious way down toward Rigolets Pass, connecting Lake Pontchartrain with Mississippi Sound.

With danger on the wane, Faustine felt Sherrod's intent blue eyes on her. As she hurried to her cabin, she heard him order one of his blacks to the wheel. She waited breathlessly, hoping almost to hear his rapping at her door, though all that reached her ears above the creaking of ship and the swish of water down the sides were the distant sounds of thunder. The rumbling was from the south. It rolled low over the swamps, faint on the wind but ominous, and she knew that the Federals and the forts were slugging it out.

At the pass next morning an old fisherman looked up from the net he was mending and said it was strange, with everybody leaving New Orleans who could, that anyone should wish to go there. The thugs were looting and murdering and the flooded Mississippi was eating at the levees and threatening to plunge in on the city. And down-river the Federals were hammering at the city's first line of defense.

Against his better judgment, Fisher left Sherrod in Lake Borgne and, with Faustine and her maid, he managed at considerable cost to reach New Orleans and find a carriage for hire. He ordered the driver to Hotel St. Charles in the American quarter despite Faustine's desire to go to the St. Louis, the center of the city's Creole social life.

Faustine could not adjust in her mind the change that had come over New Orleans. The closer they came to the river, the greater were the number of boarded doors of shops and business houses.

In reply to her question, the mulatto driver said, "Mam'selle, she is one dead place. No employ, no ship, no trade, no gold, no silver, just Confederate and State paper money and shinplasters! *Nom de Dieu!* Food prices she's go up and the money she come down."

Harold asked for news of the siege down-river and learned that everyone believed the forts would hold the enemy in check. Furthermore, the ironclad *Louisiana,* the ram *Manassas,* the *Governor Moore,* and *Stonewall Jackson* would drive the enemy to the sea. "But the great ironclad ship *Mississippi,* let us complete her and the river she is open all the way to the Gulf! Then we see the trade again."

New Orleans was under martial law, they learned. The Commander of Confederate Department No. 1, Major-General Mansfield Lovell, allowed the city government to continue as usual, perhaps because he realized that only that which represented New Orleans could command respect from its citizens.

Before they reached the hotel, the driver drew up sharp to allow a patrolling squad of Mayor Monroe's Foreign Legion time in which to subdue a gang of river ruffians.

Faustine watched the officer in glittering uniform of green and gold with fond thoughts of Estève Decloux and Toulouse Street; the lovely house, its patio, the ringing laughter of the dear girls. A little gladness roused her spirits and she was thinking that surely only the surface of the city had been revealed to her this morning. Somewhere behind the grilled balconies they still sang "Blue-Eyed Mary" as well as "Dixie," swung into quadrilles with hoops and crinolines swaying. Somewhere a brilliant *soirée* in someone's honor, tonight perhaps. Ah, for the memorable bouquet of a Frenchman's champagne, the tilt of a glass with deep masculine eyes over the rim of crystal saying silently, eloquently, "*Ma chère*, my sweet one, a moment with you in the moonlight."

She blushed, deliciously, even as the lieutenant struck one of the ruffians over the head with the flat of his sword.

And she was hungry. What she wouldn't give for the sight of a Negress with a tray of pralines. And how she hungered for that famous Creole dish *pompano en papillote*, or a bowl of Louisiana gumbo, the New Orleannais improvement on Marseilles *bouillabaisse*.

She could see the St. Charles now, regarded in years past as an architectural wonder of the world by many travelers. She had seen and marveled at the hotel's famous gold service, said to be valued at sixteen thousand dollars. And now the great structure on St. Charles Avenue at Common Street represented the thing she wanted most, excitement in a lavish setting.

Faustine's first disappointment came upon finding the lobby seething with people seeking escape from the lawless elements and the threatening Mississippi. Others were waiting for a train to take them out of the city or a means of crossing the thirty miles of Lake Pontchartrain. A man rubbed against Faustine, his breath foul with whisky, his eyes dancing as he espied the jeweled necklace reaching toward her bosom.

The clerk repeated to Fisher, "I have no rooms." His trim brows lifted. "Sir, did you say gold? Allow me, please, to warn you. Whisper if you own gold." In hushed tones he added, "Or American greenbacks."

Fisher then asked for a suite of rooms, and drew a hopeless smile from the clerk. In the end, he was glad to accept one small room, though not Faustine, who advised the clerk that she was the wife of a Confederate States lieutenant who had sailed aboard the *Sumter*.

"Sorry, ma'am. If you were the wife of President Davis, I'd have to say the same."

Couching her winning smile, Faustine turned her back. Looking up, she was pleasantly surprised to find herself the object of a young naval officer's attention.

"Ma'am, permit me. I overheard your remark about the *Sumter*. Lieutenant McKeever, of Richmond, here to speed up work on the ram *Mississippi*." He bowed, stroked a neat auburn mustache, and returned her smile.

Behind her show of calm, Faustine's heart beat fast. Here before her eyes, in the shape of a very handsome and young naval officer, was hope for entertainment. She awaited breathlessly his reason for accosting her.

"My quarters are small, ma'am, but your party is more than welcome. For a week I've scarcely opened the door except to change uniforms. We're working round the clock, off and on, readying the ram *Mississippi* for service against the bluecoats."

"Oh, how very generous of you, Lieutenant! But——"

Young McKeever escorted them to a modest apartment a short distance away on Common Street, all the while talking of home, the *Sumter*, the forts that nothing afloat could pass, their 8- and 10-inch columbiads and rifled 32-pounders which would play havoc with the wooden Federal ships fighting the current of the river. Bidding them enter his place, he presented a small parlor and a bedroom with a single four-poster. He took his meals out, he said, though of late food had become a problem. Rather, the money with which to pay for it. He showed car tickets worn slick from handling, which were used for five-cent pieces in the city.

Rising to depart, he said, "Ma'am, if I may presume to warn you, stay off the streets at night. You too, Mr. Fisher." Then he presented his pistol to Faustine, saying, "Just in case you need it, ma'am."

"Oh, you kind, dear boy!" Faustine exclaimed, holding the gun awkwardly. "But I know nothing of firearms. Besides, this is New Orleans."

"That's what I mean, ma'am."

Harold departed shortly after the Virginian took his leave, and Faustine sent Cora out to hire a messenger boy. Soon a note was on its way to the Decloux house on Toulouse Street. The boy returned with it, advising that the house was closed. She sent him in search of other acquaintances before giving up.

"A horrid place!" she cried in exasperation.

At dusk Lieutenant McKeever brought two bottles of wine and three tired officers who had known Adam, and who, like himself, were off duty that evening. Delighted, Faustine made them sit while she served. For more than an hour they laughed, talked of Adam, the Navy, and the war in general, with not a word about New Orleans. It seemed they had pledged themselves to silence on the subject. The wine left them gay, Faustine no exception, and anxious to prolong the brief respite from toil and worry. When the senior officer proposed a dinner for the lovely lady at a café still famous for French cuisine, and of late notorious for prices beyond the reach of all but a few, the foursome pooled their resources and exchanged hopeless glances.

Faustine smiled. "You're all too sweet." Opening her reticule, she dropped one Confederate note after another atop their wealth until tall, dark Lieutenant Bascom said, "Enough!"

At half past two in the morning Faustine returned to the apartment and flung herself on the sofa. With head spinning under the fumes of old wine and fresh, exciting memories, she smiled up at Fisher and Cora, who had spent long hours worrying about her safety.

"What a wonderful, glorious city," she said, sighing contentedly.

From the street came sounds of fighting. The crash of glass on the banquette and cobbles was followed by mingled oaths and cries of pain. A shriek split the night and fell away in a long unearthly moan. Then all seemed still and quiet in the restless city.

3

Faustine opened her eyes and said sleepily, "Go away, Cora. And close the window. That noise!"

The Negress continued to shake her. "It's dem fire-alarm bells, Miss Faustine!" Her voice quivered with fright. "Twelve strokes, fo' times repeat!"

Faustine leaped up, staring, listening. This was the warning that New Orleans was in grave danger, that called every man to his point of muster.

But it could not be true. She shook her head to clear it, to prove to herself the bells were not ringing. But the harsh clanging kept on. Then suddenly it ceased.

"Dat's it—the fo'th time! Lawd God!"

"Cora! Calm yourself. A levee has broken somewhere. But we're on the second floor."

"No'm, 'tain't no lebee, 'cause they ain't no water in de street. Jest folks."

Faustine looked down at the milling crowd in the street and turned away, her face pale. "Where is Mr. Fisher, Cora?"

"He left 'bout a hour ago."

They barred the door and waited. As the morning advanced, the crowds grew larger and citizen companies and Confederate troops tramped the streets. Groups huddled about men of the Louisiana State Navy and listened, while roving squads of the Foreign Legion exhorted all citizens to join their companies in defense of the city. But a starkly practical man almost under Faustine's window asked how mere men could hold back the Yankee horde when the forts had failed to stop them. It was generally believed that New Orleans would suffer the fate of Carthage.

By midafternoon Faustine was desperate. Cora pleaded with her to escape while they could, though Faustine insisted on waiting for Harold. When a pounding on the door caused her to grab the pistol in both hands, she realized that she could no longer pretend for Cora's sake. She almost swooned with relief upon learning that the visitor was Lieutenant McKeever.

Weary, his fine gray uniform water-soaked and dirty, he sat down and told them of the battle down-river and the destruction of the Confederate flotilla. The mighty *Louisiana* had blown up; the river ram *Stonewall Jackson* had been forced into shoal water. There she sank to her topgallant forecastle. The crew of the *Manassas* had swarmed ashore, deserting the ship, and the *Governor Moore* had gone up in flames. The forts had been so weakened by five days of constant mortar fire that they were in no condition to halt the great Union squadron. And now the enemy was steaming in force for New Orleans.

"The impossible has happened," McKeever said with almost pensive incredulity.

Faustine stared at him, wondering behind her apprehensive expression how men versed in military affairs could be guilty of such an error in judgment. It was almost a betrayal.

"We've been trying to save the *Mississippi*, trying to lighten her so we can tow her upstream."

He rose, sat down again, and said, "General Mansfield Lovell is seizing all available steamers. He has ordered our shipyards burned as well as all craft he won't need, and the order has been given to burn all the cotton on the levee. There must be fifteen or twenty thousand bales."

After gathering up a few of his belongings, he walked to the door and stood in troubled thought. "I'm off, ma'am. Where, I don't know, but the Navy needs her men more than ever now. Thanks for your company last night. You helped us more than you'll ever know."

Then he was gone.

Faustine barred the door again and stood with her back to it for long minutes. From the street the noise and frantic cries of the increasing mob rang in her ears. A gun went off, and another. Faustine knew she was trapped. Her head sank to her chest and her eyes closed in prayer. She wanted to run, run, run. She wanted her baby.

Slowly she pulled herself together.

Harold arrived at dusk. His first remark was, "Well, I got my money, though I discounted the sum in order to get United States greenbacks."

Faustine despised him then and said as much before ordering him to find a way of getting them to Rigolets Pass. He departed, only to return hours later with the news that the city had gone mad. Not a horse or carriage could be found.

The horrible nightmare began with the fires. From her window Faustine saw the flames licking up from the levee. All that night the red glow lit up the streets and buildings. Toward morning the crowds thinned and Faustine left the apartment in search of a carriage or wagon.

As she made her way toward the St. Charles Hotel, a drunken sailor accosted her. Ahead, a group of men were rolling a barrel down the street. One turned and fired into a pursuing body of men and ragged, screaming women. Faustine saw a woman clutch at her stomach and sink slowly to the cobblestones. Then someone or many smashed the barrel open and flooded the gutter with molasses.

Everywhere she turned there were people shouting, "Betrayed! Betrayed!" And men with cases of meat or other provisions snarled like rats and mouthed vile oaths to those who came near them.

Caught up in a crowd rushing toward the levee, Faustine ran with them. The alternative was death by trampling. When they seized a dray, she broke from them. An overturned wagon offered shelter and she hid, praying for escape even as she stared in horror at the oily river under the glare of yellow flames. It stretched for miles and miles. The water licked at the edge of the levee, and out in the swelling stream men were putting the torch to ships. Up soared one blaze, then another. Sounds came and fell away. A fusillade of shots was followed by high-pitched screams and the frenzied howls of a surging mob.

Something struck with a smash of glass near her head. The fumes of rotten liquor assailed her nostrils and she turned her head away from the sickening smell. The reek of burning cotton was bad enough. Then two burly flatboatmen were searching the wagon.

"Wal, God help me, Joe, a female! Grab her, boy!"

"Hell with her, Pa. We need whisky and grub. 'Sides, Ma catch ye fiddlin' round, she gut you like a shoat."

The older one chased after Faustine and caught her just as a band of spoilers raised a cry of, "Whisky warehouse!" For a moment the foul-smelling boatman seemed undecided. Then, tired of her continued screams and clawing nails, he clapped a hand over her mouth, pinched a nipple of her breast again, and said, "Hell, gal, Joe's right. Whisky's mo' impo'tant."

Faustine ran, stumbled, fell, got to her feet again and kept on. Wild with terror, she dodged a party of Negroes laden with hams and sacks. Cries of animal delight sounded all about her as the plunderers discovered cases of canned fruits and meats, barrels of potatoes, hominy, and beans. "Looky hyar, a firkin o' butter!" was answered by a harridan. "Shet yore damn fool mouth! Want it took from ye?"

Faustine threw herself into the arms of an officer of the Foreign Legion, who stood with smoking gun in hand. "Oh, God in heaven, save me!" she cried.

The bleak dawn was breaking over smoky New Orleans when the officer led her into the lobby of the St. Charles Hotel. There she remained, trembling, on her feet when she wanted to fall, amid hundreds of others like herself. With full daylight, she ventured out again, this time toward the apartment on Common Street.

Faustine was not prepared for what met her eyes a half block up the street. A crowd gathered about a lamppost was staring up in silence at a figure dangling by a rope. Fixed to the man's coat was a crudely lettered sign reading: YANKEE.

Shuddering, she turned her glance away from the horrible sight. Then suddenly she jerked her head back and stared in frozen horror at the purple face of the victim.

A soldier on horse hacked the rope in two just as she sank to the pavement with a piercing scream: "Harold!"

Everything seemed vague and distant after that. She remembered spitting fiery whisky and finding herself sitting on the sidewalk.

Then dazed, uncaring, she was walking, walking, surrounded by what seemed thousands of men, women, and children, all staring down-river. The sky was dark and heavy. Nobody seemed interested in the threatening rainstorm.

"Can you see the Yankee ships yet?" someone asked. "It's past noon now. Reckon they're coming?"

A cannonading was the answer, and a man with tears running down his cheeks said the Yankees were engaging the last defense batteries at Camp Chalmette, where Andrew Jackson had defeated the British in 1815.

"I see them now!" The cry rippled through the mass of people and fell away, and Faustine saw the black, naked masts of the Union squadron. They were creeping around the big bend of Slaughterhouse Point. The cannonading had ceased. They came on, bleak, grim, silent, their yards heavy with bluecoats. Closer, closer, until the Stars and Stripes of the terrible conqueror were sharply etched against the threatening sky.

A cry, a cheer, went up: "The *Mississippi!*"

It was followed by howls of rage, for the unfinished *Mississippi,* the sole Confederate hope, was floating down to meet the invader in a mass of flames.

Then the enemy was close to the crowd that still howled its defiance. A silent enemy, except for the splash of anchors, its black guns trained on the defeated people of New Orleans, who cried as in one voice, "Hurrah for Jeff Davis!"

Faustine breathed a heavy sigh and stared indifferently up at the flag of Louisiana standing straight in the breeze above the city hall. Its red, white, and blue stripes, union of red with a single yellow star still flew. Proudly. Suddenly it wilted under the downpour of rain and hung there drenched, limp.

The rain fell in torrents. It didn't matter to Faustine. Nothing mattered.

A man behind her said, "Reminds me of the speech of old Umbrella Jim, king of the shell gamblers.

> *"Select your shell; the one you choose;*
> *If right, you win; if not, you lose."*

Then the man took Faustine by the arm. She looked up at him without any change of expression for a second or two. Then she seemed to go limp before giving in to tears of relief.

"Let's get out of here," Sherrod said. "The humor of this mob is likely to provoke cannon fire."

"Just take me home," she begged. "Take me home."

## 23.     Escape of the *290*.

1

WITH THE APPROACH OF EVENING IN LATE JULY OF 1862, Adam Cutler, in civilian dress, departed from the shipyard of the Messrs. Laird in Birkenhead and crossed the Mersey River to Liverpool. As was his habit, he went directly to Abercromby Square, secured a copy of the London *Times*, and entered a restaurant which he had patronized for several months.

Mr. Trimble, the proprietor, greeted him with, "A fine evening it is, Mr. Sheridan." In subdued tones he said, "Mr. Bulloch left a message, sor. Says he, ' 'Tis a matter of extreme urgency, so advise Mr. Sheridan to be at the offices of Fraser, Trenholm & Company at eight sharp.' "

Adam glanced at his watch, asked for ale and lamb, and moved to his favorite corner table. He glanced at *The Times*, then put it aside and gave serious thought to Captain Bulloch's message. It concerned the *290*, of course, for she was in peril. A deplorable situation, that. The vessel had recently leaped out of total obscurity into international limelight.

Actually, Adam admitted reflectively, the present trouble stemmed from the *Sumter's* success. Before the Union warships *Kearsarge* and *Tuscarora* bottled up the *Sumter* at Gibraltar in the spring, her boilers crippled almost beyond repair, she had captured seventeen enemy merchant ships and had so alarmed Yankee shippers that Northern carrying trade fell off noticeably. Furthermore, the enemy had kept five of his best ships-of-war engaged in chasing her for more than six months. And now the *Sumter* no longer posed a threat.

However, the Lincoln government was naturally anxious and determined to do all in its power to prevent another *Sumter* from preying on its commerce. In keeping with this policy, Mr. Seward, the United States Secretary of State, had instructed Mr. Charles Francis Adams, his astute Minister to the Court of St. James's, to double his efforts in uncovering information pertaining to any vessels being clandestinely built for the Confederate States by English shipyards.

As everyone connected with the naval affairs of the South could testify, Mr. Adams lost no time in putting a host of undercover agents to work. Hence Lieutenant Cutler of Confederate States Navy became Mr. Sheridan, civilian.

Adam accepted the ale and drank deep. Smacking his lips, he thought of the vessel they had slipped past the Federal spies. The *Oreto* left England unarmed, unmanned, as prescribed by the Queen's neutrality law, and was delivered to the intrepid Captain James Maffitt, C.S.N., to be commissioned the *Florida,* a commerce destroyer. But once she had flown, Mr. Seward in Washington raised such a cry that the *Oreto* was hailed into court in Nassau for an alleged breach of the British Foreign Enlistment Act.

Adam was versed in every detail of the neutrality law. He realized also that the Queen's officers stood ready to enforce the law. But of greater moment was American Minister Adams's insistence on official attention to any infraction of the law that might favor the Confederacy. His persistent efforts had been rewarded, in part, when his agents found reason to doubt the good intentions of the Messrs. Laird regarding the 290th ship to be built in their yards. So . . .

Claiming the *Oreto* as just cause for a belligerent attitude toward England, the United States was, through Mr. Adams, bringing such pressure to bear regarding the 290 that in London, Foreign Secretary Lord John Russell interpreted the American demands as a serious threat of war. Thoroughly intimidated, Lord Russell was advocating caution.

Recalling how England had swallowed her pride in the *Trent-San Jacinto* affair, Adam and all Southerners in England were wondering if caution in this instance would result in the detention of the 290.

Mr. Trimble appeared with cold lamb and asked if Mr. Sheridan wished for more ale.

"Yes," Adam replied absently. To himself Adam said, "If only 'Beeswax' Semmes would hurry to Liverpool with his officers."

After Semmes was forced to abandon the *Sumter* at Gibraltar, he spent a month in England before sailing for home by way of Nassau.

There he received a letter from Mr. Mallory instructing him to return to England and assume command of the 290, which was to be commissioned the *Alabama*.

A proud name for a fine ship, Adam mused. But would she ever leave the Mersey for her christening on the open sea?

A strong sense of urgency assailed Adam as he thought of the blockaded South's great need for the *Alabama*. The Northern fleets under Farragut and Porter had literally cut the South in half. Only Vicksburg and Port Hudson held out on the Mississippi. And never had he been more shocked or depressed than on the day he learned of the fall of New Orleans. He would have gambled all he owned that the Federal squadron could not gain past Forts Jackson and St. Philip.

Faustine's account of the tragedy of New Orleans had upset him greatly because of her part in it. Although he refused to censure her, since his family had sanctioned her trip, he could not put down a feeling of jealousy and resentment every time he thought of his wife in the company of notorious Captain Sherrod. On the other hand, he was forced to agree with Faustine, however grudgingly he did so. Parts of her letter flashed through his mind:

Cora has simply disappeared, Adam darling, and I feel responsible. But on that horrible day I was almost out of my mind. We owe Captain Sherrod a debt of gratitude beyond our ability to pay, for had he not arrived when he did there is no telling what might have happened to me. But he hired a dray for $20. and took me to Rigolets Pass, where he found the *Gulf Wind* in flames. He watched his gallant schooner settle with no outward sign of regret, just a shrug and a statement about her usefulness having come to an end long before she went the way of all ships. He then hired a fisherman to take us out to the Federal gunboat *Water Witch* and demanded passage to the entrance of Mobile Bay in return for the destruction of his vessel. He got it, much to the surprise of the Yankee crew and myself. He is leaving for England to purchase a steamer to run the blockade. Please assist him there if you are given the opportunity, for he saved me for you and our darling little Joseph Adam. . . .

Joseph Adam. He would be close to five months old now. Just what did a baby look like at that age; had he teeth; could he walk? Adam was missing the answers to his questions, though he felt again that strong desire to see his son. Only a sense of patriotic duty had kept him in Liverpool. Only that restrained him now.

His appetite gone, Adam put down his fork and stared at the

plate, at Bay Oaks in his lonely mind's eye. A wife and son were far away, no matter how deep in the heart one carried them. Only war and the machinations of war were in reality close.

Slowly he got to his feet and walked out of the place.

2

Entering the house of Fraser, Trenholm & Company, Adam admitted to the feeling of awe and respect which the very name of the firm evoked in Southerners. At the beginning of the war Mr. Caleb Huse, general purchasing agent for the Confederacy in England, had approached the firm regarding supplies for the South. Despite the limited finances and unestablished credit of the new republic, as well as its lack of recognition by European powers, who admitted only a *de facto* government, Fraser, Trenholm & Company had responded by sending ships laden with arms and supplies through the ports of Nassau, the Bahamas, and St. George's, Bermuda. The Liverpool firm was virtually the bank and supply house of the Confederate States, which resorted to making regular remittances in cotton instead of cash after President Davis abandoned his policy of "cotton-starving" Britain into the conflict.

Awaiting Adam were: Mr. Prioleau, member of the firm; Mr. Laird, junior partner of Lairds; Captain James D. Bulloch, Adam's superior and Confederate Secretary of Navy Mallory's confidential emissary abroad, by whose genius and untiring efforts the *Oreto* and 290 had been contracted for and built; Captain Matthew Butcher, of the Royal Naval Reserve and formerly of the Cunarder *Kamac*.

As Adam took a chair, Mr. Laird read a message from his brother, John Laird, Member of Parliament, in which he stated that:

At the time the 290 was contracted for by Mr. Bulloch, no question had been raised in England regarding the right of a neutral to build and/or sell ships to a belligerent; that despite the fact that the existing laws of nations did not prohibit such, the Government of the United States continued to insist that English shipyards should not be allowed to supply the Confederate States, with even unarmed ships; that while he felt that everything had been open and aboveboard in the building of the 290, and government inspectors and customs officers had verified this, it remained a fact that the Northern states had been and were bullying the British to the point that the 290 would be detained.

Mr. Laird raised his glance and concluded with, " 'Unless,' my brother states, 'something drastic is done at once.' "

A grave silence fell over the group. Bulloch got up, walked to a window, striking his fist against a palm in absent manner. "Thanks to Messrs. Laird, Fraser & Trenholm, and Lieutenant Cutler, the batteries, various arms, ammunition, and stores are ready to precede the 290 aboard the *Agrippina* to Terceira in the Azores, and the *Bahama*, also loaded, awaits Captain Semmes and his officers."

Standing with hands rammed into trousers pockets, Adam intercepted the exchange of glances between Messrs. Laird and Prioleau. He knew these men, realized that the former had an investment upwards of two hundred thousand dollars in the 290, that the latter was carrying the South to the tune of several millions. He knew also that their present anxiety did not emanate from fear of monetary losses, or from any "purely British reasons" as the Yankees charged, referring to England's secret pleasure and profit every time an American merchant vessel fell prey to a "Rebel pirate."

But they were withholding something. Captain Bulloch saw as much, and glanced from the shipbuilder to the letter in his hand.

"All right, Mr. Laird," he said, "you can lay the cards on the table."

"Very well," said the very proper Englishman, stroking his chin with a forefinger. He eyed Captain Bulloch sharply. "My brother goes on to advise that if the 290 is not in the Irish Sea under a British flag and a British captain by this time tomorrow she will be tied up in court indefinitely."

Adam stared at him and slumped into a chair. "Impossible," he said. "Under the present political fire she would not be allowed to clear for the sea. And a British captain—who?"

As Bulloch smiled wisely, Mr. Laird narrowed his gaze on him. "Does this account for the presence of our friend Captain Butcher?"

"It does, sir," Bulloch replied. "As we realize, all of us, once the 290 reaches the sea, the command is a matter of concern. The master in the stream is an absolute monarch. And I have considered how large the Yankee reward might be for the betrayal of our vessel. Therefore, I sought first a soul of honor, then a captain. I am pleased to say I have found both in Captain Butcher."

As the English seaman's face reddened under the compliment, Bulloch said, "But beyond that it's up to all of us to discover some ruse by which we can put the 290 to sea without delay."

"Ruse?" Adam cocked an eyebrow at him. "At least we're beginning to think in the right direction."

As Prioleau passed out panatelas and produced brandy, Bulloch said, "So far, so good. Captain Butcher will command our vessel on her maiden voyage to the Azores."

Adam smiled and trained his black eyes on his superior. "Maiden voyage," he scoffed amiably. "The 290 will be lucky if she so much as splits a wave in a trial run."

"Trial run!" Bulloch exclaimed.

Every man present started, including Adam. Bulloch smiled, Prioleau's heavy brows drew together, Laird leaned forward, tense with discovery, and Butcher almost leaped to his feet. But all were eying Adam curiously, for he had hit on an idea. Though the 290 had been launched in May, she had not put out of the Mersey on her trial run.

"God bless you, Adam!" Bulloch cried.

For several hours they made plans. Then they shook hands around and raised glasses to the success of the 290's trial run next day.

3

Adam arrived at the Birkenhead yard as the summer sun threw its first rays across the wide Mersey. Pausing with eyes squinted nearly shut, he stared back at Liverpool for a time before making his way toward the ship he had helped build.

She sat the water proudly, about a thousand tons' burden. She measured 235 feet over all, beam 32 feet, depth 20 feet. Barkentine-rigged, her lower masts were long and fashioned of the finest yellow pine. Looking at her from a distance, he noted with pride how magnificently sparred she was, how gracefully she floated. Everything about her was new and modern. Unlike the *Sumter*, the 290 had been built to fulfill her purpose, and the Lairds had done their job well. Her rigging was of top-grade Swedish iron wire. No hemp to constantly tighten at sea. In a gale her strings would play a tune; "Dixie," Adam hoped, over the seven seas.

She gleamed like a thing alive and fresh in the morning light, and beneath her handsome exterior two powerful engines awaited only steam in the boilers. Nor would her two-bladed screw ever become a drag on her sail power, for it was so designed that it could be triced up to the propeller well when a fair wind cried, "Use me, Mr. Rebel. Spread your acres of sail and save your coal."

Casting an admiring glance at her long bowsprit, Adam approached her with an eye to her armament. She would carry six 32-pounders in broadside and two pivot guns; would ship before the mast one hundred and twenty men, and one fifth as many officers.

Touching her hull timber, he thought now, as in the early spring, that the lightness of her scantling was her one weakness, in that she would be vulnerable to a shot below the water line. However, she was supposed to chase merchantmen, not engage Yankee cruisers.

Boarding her, he gazed across at Liverpool again. The city was coming alive. The Mersey was floating barges, skiffs, and steamers now. The customs boat was pointing her nose toward Birkenhead.

Frowning, Adam wondered if the order had come through to detain the 290. Perhaps the customs craft put across this early every morning. He was suddenly suspicious of every boat that flew an official banner. Such a feeling left him impatient of further delay.

Workers were arriving at the yards, among them Bald Peters, the finest fitter in the business. Seeing Adam on deck, he paused, worked his large mouth into a grin, and said, " 'Ow goes it, Mr. Sheridan? 'Ave ye lost yer best friend or be ye thinkin' o' departin' this 'ere fine vessel?" Seriously he said, "Hi 'ear she's in trouble. Eh, wot?"

"She is. Charged with being a Rebel cruiser in disguise."

"Well, spit in me fyce! 'Tis a bloody, dirty-livered aipe who'd call this merchant lydy a cruiser." His grin reappeared. " 'Twixt us, sor, hi'll guarantee the foc's'le to support 'er for'd pivot."

Adam was in a better humor when Mr. Laird and Captain Butcher arrived.

Within the hour the English crew had acquainted themselves with the 290's decks, rigging, and engines. A wisp of smoke lifted from the single funnel amidships and, caught by the wind, jerked straight alee. The chief mate glanced from the smoke streamer to the lower main yard. "The main course," he said, "will foul the smokestack, so we'll keep her set flying." Turning aft, he smiled at Adam. "But she's got a bloomin' fine teakettle below."

A spic-and-span tugboat churned the water alongside the ship, and Captain Butcher ordered deck chairs heaved aboard and placed on the quarter-deck. Then he gave instructions to the stewards regarding the chilling of two cases of champagne, which were hoisted aboard in a most gentle manner. Striped awnings soon shaded the afterdeck, and additional seats were set up for the band, which would go along to furnish entertainment.

The engineers banked their fires lest the smoke annoy the visitors soon to board the ship. When at last a white steam launch with Laird on the nameplate approached with the ladies, only heat waves were visible atop the funnel.

Mr. Prioleau introduced his wife and daughter as well as executives of his firm, their wives, and several young ladies. Mrs. Laird's guests included members of her set, a baronet and, perhaps the most attractive young woman Adam had met in England, a Miss Cornelia Earle of Barrow-in-Furness. Her bright smile slowly departed as she studied Adam with deep, inquisitive eyes. Twice within the next hour he found her attention full upon him.

As the uniformed band arrived and placed their instruments abaft the mainmast, Mr. Laird called Adam and Captain Butcher aside. His expression was grave and tensely alert as he advised of the latest developments in London.

The evidence against the 290 placed by the American Minister Adams in the hands of the Queen's advocate had caused officers of the Crown to render an opinion that the vessel was undoubtedly intended for warlike use against the United States. They recommended that she be seized at once.

Adam felt the blood draining from his face. The order to detain the vessel could be expected at any moment now, and their pilot was not due for another thirty minutes.

Every tick of Adam's watch seemed to prolong the suspenseful agony of waiting. He paced the deck forward under pretext of checking this or that. Pondering his old-womanish fears, which were something new in his calm life, he excused himself on the reasonable grounds that the South stood in peril of losing her greatest potential naval asset.

The pilot's appearance did nothing to appease his anxiety, for in his company were the chief customs officer and two government men Adam had never seen before. There followed a thorough inspection of the vessel from stem to stern. Then the Crown's men stood with Laird, Butcher, and Adam at the port gangway, where they darted puzzled glances at the ladies in fine dress and the colorful uniforms of the bandsmen. Curious, they were told that the ship was to make her trial run up the Mersey with the ladies and the band aboard; that once in the Irish Sea, they would swing her a few times under steam and sail before returning.

Then Mrs. Laird was addressing her husband with a question: Would they arrive back in Liverpool in time for tea?

The Crown officers spoke of orders expected within the hour, pondered aloud the ship's company, and said in conclusion they had no authority to interfere with a trial run. Another look at the pretty ladies who were to go along seemed to assure them of the ship's return. They said as much, then took their leave.

The tug snorted signals to declare her right to the road, tightened the hawser, and churned forward. The first motion of the *290* was to Adam the answer to a prayer. She shuddered, eased to starboard out of the slip and into the Mersey for the open sea.

As the English colors lifted to the breeze and broke wild and free in the wind, the band began to play "God Save the Queen."

The gentle wind blew straight across the water, ruffling up whitetopped wavelets on the broad Irish Sea even as it played havoc with the full skirts on deck. Miss Earle seemed unaware that her dress was flattened against her long-limbed figure. Her full red mouth was parted, revealing even white teeth, and her eyes were fixed admiringly on Mr. Sheridan, who, on his sea legs, was handing her a glass of champagne.

"Thank you, sir." She smiled, touched her lips to the glass. "This ship means very much to you, doesn't it?" As he made a light shrug, she dropped a hand to his. "Why?" she asked.

Her touch quickened his pulse, causing him a sense of guilt. He had been a long time away from home and Faustine.

"I'll tell you when we pass the marine league," he said, raising his glass. "Until then, my fair lady, let's talk about you."

Mrs. Laird's pleasant voice lifted with, "Trial voyages are such fun." Then she said, "Cornelia, you've completely monopolized Mr. Sheridan. Rosamond would like to talk to him about her brother in New Orleans."

Bowing, Adam left Cornelia to the baronet and sat out a quarter hour of desultory conversation, during which the mouth of the Mersey fell farther astern, he observed, and the steady eyes of Cornelia seemed to dwell only on him. Ahead, the tug was casting loose, and Captain Butcher's able crew were setting sails to the wind. The *290* surged forward on her own for the first time.

It was her virgin run, her wedding with the deep stream and the sea wind. There was, Adam reflected, a strong kinship between a lovely woman and a sailing ship, for both, one and the other, radiated an ineffable joy that was born of and sustained by beauty and grace and challenge.

His glance was drawn to Cornelia Earle.

Captain Butcher ordered the bell eight. It was high noon. He accepted champagne, clicked his heels together, and raised his glass.

"With the marine league one mile astern, ladies and gentlemen, I propose a toast to Lieutenant Adam Sheridan Cutler of the Confederate States Navy."

Amid the merriment on her decks, the *290* ran on, taking her swings, her tacks aboard, like the thoroughbred she was. After an elaborate lunch was served, she took her wind over the port quarter and ran under steam. Mr. Laird asked for full speed ahead, and called for a cheer when the *290* logged above eleven knots.

As the English were in sympathy with the South, Adam found Lieutenant Cutler, C.S.N., exceedingly popular. Besieged with questions, he dodged the slavery issue in favor of hunting and hounds and tales of Bay Oaks. Then he was telling them about the new arithmetic book in the South.

"Problems like this," he said. "If one Confederate soldier can whip seven Yankees, how many soldiers would it require to whip forty-nine Yankees?"

The laugh that followed ended with curious glances when Captain Butcher slowed the ship and hoisted a signal. As the tugboat aft steamed up and slid in for the gangway, a lady was heard to say, "What on earth is Mr. Laird up to?" The wife of the shipbuilder was no exception. She asked why the tug had followed them to sea. With Laird's reply, she and her guests, the members of the band, even Butcher's crew, showed genuine surprise.

"The tug will return us to Liverpool."

Slowly it began to dawn on them that they had had a hand in as clever a ruse as one could ask for and relish. Indeed, for while the tug would steam for the Mersey, the *290* would run to sea and thereby escape detention.

As smiles blossomed in full appreciation of the joke played on the American Minister Adams, Captain Butcher and Mr. Laird gave Adam full credit for saving the ship for the Confederacy.

Cornelia Earle seemed to convey the sentiments and admiration of all aboard when she took Adam's hand in hers and said, "You're simply wonderful, sir!"

She studied him a moment, searching deep behind his eyes, and he felt in her look a serious longing and devotion for something she seemed to find in him. Then she drew his face down to hers and kissed him full on the mouth.

"I'll never forget you, Lieutenant Adam. May God bless you."

As the tug pulled away, the band struck up "Dixie's Land." The strains floated across the water until they grew faint.

> *In Dixie's land I'll take my stand,*
> *To live and die in Dixie . . .*

How appropriate, thought Adam. The English people had built, honored, and helped save the future cruiser *Alabama*. They could justly sing the stirring air of the South.

Adam watched the tug fall away over the port quarter as the *290* under sail and steam pointed her jib boom down for the distant Azores.

## 24.    *Aide Toi, et Dieu T'Aidera*

ADAM mopped sweat from face, neck, and bare chest and gazed tiredly over the rail at the foul-smelling town of Porto Praya basking in the hot August sun.

"Damn this waiting!" he mumbled under a two-week-old beard before shifting his glance toward the storeship *Agrippina*, anchored alongside. "Damn Captain McQueen's motley crew." He was about to extend his imprecations to the *290's* decks, where guns, gun carriages, barrels of salt beef and pork, and the assorted confusion of paymaster's, gunner's and boatswain's stores reminded him of a hurrah's nest. But just then Captain Butcher, looking like anything other than an officer of the Royal Naval Reserve, cried a warning.

Adam turned his eyes to the east and stared at a vessel opening the harbor. She was inbound and she could be a Union cruiser. In fact, both he and Captain Butcher thought she was and were crying orders to the crew, who for once jumped handsomely to cover the guns and carriages with tarpaulins. Adam knew that the Portuguese would offer little resistance to the demands of the haughty Federals. So if she turned out to be the enemy in pursuit of the flown *290*, the game was up.

The ship came on with British colors whipping forward, bows dipping and rising, as some sea was on and the wind was freshening. With spyglass up, Captain Butcher laughed out of sheer relief.

"The *Bahama*, Captain Tessier!" He added, "And the man with the spikes for mustaches must be your 'Beeswax' Semmes."

Presently the voice of Semmes came on the wind. "Follow us to the lee shelter in Angra Bay!"

A few hours later Captain Semmes and Lieutenant Kell stepped aboard the future *Alabama* for the first time. Both greeted Captain Butcher.

Said Semmes, "I was told that Lieutenant Cutler sailed here."

"Aye, sir." The Englishman laughed. "The man is hiding behind that coal-black beard over there."

"By all that's holy!" Semmes exclaimed, stepping forward with outstretched hand. "Mr. Cutler, I suppose you'll refuse to depart once this ship is put in order."

"Correct, sir," Adam replied, grasping the other's hand.

Turning to the group of officers who had boarded the ship on his heels, Semmes said proudly, "I've told you of Lieutenant Cutler, gentlemen. Well, here he is; at a disadvantage, of course. But in uniform he's apt to outshine any of you. Am I not right, Mr. Kell?"

Tall, auburn-bearded Kell grinned mischievously and replied in his best Georgian voice, "I am sure the pretty doñas of Cienfuegos will vouch for that, sir."

Adam's eyes twinkled with the memory of all his silence regarding events in the Cuban port had evoked in the wardroom. For days they had ribbed him about pink-scented sheets and Castilian beauties. Thank heavens they didn't know that he had walked out on a lusting doña.

Adam was introduced to Lieutenant Arthur Sinclair, of an old naval family in Virginia, Lieutenant John Low, of the Royal Naval Reserve, Midshipman Maffitt, son of Captain Maffitt of the Old Navy and at present in command of the *Florida*, and Acting Master Bulloch, brother of Captain James D. Bulloch.

Adam greeted his friends from the *Sumter*, Lieutenant Armstrong, promoted to Chapman's place when the latter missed Semmes at Nassau, and former midshipman Joseph Wilson, now third lieutenant, in Stribling's place.

"Captain Maffitt took Mr. Stribling away from me," Semmes declared.

"Where's Lieutenant Evans?" Adam inquired, only to learn that he, as Chapman, had failed to reach Nassau in time to sail with Semmes.

Surgeon Galt, First Lieutenant Howell of Marines, and bluff and hearty Miles J. Freeman, engineer, all of the *Sumter,* greeted Adam.

Freeman said, "Mr. Cutler burned the first damn Yankee and I steamed him to her."

"Boilers foaming," Adam jested.

"No such thing! That was when we showed the *Brooklyn* our heels."

Staring at the uninviting disorder of decks, Semmes drew his brows together. He twirled a mustache tip and said, "Well, gentlemen, do we splice the main brace or fall to work?"

It was Adam who ventured a reply. "Sir, I'm prepared for just such an emergency. There is chilled champagne below awaiting the splice."

In that moment Lieutenant Cutler was undoubtedly the most popular man aboard.

The work of transshipment of guns and stores was renewed that afternoon, with the crews of all three ships straining under the weight of pivot guns, fitting side and train tackles to the broadside guns, stowing the shells and magazine lockers, the sailroom, putting down the circles for the pivot guns, and answering the call to myriad other duties as well. Boatswain, gunner, engineer, sailor, marine, midshipman, and lieutenant fell to with a desire to complete the gigantic task. Far into the night the work went on.

Next day it began anew, and if the Confederate officers needed anything to spur their activities, they had only to remember the words of Captain Semmes during the brief respite for refreshments the afternoon before.

"Gentlemen, you will do well to remember as you strive to bring order out of chaos here that we have no crew whatever to back up our authority should we be discovered by the enemy. Captains Butcher, McQueen, and Tessier shipped British subjects for their crews for a voyage from Liverpool to the Azores."

The effect of Semmes's statement was sobering. They had a ship, but no crew. It was something to think about.

Day after day they kept after it, steaming offshore beyond the marine league by day, hauling under the lee of land for night anchorage. With decks cleared, her armament secured, battery and brasswork gleaming in the late August sun, yards squared, with rigging hauled taut, the 290 was ready to be commissioned. She was ready for sea, with one exception—

Once placed in the service of the Confederacy, she would be minus a crew to sail her.

On Sunday morning, the day of August 24, 1862, the three vessels put out in a sea made to order for the occasion and sailed to an offing beyond the marine league before transferring all but the working crew of the supply ships to the 290.

As the sailors from the streets of Liverpool boarded the ship, their eyes widened in genuine surprise and admiration. The captain and officers of the 290 were dressed in fine gray uniforms bedecked with gold braid and gleaming dress swords. To further impress the Liverpool Jacks, the boatswain mustered the men aft, and Semmes mounted a gun carriage and read his commission from the President of the Confederate States. Next he read the order of the Secretary of the Navy, directing him to assume command of this ship.

This done, the flag and pennant of the Confederacy were thrown to the wind at the peak and mainmast head. A gun boomed from the deck and a quartermaster hauled down the English colors.

Amid the cheers, the *Bahama* fired a gun in salute and the band struck up "Dixie." With the first hush in the wake of the excitement, Semmes said:

"Gentlemen, the 290 now becomes the Confederate States ship-of-war *Alabama*."

The gaping sailors in ill-assorted sea toggery stared from this strange new flag to a handful of men in the strangest and dressiest uniforms ever to parade a deck. By comparison, Her British Majesty's Navy's blue at the moment seemed dull and drab.

Semmes was astute enough to grasp the moment for all it was worth. The ceremony, his own bearing commanded full attention as he thanked the sailors of Britain for their sense of justice with a brief account of the war between oppressor and oppressed. They would, he said, be fighting for a just cause if they enlisted for a cruise of excitement and adventure, with shore liberty on proper occasion. Gradually he built up to the items most likely to appeal to these "noble and generous sailors."

They would receive, he told them, double the wages paid by the British, and in gold. In addition, one half the value of vessels destroyed or bonded as prize money. Furthermore, they were assured of their grog twice a day, the finest rations on the high seas, and fair treatment

On the other hand—"I give you to understand that the *Alabama* is neither privateer nor irresponsible nondescript created to roam the seas for the purpose of plunder without discipline or order, but a *bona fide* Confederate man-of-war commissioned by the President and subject to the rules and regulations of the Confederate Congress. And to disobey these rules will subject you to certain and perhaps severe punishment."

The speech ended with a brief account of the hardships of such a cruise and the mention of a possible rope collar slung from a yard-arm in event of their capture.

Adam smiled. Semmes had spiced his bid with enough of the bitter to make the sweet sweeter, but had he talked a crew aboard the *Alabama?*

Then the boatswain piped down and the sailors were free to discuss the matter among themselves. The paymaster appeared with his shipping list and took a position amidships to await the decision of the sailors to sign on or depart.

Tension mounted aft as Semmes and officers waited. Adam considered the utter uselessness of a ship and gleaming battery without men to operate them. Below and forward of him were ninety-five English sailors, all green, all in need of soap. On these men the hopes of the Confederacy at sea rested at the moment. An incredulous situation, he admitted, a power's dependence on a handful of unkempt seamen. But this was war, and war brought about strange things.

Adam turned to young Maffitt and suggested a stroll forward. The twinkle in his eye was not lost on the midshipman, who soon caught on to the game afoot. As though unaware of the groups of English sailors on all sides, Adam walked slowly to the bows and back, all the while praising the quality of grog aboard ship.

Young Maffitt felt like a dummy, though a useful one when a listening sailor wet his lips in anticipation of grog twice daily.

The sailor moved toward the capstan. A moment later he was signing the articles. Others followed. A line was forming now.

The heavy sighs of relief all about Adam were in reality cheers suppressed. However, the suspense, though lessened, remained. The question now was: How many will sign; half a crew; all; just how many?

In the final count all but ten men had cast their lot with the Confederacy. There were eighty-five less Englishmen in the world when the signing was done.

Semmes looked tired but happy.

"Well, gentlemen," he said, the fire of a zealot flashing across his gray eyes, "the *Alabama* is ready to sail the seas, to destroy or court her own destruction. Whatever her destiny, may she win the admiration of the world."

So saying, he led his officers to the *Alabama's* wheel and read the motto inscribed in French thereon:

Help yourself, and God will help you.

Toward midnight the *Bahama* departed, and the *Alabama* pointed her head to the northeast under easy fore-and-aft sails. Where she was going only Semmes knew, though Adam, as the others, suspected strongly that she would hunt the quiet of the ocean in order to train and drill the crew.

Her destination, however, was of small concern to Adam, who had too long been out of uniform and absent from service afloat. A deck felt good under him, a rolling deck, and the splash of water at the bows and under the propeller well sang sweetly a song of the sea. But beyond such things, he felt a sense of having filled his position with dignity and credit. His right here had been earned. He had, in the way Mr. Mallory instructed him, helped build this formidable engine of destruction, had watched her grow rib by rib, plank by plank, had helped arm her. Then he had worked and fretted in an endeavor to keep her identity secret and, failing that, had aided in her escape.

That was of the past, yesterday, gone. As he stood under the bright stars, he felt somehow that the present was but a fleeting stage under him, a deck rising and falling to the scend of the waves, an ever moving bridge impelling him forward with hope and wonder and mystery as he looked ahead. But it was a good moment, the present, a clearinghouse for the mind and the soul.

As for the future, the long, sleek *Alabama* would transport him there. Indeed, she was doing that now, running full into the night, racing to her destiny, and his, on wings over the sea.

## 25.     The Belle of Mobile

1

ON THIS PLEASANT DECEMBER DAY OF 1862, Adria looked inquiringly up from her sewing to her father, who was saying:

"Leland Jarvis, I believe you're still living Stonewall Jackson's triumph at the Second Battle of Manassas."

"Rot!" Jarvis said with gusto. "You always miss the point. I was merely saying that we're always from five to twenty-five thousand men short of what the Federals put into battle, and yet we win. At Manassas, Yankee General Pope had eighty thousand to our fifty-four."

Joseph flicked ashes, wet his lips, and said, "So Lee invaded Maryland, and Stonewall Jackson advanced twenty-five miles north of Washington, went on to take Harper's Ferry on the fourteenth of September, and Lee beat the hell out of McClellan at Antietam on the seventeenth."

Jarvis leaned forward. "And Lee with sixty thousand men against McClellan's eighty-seven thousand. That's what I'm trying to get through your hard skull."

"St. Peter's nightshirt! Can't you see a foot in front of your nose? Why, the goddamn Yankees——"

"Father!" Adria cried indignantly.

Joseph jerked his head around, glowered at her, puffed up a smoke screen, and said in a lowered voice, "The Yankees own the northern part of our state, Leland. And with the enemy that close to your Marengo County plantation, you're still celebrating Second Manassas."

Annabel entered and paused to raise her brows before moving to Adria. "Have they gone back to finish the Seven Days' Battle yet?" She sat down and inspected the dress critically. "Oh, Adria, will you never learn to backstitch? And just look how you've basted the seam."

Adria gave a toss of her head. "Anyhow, I can tell you how many men Lee had when he beat the hell out of McClellan at Antietam. But, look, Mother," she said, glancing despairingly at the work in her lap, "do you think I'd be too terribly conspicuous if I wore the new dress from Havana to the relief bazaar?"

"I most certainly do. Everybody would know the moment you arrived that it was blockade-run. You know the feeling around Mobile."

"Then what shall I wear?"

Annabel studied her a moment thoughtfully. "I've offered twice to make over your rose ball gown."

"No."

"But you haven't worn it since the Christmas ball of 1860. Two years, Adria."

"Just the same—no."

Adria inhaled deeply and looked out the window. Beyond the green live oaks, which were oblivious to the change of seasons, scarlet and yellow leaves bent to the wind off the bay. A squirrel ran across the limb nearest her and hid behind a clump of Spanish moss.

Adria was unaware of color or life or scene. All she saw was her image in the mirror as she wore the rose ball gown for the first time; as, enchanted by its beauty, she met James. In that dress she had fallen in love. And all that had happened since had failed to release her. She still loved James Hillyer.

She was deaf to the conversation about her. Joseph was talking of the terrible drought of 1862, and Jarvis replied that as if a dry year wasn't bad enough, the government had imposed restrictions which no sane planter could approve. By advice and by law, he vowed, plantation life had changed.

"Less and less cotton," Jarvis complained, "and more and more corn, speckle-jack peas, goobers, and chufas. And sweet potatoes. The niggers don't know how to raise such crops. Fact is, Joseph, I've done more field work this year than in all my years put together."

"I know. I know." Joseph glared at the end of his cigar. "Sending all my meat to the Army and up on my Clarke County plantation we're having to make syrup out of watermelon juice, soap and whisky out of chinaberries. We're even mixing dogwood and willow bark with tobacco for the slaves. But we don't know what hard times are. Upstate folks are living on bread and syrup and making buttons out of pine bark and persimmon seeds, dying homespun with bark and leaves, blacking their shoes with soot and lard.

"And you know, Leland, since the conscription act of last April, I've had a dozen distant relatives pop up, each asking for five hundred dollars to buy his way out of military service. Even had one distant cousin to start preaching when I refused him the money."

Jarvis crossed his legs and laughed.

Joseph tossed his cigar into the brass cuspidor. "It's not funny, Leland. Neither are the things that are slowly draining us of our money—taxes, feeding the poor, caring for the droves of refugees from New Orleans, building gunboats and high prices.

"Bacon nine dollars a pound."

"Ten, Joseph," Annabel corrected.

"Ten? And a year ago we were howling because it had jumped from twelve to thirty cents. Tea is up to twenty dollars a pound. Think of it! Why, we could live cheaper at the Battle House, with board still three dollars and a half a week."

"You just look at the worst side, Joseph," Annabel said. "Remember how pleased you were when cotton jumped from ten to seventeen cents a pound last week?"

"For how long was I pleased, ma'am? Ten minutes maybe. Then I found out that two bushels of salt had cost me fifty dollars."

"That Captain Sherrod is to blame!" Jarvis said vehemently.

Adria started at the mention of Sherrod. Instantly James was forgotten, and she cocked her head inquiringly.

Faustine suddenly entered the room. "Did I hear someone speak disparagingly of my benefactor?"

"You did," Joseph said.

Faustine smoothed her full black skirt and sat down. "Adam is asleep at last. What on earth would have given him the colic, Mrs. Cutler?"

Joseph chuckled. "Speculation, scarcity, and depreciation of the Confederate dollar. Besides, aren't you all forgetting his first name is Joseph?"

"Vain, isn't he?" Faustine winked an eye at Jarvis. "Was there any mail today?"

"Erasmus has gone to the landing," Adria replied, studying the scalloped neck of Faustine's dress, admitting in silence that it was rather becoming. Faustine had a pretty neck and bosom, she reflected. And the baby, whom she had nursed herself, had done little damage to her breasts. Now if she ever had a baby she'd be on the lookout for a slavewoman with freshening udders.

Jarvis was saying, "I suppose you've heard about Sherrod's scandalous trade with the Yankees in New Orleans."

"Well, I haven't," Adria said curiously.

Jarvis eyed her, then looked at Joseph. "You don't tell your womenfolks everything, do you?"

"Well, no. Sherrod ships a little cotton for me now and then, and——"

Adria sat up stiffly. "If he's good enough for you to trade with, I suppose we can bear up under the story, Father. Unless it's unfit for women's ears."

"It's not that bad," Jarvis said. "Or it might be worse. You know about Yankee General Butler in New Orleans. Butler the Beast, they call him."

"Who doesn't?" Adria asked, recalling the wave of world-wide indignation Butler's order of last May had aroused. It was called the "Woman Order," since he declared that "hereafter when any female shall, by word, or gesture, or movement, insult or show contempt for any officer or soldier of the United States, she shall be regarded and held liable to be treated as a woman of the town plying her vocation."

"Oh, the way I hate that man is a sin!" Adria declared. "Do you mean that Captain Sherrod is doing business with *him?*"

"I do," said her father. "And furthermore, Mobile is up in arms. They're circulating a petition to be sent to Montgomery and on to President Davis asking that Sherrod be barred entry into any Southern port."

"Did you sign it?" Adria demanded.

"No. No, I didn't. You see—I—well, to begin with, it's common knowledge that Butler made use of his military power to get rich. He closed the gambling houses in New Orleans and let them reopen when they paid a license fee to his brother. From there, he began to take this and that and engage in any kind of trade that was profitable. He didn't overlook cotton."

Faustine leaned toward Adria and whispered, "I heard that after Butler issued the Woman Order, the women of the red-light district resented his putting them on a level with the decent ladies and pasted Butler's pictures on the inside bottom of their tinkle-pots."

Adria's mouth formed an O and her eyes twinkled brightly. "Why, Faustine!" she cried, suppressing a titter.

"And they say the general ordered the red-light district raided and all the pots destroyed."

"How perfectly awful!" Adria gasped.

"Whisper! Whisper!" Annabel scolded. "Shame on you two."

Joseph was saying, "It's no secret that the North's need of our cotton has kept up a steady trade between our blockaded ports and Havana and Matamoros."

Adria looked shocked. "Do you mean to say we're doing business with the Yankees, Father?"

"I do. The North wants cotton and allows a contraband trade, and the Confederate Government can't stop it all. But it's trying to, because if the trade continues Europe will say old king cotton is a weak sister and never will recognize the Confederacy."

"It's all Greek to me," Adria admitted with a toss of her head. "But what has all this to do with Captain Sherrod?"

"Plenty," Jarvis replied. "Back in April our Congress made it unlawful to sell the enemy in possession of any part of the South cotton, tobacco, rice, sugar, molasses, or naval stores. However, our Secretary of War granted licenses in certain instances to allow this trade—in order to secure drugs and medicines which the Federals wouldn't allow to come through the blockade. Our soldiers were dying.

"So Captain Sherrod works himself up quite a trade. I heard that he went from Richmond with his license direct to Beast Butler and made a deal—so many pounds of cotton for one of bacon. The same with salt and other items we needed, including medicines. In this way Butler built up a supply of cotton, which Sherrod helps export to Havana for him. Then Sherrod brings us bacon and salt, and the prices go up and up. Governor Shorter is howling loud about it, but Sherrod says it's legal and, dammit all, it is."

"Why, it's simply awful," Adria said, shaking her head curiously. "But fascinating."

"And they're saying," Joseph continued, "that Sherrod, Butler, and the English houses in Mobile have contracted to export two hundred thousand bales of cotton by way of New Orleans. They expect to make a profit of ten million dollars."

"Ten million?" Faustine said. "But how can Captain Sherrod run past the Federal blockade?"

Joseph laughed at her ignorance of such affairs. "Butler and Farragut give him clearance, that's how."

Adria looked at the mantel, her mind speculating on what Lawrence's investment of two thousand dollars in Sherrod's trade, which Lawrence knew nothing about, would bring her. Covering her secret elation, she said:

"I wonder how long this sort of thing can go on."

Jarvis said, "As long as we're getting medical and army supplies, clothing and blankets in exchange for government cotton, Sherrod can ship private cotton on the side and bring in all the luxuries and fancy goods he desires."

"Except for a rumor," her father added, "which I hope is a fact—the Federal Government is sick of Butler and plans to recall him."

Adria gave him a quick glance. "Really?"

Leland Jarvis rose and walked to the window. "Speak of the devil," he said. "Here comes Sherrod."

2

Sherrod doffed his cap and bowed as elegantly as any planter's son before ordering his huge black servant to bring in "a few trinkets." He appeared not to notice the cool reception accorded him by Messrs. Cutler and Jarvis, though he remained standing as he declared with perfect ease and sincerity that Bay Oaks could claim the distinction of sheltering the prettiest ladies in Alabama.

Then he turned his dancing eyes from Adria's and Faustine's provocative curves to the sullen faces of the men. "I suppose," he said, extending his cigar case, "you've heard the news from Fredericksburg. It was slaughter."

"No." Joseph thawed instantly. Accepting a cigar, he said, "Have a seat, Captain?"

Jarvis's hands gripped the chair. "Our troops or Federals? Hell, man, I've got a boy up there!"

"So you have, sir."

Adria glanced at her mother, who sat as though awaiting the amputation of a limb. As she turned to Faustine, she intercepted the admiring and speculative look her sister-in-law gave the blockade-runner.

"Yes sir, gentlemen, it was a bloody day. General Burnside had, they say, one hundred and fifteen thousand men against Lee's seventy-seven thousand. But Lee had Jackson and Longstreet, and the despair is up North, for Burnside did no better than McClellan, and another great battle went in our favor."

Leland Jarvis was on his feet shouting with joy. Joseph was grinning, ordering the best whisky served the bearer of such good tidings. Sherrod began distributing gifts from abroad, pausing to eye Adria and Faustine as they uttered exclamations of delight.

"I'll love you always for this," Faustine cried, holding up a wide roll of expensive silk.

Adria stood with a European hat in each hand. "You shouldn't have, Captain Sherrod. Such extravagance!"

As Joseph's disapproving frown faded under the fresh memory of a great military triumph, Sherrod, aware of his moment, produced a picture and extended it to Joseph, saying:

"There she is, Mr. Cutler. The fastest steam vessel in the Gulf of Mexico. Four hundred and fifty tons, ten times as long as her beam width, with feathering paddles. I just ran her in from Havana."

Soon all were looking at a picture of the long, rakish side-wheeler and listening to Sherrod. "Her funnel is short and can be lowered level with the deck. Painted lead gray, this vessel can't be spotted by a Federal at three hundred yards. And listen to this—she's equipped to blow off her steam under water."

He added, for effect, Adria thought, "Think of the arms, clothing, quinine, ether, opium, and rhubarb she'll bring to our armies."

Joseph frowned. "And fancy goods at high prices."

"Confederate agents abroad will guarantee that needed supplies are loaded on first," Sherrod replied convincingly.

Leland Jarvis pursed his lips and squinted one eye shut. "It's what she carries out of our ports that makes her ride a profit, eh, Captain?"

"Right. No cotton, no guns or medicine. Now down to cases, gentlemen," Sherrod was saying.

After a brief business discussion, Sherrod said, "I'm open for suggestions regarding a name for my new vessel. At the Battle House, some of the boys wanted to call her *Shoot the Works, Belle of Mobile, Dead of Night,* and so forth."

"I like *Belle of Mobile,*" Faustine said.

Adria agreed.

Joseph said, "Why not *Belle of New Orleans?*"

"Father." Adria tensed.

Sherrod pretended not to have heard. "You know, I've had a name in mind for some time. Funny thing, a ship. She's so much like a woman that you see in her the qualities of certain women. This steamer of mine is no ordinary Ruth or Mary, but a spirited creature. Aye, with a mind of her own."

Erasmus arrived with a letter for Faustine. "From Adam!" she exclaimed, bowing out.

Adria was staring anxiously after Faustine when Sherrod said:

"Miss Adria, I've been wondering if I might have the honor of naming my ship after you."

Adria stared at him with open astonishment.

A silence fell over the room. Joseph's eyes thinned to slits as he fought back impulse with policy. Leland Jarvis stiffened and glared at the seaman. Annabel nodded thoughtfully but withheld judgment.

"Well, Miss Adria?" Sherrod said.

As Adria sat down and gazed quizzically from Sherrod to her father, Annabel said, "Captain, I am sure you could find no more suitable name for your ship. Also, I am equally sure that the honor you wish to bestow upon our daughter is one likely to be coveted by many of our patriotic ladies. I suppose you mean well. In fact, your coming to our house with such a proposition is in your favor. And yet, sir, in all honesty, I must admit that your temerity amazes me."

"How so, ma'am?" Sherrod asked.

"Captain, I do not presume to say that there is or is not any basis for the constant flow of unfavorable comment regarding your affairs."

"Gossip," Sherrod replied, with a wave of his hand. "I'm used to that."

Annabel said in even conversational tones, "We aren't used to gossip. Futhermore, my dear Captain, we shall continue to take every precaution necessary to protect the Cutler name."

Sherrod nodded, smiled, made a slight shrug, and said with no loss of composure, "Then she'll be the *Belle of Mobile.*"

"Thank you, Captain," Annabel replied. "And now, sir, since we've gone this far toward establishing a purely honest relationship between us, there is the matter of an investment made by my daughter and her husband in this steamer of yours."

"Please, Mother! Not here!" Adria felt the crimson surge up to the roots of her hair as the hard questioning eyes of Leland Jarvis fell on her. "Mother, I—I didn't explain in full. Lawrence doesn't know."

Joseph rose, an angry red in his face. "Then the cat out of the bag takes on an ugly stripe."

"Sit down, Joseph." Annabel bit her lip and faced Adria. "I didn't know, child. I'm sorry. But now that the damage is done, we'll see if it can't be remedied once and for all." Observing a brief pause, she addressed Sherrod.

"It is my fondest wish that the business transaction between you and Adria be terminated at once."

"Look here, ma'am, do you realize that her investment of two thousand dollars has already made her three thousand above that?"

Annabel looked incredulous, as did Adria and Joseph. It was Jarvis who stood, waved a hand, and said in trembling rage that his son's wife wasn't for sale at any price, that for a hundred times the sum he would not allow the Jarvis name to be associated with that of any traitor who hobnobbed with Beast Butler.

Sherrod laughed in his face.

Annabel felt all eyes on her; Adria's anxious, Joseph's alert and vacillating, Leland's stormy, and Sherrod's cool and collected. She admired this bold man, rake and adventurer that he was, saw in him a physical attractiveness that in her youth might have swept her off her feet. Adria was young. Her glance darted to Adria's face, and she was not surprised to find her own impressions mirrored in her daughter's eyes. It was as she feared, and for all her outward calm Annabel trembled inside.

Joseph said, "I'll buy Adria's shares and put an end to this business."

Sherrod smiled his opinion of Mr. Cutler. "Aren't you afraid the war won't last, sir?"

"Captain, I'll have you understand it's a sacrifice on my part."

"Yes siree," Sherrod agreed. "A matter of gilt-edged principle."

"Adria," Annabel said quietly, "must I do your thinking and talking for you always? Or," she added in vexation, "shall I send for Mammy Rose?"

"Frankly, I've had enough of this." Making no effort to hide her pique, Adria said, "Since when is it a crime to make a good investment? Don't bother, Mr. Leland, I know your reply. But let me tell you something, sir. When I put myself up for sale, you can gamble that I'll fetch more than even you think your plantation is worth, and the price of a gunboat to boot."

"But, darlin' child——" Jarvis spluttered.

"And furthermore," she said to her parents, "I'll do nothing regarding the shares until I talk to Lawrence. It's his money, not yours."

Annabel said determinedly, "And it's his wife's and my daughter's name in jeopardy. Now, Captain Sherrod, I beg to advise that as of today Adria is getting out of the blockade-running business."

Adria stamped a foot and said defiantly, "I'm not! It's my investment, and it's a good one!"

Sherrod lifted his palms and walked casually out to the gallery. The argument inside reached his ears and evoked an expression of sardonic amusement on his face. With hands rammed into trousers pockets, he leaned against a great white column and considered the outcome.

"Win or lose," he said, "I've got a foot planted inside this house."

## 26.     Strangers in the Night

1

WITH LONG YEARS OF SERVICE IN THE NAVY BEHIND
HIM, Acting Master Porter did not flinch when the Parrott 30-
pounder belched flame and smoke, but watched expressionless as the
shell shrieked its way to the island and exploded over Galveston.

"You know, Mr. Hillyer," he said, "it's odd that the damn Rebels
don't know when they're licked."

James acknowledged the executive officer's statement and no
more. The roar of guns from three other Union warships beat at his
eardrums. Any second now the flagship *Brooklyn,* nearest the *Hatteras,* would blast the January air with a thunderous broadside.
Already, Assistant Surgeon Matthews was stopping his ears with
forefingers. Then it came and the *Brooklyn's* masts seemed to leap
back in recoil as the roar shook the very water.

Commodore Bell of the Union squadron was at least persistent,
James admitted to himself. He was literally giving the Texans hell
in big doses.

It was a quarter past two on this afternoon of January 11, 1863,
James observed. The bombardment would drone on, wearily, monot-
onously, into the night, he supposed. Now Captain Clyde was ordering the ship swung portside to island in order to allow the starboard
battery to cool.

James stared abjectly across the water at the town, recalling that
Adria's aunt, Miss Eugenia Temple, lived in Galveston. On Tremont
Street, he thought.

Damn! The 32-pounders were exploding shots on the swing, into
his brain almost. But service aboard the *Hatteras,* as much as he
secretly disliked this sort of thing, was better than none at all. His
ambition to chase the commerce destroyers had been thwarted by
a brief period of glory and subsequent disfavor.

His mouth tightened automatically with the memory. Thinking of
the peculiar nature of the human animal, loud with his cheers one

day, louder with jeers the next, he felt that he could in aroused anger almost spit a 20-pound shot over the "City of Oleanders." He could hardly blame Captain Wilkes of the U.S.S. *San Jacinto* for pausing in his chase of the *Sumter* late in 1861 to capture what he considered a bigger prize, the Confederate commissioners to England and France from the British ship *Trent*. Nor did he blame Wilkes when the North hailed the officers of the *San Jacinto* as heroes. How he had basked in the glory. He recalled his father's praise of his son. How the people of Boston had wined and dined the gallant naval officers until the act of the fiery-eyed zealot Wilkes had almost brought on war with England. After that, they might have received a better reception in Richmond or Charleston. Of course, the government had already made a hero of Captain Wilkes. Mr. Gideon Welles, Secretary of the Navy, was stuck with him and, to his credit, sustained him.

But Lieutenant Hillyer? Why, they simply forgot him. And after months in the Boston Navy Yard, where he was ribbed and was called, "Rebel Ambassador to Britain," among other things, he was unhappily anchored aboard the *Hatteras,* off Galveston, Texas.

Here because dashing Confederate General Magruder had on the night of January first recaptured Galveston. The timely Rebel action had turned the planned invasion of Texas by General Banks with thirty thousand New England troops. Banks, who had been "chased ragged" by Stonewall Jackson, had been due with his army on the tenth, only yesterday. But he was in New Orleans awaiting the fall of Galveston.

James stared at the gunners with unseeing eyes that next followed a streamer of powder smoke to leeward. Turning his glance on Acting Master's Mate McGrath, he tried to close his mind's ear to the continuous shelling of the Texas port.

"We're wasting Mr. Lincoln's shot," vowed Matthews. "I'd a damn sight rather turn a Parrott on our disgraceful General Butler."

"Well, since he's been recalled to Washington, thank God," spoke up McGrath, "let us wish for real sport, the pirate *Alabama*."

James brightened for the first time in hours and came forth with an enthusiastic "Amen!"

As he had followed the career of Adam, so had he closely, anxiously, kept up with the depredations of the new and greater threat to Yankee commerce, the elusive *Alabama*. The news of Adam's capture by and escape from the *Minnesota* had reached him in Boston, and shortly thereafter came the rumor that Adam had gone to England. Then, not a month past, a lieutenant of the *San Jacinto,* which ship had the *Alabama* bottled up at Martinique only to let her slip out to sea in the dead of night, had declared that Lieutenant Cutler was aboard the English-built Confederate cruiser.

Raphael Semmes had lost little time since leaving the *Sumter* in renewing his destruction of American vessels. In the Azores he had captured and burned whaling ships to his heart's delight, first the *Ocmulgee,* next the *Ocean Rover,* then vessels too numerous to mention. From the captains whose craft he captured came accounts of the *Alabama's* speed in chase. She was swift, no doubt about it. The New York papers listed regularly her crimes, the places she was last seen, her probable course. At present she was supposed to be cruising the northern coast of Brazil. They named the gunboats sent in pursuit of her. The New York Chamber of Commerce sent numerous resolutions to Mr. Seward, Secretary of State, branding the *Alabama* as privateer, plunderer, British pirate, and brigand, demanding that the Secretary of the Navy send more warships in chase of her, lest the commercial marine of the North be destroyed and driven off the seas. Said the resolutions, "She is burning everything right and left, even British property. Will the Lion stand it?"

Fresh in James's memory were bits from Boston and New York papers regarding Yankee shipping.

ADVANCES ON MARINE INSURANCE—In consequence of the destruction caused at sea by the privateer steamer *Alabama,* the officers of the insurance companies of Boston have fixed the present war rates on different voyages as follows . . . These rates are liable to be altered according to the necessary requirements of the times, consequent upon the unusual hazards to which commerce is now exposed.

NEW YORK: The damaging effect of the *Alabama's* raid on our shipping upon the maritime interests of this port were as conspicuous today as yesterday. . . .

The *Alabama* was indeed a thorn in Secretary of Navy Welles's side. He had blocked the ports of the South, taken New Orleans and most of the Mississippi River, but could neither find nor capture the one single, solitary Confederate cruiser that was virtually blockading the North.

James muttered an oath. It was galling to be where he was when his heart's desire was to go in search of pirate and arsonist. He wished to return the favor of his former closest friend. Let Adam be the prisoner next time.

As the ship's bell sounded the half hour, the *Hatteras* suddenly came alive. From the flagship *Brooklyn's* signal halyards fluttered an order to Captain Clyde: Chase a sail to the southward and eastward.

Although the sea-wrinkled captain did not comment on the pleasure Commodore Bell's order evoked in him, James thought his eyes responded with something like, "Gladly, sir." As for the officers, only the serious business of getting under way, plus naval discipline, restrained cheers and a lively chorus of "Yankee Doodle." The captain sent his compliments to the engineer with a request for a full head of steam. Orders rang, and presently the *Hatteras* cut loose from the assaulting flotilla with her wheel boiling the water on a course for the opaque horizon of the Mexican Gulf.

The run began as a lark, a respite from the eternal shelling, and nothing happened to change the outlook during the first hour. The chop of the sea increased, the weak, uncertain wind blew across the level reaches, and a murky sky moved nearer the zenith. Then the strange sail came in sight and the excitement of chase offered sport to officers and crew. She was a steamer also, though a screw vessel. The news was relayed to the flagship by signal.

At four-thirty o'clock the *Hatteras* brought the other ship closer. A half hour later Captain Clyde shed his all's-well expression. The very fact that he was gaining rapidly on the stranger aboard a craft known for her slow speed caused him to suspect some deception.

"What do you make of her, Mr. Porter?"

"I'm afraid, sir, you'd laugh at what I'm thinking."

"And you, Mr. Hillyer?"

"I've been thinking also, sir," James replied evasively.

The short January day was fading into night when the deck estimated that the suspicious craft was no more than five miles ahead. The captain was by now thoroughly alert. He spoke of "a rare possibility," though he named no vessel, just concluded his surmise with, "And perhaps a rare opportunity."

"For eternal fame, sir," James ventured.

"Which I seriously doubt, Mr. Hillyer. Just the same, we'll clear the ship for action."

Once the order had sounded, James Hillyer experienced a curious thrill that sent his hopes soaring. Strange little things, utterly foreign thoughts, entered his head: Adria's satin slipper, symbol of undying love or eternal bitterness, perhaps both, the glint of fire in Adam's eyes as the *Golden Rocket* burned; a line—"You were born to love, to hate . . ." But all these things were part and parcel of the paramount wish—

That the ship ahead might be the *Alabama*.

The gun crews were removing tompions and running powder boxes, shot, and shell on deck from lockers below. By six o'clock loaders, lever compression and springer men stood impatient for action at their various positions, and Gunnery Officer Lieutenant Hillyer looked over his crew and readied his eight-gun battery with more pride than misgiving.

Full night had descended over ship and sea when the foretop cried the deck, "She's about four miles off, sir, stopped and lying broadside to us."

Captain Clyde's voice lifted calm with, "We can now speak our minds. By her general character and maneuvers, I believe her to be the famous *Alabama*." Observing a brief pause, he addressed the crew briefly.

"There is no need to remind you that if my guess is right you are about to meet a formidable foe. You know what her capture will mean to us."

2

Aboard the lighted vessel awaiting the Federal steamer *Hatteras,* the captain who had just watched the furling of his sails ordered the beat to quarters. He smiled in response to the pattering of feet, the alertness of gunners and powder monkeys, and twisted the tip of a mustache. The days of drill, drill, drill were paying off. His ship in fighting trim, he turned to his executive.

"Mr. Kell, we have given chase pretty often, but this is the first time we've been chased."

"Indeed, sir, and I've been drawing an estimate of her. She's a large steamer, though not of the class of the old steam frigates or new sloops. I'll venture a guess that her armament is more to our size."

Lieutenants Sinclair, Armstrong, and Wilson agreed. Lieutenant of Marines Howell toyed with the wisp of hair on his chin, a miniature copy of Semmes's, and made a classic remark: they would soon find out.

"True, Mr. Howell. I've awaited this day, as you gentlemen realize, since we learned from the New York papers of General Banks's planned invasion of Texas. Now despite the fact that we find the gallant Texans have recaptured Galveston, leaving us with no confused troop landing to wreak havoc upon, but five ships-of-war, a different version of the sport I promised you in the Arcas Islands is about to commence. But, gentlemen, remember this, that while we have decoyed one enemy vessel twenty miles to sea, we must make haste in battle lest the other four arrive to pounce upon us."

That was Semmes's speech to the afterguard. He turned next to Lieutenant Cutler. "Mr. Cutler, your hunches and judgment have on numerous occasions been paradoxically apt. Now may I ask why you insist on depressing our guns?"

"I was too long at Laird's, sir, to overlook the weakness built into a ship's side."

"Damn my eyes!" The expression, typically Semmes, was no indication of anger or rebuke. "You draw attention to our own light scantling."

"With that in mind, sir, it is my fondest wish to beat our blue-bellied friends to it."

A murmur of approval from the officers followed.

The pursuer came on rapidly, a dim shape except for a few lights aboard and sparks of fire leaping from her smokestack. From the distant shore silence and thick darkness met the alerted ears and eyes of the *Alabama's* crew. The entire Union squadron had ceased its fire, as if to watch and listen on a night made for sound waves from sea to land.

The Federal grew larger, came closer. When no more than one hundred yards apart, both ships stopped their engines. A hush of excitement ran the *Alabama's* deck.

"What ship is that?" the Federal hailed.

"This is Her Britannic Majesty's steamer *Petrel*," Lieutenant Kell trumpeted. "What ship is that?"

"This is the United States ship——"

No one aboard the *Alabama* caught the name. Semmes said, "It doesn't matter. We've heard enough to know she's the enemy."

There followed a tense, awkward interval of silence out of which the low drone of conversation on board the Federal was heard. Adam shifted his intent gaze from the indistinct lines of the side-wheeler to his own deck. The gunners stood with lock strings in hand, eagerness and excitement in their faces.

Presently the other hailed again. "If you please, I will send a boat on board of you."

Kell cried into the trumpet, "Certainly, we shall be pleased to receive your boat."

Adam listened. Now he could hear distinctly the Yankee boatswain as he called away a boat. A creaking of tackles sounded as the boat was lowered from the davits. Then the men were pulling at the oars for a crossing. Adam looked up at the stars, now breaking clear, then suddenly narrowed his gaze and lowered it on Lieutenant Kell.

The boat was halfway between the ships when Semmes broke the mounting tension. "I suppose you are all ready for action, Mr. Kell?"

"We are, sir, and are only waiting for word."

"Tell the enemy who we are, for we must not strike him in disguise, and when you have done so, give him the broadside."

Kell sang out in his powerful voice, "This is the Confederate States steamer *Alabama!*"

Whirling to the crew, he cried, "Fire!"

The dark of night was instantly stabbed by a flash that lit up sky and water and Federal side-wheeler. A burst of thunder shook the sea, masts, yards, and the very deck under Adam's feet as the *Alabama* shuddered under the recoil of her guns. A bare second later the enemy returned the fire. The battle was on and both ships moved forward, the Confederate fighting his starboard, the enemy his port battery.

The firing continued, with neither side inflicting appreciable damage in what was developing into a running duel. With the ships sailing almost parallel and with perhaps two hundred yards of water separating them, both gathering headway rapidly, Adam found his target closer than at the opening of the fray.

Coughing, eyes smarting under powder smoke, Adam cried to Gunner's Mate Wier, "Depress the guns more!"

"Aye——" Thunder completed the reply, and from above Lieutenant Howell's marines sent warm musket fire at the enemy deck. Pistols were fired between cannon blasts and men tensed and cringed inwardly while awaiting the reply of 32-pounders. Then the flame, the blast, the shriek of shot which no man ever got used to. It was again high above its mark, and Adam realized with elation that most of the Federal shot was aimed at the *Alabama's* upper works.

"She's cutting toward us!" Kell shouted.

"Good!" Adam returned. "We'll flirt the battery and play Dixie on her hull!" To the gunner's mate he cried, "Loose the 100-pounder for'd on the enemy's hull amidships!"

In the flashes of exchanged fire, the big pivot gun was aimed with accuracy and speed at a vital spot and fired. A gaping hole in the Federal's side was raggedly outlined by fire inside her hold. Then a shell from the *Alabama's* pivot aft tore through the hull and exploded in the enemy's sick bay, starting a second fire. Frantic shouts from the deck of the twice-damaged Union vessel were jarred into oblivion when a Confederate shell struck the cylinder. Almost in the instant, a hiss of steam from engine room and deck followed. A split second later a terrible crashing of machinery advised that her engine room was a shambles.

Adam grinned, then stared at the masts and yards of the enemy, outlined a hellish red in the flash of fire. The ships were so close together that the blast of either ship's magazine might send both of them to Davy Jones, and a turn of either helm would have locked yardarms.

Another blast from the *Alabama* seemed to stagger the crippled vessel. But she came on, veering closer, solely on gathered momentum, her walking beam shot away, holds in flames and water pouring into her below the water line. The next flash of fire to light her up jerked a cry of joy from the Confederate deck, for she listed heavily to port.

James Hillyer found himself sprawled on his stomach shaking his head fiercely. A minute, or perhaps only a second, earlier the very deck had risen under his feet to hurtle him against a solid object, which he recognized now as a 30-pounder Parrott rifle. As he tried to rise, a sharp catch of pain near his right shoulder evoked a groan and an oath of impatience. He managed to rise. Then a cut on his forehead began to burn and he realized that there was no right sleeve on his coat. Devilishly odd, all, for he recalled little of what had happened since the first explosion below.

Steam hissed about him and a tongue of flame licked out of the smoke issuing from the buckled deck under his feet.

"Mr. Porter! What happened here?"

"You all right, Mr. Hillyer? Our engines are blown to smithereens, and we've—— What?"

James staggered aft in time to hear a report from below: "Whole sheets of iron have been torn from her side below the water line, sir. We're sinking fast!"

Captain Clyde's glance fell on the *Alabama,* now beyond the range of his guns. "She's no doubt preparing to rake our deck with fire."

"Our magazine, sir!" Mr. Porter cried. "Since the fire in our holds will reach it any second, shall I order it flooded?"

"Aye! At once, Mr. Porter. Mr. Hillyer, fire the lee gun."

"Surrender?"

"Indeed, Mr. Hillyer. I have no right to sacrifice uselessly, and without any desirable result, the lives of all under my command."

With the report of the off gun and the sharp hail of surrender, the *Alabama* trumpeted a question: Was any assistance needed?

Mr. Porter's response was instant. "Send us boats at once. We're sinking fast!"

James gripped his useless arm with the hand of the other and stared about him. The old *Hatteras* was going. She was filling fast.

"Heave all port guns overboard!"

The order finally penetrated James's brain. The necessity of the order impelled him forward. With the ship's present list, the weight of the guns posed a threat to the lives of all aboard. He had no sooner taken a step than he was thrown off his feet by a sudden lurch of the ship. For a moment all went black, and he awoke to the pain in his arm. Suddenly everything was clear in his mind again. The scream of the last wounded man was real. The blood of one of the dead ran off the deck near where he lay. The gallant conduct of Assistant Surgeon Matthews would always stand for something, as would Acting Master's Mate McGrath's performance as a gunner.

Men were frantic now. "She going down fast!" They faced death again, pushed at one another, asking questions: Would the pirates' boat reach them in time; would the Rebels hang them from yard-arms? A muffled explosion sounded below. The ship shuddered under the onslaught of fire and water. The trailing smells of powder, human sweat, smoke, and steam on a deck settling more to port frightened even the disciplined crew. Only flashes of light over the water broke the curtain of night.

"To the nor'west o' us! Look!" cried a sailor. "Our ships are comin'!"

James worked himself erect and stared. "Too late," he said dismally.

Captain Clyde's voice sounded above the crackling, gurgling, and hissing under the sinking decks. "The enemy is sending us assistance. Prepare to abandon ship."

For the first time since the guns had ceased to roar, James became aware of the *Alabama*. She was steaming close now for the rescue, her boats in the water under smart handling. She was, however, enemy, sworn enemy to him, for she was pirate and arsonist; hated enemy from powder boy to Semmes and back to Adam S. Cutler. And by the devil's own luck, she was the ship he had been so almighty anxious to sail out and capture.

Tears of anger and frustration rolled hot down James's cheeks. He could bear up under a forehead gash, steam burns, and snapped arm without a murmur. But the thought of capture again by Adam was too much.

The survivors had not reached the *Alabama* when the *Hatteras* slid bow first under the water, her pennant at the masthead. Then she was gone forever, the suck and gurgle of air and water her sob as she went to a watery grave.

A Confederate at the oars said, "The end of another Federal."

As the officers and crew of the *Hatteras* reached the *Alabama's* deck, James saw Semmes glance up from his watch. Before accepting Captain Clyde's sword, he said:

"Just thirteen minutes elapsed between the opening broadside and surrender. While this is probably one of the shortest naval duels on record, it is none too quick for us, gentlemen. I suggest we get under way before the four lights on the horizon overtake us."

Gripping his shoulder, James found himself looking squarely into the steady eyes of Adam. For a minute their glances held, calm, independent, proud, but searching. Slowly the muscles of James's face tightened, as if to hold back a cry of "Gloat, damn you!"

Adam spoke to the *Alabama's* assistant surgeon and in that gentleman's company advanced to the prisoner.

"Mr. Llewellyn, this is Lieutenant James Hillyer. Now I'll consider it a personal favor if you'll patch him up and return him to the wardroom."

Adam bowed and turned away. James glared after him, thinking it damned unsportsmanlike but typical of a cold-blooded, victorious pirate to wish his prisoner mended for the sheer pleasure of humiliating him.

Pausing, Adam looked again at his former friend, a trace of tentative humor in his face. "On second thought, Mr. Llewellyn, he's becoming such a regular visitor you might do well to break the other arm."

For a few seconds James seemed ready to break out with a genial smile. Almost he heard "Admiral Co-Co" and felt the comforting warmth of the greeting couched in other words. Whether to grin or scowl awaited his immediate decision, for such opportunities were brief. He had heard of Confederate and Yankee shaking hands after battle, as though the war ended with their handclasp. He could understand and wish his feelings were less passionate. And he could imagine a victor's generosity toward a captive. But slowly rising like an iron wall in his mind was the memory of a torch applied to a defenseless ship by the very hand that under the madness of flames and lust for destruction had slapped his face. Later events, the bloody battles from First Bull Run (or Manassas, as the Rebels called it) to the present, cemented the hate he had nursed until it became to him a symbol. Any hint of friendliness now would in effect be tantamount to giving his and his government's condoning nod to barbarism.

Such were his thoughts.

Adam waited out the moments in which James seemed to waver between conflicting desires. Only when malice emerged the stronger in the Marylander's expression did he drop his glance; then, putting his back to the prisoner, he promised himself that the Yankee would never again have the opportunity to reject his offer of renewed friendship.

## 27.    When the Bamboo Blooms

### 1

WITH PRISONERS OF A FORCE EQUAL TO THEIR OWN, the officers of the *Alabama* were more than anxious to reach Kingston, Jamaica. Forced to sleep with "one eye open," despite the fact that the crew of the *Hatteras* were on parole, the Confederates were further harassed by inclement weather. A succession of southerly gales battered the overcrowded ship under sail through the Yucatán Passage and on into her tenth day before she sighted the lighthouse of Port Royal late in the afternoon of January twenty-first.

The necessity of constant vigilance, lest an enemy warship lie in wait, caused Semmes to hoist a French flag before calling for a pilot. Once the narrow, tortuous channel had been negotiated in the darkness of early evening, the *Alabama* declared herself. The news spread fast over harbor and town, drawing visitors, enterprising bumboat captains, and a lieutenant from the English flagship *Jason,* all to welcome the Confederates to port. The ship's fame suffered no loss when it became known that she had on board more than one hundred Federal prisoners.

With boats three abreast on each side of the *Alabama,* the ordeal of port entry, so dreaded by the lieutenants, began. Adam, as Kell and the others, actually preferred battle to anchor, and for good reason; the crew to a man forgot ship and thought only of shore liberty. In order to prevent all hands from jumping ship, discipline was of necessity relaxed, which meant double duty for officers.

The following morning the excitement began anew. Captain Semmes called upon Commodore Dunlap, in command of the squadron of British Admiral Milne's fleet, and forwarded through him a report of his arrival to the English Governor together with a request that he be allowed to land prisoners and remain in port for necessary repairs. Upon receipt of a prompt and favorable reply, the prisoners were made ready for landing and their formal release to the protection of the American consul.

Captain Clyde, who had been the guest of Semmes, and his officers, who shared the *Alabama's* wardroom, gathered on deck to say farewell to their captors and excellent hosts. With one exception, the scene of blue in handclasp with gray seemed more like the end of a pleasure cruise than the disembarkation of prisoners of war. Only Lieutenant Hillyer, U.S.N., evinced open displeasure of a duty imposed by his fellow officers.

Adam stood at his captain's side as James stepped before them with hand limply extended, his silence conspicuous enough to provoke a remark from Semmes.

"Well, Mr. Hillyer, I trust you enjoyed your stay aboard of us more than back in 'sixty-one on the *Sumter.*"

James's sullen expression flared like a match into open hostility. Although he bit back all he wished to shout at Semmes, he conveyed his feelings by look and eloquent brevity as he replied crisply, "Next time, the Lord willing, I'll be the host."

He moved on, leaving in his wake a group of Southern gentlemen who were not allowed to forget that the highest aspiration of officers in the Union Navy was their capture. A compliment, of course, but it was also freighted with all sorts of conjectures regarding their fate should an ill-starred destiny deliver them up to such men as Lieutenant Hillyer. Somehow the look in his eye carried all the welcome of a stout rope dangling from a Yankee yardarm.

Watching his former friend depart, Adam frowned seriously at the future. They would meet again, he thought, and on the avenue of war, which led in only one direction. There was no turning back to friendship and warm affections between people of a kind, but a steady march onward to the harsh music of cannon in a symphony of death and ruin.

On this day the *Agrippina*, Captain McQueen, kept her rendezvous with the *Alabama* and began the transfer of coal. Captain Semmes accepted an invitation from an Englishman to spend a few days in the mountains and left the task of provisioning and repairing the ship as well as policing the crew to Kell and subordinates with an order to dispatch a courier to Flamstead, the country seat of his friend, when the *Alabama* was ready to sail.

On the second day in port, after the ordeal of searching Kingston for drunken members of the crew, the weary officers proposed that Mr. Kell name one of them the courier to Semmes when the time came. Accordingly, on the third day, Kell advised that the man he had selected, because of his long extra hours on duty, was Lieutenant Cutler, who would be accompanied by handsome Midshipman Maffitt.

Taking the captain's gig up to Kingston, Adam hired a carriage and ordered the old Negro driver to time his arrival at Flamstead so they would have to spend the night. In response to young Maffitt's wise grin, Adam said, "Perhaps you'd prefer the deck and Jack on a lark."

"Not I, sir. After last evening I'll dread port entry the rest of my days at sea."

Recalling the incident which provoked such a statement, Adam laughed. The ship's cutters and shore boats were returning one after the other with sailors in every stage of inebriation when a couple of them decided to escape irons below deck and leaped over the side. Taking charge of a passing boat, they seized the paddles from the two Negro occupants and put out for shore. Kell had a cutter manned for pursuit in short order, Maffitt in charge. As the long sweeps of the cutter gained on paddle oars, Maffitt heard one of the culprits say, "I'll tell you, Bill, there's too much cargo in this here damned craft, and I'm going to lighten ship a little." So saying, he and his companion grabbed one of the Negroes and heaved him overboard in the shark-infested waters of the bay.

Maffitt chuckled. "Naturally, we had to pick up the darky. The drunks gained on us, and just as we drew near in that moonlight race they seized the other darky and tossed him overboard. But finally we caught the rascals."

Adam said with mock gravity, "You know, 'Beeswax' Semmes may not sanction your behavior."

"Why not, sir?"

"Since he's a stickler for rules, he might find you guilty of violating British neutrality by capturing a neutral craft in neutral waters."

Maffitt's laughter was good to hear. All the officers of the *Alabama* had in one way or another tried to cheer this young midshipman, whose silent grief and concern for his father were more than justified. Maffitt had been a figure and a name in the Old Navy, ranking with Buchanan, Tattnall, "Deep Sea" Maury, and Semmes, all of whom were making history in the Confederate Navy. And Captain Maffitt, father of the lad at Adam's side, had recently earned the admiration of even his enemies in as daring and tragic an episode as naval history could boast of.

After a long and tedious trial in Nassau for breach of the British Foreign Enlistment Act, the *Oreto*, Captain Maffitt, became the Confederate commerce destroyer *Florida*. She was no sooner put into service than an epidemic of smallpox reduced her working crew to one fireman and four deck hands. Then in mid-August of 1862 Maffitt was himself attacked. A week later his son Laurens died while he was unconscious. After several days at Cuban anchorage a consultation of doctors was held and Maffitt's condition was considered hopeless. Then he spoke for the first time in three days, saying, "You are all mistaken. I've got too much to do, and have no time to die." A week later, after failure to recruit a crew or refit ship in Havana, he resolved to run into Mobile. On the fourth of September, at two in the afternoon, Fort Morgan was sighted, as were three Federal vessels which barred his entry into Mobile Bay. Maffitt was assisted on deck, being too weak to appear otherwise, where he made preparations for blowing up his ship if he failed to pass the enemy. Hoisting the English ensign, he stood boldly in until the *Oneida,* flagship of the blockading squadron, sought to intercept the *Florida*. The latter's failure to stop invited and drew Federal fire at close range. After cutting away her hammocks and smashing her boats, all three ships opened fire, broadside after broadside. One 11-inch shell passed entirely through her hull before it exploded. Masts and spars shot away, cabin shelled, and without a crew to man a battery, the *Florida* withstood two hours of enemy gunning before crossing the bar for anchorage near Fort Morgan.

That was Maffitt, Adam reflected. Words such as "brave" and "resourceful" sounded weak in describing such a man. And one could only imagine the pages of history this captain might have written with a fleet the size of Farragut's at his disposal. But fate had played a trick on this reincarnation of a John Paul Jones or Horatio Nelson, for his country had been unable to float a navy worthy of the name. Nothing more had been heard of Captain Maffitt. Every ship encountered since November of 1862 had been questioned to no avail.

"Pretty country," Adam said.

"It is, sir. And I suppose it will be much cooler up at Mr. Fyfe's plantation."

"I suppose. Anyhow, let us hope his wine is chilled."

After an hour over a paved avenue lined with cactus, towering coconut palms, and flamboyant trees, the latter stretching out like flaming banners of welcome, they began a gradual climb. Picturesque country houses appeared behind groomed hedgerows, and as elevation was gained, they looked down on fields of sugar cane. Then the carriage seemed to be riding the edge of a cliff, an alien object on a narrow roadway that cut a gash in the jealous green jungle spilling headlong toward the sea.

A lazy sail played in the breeze out from shore, and in the harbor below large ships became toy ships, lying as still as on a canvas of tropical Jamaica.

"There she is, the *Alabama*," Maffitt said.

But Adam was watching a silver sheet of rain far out to sea. A breeze lifted to his nostrils the sweet fragrance of jasmine. War, destruction, even the *Alabama*, had no place in a scene of placid beauty. This spell of late afternoon was strong and languorous. It seemed to invite the rustle of silken petticoats as ruffles and ribbons and scented ladies with seductive eyes and lips as red as mountain strawberries smiled and walked across the stage of his mind.

Such beauty resolved itself into one woman: Faustine.

Ahead, a bamboo thicket appeared out of a forest of tree ferns and mahogany. Along the road wild orchids blossomed.

His mind played tricks with him. He felt Faustine in his arms under his touch, and the desire for her seemed to drive him mad. He cursed the tropics and the long war.

The old Negro driver in top hat pointed a bony finger at the feathery bamboo and said, "We pass this place in hurry-up, 'cause bamboo said to be in bloom." Questioned by Adam, he explained that it was talk all over that only once in a hundred years did the bamboo bloom, but that some "niggers" had seen it and had fled in fear.

"Stay away from it, master. Strange things happen when it bloom. Evil spirruts cause wrong people to be 'tracted to one another."

Adam's brow rose and fell. There was tragedy and life and drama in their superstitions, and there was something fascinatingly cryptic about even the land.

The sun was cutting the arch of sky near its base over the sea when the carriage rounded a curve and entered a stone gateway into a flower garden of great size and beauty. This was as far as a vehicle could travel. After refreshing themselves on tea at the inn, Adam and Maffitt mounted saddle horses and followed bridle paths up the mountainside. As they sighted the garden and lawn of Flamstead, the sun dipped under the Caribbean.

Suddenly from under the western horizon a great shaft of emerald light leaped toward the zenith of the sky. Adam reined his horse to a stop and sat still in the saddle, content to watch God's universe troop the colors. The afterglow faded swiftly away, and the day fell back into a wine-dark sea. Then the soft tropic night fell over the land. A nightbird sang in the rosemary trees and a large moon began to paint every surface in pale silver against the deep shadows of evening.

Maffitt's voice sounded an intrusion on the perfect setting. "A man could easily fall in love on such a night, Mr. Cutler."

"Aye. So be careful, Mr. Maffitt," Adam replied.

2

Inside the Fyfe house, the Confederates found all the hospitality and elegant leisure of an English home in evidence. Far above the sultry coast a fire of cedar logs burned in the hearth and several Englishmen of wealth, learning, and distinction looked into its cheery brightness and discussed this and that. The Governor of the island was present, as were the owners of neighboring mountain estates.

Mr. Fyfe showed Adam and Maffitt to a room overlooking Kingston and the sea far below them. "Make yourselves comfortable, gentlemen. If you like, join us below in bloody debate. The ladies should arrive soon. Odd, not a one in the house, but all over to Bloxburg, a neighbor's house, for a bit of entertainment."

When Adam joined the men before the fire a half hour later, the trend of conversation had to do with Jamaica's economic history. Soon the dominant subject was slavery, which had written its turbulent chapters across the island's life as a crown colony. From chief resort of buccaneers on the Spanish Main to one of the world's greatest slave marts, Jamaica had thrived on free labor. Then, twenty-nine years ago, her slaves had been given their freedom.

The host beckoned to his gray-haired Negro butler and glasses were refilled. Outside, the moon played on the cedars, though it went unnoticed as the Governor delved further into a subject of paramount interest to the Southerners.

"Before the emancipation of the slaves here in Jamaica, our planters were rich. It was a sugar, coffee, cocoa, pimento, and ginger prosperity. In keeping with the argument at home, in 1831 the slaves revolted, believing they had been freed. Two years later the act was passed and 125,000 slaves were set free. Jamaica lost her trade because she lost her crops, because she lost her labor. She has never regained her place in the sun."

Said portly, pink-faced Mr. Fyfe, toying with a glistening taffy-colored mustache, "By Jove, His Excellency would have us thinking 'e favored a return of the bloomin' slave system. Eh, wot, Captain Semmes?"

Gray eyes twinkling, Semmes ventured a cautious reply. "Whatever His Excellency's private opinion, he admits with facts the deplorable economy of an agricultural people without slave labor."

Adam silently applauded Semmes for his reply.

"My opinion," said the Governor, "is like a grain of sand against the tide. I drew the comparison regarding our prosperity to emphasize the determination of our people when a principle is involved. Despite the terrible cost of freeing the slaves, Great Britain did not look back. She never will, gentlemen. Nor, if I may be so bold as to say so in the presence of our Southern friends, do I believe Great Britain will recognize a republic of slave states."

The handsome secretary to the Governor spoke up. "Even in the spring of 'sixty-one you said that, sir. And events of recent date seem to prove your judgment correct."

"Eh? Events?" Fyfe asked. "What events?"

Adam's glance narrowed on the secretary, and Semmes leaned forward, with a sharp frown creasing his brow.

The Governor laughed. "I'm sure we're sounding off too much, my dear Fyfe. My unofficial sentiments are with our gallant Confederate friends, so let us speak of other things. You, sir, Lieutenant Cutler, did I not hear Captain Semmes say you were a party to the escape of 290 from Birkenhead?"

"I was, Your Excellency."

The Governor's thin sandy brow rose as a smile spread across his jolly face. "My niece was a guest of Mrs. John Laird that day, Mr. Cutler. Perhaps you remember Miss Cornelia Earle of Barrow-in-Furness."

Adam's pleasure equaled his surprise. "Of course I remember Miss Earle."

"Then would you believe it if I——" He broke off in midsentence at the host's insistence.

"I say, Governor, Hilary is cornered by Captain Semmes, who wishes to know what recent events prove that the Lion of Britain will never recognize the Confederacy."

"Prove?" said the Governor. "He said, 'Seem to prove' if my memory is correct."

"A pure technicality!" Fyfe blustered amiably. "Which men of state use to evade issues. Come now, you're not the Captain-General of Jamaica before the Privy Council, Your Excellency. What's said at Flamstead goes no further."

Nudging Adam, the Governor said, "Seems I'm surrounded by the enemy, Lieutenant Cutler."

"Indeed, sir. Your Excellency has no means of escape."

"Very well, gentlemen. This is forced upon me, as Captain Semmes will verify. So, my answer to the question upon which my impolitic secretary focuses all attention is just this:

"The events of which he speaks are President Abraham Lincoln's Emancipation Proclamation, delivered last September, I believe, and declaring all slaves of the South free as of January first of this year of 1863, and the reaction to this act in the capitals of Europe."

Semmes twisted one mustache and then the other, Adam observed, aware that his own curiosity was no hidden secret here. He tensed in every muscle as the Governor said:

"This proclamation by the President of the United States has not helped the Southern cause in London or Paris. If there was ever any thought of European intervention on the side of the Confederate States, I'm afraid it simply evaporated into thin air—because Mr. Lincoln's order to free the slaves convinced anti-slave Europe that the American issue is slavery and nothing else."

Feeling as though his stomach hung suspended as the result of a

long fall, Adam turned troubled, astonished eyes upon his commander. Semmes's expression, he decided, could have admitted no
greater shock had an enemy shell exploded the *Alabama's* magazine.

The Englishmen were not blind to the bombshell dropped by the
Governor, nor was His Excellency, who broke the tension with, "For
God's sake, my dear Fyfe, have the glasses filled!"

Before the host could relay the order, feminine voices and gay
laughter sounded from the entrance hall. Instantly sighs of relief
became audible and long faces of seconds before brightened because
of the timely interruption.

Adam felt like a mechanical man as he bowed before the wives
of the Englishmen and their friends and daughters. His mind was
still busy with the depressing subject of European opinion when he
suddenly found himself staring into the lovely, surprised face of
Cornelia Earle of England. Under her excited hazel eyes he forgot
Mr. Lincoln and Europe and thought of her last words aboard the
*290*.

As he accepted her extended hand, a current of thought, an expression of admiration or an attraction stronger than either of them,
flowed from her fingertips through him like electricity. In the
moment his head spun and his blood coursed fast and warm in his
veins. Faustine was a long way off; Cornelia was very near.

3

Perhaps no set of warnings or superstitions could have kept them
apart that evening. Aroused feelings of curiosity, one for the other,
the crisp mountain air, the sea and mountainside under a bright
tropical moon were not to be denied. Leaving the company in the
house was not at all difficult. Nor was their departure arranged. It
just seemed to happen.

Near the curve of an upper bridle path, they looked down upon
the twinkling lights of Kingston several thousand feet below. Nothing personal had been spoken between them. Her remarks had been
for the *Alabama*, the *290* she had ridden to sea, and the vessel's
amazing career as a commerce destroyer. After a silence she spoke
of her visit to Jamaica for the winter.

"Strange, isn't it, Lieutenant Adam," she was saying in low,
throaty tones, "that every few hundred feet of elevation here brings
about changes in the plants and forests equal to degrees of latitude?

Here we are in the tropics, but the flora and climate of Flamstead are of the Temperate Zone."

Adam caught himself searching her statement for some hidden meaning. Finding none, but still unsure, he spoke of the orchids growing at a lower level, wondering as he did so what emotions really dominated her at the moment. As for himself, he was lonely. She had matured since last summer, or did her dress or hair create the illusion? She seemed prettier, but this opinion could be influenced by the moonlight or his memory of her. In any case, she represented temptation in an ideal setting under a bright holiday moon.

Feeling the general pressure of her long fingers at his arm, he looked at her half-averted face as she said, "I learned a little about you after that day." Slowly she raised her clear, direct eyes to his face. "That you have a wife."

Adam said nothing. He saw her glance drop under his gaze, then lift, calm and challenging. "Please believe me, sir, I am not a silly girl who strikes up a romance before tea every day."

"I can readily believe anything you say," he returned politely.

"But you are curious as to what I shall say next. Oh, I could go on talking in circles, but I won't. Not to you, as least. I fell in love with you, Adam. You left. I never expected to see you again. Upon learning from Mrs. Bulloch up in Waterloo that you were married, I was not surprised. Nor was I jealous of your wife. Can you explain that?"

"I'm afraid not."

"Neither can I," she said, almost wonderingly. "I thought one in love could not bear the thought of another's claim to a sweetheart. But I guess," she said, looking down at the sea, "it was all so sudden and unexpected that I became confused. Then after I had time to piece everything together, nothing of the past really mattered. Just the future."

"Future?" Adam's gaze narrowed on her. "Just what did you see there?"

Her pensive eyes were steady and full upon him as she said softly, "A memory of something beautiful in my life, Adam."

Now he was truly astonished. Never had he met a girl who lived under the influence of ideals formed in her mind. She was flesh, blood, and bone and therefore subject to the desires and aspirations of mortals. The same as he. She would melt under his kisses.

He laughed lightly. "Now if that isn't like a woman. After saying you wouldn't talk in circles, you do just that." With her denial, he said, "I can prove it."

"How could you possibly disprove the truth?"

"By taking you in my arms."

She studied him closely, her glance touching his eyes, jaw, shoulders, then his mouth. Smiling, she said almost eagerly, "I would like that very much."

She waited a few seconds. "Why don't you?"

He glared at her and felt a sudden desire to kiss her roughly. "I should, if only to dispel your fine illusions and bring you down to earth for some worthy young man. And I'd do it, except for——"

"For what? Say it, Adam!"

"You'd never be the same woman again. The stars and moon are pretty to you now, Cornelia. You're a romantic idealist. If I kissed you the way I want to at this moment your visionary world would crash like a mountain about you."

"No. That would be impossible," she said in slow and final judgment. "For you are not the kind of man who could, no matter how much you tried, be unfaithful to your marriage vows or wish to destroy what is in my heart."

He smiled and shrugged at what seemed her evident attempt to disarm him; he ran an eye over the low-neck dress that exposed the shadowed cleft of her bosom, and breathed the faint, elusive scents about her; he looked into her face and saw that she was searching him quietly, imploringly, as though she felt something strongly, deeply, and wished that he possessed her wisdom so that he too might see it. It was a warm and unsettling something that reminded him of a strange feeling under the stars over the sea, in which he seemed to have established a brief and vague contact with infinity.

Then in a wink of an eye it was gone. What it was he did not know, but it left him wiser and more temperate. Faustine crossed his mind, and he was wondering if without a wife and the love he had for her he could under the fires of passion make a move to destroy what was in this lovely Englishwoman's heart.

He supposed not. However, she had almost dared him to take her in his arms. What if he didn't? There had been times when he regretted walking away from Doña Antonina. Now he was asking if in the future he would scold himself for leaving Cornelia as he found her.

A nightbird's cry sounded from a cliff below them. The answer came nearby, alive and liquid. It left a silence, still and equally melodious.

Cornelia clutched at his arm. "We'd better return to the house, Lieutenant Adam. They say the bamboo is in bloom."

## 28.     The Blockade-Runner

ON A CLEAR MAY AFTERNOON OF 1863, the *Belle of Mobile* slid into her home port before a crowd of considerable size.

Standing her deck aft with an eye on the pier, Captain Randall Sherrod called for easy helm to lay her alongside in smart fashion. As the grinning Negro at the wheel cushioned the touch of ship to shore with admirable skill, the master ordered steam blown off under water, vessel secured to dock, and immediate anchor watch to the fore, stern and amidships. Only after serving the ship that served him did he scan the sea of faces beyond the iron rail.

Captain Sherrod knew as well as any man that the arrival of a blockade-runner in Mobile was cause for celebration. Since Captain Maffitt's daring entry into Mobile Bay in September of 1862 had been matched by his equally bold and successful reach for the open sea in January, the Federal blockading squadron had doubled its vigilance. As a result, fewer ships won past the Yankee watchdogs, and the skippers of vessels who did so were nothing short of heroes to the general public and devils of the first water to the small group of citizens who claimed that blockade-runners were largely responsible for gross speculation, extravagance, depreciation, and resulting poverty and suffering.

Sherrod was not blind to the fact that he, himself, constituted one of the major reasons for the spread of the latter opinion. However, it caused him no twinge of conscience. The risks were big, the Federal guns did not fire blanks, and there were profits and fees to be handed out at home and abroad.

He spread his lips in a downward grin, for standing on the dock were members of the Mobile Committee of Public Safety, which body had earlier branded his "unpatriotic business dealings at home and with the enemy in New Orleans in the year of 1862" as "gross and atrocious and typical of the injury to public welfare inflicted by blockade-running." In spite of regulations by the Richmond government, the committee went on to say, men of Sherrod's type continued to bring in more luxuries than necessities.

Sherrod's business agent greeted him and came aboard. A Creole of small stature, Henri Devol said, "Ze messieurs of ze committee wish to engage you in talk, *Capitaine*."

"Apparently," Sherrod replied. "But what's the latest news in Mobile?"

Devol fingered a line mustache and advised that General Lee had won a signal victory at Chancellorsville over Yankee General Hooker. "But, m'sieu, a sad thing she happen. Stonewall Jackson was kill."

"I heard that in Nassau. But tell me, has Vicksburg fallen yet?"

"*Mon Dieu*, no! She is hold out against the Federals. All ze South cheer." He talked on, about the refugees pouring in from New Orleans and upstate, trains bringing in wounded soldiers, the citizens of Mobile feeding four thousand people daily in the free market, and the new taxes. Then he was asking about the blockade-runner's expenses for the voyage completed.

"Sixty-two thousand," Sherrod said.

"*Sacrebleu!* So much?"

"Considering five pence sterling paid by the Confederate Government on outgoing freight and one hundred dollars a ton in cotton to be received in payment here, I figure the gross profit to be around a hundred and forty thousand dollars."

Devol's smile was broad. "Leaving ze net gain seventy-eight thousand." He sobered quickly. "*Mon Capitaine,* to let ze gilded cat out o' ze bag here would be mos' tragic."

"True, Henri. Now acquaint me with the latest, socially."

"Ze pleasure? M-m-m, let me see. Ah, *oui!* Tonight one new companee of soldier is fit out and assemble at a barbecue in Bienville Square."

"Wonders never cease. Now who would have believed that Mobile could raise one more company? But what's social about that?"

"Your frien' ze Mrs. Jarvis of Bay Oaks, she is present ze colors tonight."

Sherrod nodded. "That should be worth seeing," he said, thinking in detachment that the citizens assembled on the pier seemed more unfriendly than any that had welcomed him home in the past. And there came the chairman of the Committee of Public Safety.

The hush of the crowd and the belligerent attitude of the gentlemen of the committee advised Sherrod that he was on the verge of being unofficially tried and convicted in a memorable dockside ceremony. The lawyer stood straight as a poker, using silence for effect even as he attempted at the outset to frighten the wits out of the "defendant" with a pair of black eyes. After a minute of this he said:

"Captain Sherrod, as master of an outgoing vessel, did you not sign a bond to return with one half your cargo for the government and the other half to be comprised of articles of importation allowed by the Confederate Government?"

"I did. But what sort of inquiry is this?"

"Public, Captain. You know the purpose of this committee." The lawyer spread feet apart, hung thumbs in his belt, and asked what cargo Sherrod returned to the government.

"Machinery for the naval foundry up at Selma, the same for the navy yard on the Tombigbee, plus three hundred pigs of lead, twenty barrels of steel . . ." On he went, rattling off item after item from cartridges to medicines and drugs, the greatest items in demand, "Quinine, laudanum, ether, morphine, calomel, and cork."

When Sherrod finished, the spokesman asked, "Just what does your half of the cargo consist of?"

"Calico, silk, scented soap, French perfume, champagne, and hoop skirts."

"Indeed!" A note of triumph sounded in the lawyer's voice. "Luxuries." The leader consulted with members of his group and looked over the crowd of bystanders. "Do you realize that one fourth of the white population of Alabama was supported by the state last winter? Yet despite such hard times, speculators who bought your goods at public auction have so pushed the prices up inland that coffee sells in places at fifty dollars a pound. You blockade-runners are responsible. Not only are you draining the country of hard money, but you are setting examples for ambitious men with less experience, causing the loss of valuable ships and machinery."

"Amen." It came from deep in the crowd. An ominous buzzing ran the dock, and men were beginning to glare at the accused. The leader continued:

"Regarding your private dealings with the enemy, Captain Sherrod, it was rumored that you, together with several English firms of this city, built up a cotton monopoly in New Orleans with, and under the protection of, General Butler, in command of New Orleans; that upon Butler's removal by the Federal Government, you lost a fair share of the anticipated profits, said to exceed ten million dollars, and went on a three-week drunk——"

"Two-week, counselor," Sherrod interrupted. A portion of the crowd seemed amazed at Sherrod's temerity, though the majority laughed out loud. Quick to grasp the situation for its full worth, Sherrod grinned and said:

"I've had the pleasure of robbing the Yankees more than once during this war."

A merchant in the front ranks cried so all could hear, "But not as regularly as you've robbed the Confederates. Eh, Captain?"

"Right," Sherrod replied evenly. "But, gentlemen, for every pound of cotton I've shipped free past Farragut's fleet, I've brought to Mobile a pound of medicines and drugs and necessities. As for robbing you, figure the current rate of exchange on the Confederate dollar at five or six to one and place the blame on me if you can."

"So ye're lily white, Cap'n." The foghorn voice of an old salt drew a titter from the gathering.

"Not quite," Sherrod said. "But there's not a man among you who would sink a fine ship just because she had a barnacled bottom."

"A fine speech, Captain Sherrod," said the lawyer with a politician's lambent humor. "We agree that you are heavily barnacled." After a pause he said, "Because your kind have shown by your practices that you are an influence toward luxury and indifference at a time when greater sacrifice is demanded, and that you constitute a detriment to the war effort, we are submitting a resolution demanding that blockade-running on private account be prohibited and that only public vessels be allowed to depart from this port."

Sherrod fingered the visor of his cap and waited for silence. "Sure," he said. "You've sent other resolutions to Montgomery and Richmond, haven't you? Just because you won't admit that the need for supplies outweighs the evils of my business."

"Hear the man!" The lawyer addressed the crowd. "He admits all we charge him with."

"Aye. Randall Sherrod never argued that water wasn't wet." With indifference and insolence on a par, he sauntered down the gangway eying this man and that. "Any man who stands up for what he thinks is right and honorable is to be admired," he said. "But I have small use for one so damn shortsighted that he rallies to stock principles against the best interests of his warring people and government. Which is exactly what you gentlemen of the committee are doing when you prattle on the evils of blockade-running and try to eliminate them.

"Why, every man of you ought to know that in this business of supplying the South, those evils are the things that keep the trade alive."

The group stirred, though no one spoke out.

"Take away the big profits and trade in luxuries, gentlemen," Sherrod went on, "and the South, minus a navy and undesirables, like me, who take the big risks, will find herself strangled into defeat by the blockader a damn sight quicker than you can imagine."

Sherrod paused near the lawyer, looked level with him a minute, then instructed Devol on deck to pass out rum and Havanas to his host of friends gathered to welcome him home. Following this bit of irony, Sherrod grinned broadly and said:

"Now when I put my fancy goods up for auction, don't you gentlemen stumble all over each other in outbidding the public."

He left it with them and made his way toward the city.

## 29.     "Never Surrender"

### 1

ON THIS SAME AFTERNOON everyone at Bay Oaks was preparing for the big event in Bienville Square that evening.

Abel, Erasmus, and Mammy Rose, even saucy Claribel, had vowed they wouldn't miss the big honor which, in Mammy's words, "de state o' Alabamy, de city o' Mobile, and de Confed'racy done heap on Miss Adria."

Every spoke and surface of the carriage had been polished to mirror brightness. The horses shone as though oiled, so diligently had Abel used the currycomb. In the shade of a live oak Abel, in top hat and blue coat, rubbed at the brass of a coach lamp while waiting for the family. Close by were Leland Jarvis's handsome gray conveyance with green wheels, fine sorrel horses, and coal-black driver Ezra, in 1860 livery, now several sizes too small for him.

The Jarvis Negro looked solemn as he told of the return of "Marse Law'ence's pussonel nigger" Joe Bob from Virginia. It was the custom for any Southerner to take along a servant, since white soldiers did not wish to dig trenches, split wood, drive teams, or play in the bands. Congress allowed this, and authorized employment of four cooks to each company. But Ezra was saying:

"Joe Bob he git home after walkin' his feets off nigh up to de ankle and say Marse Law'ence done been took prisoner at de battle o' Chancellorsville by de Yankees. He say, Abel, dey got ho'ns growin' outen de haid, dem Yankees. Dey try to set Joe Bob free but he don't like nothin' 'bout it and he 'scape."

"Po' Mistuh Law'ence," Abel said mournfully. "He a prisoner and won't be a huntin' no coon 'n' bobcat in de bottom land this summer."

Ezra wiped sweat from his neck, stared up at the pillars of Bay Oaks, and said, "Sholy won't. But how come, Abel, yo'alls don't paint where de wood show through?"

"Reckin we's a-waitin' fo' summertime, Ezry," Abel said, not wishing to repeat what he had overheard, that Marse Joseph hadn't enough cash on hand to afford the luxury of paint this spring.

From the house came a child's squeal of delight. "Little Adam some chile," Abel said, grinning. As if to cover the unpainted boards of Bay Oaks with glory, he said, "Ezry, I reckin yo' done hear 'bout Mistuh Adam and his ship *Alabamy* sinkin' de Yankee ship at Galveston. Yassuh, Ezry, we is got reasons fo' to be proud at Bay Oaks."

From the interior the raised voice of the owner gave Leland Jarvis to know that he was not a member of the Peace Party; all he had said was what everybody knew, that there could be peace between the North and South whenever Jefferson Davis wanted it.

Abel grinned. "He layin' it on, Ezry."

Joseph was. His words reached the drive distinctly clear. "And Chancellorsville proves our military superiority. Sure I cussed Lee two years ago. But not now. Hooker tried to trap him and he trapped the trapper. Now Lee can take Washington or invade the North. All I say about peace is this—if we've won what we want, let's make peace. The sooner the better. This damn war is pinchin' me where it hurts, Leland."

Abel said importantly, "What us wants, Ezry, is peace iffen we done got what we wants, understan'?"

Upstairs, Mammy Rose was helping Adria get into a dress Annabel had made especially for the occasion. "Dis heah honor yo' sholy deserve, honey baby. Ain't nobody done work harder at dem benefits from Mon'gomery to Mobile."

Adria watched Mammy bring the dress down over her bosom and waist. Staring at a maze of ruffles, she thought of all the things that had occupied her waking hours for months. She had planned and worked up bazaars and staged *tableaux vivants* to raise money for hospitals, had sponsored money-raising events in Tuskegee and other towns to build a gunboat for the defense of Mobile Bay, had presented the colors to this company and that in Clarke, Marengo, Dallas, and Lowndes Counties, and laid flowers on the graves of dozens of soldiers in public ceremonies in as many towns.

"Gittin' so Mistuh Joseph and Mistuh Leland both fightin' to see who go wid yo' to de next town. But don' go gittin' stuck-up, chile, just 'cause yo' is 'bout de mos' important lady in de state."

Adria drew a deep breath and exhaled. "I was just wishing I could get stuck-up, Mammy." Her eyes narrowed in alarm at her waist. "Why, look! I do believe I'm inches larger than when I left for Selma."

"Nope. Been watchin', honey chile."

"You? Why?"

"Got a husband, ain't you'? Ain't it plumb natcheral fo' married womens to hab babies?"

Adria shuddered slightly. "Oh," she said. Then her thoughts turned back to the holidays of 'sixty-two. Her lips parted and her eyes lost their sharp focus as she recalled turning away from puzzled Erasmus on that clear December afternoon. She had just ordered him to find and bring a holly tree into the house before Christmas Day.

Erasmus had every reason to look utterly confounded, since the year before she had strictly forbidden him to enter the house with holly before Christmas. But Erasmus didn't matter. It was what she saw next. There in the doorframe, standing with feet planted wide apart, a dark and bitter look on his face, was Lawrence! She saw him now as clearly as five months back and recalled her feeling of shock. . . .

She simply stared at him, unable to believe her eyes. "Lawrence!" A hand was pressed to her bosom to stop her wild-beating heart. Oh, but there was black anger in his eyes!

"Lawrence, you—why, what a surprise!" she stammered. Then she was inviting him into the parlor. But he just stood still, as though deaf, for a minute or so.

"What I have to say is to you alone, Adria. Behind closed doors." Then he said crisply, "We'll go to your room. Now."

More curious than defiant, she obeyed his command and led him to the privacy of her room, where he stood, thinner, older, and angrier than she had ever seen him, and called her liar, cheat, and scheming woman. Too astonished to speak, she sat down slowly and tried to take her eyes off him. Then he was telling her why she was the things he called her. There were two reasons, he said, moving to within a foot of where she sat on the bed and glaring down at her until she leaned backward in trepidation.

Lord in heaven, he was furious! He drank red wine, wiped his mouth with the back of his hand, and repeated some of the things people in Mobile had said about him following his wedding night.

"And you knew about this talk when I was here last year? Didn't you, Adria?"

He towered over her, black-eyed, ominous.

"Y-yes," she stammered, lying flat of her back as his face drew closer and his hot breath steamed from distended nostrils.

"Mrs. *Virgin Jarvis!*" His face was too near and distorted, and his hands were working spasmodically at his sides.

"Lawrence Jarvis!" she cried. "Get back from me!"

She rolled across the bed and on the opposite side she stood facing him. He sat down, still red and purple of face, and drank more wine. Taut with anger, he said:

"Here, Adria, you'd better drink some too. That's not all I heard."

"What do you mean, not all you heard?" she asked, easing nervously for the door.

Rising, he threw the latch on the door. "The diamond brooch I was going to buy for you. Remember?"

"What about it?" she asked, backing slowly to a bedpost.

"You ask that? Suppose you tell me the only reason you decided to toy with my affections, to keep me dangling, the husband in name only, was so I'd advance you the money which your father refused you to invest in Randall Sherrod's Yankee cotton venture. You knew how I despised him, and yet you were willing to carry my name and risk it to more scandal by putting in with him."

Adria bit her lip, looked away, then said defensively, "It was a good investment. Deny that."

"Investment! Hell! I can make my own. I'm the man of the family. My mother and your mother didn't deal in business. And by God, my wife won't! Not any more she won't."

Adria's eyes danced angrily, cautiously, and her head cocked from one side to the other. Threats from an enraged Lawrence carried a sterling authority. The very fact that he was absolutely right would justify whatever he had in mind. As he walked toward her, slowly, his eyes mere slits, she suddenly knew what he had in mind.

Her jaw dropped and she stood rooted in fear, heart pounding, pulses stepped up. Her breath came in short gasps as he cut off all avenues of retreat and took her shoulders in his hands.

He did not shake her hard until she dropped her glance. Then, forcing her to look up at him, his lips drawn back tight against his teeth, he said fiercely, "You couldn't sleep with me on our wedding night because I wasn't a blond-headed Yankee from Maryland. And if you had, you'd probably have closed your eyes and made believe I was him."

"Lawrence!" Her astonishment and insult were complete.

"I mean it. Just like I used to lay up with a whore and pretend she was you. But I haven't touched a woman since I married you—fool that I am." He laughed crazily.

"Oh—oh, no!" The things he said shocked her down to the depths of her very soul. She tried to break from him but he held her with his hands and with the intensity of his eyes.

"Unfaithful in your heart, in your dealings with me before, during and after our wedding. Me—think of it—married to a woman like you! Me flat of my back in a makeshift hospital, cold, starved, wet. Lice crawling over me, blood running out of me. Shells exploding on every side and me, fool, calling your name—Adria! Calling for my wife—

"'Adria! My love!' Again and again, and my nigger Joe Bob saying you weren't there when I had to see your face or go mad. And I did go mad, so mad they had to tie me to a tree.

"And I'm still mad!"

He was indeed, she admitted. Not a half hour in the house, his anger and frustrations were running away with him, tearing him to pieces.

She broke for the door to the upper gallery, but he was too fast for her. His hand fell short of her shoulder though it caught her dress at the neck and, as she ran, ripped it down past the waist.

Then his hands caught her to him roughly and one of them

slipped under the torn dress and touched her bare skin. She cried out, and he shook her, then drew her, resisting and fighting, to him and tipped his head to her face. He bruised her body with his tight grasp even as he seemed to bruise her numbed mouth with his. Then he was swinging her up into his arms, kissing her madly, holding her tightly and running his lips down her throat and the divide of her bosom to where the dress had fallen from her. For moments on end he stared at the uncovered sweep of her bosom in fascinated wonder. Then he lowered her gently or savagely, she did not know which, and strange sensations of trembling and whirling through space mingled with an awareness of pleasure at the touch of his mouth to hers. Came a strong memory of Randall Sherrod's firm, muscular kiss during the storm, of sweet laziness. She tried to cry out in protest of something, but no sound came through. Lawrence closed off sound, everything. She despised him for this! How she hated him. Then she felt all tightness about her lips and arms dissolve.

She was crying under the strength of his arms, shaking with horrible fear. Then she was running her hands through his hair, reaching eagerly for his kisses, feeling gloriously wild, then wilder, with sudden joy. The world seemed to fall away, the heavens to burst about her. On she soared into the all-wonderful universe.

Later he held her in his arms, forced her shamed face up to his and her eyes out of hiding. The memory of surrender and rapture was too fresh to deny. She trembled closer to him and felt herself go dizzy under his gentle kiss.

Then he slapped her hard and arose. As she studied him, more dazed than resentful, he said:

"I've got to get back. I came without leave to kill a few men in Mobile, to hurt you. Reckon I've done enough." He got into his coat and turned his back before saying, "Fool that I am, and this guarantees it, I still love you, Adria." He laughed without humor.

"I'll probably call your name from a muddy bed up in Virginia again."

"Yes, Lawrence," she said.

He studied her, half smiling, half frowning. "You know, I might one day learn to trust you, Adria. In the meantime——" He broke off. At the door, he turned and his voice lifted bitterly.

"I hope by summer you're showing Mobile a belly as big as a watermelon, Mrs. Virgin Jarvis."

She cringed. Had a club been brought down across her head she

would have felt less hurt. She felt cheap then, as though she had
suffered him for gain, and buried her face in shame.

## 2

The memory fell away and Adria stood as before in front of her
mirror. Mammy Rose had just told her that it was perfectly natural
for married women to have babies. But the mad experience of last
December had produced no sign of child. She said:

"I suppose little Adam is enough to keep this family busy."

Mammy said reprimandingly, "Always room fo' one mo' chile in
any family. Mistuh Adam done give Miss Annabel and Mistuh
Joseph a gran'chile. Yo' time is come now."

"You know, Mammy, I sometimes wish for a baby of my own.
Perhaps I wouldn't have time to be lonely."

"Lonely?" Mammy thrust her head forward. "Jest when is yo'all
had time to be lonely? But maybe yo' misses Mistuh Law'ence."

"No."

Adria turned a shoulder to the mirror and followed it critically
until a side view of her figure presented a full bosom and slim waist
under the palest blue cotton and lace. How becoming was her gown,
even though it was cut to reveal more of her than was respectable.
It was Faustine's idea. But Mammy was scowling at her for another
reason, saying:

"If yo' ain't lonely fo' yo' husband, den who?" There was no reply.
"Look heah. Done been mo'n two year. Time yo' fo'got dat no-count
Yankee man."

Adria ignored this. Her image pleased her. She looked so young,
so virginal. Actually, it seemed incredible that she had been married
as long as Faustine and Adam, lacking a week.

"Sides, po' Mistuh Law'ence done been took prisoner by dem
monster Yankees."

Adria lowered her head slowly. She felt mean and stubborn
even though she made every effort to feel sorry for Lawrence.

From downstairs came a rousing yell. Adria started, then relaxed.
It did beat all how her father insisted on spoiling Adam's son.

Faustine stuck her head in. "We're all ready." She entered the
room examining the dress Adria wore under a critical frown. "Oh,
heavens, no!" she exclaimed.

"Now what?" Adria demanded, whirling.

Faustine drew her nether lip between her teeth and slowly shook her head. Then she said firmly, "The neckline is entirely too low, Adria."

Adria's hands came to rest on hips and her eyes narrowed with sudden wrath. "Well I'll be damned!" she said. "Coming from you, Faustine, I should think it would have to be cut to the navel."

Faustine's delicately arched brows lifted, then slowly knit in a puzzled frown. "We'll be waiting downstairs," she said.

On the stairway, Faustine admitted it was all her fault. However, she saw no earthly reason why an innocent mistake in sewing should provoke Adria into a temper, actually the first sharp outbreak between them in months. Somehow they had resolved to accept each other and had done very well with it. In fact, they took sides together at times, laughed, and exchanged secrets. But a wall continued to separate them. Perhaps it was just as well that Adria's war work kept her away from Bay Oaks half the time.

Suddenly Faustine decided to spend the night with Elvy, if only to be away from Adria. She craved excitement, something she could not find here or, for that matter, at Elvy's house. Glory be! What she really needed most was attention.

At the stair landing, she paused and said to herself, "Anything to break the monotony of this horrible war." Frowning, she looked upstairs. "And that's what Adria needs and doesn't know it."

It actually went beyond mere monotony, she admitted, moving down a step at a time. She stopped suddenly as her son toddled out into the hall with Joseph Cutler after him in pretended full pursuit. What was happening to everyone at Bay Oaks, perhaps to all Southerners of the old aristocracy, seemed to be mirrored in the face of her father-in-law. Perhaps that was one reason why Adria's temper was on edge. Then Faustine admitted that it could be the reason she desired to lose herself in a nirvana of pleasure.

Poor Joseph, his eyes had sunk deep into their sockets during the last few months. Reddish-brown hair and long mustaches had taken on an ashen hue. He stared into space with worry in his expression. Annabel, even the slaves, spoke in hushed tones about how he had aged; all of a sudden, it seemed.

Faustine did not move until Joseph led Adam by the hand on outside to the carriages. When the hall seemed empty, she raced down in a swish of petticoats and ran to the dining hall. At the sideboard, she reached eagerly for the decanter of brandy. Pouring, she drank and felt the liquid burn its way down. She relished the light pain of swallowing; because, she thought, the searing path it cut was to some delicious flame, if only of the mind. It settled her nerves, slowed the trembling inside her; it closed off the future.

But she had not drunk enough to forget the many reasons why Joseph had changed. The crease deepened between her eyes as she admitted that Joseph, as Leland Jarvis, was still rich in land, cotton, and slaves. But oh how false was this wealth now! The real things, the earth, its produce and the reapers, the bulwarks of any economy, seemed to have turned into cannibals bent on devouring themselves. Crops had been reduced, planting had been geared to the war effort instead of individual profit. Then the land taxes grew and grew, and there was a heavy tax on slaves, and cotton piled up awaiting shipment. Since 1861, Joseph had contributed to this benefit and that until it hurt, had invested cash in state and Confederate bonds.

Then money decreased in value and prices soared higher, higher, and with over one hundred slaves to feed and clothe, Joseph was staggering under the increased burden. He borrowed here and there and, finding himself in need of a more stable medium than Confederate money, issued notes and promises to pay. As private credit was better than public, these notes were swept into circulation along with those of other men at face value. The vicious circle continued; the steady depreciation of currency was making Joseph poorer. The more money he received for cotton, the less the paper dollar was worth.

"Poor dear," Faustine said aloud. Joseph Cutler seemed to know he was headed for ruin on a runaway economy and that there was nothing on earth he could do to stop it.

Faustine looked at the decanter. Her desire for brandy was greater than she cared to admit. Too bad, she told herself, that she had the mentality to understand what was happening to the wealth and position she had married. Why, another year of war would——

"No!" her voice lifted in protest. Then she was saying under her breath, "God forgive me, but I would enjoy getting drunk enough to forget there was ever such a thing as war."

She poured generously with trembling hand. "Or how much I need you, Adam darling."

3

By dusk that evening Bienville Square was running over. Men, women, and children stood in Dauphin and St. Francis Streets watching the carpenters hanging lanterns atop the wooden stand decorated with bunting, sniffing the tantalizing aroma of barbecued beef and mutton. Ladies in dresses that were new in 1860 or '61, some in hoop skirts made from the remains of old ones, smiled and talked with genuine and pretended gaiety that made the sacrifices of war seem far in the past. Soon the call to food stirred the crowd. When the pastor of the Government Street Presbyterian Church invoked God's blessing on the food and gathering, neighbors and strangers of a kind seemed to forget war and uncertainty and wonder as to what the future would bring.

Adria listened to the handsome medical officer who would deliver the main address. Major Faber had served in Tennessee under General Bragg and later upstate to the credit of his branch of service. For a time she studied in detachment the black facing of his collar and cuffs which, with the black stripes down his trousers legs, distinguished medical officers from others. She had scarcely tasted the meat, and even as she tried to appear attentive she was on edge, wondering when Joseph Adam would ruin his white costume and Annabel's dress. Then Faustine claimed her attention. Actually, she was flirting with a banker's son, one said to have paid a substitute two thousand dollars to serve in his place in the Army. Shame on Faustine, she charged in silence. Suddenly she realized that the medical officer was talking to her.

"You know, Mrs. Jarvis, although those new recruits are the scrapings of the barrel, mere boys and old men, God knows the South can use them." Following the glance of pity and concern she bestowed on the volunteers, he said, "There's nothing like a lovely woman to stir up patriotism in a man."

"Unless it's a band," Adria replied, forcing a gay smile.

The major departed as the captain of the company of recruits assembled his men before the stand and the band began to play "The Bonnie Blue Flag." The mayor of Mobile, and General Maury, in charge of defenses of Mobile, a flag-bearer, and two uniformed officers from Fort Morgan approached Adria and, following her curtsy, escorted her up the steps to a seat of honor.

General Maury spoke briefly, pointedly, regarding the new and second Confederate flag formally adopted on the first of May. A change had long been necessary, he said. Even at the First Battle of Manassas, the Stars and Bars so resembled the Stars and Stripes that there was confusion on the field of battle. And now the Battle Flag, the square Southern Cross, formed the union of a banner of white.

He then produced the new flag and unfurled it. "The Stainless Banner!" he cried, and Mobile cheered loud and long. Once the demonstration ended, General Maury concluded his speech with two words:

"Defend it!"

Major Faber, a dynamic speaker, urged the people not to write their troubles into letters to the soldiers, as this was the greatest single cause of desertion. "Suppose you are down to a dozen grains of corn to eat, shall you write your husband or son of this? To do so may cause his name to appear on the Black Roll, may get him fifty lashes, or a D branded on him, or worse. I've seen worse, just as I've seen the terrible results of the enemy invasion of our own state of Alabama.

"In a recent report by Federal General Dodge up in northern Alabama, he openly boasts of carrying off fifteen thousand bushels of corn, thousands of pounds of bacon, a thousand horses and mules, and fifteen hundred slaves, of destroying tanyards and flouring mills. You know what General Mitchell did up there—turned his troops loose on Athens to sack the town after the old European custom, to curse, abuse, rape, burn, and pillage."

The new troops were getting angry, Adria observed. So were the people. So was she.

"They turned former Governor Chapman out of his home to make room for a Negro regiment."

Adria's glance collided with Randall Sherrod's. She felt a solid impact, as though concrete matter had struck head on. His supercilious smile caused her to realize that the crowd-moving speech was to him a source of amusement. He was laughing at patriots, at the speaker. She was angry at him now. In fact, she decided that she had never ceased to despise him.

She was glad and thankful now that Lawrence had won over her where her mother had failed and forced her to take his money out of Sherrod's despicable business. She had not felt the loss that came with Butler's removal from office in New Orleans. And now she was wondering how on earth she could have for one minute even considered doing business with the Yankees.

As she looked down at Sherrod again, she saw him moving toward Faustine and Elvy.

"And now," Major Faber was saying, "it is my honor and pleasure to present a lady of the South who has done as much for our hospitals, aid societies, gunboat building, and war relief as any one person in Alabama—Mrs. Lawrence Jarvis, who will present the colors to Captain Hayne of the new company."

As the drums rolled and the crowd applauded, Adria could not help but look at Sherrod; rather, she looked down on him, from, she felt, a towering pedestal reserved for only true patriots. A spirit of greatness and devotion to a cause flooded her. Under her look, Sherrod neither cringed nor removed his glance from her face, but stood with head tipped to a match in his hands just beyond the end of his cigar.

Two soldiers on crutches commanded her attention then. One was minus a leg, the other a foot. Both stared up at her out of cold, hollow faces.

Adria knew that every eye was upon her, that she was beautifully, appropriately dressed for the occasion. Futhermore, she represented something, the Southern woman, the bravest, truest, and fairest lady on the face of the earth.

Poised, in no hurry, she held forth the new "Stainless Banner" with the legend she had herself embroidered on its field of pure white: NEVER SURRENDER.

In voice strong and clear she addressed the captain, who stood in stiff salute. "We are proud indeed, noble sir, to confide to you this emblem of our zeal for liberty, hoping and praying and trusting it will nerve your hearts and strengthen your hands in the great hour of trial—that its presence will forbid the thought of seeking any other retreat——"

Adria paused for effect. "—Than in death," she said with emotion.

As Captain Hayne bowed in acceptance of the pledge, Adria's glance was drawn again to the crippled soldiers from the front. The one without a leg glowered at her, shook his head pityingly, and turned away.

Adria tried not to wince, but failed.

The band was playing "Dixie's Land" and the cheers of the crowd rang deafeningly. General Maury and the dignitaries crowded about her, each touching lips to her hand. She was very happy. She felt her blood tearing strong, red and alive, into every fiber of her being. She could not deny that she was being swept up and away on a tide of patriotism and personal glory again, as in Selma, Montgomery, and in other towns, or that she was joyously drunk on it.

In her ecstasy the look on the crippled soldier's face was forgotten, and it didn't seem to matter that Randall Sherrod was leading Adam's wife away from Bienville Square.

Sherrod's grip was tight on Faustine's arm as he stopped still and looked back at the lanternlit stand. His silence seemed too taut, too alive with interest, a bitter interest that was darker and more unpleasant than his reckless expression at first conveyed.

Faustine looked from his half-closed eyes to Adria, surrounded by admirers. "What are you staring at?" she asked, an edge of jealousy creeping into her voice.

Sherrod's chuckle was minus humor. "Look at her," he said mockingly. "To men old enough to be my father and boys I could have sired, she advocates no other retreat 'than in death.' Impressive, all right.

"*Than in death,*" he repeated slowly. "And she's pretty enough to fill the hearts of the boys to overflowing with valor. I know." Almost pensively, he added, "I wish to hell I was that young again. She'd be the faultless angel with wings as white as snow."

Faustine eyed him with mounting curiosity. "And what is she at your ripe experienced age?"

"A handsome woman."

It was the way he said it, the way he looked at her. Faustine felt as only a woman could his true sentiments, and she burned with jealousy in the instant before she decided it didn't matter, that she despised him.

"How very interesting," she said, drawing his glance slowly away from Adria.

He was amused and laughed. "And you're the nicest people," he said, lifting a black eyebrow speculatively. "Lonesome, in need of excitement—some admiring fellow to drink champagne from your slipper."

Faustine swept him with a glance that conveyed a poor opinion of him.

Ignoring this, he pinched her cheek playfully and whispered, "I happen to have chilled champagne. And for every drink I take from your slipper, I'll give you a new pair with heels three inches high—plus a pair of stockings, silk all the way to the top, my dear. Does it sound interesting?"

Mustering her scorn, she stared levelly at him. "Really, Captain, I wouldn't know whether it's a good proposition or not."

She was walking away from him, head high, when his hand fell to her shoulder. "I'm taking a chance also," he said, his lips at her ear.

Whirling, she struck his cheek with open palm. Unaware of anyone near but him, she stared, somewhat dazed and confused, as he threw back his head and laughed. Then, in the shadow of an oak, as hundreds walked past in the night, he took her in his arms and bent her head back and kissed her softly, roughly, until her every nerve and blood cell responded eagerly and she was returning his kisses.

"Stop! Please stop!" she begged, turning her head this way and that. "You're hurting me!"

She stared dizzily into his blazing eyes as he said, "You've wanted to be kissed like this, haven't you? Answer me, Faustine."

"I don't know. No! Let me alone! Please——

People in the darkness passed on by. The lanterns were dimming, and he was pressing her for a reply to his invitation to board his ship. She was saying no over and over, trying to break away. Then his mouth was on hers again and she surrendered without any struggle.

BOOK FOUR


*The Hell and the Fury*

1

THE STILL GRAY SKY OVER BOSTON reminded James of a frozen shell that held back another flurry of snow. The ground was a brittle white and icicles hung from the eaves.

He turned from the window to a mirror, counted the heavy brass buttons on his coat in detachment, two rows of nine each against navy blue, and examined the curly mutton-chop whiskers adorning his face. Although he thought himself far better-looking clean-shaven, Jane Fenwick insisted in her deep, imperious voice that he would merit the respect due an admiral with his distinguished face behind the brush. Thus the experiment, and not once had he been mistaken for a Du Pont or Farragut.

Oh well, it cost nothing to humor the widowed sister of his friend Stephen, who had departed for New Orleans and service in the Gulf squadron. Jane was not beautiful, James thought, though her face was interesting, alive, and demanding. Her figure was slender and she moved gracefully, with a certain gallant defiance and pride he could not help admiring. But despite successive attempts on his part to respond to her romantic interest in him, nothing came of it.

His trouble was like a disease, a memory of Adria.

How many times had he told himself that a man with any brains or gumption whatever would forget a former sweetheart who was married to another man? One thousand times, perhaps. But what was wisdom of the head when the heart ignored it? To a crazy sentimentalist like himself, nothing. So he would go on thinking about Adria, by day, by night. She would continue to laugh at him, to punish him for his indecision by dominating his waking dreams, his restless nights.

It had been more than three years now since he had seen Bay Oaks. And yet, on this wintry February day of 1864 Adria remained as fresh in his memory as when he and Adam departed for Pensacola. The warm, fragrant scents about her, the tiny coil of hair at her forehead, the talkative, changing curves of her mouth, the un-concealed yearning in her eyes. She who could have been his!

As though seized by panic, he threw on his cap and jerked up the heavy blue coat on the way to the door. Escape was imperative. It was always that way. And if pictures of Adria were not enough to torment him, the memory of his humiliation at the hands of Adam, twice, together with his inability to do anything about it, tightened the thongs of frustration about him.

A little over a year had passed since the sinking of the *Hatteras.* James paused at the door and stared at a newspaper. The story of the *Alabama's* career, from escape at Birkenhead to her capture of the Boston bark *Amanda* off Sunda Strait, Dutch East Indies, caused his blood to boil. His anger was directed at a navy that could blockade over three thousand miles of coast line and yet could not locate, much less capture, one small ship that was day by day de-stroying the American merchant marine on the high seas.

Incredible, the *Alabama's* luck and success. She was always some-where else. Now off the coast of Brazil, in the lower Atlantic, stand-ing down the South African coast. Federal ships-of-war chasing after her, to where she had been, but never to where she had fled in the shadow of funeral pyres she lit across the seas. The highways of the ocean were hers, free to roam as she captured, cut down, and burned the commerce of a nation. She was headed for Africa, but no sooner was the Federal flying squadron off in chase than she appeared again in South American waters like a shark in a school of fat trout. Blazoned across Boston and New York papers were the losses of Yankee ships *Washington, John A. Parks, Punjaub, Morning Star, Kingfisher,* and *Nora.* And on and on, ship after ship, cargo after cargo. Splendid conflagrations!

James's eyes narrowed on the doorknob in his hand as he saw again the hungry flames devouring the *Golden Rocket* and felt again that horrible fascination as he watched her burn and heard her crackle and hiss and roar. Her cry was that of a wild thing wounded. Hers was a death without pain; mortals absorbed the agony. The deed reeked of hell's brimstone; it captured in the glow of fire the worst in man and war, a complete abandon. In the excitement of fire one felt the presence of some conflicting vision or feeling and caught for an infinitesimal moment a glimpse of quivering beauty against a darkened sky.

James opened the door and felt the inrush of chill air. It tasted good. He forgot Semmes and the *Alabama*. A little later he was walking toward Beacon Hill.

Jane Fenwick insisted that James sit near the marble fireplace. In a dress of palest blue secured by tiny bows of lavender, she gave a sinuous twist of her body and poked at the log in the fireplace until a shower of tiny bright stars danced madly up the chimney. Then she turned her violet-colored eyes on him and struck a serious contemplative pose. With her face and figure partly highlighted by the mellow flame against soft and dark-toned shadows, she reminded him of a portrait by an old master suddenly come alive. He liked the deep cleft of her chin, her long aristocratic nose, but most of all her firm, energetic eyes and wide mouth.

Her husband, twenty years her senior, had fallen at Shiloh back in 1862. He left her a tidy fortune, a fine house, and a respectable name. Beyond these things she seemed a mystery, though James was reasonably sure that this healthy, attractive woman of twenty-two would not long remain a widow.

"Dear me, James, you look so very serious." Her finger touched the tip of his nose. "Why?"

"The newspaper, I suppose. It opened old sores."

"The *Alabama?*" With his nod, she whirled and her petticoats lifted high, exposing trim legs. Aware of his mounting interest, she gave a careless little laugh. "Sometimes I believe you feign seriousness for two reasons, so I will give you a glass of Colonel Fenwick's honey cordial and make over you until you laugh."

He smiled, his gaze narrowing on her slim waist.

"It isn't normal for a grown man to brood because of a ship. I can't understand you. Suppose it has by some miracle escaped our warships and destroyed much of our commerce, haven't we avenged the *Alabama?* Think of last summer and General Lee's defeat at Gettysburg on the third of July, of the fall of Vicksburg to General Grant on the Fourth. Our flag waves over half the territory of the rebellious slave states and our armies are marching deeper."

"I know. I know," he said impatiently. "But if I don't ever——"

She ran to him and laid a silencing finger on his lips. "Oh, James! What a stubborn, silly fool you are. Come, let me warm you with the colonel's cordial." She moved to a sideboard and returned with bottle and glasses. Pouring, she pressed a brimful glass upon him, filled her own, then dropped into his lap.

The knocker sounded and Jane went to the door. James heard his name mentioned. Before he decided to rise, she closed the door and rounded the corner from the hall staring at a flimsy envelope.

"A telegram for you," she said, puzzled. "Nor would the insolent fellow tell me how he knew you were here."

"I left a note on my door," James explained, eying the telegram. "Open it, Jane."

"Sure you want me to? It contains your orders, no doubt. Where, Lieutenant Hillyer? Does Rear Admiral Farragut call you to the Gulf to be with my brother Steve, or does Wilkes want you to help intercept blockade-runners, or——?"

"Give it here, Jane," he demanded amiably.

"Or shall it be your good fortune to go in chase of the awful pirate Semmes?" She placed the telegram out of his reach behind her. "Sit and close your eyes."

He obeyed, and she sat in his lap again. She kissed him passionately and studied the expression on his red face. Pressing his forehead to the bows at her bosom, she tore the envelope. At the moment he didn't care what his orders were, for he was a man on fire.

"Captain John A. Winslow," she said curiously. "You're supposed to report to him aboard the *Kearsarge*. Does that mean anything to you?"

James started, then settled back. "The *Kearsarge* bottled the *Sumter* at Gibraltar. Maybe it's what I've prayed for." He drank his glass dry and handed it to her. "What else does it say?"

She made no reply, but sauntered across the room. Soon she filled his glass and came to him again.

"What else does it say?" he asked again.

She eyed him speculatively a minute, poked the log, and turned her full attention on him once more. Under his questioning glance she said, "I suppose I must say it. You're to go in chase of the pirate *Alabama*."

A dubious grin crossed his face. "The telegram, Jane," he said.

She tossed her head and made an unsuccessful attempt to evade his hand. Drawing her to him, he removed the telegram from her clenched hand and read it.

Watching him closely, she saw his face take on a new energy and purpose. Soon his eyes lost their sharp focus and he breathed a contented sigh.

"Jim Hillyer!" She could not suppress the outburst. "The expression on your face now is the one I had hoped to bring out of hiding."

James said nothing, though a reply seemed to flow out of his silence, to advise in a voice she could understand that he had a score to settle before any woman could ever hope to claim him.

2

There was scant food on the table, though it wasn't so noticeable if one's head was properly bowed when Joseph said grace. Adria's eyes fluttered open and lifted in time to see her mother wipe a solitary tear. Faustine was lost in thought, her lips parted and loose. Little Adam, two years and one month old, stared at his grandfather, who, in trembling tones, wound up his petition to the Lord, saying:

"And now help us to remember Thy grace and Thy blessing even as we turn our puzzled eyes to heaven and ask why Thou gavest us a Gettysburg and a Vicksburg, O God. Bless us, bless this food to the use of our bodies, we ask it in the name of Thy Son Jesus Christ." A pause followed. "Amen."

Adria said, "It seems the less we have to eat the longer you pray."

Before he could form a reply, Annabel said, "Joseph, you keep throwing Gettysburg and Vicksburg up to the Lord. Aren't you afraid He will resent your feelings?"

"The Lord knows me. He made me, Annabel, and He'll forgive me for hating Yankees and begrudging them one success after another." His desolate eyes took in the table, and he said, "Just look before you at what——"

"Don't, Joseph!" Annabel commanded. Not one of them, Mammy, Erasmus, and Claribel included, had failed to stare at the Cutler table without memories of the groaning spread of good things to eat; things taken for granted; blessing unrecognized in time of plenty. And now meat was served only after Joseph or a slave returned from a hunt with squirrel or deer. During 1863 the raising and storing of meat and garden produce had not been taken too seriously since the war had been nearly won in the spring. But cabbage had flourished, and despite its terrible odor they ate it regularly. By the time Gettysburg and Vicksburg sobered the South, it was a little late to raise food for winter. To make matters worse, the rate of exchange on the Confederate dollar was ten to one shortly after Gettysburg. It had been a bad year for cotton, and the price it brought, forty cents and up in coin, was offset by the tremendous increase in prices. A pound of beef or an ounce of quinine cost over a hundred dollars; flour, forty dollars a barrel in 1862, was now two hundred and fifty dollars.

A fifty-cent cotton shirt from New England sold for fifty dollars in Mobile.

Annabel swallowed hard and forced a smile. "We can give thanks to the Lord that we are not in the path of the invading Northern armies."

They could. They did so in silence. The new crop of Yankee generals were not like McClellan, who respected Southern property and opposed abolition of slavery. With General Grant now in full command of Northern forces, Sherman in Tennessee was looking at northern Alabama and Georgia with fire, slaughter, and destruction in his eyes. "The Yankees," a Southern general wrote Governor Watts of Alabama, "spared neither age, sex, nor condition."

Faustine tiredly helped Adam's plate, then gazed at her son. "The Yankees will never have another chance to take me or mine."

"Don't challenge the Lord, girl," Joseph said.

"I didn't mean it that way," Faustine replied.

Adria had no appetite for leftover squirrel dumplings, corn pone, and bean soup. There was business to attend to in Mobile—cotton from upriver to dispose of, debts to settle, and food and clothing for the slaves to haggle over with the merchants. Poor Joseph. She sent him a sidewise glance, then looked at her plate. Since the loss of Vicksburg he had put off this and forgotten that until one day last August overseer Paul Angleton let it slip that the Clarke County slaves were without flour and molasses. As one thing followed another in the fall and winter, the responsibility of running both Bay Oaks and the upriver plantation gradually shifted from Joseph Cutler to Adria and Annabel. In November, Aunt Eugenia had broken her hip and just before Christmas, Annabel had caught a cold while nursing a sick slave. Pneumonia followed. As a consequence, Adria was forced to accept the full burden.

Joseph said, "Abel should have the carriage ready soon as we eat, Adria. The meeting of the Peace Society is at three——"

"Father, I'd rather you didn't attend."

"Look here, Adria, we've had enough of war. Why should we keep on fighting when all we have to do is signify to the North our willingness to stop fighting? The Yankees have had enough of it. We've won our point. With peace, England will recognize us, and——"

"No," Adria said firmly. "I believe, as Governor Watts said when he was elected, 'If I had the power, I would build up a wall of fire between Yankeedom and the Confederate States, there to burn forever.'"

Annabel frowned. "Adria, you sound more bitter as time goes by. Now what's wrong with your father or any Southerner petitioning for peace?"

"Everything. You forget the lives of Southern men sacrificed to the principles we are fighting for; you forget the atrocities of the invader upstate. I don't. I can't. I won't. And I don't want a Cutler groveling and simpering for peace.

"Nor would Adam have it. Remember what his ship and he and all aboard the *Alabama* are doing. It fills my heart with pride and joy when I read about her sinking another Yankee vessel. She's terrible and ruthless, the Yankees say. Praise God! Let her send all the Federal ships to the bottom. And—while the *Alabama* flies our flag—let none of us talk peace."

Joseph's eyes fell on her sharp and intent. He tugged at a mustache. "Maybe you're right, and maybe you're wrong, child."

"Child? Father, I'm twenty-three, twice as old as a woman my age before the war. So we won't talk any more about peace or attend any meetings of the Peace Society. Instead, we'll think about settling a few debts to several merchants."

"With what, Adria?" her mother asked.

"Well, Mr. Acres gave me an idea a few weeks back. I was trying to get together enough paper currency to pay for the ten yards of calico for your new dress—imagine fifteen dollars a yard!—when he said, 'Miss Adria, if you'll just have your niggers dray several boxes of goods from the wharf, I'll call it even.'

"It's simpler than you think," Adria advised. "Father and I are paying off several thousand dollars in debts with labor. And I—we—are having Mr. Paul send ten slaves down-river to work out what we owe for the seed corn we're planting up on the Tombigbee."

"Along with cotton," Joseph reminded her.

"Naturally, Father," Adria replied. "Cotton is our sin and habit. If we knew it would ruin us, we'd still plant it and stake our future on it."

"It built this house and furnished it," said Joseph with a hint of his former gruffness. "It built this state and the port of Mobile and wrapped you all up in luxury."

"But it won't pay our debts now," reminded Adria, starkly practical. "Nor can you cook it or eat it raw."

Joseph slumped in his chair, pallid, weary, and bitter. "You are right, Adria. And yet cotton is making millionaires out of men like Sherrod."

Adria was ready to argue that risk had more to do with it than cotton when she noticed Faustine suddenly emerge out of dreamy thought at the mention of Sherrod.

Now there was more to this than met the eye, Adria admitted again, thinking back to last May when she presented the colors to Captain Hayne, since killed in battle. She had seen Adam's wife leave Bienville Square with the blockade-runner, though she thought no more about it since she supposed Faustine spent the night with her widowed sister as planned. It was about a week after Gettysburg that Elvy unwittingly corrected Faustine regarding her whereabouts on that night. Since then Faustine had gone to Mobile at regular intervals.

Adria rose from the table without glancing at Faustine, whom she suspected but didn't dare spy upon. Despite all she had been taught, she kept telling herself it was far better to harbor doubt than risk uncovering something too sordid and revolting to live with.

Abel waited with the carriage. Kissing little Adam on both cheeks after a promise to bring a bag of candy, Adria left the house.

Seated by her father, she made every effort to keep a pleasant expression on her face as the unpainted columns and shabby fences of Bay Oaks seemed to close in and smother her. Paint was a symbol of something lost. Bread she could do without, but not paint. She wanted to cry out in defiance at the cause of neglect, to clench her fists and flash her angered eyes and tell the world that she would paint those once magnificent pillars if she had to sell her soul to do it.

She closed her eyes and forced the violence of feeling out of her mind. Suddenly contrite, she shook her head and wondered how she could entertain such frightening thoughts. And the way she thought of Faustine was anything but Christian. The war itself, so big and vast, belittled her and her small problems and responsibilities. How could she covet enough paint to dress Bay Oaks in dazzling white when not one soldier in ten wore the lauded gray of the Confederacy? They wore homespun and rags. And how could she think of paint when daily the Mobile and Ohio Railroad emptied more wounded soldiers into the city, some without an arm or leg, others without the will to live. How could she? She had nursed these men, shuddered and trembled and nearly fainted because of what she saw and smelled and heard. The very sight of a yellow flag that marked a Confederate hospital seemed to age her.

And she could think of self, of regaling her own false pride with a layer of white paint!

She looked at Joseph, who nodded his head half asleep, and smiled with concern in her eyes and a gentle scolding on her lips. The paint was less for herself and more for her father, the same as her self-appointed vigil over Faustine was sustained out of love for Adam. So she was, in fact, guilty of nothing.

She looked back at the retreating pillars. "I'm going to do it," she said, and at the sound of her voice courage flowed through her again.

A few hours in Mobile sapped at that courage. Debts, opposition, men, supplies, money, lack of money, men again, and more debts all joined together in a relentless hammering away at a woman's fragile armor. She was not toughened to the blows of men in business. They took her in with pleasure in their eyes and did their best to rob her. She traded with them, giving and taking, compromising, but when she had done with it she felt as on her last visit, a little tougher, a little less like an aristocratic Southern belle. But more sudden and to the point, she left the city unhappily aware that she had not once been allowed to think of such a luxury as paint.

On the way home she sat back wearily and gave in to the jostling of the carriage as she tersely convinced her father that he had done well in ridding himself of several debts and taking on others. Her voice fell away in a sigh and she seemed to be sitting before a long gilt-framed mirror gazing back into the ante-bellum days at the joy and peace, the beauty and finery that were once, that might never be again. And just inside that borderline, floating on a cloud as white as magnolia blossom and soft as a lover's lips, was the one romance of her life. For a moment and another she was with James. Then gently, politely, the keeper of one's memories removed the forbidden mirror and placed another before her. She saw Lawrence in the background, and on his face was a look of judgment as he pointed an accusing finger at her.

Hastily she put both men out of her mind.

The late afternoon sun flooded through the trees, creating fairyland patches of garish light against long shadows. Ahead, a man and a woman were alighting from a carriage, and then they were walking toward the bluff overlooking the river. Suddenly she realized that they were real. Furthermore, there was no mistaking their identity.

Watching them through the carriage window, Adria tightened her mouth into a hard, thin line. She put down an upsurge of anger, for the moment at least, and thought of following them, not to eavesdrop but rather to advise Faustine and Sherrod, politely, firmly, against being seen together again. But when they disappeared behind bushes of verdant oleander, a desperate feeling of fear and loss engulfed her.

She seemed to see Sherrod kissing Faustine passionately. And she was clinging to him, and he was saying something about a woman made up of half joy and half regret, his level, hungry blue eyes mocking as he told her he had no objection to either emotion, he just didn't like both at the same time. Then his mouth was on Faustine's again and she was surrendering without a struggle.

Adria's eyes opened wide. Though imagined, the scene seemed too real. Anger rose up in her. She despised Sherrod, she despised Faustine, loathed them, wanted to hurt both of them. The temptation was so great that she considered stopping the carriage and running after them with the buggy whip in her hand. She seemed to hear the hiss of the thin willowy whip as it cut through the air like the voice of an avenging angel.

Adria breathed fast, her sharp gaze still fixed on the bluff. There was something satisfying in her imagined violence, if only for a moment. But it fell away and left her trembling, shocked at what her rational mind could not help but see and admit.

Her wrath had not been directed at Adam's unfaithful wife but at the Faustine who was again, as during James's stay, trying to take something from her.

Randall Sherrod!

It was indeed a shocking realization. But there was no truth in it, no grounds for it whatever, Adria thought in defense of self. The strain of the time, the ordeal of the day, war and privation, these things created false, utterly impossible pictures. A tired mind responded, heard things: "You don't need to wear patches on your petticoats. Just stick with Captain Sherrod, notorious speculator and blockade-runner that I am, and your pretty trim-stockinged legs will be gartered in jewels."

He had not spoken those words to Adria. His glance had. To Faustine, perhaps, she who had cried out against the war and poverty only a few days before, saying she hated all men, God and cabbage. But the look in Sherrod's eyes——

Adria sat with eyes transfixed, fingers at her open mouth, and a hand clenched into a fist at the cleft of her bosom. She could no more believe that she entertained a jealous thought where Sherrod and Faustine were concerned than she could account for the pounding of the blood at her throat and temples.

With an effort, she forced her gaze from the oleanders to the drab pillars ahead.

## 31.     The Terrible *Alabama*

THE CRY "SAIL HO!" rang down from aloft, and Lieutenant Cutler responded with the usual "Where away?" without shifting his gaze from the clouds piling up above a colorful sunset.

From the Cape of Good Hope in late March, Captain Semmes had cascaded sail and thrown the *Alabama* into the fairway of the South Atlantic for a zigzag run up to the equator. Near St. Helena, the terror of Yankee merchantment had waited, as always, on an edge of the sea, for any luckless Federal ship and, finding none, loafed under topsails into the track of ships homebound from the Pacific.

Adam looked at the calm sea around the horizon to a spot over the bows where the stranger had been sighted. Nothing was visible from deck other than very quiet sea and sky. However, on this waning afternoon of April 22, 1864, there was a possibility that the patience of officers and crew might be rewarded by the usual Yankee earmarks of cotton sails and rakish masts. One might think the officers in gray had lost their occupations, since the last capture had been in the Indian Ocean in January.

Slowly the horizon narrowed on the ship ahead and presented an American-rigged sail standing their way. Under telescope she seemed to come alive, like a tern forewarned, to flap her wings, as it were, by piling on clouds of canvas. As the brilliant colors of sunset faded over the sea into the matchless tones of ever deepening reds, the stranger helmed into a "keeping off" position and rigged out crimson-tinted studding sails. She seemed aware of the company she had fallen in with and she made it plain that she meant to run for it in the night.

And run she did. As she worked this sail and that with consummate skill in an endeavor to wring every ounce of speed from the sea wind, the fire in the western heavens fell into the flat purple sea. Stars winked on and a bright moon paled the sky and painted the water as far as the eye could reach in silver and sprinkled it with sapphires. The *Alabama* raised sail and gave chase. The watch changed and the ship's bell sounded the hours, though the ships changed neither sheet nor tack.

Adam looked from gauzy clouds overhead down to the serene, jeweled sea, and up into the faces of Lieutenants John McIntosh Kell, Arthur Sinclair, Joseph Wilson, and Richard Armstrong. He saw in their expressions a startling reflection of his own strange apathy. Strange, and yet it was not at all strange, considering that there was a credible explanation for the feeling of weariness and indifference that a few months earlier not one of them would have believed possible. But one had only to look back, and the moon over the sea helped a lonely sailor do just that. Adam stared beyond the great jibs and, in the language of the sea, "whistled up" the past, the sweet and the bitter, as succinctly recorded in his daily journal.

From Jamaica and lovely Cornelia Earle, the *Alabama* ran on to capture the *Olive Jane* and *Golden Eagle*. The former vessel, laden with French wines, brandies, and delicacies, was put to the torch without a single basket of champagne coming aboard the Confederate. And how the captain's steward Bartelli had cringed at the thought of rich olives and *pâtés de fois gras* burning without his having so much as a short run among them.

There followed capture and capture, and still other captures at this "tollgate of the sea." For something to do, the officers and crew studied the phenomena of the currents. Marine philosophers, they called the sun the Father of the Winds, and learned that he was also the father of the currents. In the cool waters under a canopy of clouds evaporation almost ceased, while under the sun it continued, changing both the temperatures and specific gravity of the waters, which in a placid sea should be the same. Therefore there was no rest, and a movement of water followed. A current formed, moved, and another body of water was forced to take its place.

The sea and the heavens were also a source of beauty. Like mortals, they had moods. Tempers flared and the elements raged, wept, dried their tears, and the bosom of the sea heaved and sobbed and slowly returned to normal. Colors warm and bright flooded surface and sail. A blue bluer than blue rose up out of the sea and stood against the sky a bladed peak, and colors as from an artist's palette lifted in fairyland shapes from the undersea.

April, May, June. The *Alabama* was fast changing her skies. Again Adam knew loneliness, a yearning for Faustine, his son, the fields and gardens of Bay Oaks. Another capture. A prize master boarded a ship in all kinds of weather. Vicious seas might toss the boarding boat up to stand on its stern or send it plummeting down into the trough of mountainous waves, but the boarding officer and crew kept doggedly on. Ship and man battled the brave and the weak winds and made a fair weather gale of any and all obstacles along the byways of the sea.

And many were the Yankee ships that were boarded and captured. The whaler *Nye*, greased to saturation with her own fat, 425 barrels of oil, made a splendid fire. The *Dorcas Prince, Union Jack,* and *Sea Lark* were burned, all because there was not a nation on the face of the earth that would receive prizes of the belligerents. There followed a meeting between Semmes and Commander "Deep Sea" Maury at Bahia. Maury commanded the Confederate commerce destroyer *Georgia,* and with him were two of Adam's shipmates of the *Sumter,* Chapman and Evans. Friends met and departed again, and new yearnings joined the old. The seas were empty and wide and silent.

Down in the cold South Atlantic on July 4, 1863, Semmes wrote into his diary: "This is 'Independence day' in the 'old concern'; a holiday which I feel inclined to throw overboard because it was established in such bad company. . . . Still . . . it will not hurt Jack to give him an extra glass of grog." Two days later the *Express* of Boston was captured and burned. Midwinter below the equator, the Southern Cross replacing the North Star, the *Alabama* bore southeast in search of India-bound ships. Off Cape Town the spectacle of the capture of the Yankee *Sea Bride* before the eyes of a city lifted Adam and the entire crew to new heights of glory. The pinnacle was reached in the China Sea after the gallant Confederate ran her easting down in the roaring forties of the Indian Ocean and stood up through Sunda Strait for the free port of Singapore, despite warnings from the Dutch and British of the presence of the Federal steamer *Wyoming.*

Great was the *Alabama's* fame. Perhaps no single ship in all history had attracted so much world-wide attention. She was more than a ship, Adam reflected; she was a legend, a valiant argosy favored by Neptune, a spark to the public imagination. To friend and foe alike, she was an incredible something to be admired. No single ship could go on defying and eluding the great United States Navy, said the world late in 1862, again in 1863. In 1864 the *Alabama* was still do-ing that very thing.

Adam recalled the reception given them in Singapore. As in Cape Town, it seemed to be as Semmes put it, "a generous outpouring of the better classes." Equally as gratifying was a look over the forest of masts in the harbor.

Twenty-two American ships, large Indiamen, were laid up there. They had taken refuge after the capture of the ship *Amanda* off Sunda Strait. And the word reached Semmes that the China Sea was bare of Federal merchantmen. Fearing the *Alabama,* they had run for cover to Shanghai and other ports.

The Singapore *Times* of the ninth of December, 1863, spoke of seventeen American merchantmen, some of which had been lying in port for over three months, and at a time when there was no dullness in the freight market. ". . . It is a picture quite unique in its nature; for the nation to which these seventeen fine ships belong has a Navy second only to that of Great Britain, and the enemy with which she has to cope, is but a schism from herself, possessed of no port that is not blockaded, and owning no more than five or six vessels on the high seas . . ." The *Times* went on to say that the tactics which the Federals had to combat were without precedent, "and the means to enable them successfully to do so have not yet been devised."

Adam frowned out over the moonlit sea. At Singapore came the first dismal realization that all was not well. The *Alabama* was in a state of bad repair. The fires had seldom gone out in her furnaces. The engineer could not clink his bars and remove the incrustations of salt from the bottom of his boilers. The copper on her hull had worn so thin it was constantly dropping into the sea. Shades of the *Sumter,* where could she go for a ship's rest and recuperation?

Home. Any port was home where they could lie out days for re-pairs, so they turned toward the Bay of Bengal, ran on for the Ara-bian Sea, on down through the Mozambique Channel, burning on the way more Federal ships. From Cape Town again the westward voyage slanted north. But gone was the excitement, the joy of chase and capture. They appeared sated on destruction, though Adam knew that this was not so. Every man was lonely; but worse, every man was beginning to wonder, actually doubt, if the cause of free-dom was a lost one.

The last batch of newspapers captured advised that the Yankee hordes occupied strategic positions in the heart of the South. The Federal blockade was strangling the Confederacy, now cut in half after the fall of Vicksburg. Beginning then, the shadows of the future fell heavily over the spirits of the officers.

Kell stared into space, and Armstrong gazed at the moon with prayerful and unfocused eyes. It was so yesterday, and so today, Adam reflected.

The stranger in the night held her distance. With dawn, Engineer Miles Freeman would lend his steam to the chase. Night boardings were not favored. The ship's bell gave off the hour and the moon slipped another notch toward the western edge of sea and sky. A fish leaped up silver and the freshening wind sent wavelets to heal the rent in the sea. An air of unrest was felt fore and aft.

The watch changed. The night moved on, ran out, and morning came. Adam appeared on deck again, breathed a sigh of relief. The stern chase, always a long one, would end now.

The blank cartridge was fired and, two miles away, the vessel luffed to the breeze, her maintopsail aback. Adam boarded her, the *Rockingham* bound for Cork with guano, the cargo covered with the usual false certificate of the Yankee. With her crew transferred to the captor, the vessel was made a target for the gun crew. At five in the afternoon she was consigned to the torch and the *Alabama* filled away.

One week later she took another prize, the *Tycoon,* from New York. Small excitement attended her capture or burning. She gave no chase, no resistance. A listless crew fired her. The commander watched her burn, and Adam cast worried glances at Semmes.

"Old Beeswax," like his worn and footsore ship, showed the effects of toil. The fiery zeal that once flashed like sheet lightning behind his eyes seemed dimmed by sad news from home. Famous, praised, damned, and feared, the "vulgar freebooter" who had destroyed fifty-eight Yankee ships, the great hero of Alabama who gave the weakening South a reason to boast even as she licked her wounds stood in his weariness with still a stamp of ruthless dignity about him. The fire continued to burn inside him.

Another capture would feed the fire, perhaps. It had to burn on something other than itself. But what had it fed upon? And what else but hope for success of the cause of the South could serve as fuel?

Adam turned away. For the first time he admitted to himself that he was afraid of what the future held in store.

## 32.     Spectacle off Cherbourg

1

LIEUTENANT JAMES HILLYER sat at the stern sheets of the boat with back to the long Federal steamer *Kearsarge* on that Sunday afternoon of June 12, 1864. The ship-of-war dedicated to the chase and destruction of the Confederate "pirate" *Alabama* rode anchor in the Scheldt, while James and a fellow officer approached the town of Flushing, Holland, in one of the ship's boats.

"Terrible," said James's companion. "Try it again, slowly—*Mijn vriend, neen* is no, *ja* is yes, *dag* is day. And if you wish to reply to something about which you don't know from Adam's off ox, just exclaim, '*Groot genade!*'"

"What does it mean?"

"Great grace. As we'd say, 'Heavens alive!' But you may run into low Dutch."

Behind them a gun was fired. Turning, they saw white powder smoke rising from their ship's deck. Suddenly the cornet appeared at the fore, causing them to stare at one another. These were unexpected signals demanding the return of all officers and men to the ship. Why? They had not the slightest idea. The boat that passed them minutes earlier must have carried a messenger. In any case, their brief holiday was nipped in the bud.

With land invitingly near, James gave the order that sculled the craft about and sat in sharp scrutiny of the *Kearsarge*. She was practically new, as ships go, having been built in 1861 and, with her sister ship the *Tuscarora*, sent in chase of the much advertised *Sumter*, which the pair bottled up at Gibraltar in the spring of 1862. She was a screw sloop of 1,461 tons' displacement, her armament consisting of two 11-inch smoothbore pivot guns, one 30-pounder rifle, and four 32-pounders. But more than these things of metal, wood, and sailcloth was the man of rare patience who commanded her.

With mind constantly tuned to their mission, which in sharper definition seemed a design for manifest failure, James could not help connecting the emergency to the *Alabama;* and despite all attempts to quell the hope surging through him, he reached the deck with eyes burning so inquisitively that Captain John Winslow found himself hard put to hide a twinkle of amusement.

The stout, round-faced captain paced the quarter-deck while awaiting the return from shore of his missing crewmen. Having already ordered steam raised, he spoke tersely of making all speed to Dover, there to pick up dispatches before proceeding on to Cherbourg, France. Eying speculatively the circle and forward pivot gun, he slowly stroked short-cropped, curly side whiskers to where they dropped under his strong clean-shaven chin. As though he expected the men to have the patience of Job, or himself, he kept them on tenterhooks, on one foot and then the other, until all were aboard and the *Kearsarge* was slipping out of the West Scheldt into the North Sea. Mustering all hands, he stood a half minute stroking with bent forefinger the mustaches curling close about a small, tight mouth before speaking.

With heart pounding, James listened avidly as Captain Winslow read a telegram from William L. Dayton, the American Minister to France, advising that the much sought after terror of the seas, the Confederate States Steamer *Alabama,* had arrived in Cherbourg on Saturday.

"Hence," Captain Winslow said, his face beaming, "the urgency of departure. There is a probability of an encounter and, of course, the expectation of the capture and destruction of this notorious and elusive enemy."

Lieutenant Hillyer scarcely heard the rest. Even though he cheered as loud as any man aboard following the brief address, he repeated over and over a silent fervent prayer:

"Lord, don't let the pirate get away this time."

Before his mind's eye as he said it was the face of Adam. And blurred red in background, his face painted by the glow of the burning *Golden Rocket,* was Raphael Semmes.

Three days later James wrote into his journal the following:

"CHERBOURG, FRANCE, JUNE 15, 1864—Small wonder I scarcely slept last night, for yesterday, sure enough, as we approached the French port of Cherbourg we saw the Confederate flag flying within the breakwater. The feeling that enveloped me as we steamed inside defies description. Neither Christian nor brutal, I can best define it as a fever pounding at my temples. The demand for justice, cold retribution, a personal and national vengeance, the latter excusing the former, became stronger as the officers and crew of our ship gathered on deck for a look at her at close range. Their various expressions of admiration for her grace and beauty in the water, as well as their appreciation of the daring rover's charmed life for nigh on to two years, angered me immensely. But worse, I found myself caught up in spellbound wonder. I, who had fought with her, who had felt in the night off Galveston her guns pounding a deck from under my feet, who had been a prisoner aboard her, actually felt a conflicting surge of pride for this craft whose career is unprecedented in the history of ships.

"Dropping our surgeon in quest of pratique, we sailed on through one pass and out the other and dropped anchor outside the breakwater. Our officer returned with the unpleasant news that the *Alabama* was going in dock for general repairs, pending permission of the Emperor upon his return from Biarritz. As the French Government owns the yards, there is a possibility that French neutrality may be so enforced as to send Semmes out to sea. But we learned also it was general knowledge that all officers and men of the *Alabama* would soon be given several months' leave of absence. So we asked the port admiral for permission to enter port for the purpose of receiving on board the prisoners recently landed by Captain Semmes and taken from Yankee ships *Rockingham* and *Tycoon,* which was refused because Semmes advised that such permission would constitute an act by the French of aiding and arming us, one belligerent over the other. It looked for a time as if we were in bad luck.

"We could scarcely steam in and take the enemy under the nose of the French fleet anchored at Cherbourg, though I in my temerity would have by fair means or foul cut her out from under the Emperor's wing regardless of consequences. Which is why I shall never command, I'm quite sure.

"Then, today, comes the unanticipated, the incredible. The whole port is agog, we hear. The news has been telegraphed to Paris, has been verified by the Confederate officer in charge of naval matters abroad, though it is still difficult to believe.

"Captain Winslow returned from an official visit to the French admiral commanding the maritime district and hastily assembled his officers and read to us a letter, from Semmes to the Confederate States commercial agent, who in turn passed it on to the Federal agent, as follows:

C.S.S. ALABAMA, CHERBOURG, JUNE 14, 1864 TO A. BONFILS, ESQ., CHERBOURG. SIR: I hear that you were in-

formed by the U.S. Consul that the *Kearsarge* was to come to this
port solely for the prisoners landed by me, and that she was to depart in twenty-four hours. I desire you to say to the U.S. Consul that
my intention is to fight the *Kearsarge* as soon as I can make the
necessary arrangements. I hope these will not detain me more than
until tomorrow evening; or after the morrow morning at furtherest.
I beg she will not depart before I am ready to go out.

I have the honor to be, very respectfully,

Your obedient servant,

R. SEMMES, CAPTAIN

"Believe me, all of us were, and remain still, amazed by this challenge. The policy of the *Alabama* has been regarded by nearly all
observers of naval affairs as opposed to conflict, despite the *Hatteras*
affair. Said Captain Winslow in the conference today:

" 'Why Captain Semmes should imperil his ship we cannot understand. He, the selected champion of a cause, is risking everything to
a needless disaster. If we are taken or destroyed, we can be replaced.
He and the *Alabama* cannot. Which proves, gentlemen, that he will
fight because he believes that he will be the victor.'

"For what it was worth, I was asked to give an account of the
*Alabama-Hatteras* battle seventeen months earlier. The captain
noted a few facts, that the battle described raged at short range, that
our 11-inch pivots should force a better distance. We decided that
the ships would perhaps engage on parallel lines, that the enemy
would seek neutral waters in event of defeat. Therefore, we would
see to it that the action commenced several miles beyond the breakwater. And to end the conference in a glory which I shall not soon
forget, we voiced determination not to surrender.

"If need be, we will go down with colors flying.

"Tonight I shall pray for victory. Beyond that, I ask only that
Adam be spared to witness the destruction of his savage ship and
find an end to his unholy vocation a prisoner aboard of us."

2

As the coaling of the *Alabama* proceeded, crews here and there
labored to make the ship ready for battle. Lieutenant Kell's eye was
a moment aloft where Boatswain Mecaskey's gang sent down light
spars and disposed of top-hamper, and another on the thorough
examination of the battery by Gunner Cuddy. Little Dave, the colored wardroom boy, said, "Mistuh Kell got eyes all over, back o' his

haid, too." While Lieutenants Armstrong and Sinclair attended to one chore, Lieutenants Wilson and Cutler supervised the overhauling of the magazine and shell rooms. Gunner's mates, quarter gunners, boatswain's, carpenter's, sailing master's mates, the captains of foretop, maintop, forecastle, and hold had their work cut out for them.

The work continued and the crew talked of the battle ahead with confidence. Other than the wardroom officers, the *Alabama* shipped eleven steerage and four warrant officers, some thirty petty officers, and almost a full complement of firemen, seamen, ordinary seamen, landsmen, and boys. Counting officers and crew, 149 men awaited the engagement with grin, jest, and no end of fancy naval strategy. With the stoppering of standing rigging complete and guns and shot and shell made ready, the treasure chest sent ashore along with the maze of captured ships' papers, chronometers, and other valuables, with swords, cutlasses, and boarding pikes sharpened, the ship was declared ready for battle, and Semmes advised that he would sail out on Sunday, June nineteenth, to meet the Federal *Kearsarge* in battle.

Saturday evening found the *Alabama* in fine inspection order and the port of Cherbourg in a state of excitement. Special trains continued to arrive from Paris. Hotels were filled and still they came, for the battle was heralded as the only major naval duel between the North and the South other than the Hampton Roads battle between the *Merrimac* (*Virginia*) and the Union fleet.

That evening Adam and Lieutenants Wilson and Sinclair were guests at a supper party in Cherbourg. Pressed for a statement beyond the trite "We are confident of victory," Adam's fellow officers called on him to turn a neat and gallant phrase. Such was expected of the intrepid Southerners. The crowds lining the streets and docks for a glimpse of the famous Rebel ship were hungry for some fitting remark that would stir the soul. The people wanted to feel the thrill of the colors flying amid shot and shell, to hear in words the roll of Confederate drums. For these were the people who had chosen another Napoleon to rule over them. They cheered him even as he used the struggle between the North and South to install Maximilian as Emperor of Mexico in a full-scale colonial venture. *"Vive l'Empereur!"*

Sitting there, eyes narrowing with intense thought, with the full attention of fashionable Frenchmen and lovely, smiling ladies upon him, Adam recalled in a flash his feeling of shock and incredulity upon learning of Semmes's intention to fight. "Why? Why, when we're all the South has left at sea? Why, when our purpose is not to fight but to destroy a greater weapon the North uses against us, supplies?" These things he had cried in silence. And in silence the answers to his questions came.

Beyond Semmes's unquestioned gallantry, his faith in his ship, officers, and crew, his honest belief that he possessed two guns capable of sinking any wooden ship of the time, beyond these things which gave him reason to believe that he would win was the burning zeal of a patriot and dreamer who envisioned the effect of a Southern naval victory in Europe. On the personal side, he had too long listened to insinuations that he was a coward who avoided armed ships. A sensitive man, a hero of perhaps exaggerated patriotism, he was also a man who would throw the dice with fate. Win or lose. But Adam secretly thought that Semmes, sea-weary and attentive to the voices on the ocean winds, had heard the judgment of the gods.

Adam stood, eyes twinkling, and faced the hosts. In his best French he said, "We proclaim our intention to sink a Federal or gain a corsair." There followed cheers and champagne. "We promise to meet you here tomorrow night to repeat the festivities as victors."

That night Adam wrote Faustine a long and serious letter. On the eve of battle his thoughts were for her future and his son's future.

3

Sunday, June nineteenth, broke bright and clear, with a gentle westerly blowing and light sea. Aboard the long black Federal ship anchored near the buoy marking the line of shoals to the eastward of Cherbourg, the crew dressed in Sunday suits had just been dismissed from inspection. The bell was tolling for service when a shout rang out on deck. "The *Alabama!* She's heading straight for us!" The officer of the deck raised his glass and soon called down the wardroom hatch, "The *Alabama!*" The drum beat to quarters, and Captain Winslow cast aside his prayerbook for trumpet and ordered the ship put about and headed for sea, the battery pivoted to starboard.

James could not believe it. He looked stunned. Surgeon John Browne smiled, slapped him on the back, and said, "Mr. Hillyer, the general idea is to give more with your 11-inch Dahlgrens than we receive." He moved on, and James went on deck.

Seeing the *Alabama* moving out of the west pass escorted by the French ironclad *Couronne,* James shut his eyes tight and held one trembling hand with the other.

"Lord, twice you've delivered me to the freebooters. Please, this time reverse it. Amen."


Adam looked from the fore-and-aft-rigged steam yacht *Deerhound,* flying the flag of the Royal Mersey Yacht Club, to seaward where the *Kearsarge* lay some seven miles northeastward. The *Alabama* was passing the French ship *Napoleon* when three rousing cheers went up and her band broke out with "Dixie's Land." She had manned the rigging to wish the Confederate well. As the warship *Couronne* led the way from Fort du Homet around the breakwater, Semmes ordered all hands to quarters and "cast loose the starboard battery."

Soon Mr. Kell reported the ship ready for action. Semmes then directed him to send all hands aft. Mounting a gun carriage, he said:

"Officers and seamen of the *Alabama!* You have, at length, another opportunity of meeting the enemy—the first that has been presented to you since you sank the *Hatteras!* In the meantime, you have been all over the world, and it is not too much to say that you have destroyed, and driven for protection under neutral flags, one half of the enemy's commerce . . . an achievement of which you may well be proud . . . The name of your ship has become a household word wherever civilization extends. Shall that name be tarnished by defeat? The thing is impossible!"

"Never! Never!" The crew spoke in one voice.

Semmes told them that the eyes of all Europe at the moment were upon them. "The flag that floats over you is that of a young republic, who bids defiance to her enemies, whenever, and wherever found. Show the world that you know how to uphold it! Go to your quarters."

As the yacht *Deerhound* steamed on out, evidently bent on witnessing the fight, Adam remembered seeing her at the yard of the Messrs. Laird of Birkenhead. He thought of the *290,* of Cornelia Earle, whom he had seen twice since he had last laid eyes on Faustine.

"It is the hour of prayer in old England," said Lieutenant Kell. "May the God of battle watch over us and see that not one of us on this day embraces his watery winding sheet."

Adam winced, looked away. Ahead, the *Kearsarge* steamed to seaward, the *Couronne* stood still aft on the marine league line. Lieutenant Sinclair stood near the 32-pounder recently shifted from portside to the spare port. He had six guns in broadside, and the shift gave the *Alabama* a list to starboard of two feet. There stood likable John Roberts, sail trimmer, with a confident grin on his face. The decks and brassworks shone in the bright sunlight. The men were all in muster uniform, as if they waited Sunday inspection. Lying flat of deck, where they were ordered to rest while the ship approached the enemy, they reminded Adam of fine, gallant athletes.

The decks were sanded down, and tubs of water had been placed along the spar deck. All was ready.

Adam thought of his mother and father, Adria, Bay Oaks, Faustine, his son, Erasmus, Mammy Rose. They seemed so very far away. And yet—so close. Then suddenly they were forgotten. The *Alabama* had decided to "open the ball."

The *Kearsarge* was no more than a mile and a quarter off when she wheeled and presented her starboard battery. When a mile distant, she sheered off, as though satisfied to carry on her attack from this distance. Semmes ordered solid shot sent after her. With a terrific roar, the whole battery responded. Guns leaped back at their tackles and the ship trembled to her mast tips. The Federal replied with a broadside and moved under a full head of steam for the *Alabama's* stern to rake her, but Semmes sheered and kept his broadside to her. Then each ship put her helm aport to prevent the other from passing too speedily. In order to keep their respective starboard broadsides bearing, both ships began to steam around a common center. At a distance now of less than a mile apart, the *Alabama* opened upon the enemy with shell.

On the horse block Semmes cried, "A hit!"

All who could spare a moment's glance awaited signs of excitement aboard the *Kearsarge*. Nothing like that occurred, though they could plainly make out the shot marks. Through glasses Adam saw and remarked upon the ragged holes. How then could shot bounce off her wooden sides? His glance collided with Kell's, and both men were suddenly taut.

Semmes spoke an order. "Mr. Kell, use shells. Our solid shot strike the enemy's side and fall into the water." Above the noise of decks he said something about defective ammunition and tugged at a mustache in puzzled manner.

Adam noted that the shells thrown by the *Alabama's* pivot guns reached the enemy even by ricochet, while the Federal's 11-inch shells were falling short. Feeling the advantage of distance, Adam was rushing abreast the mizzenmast with the observation when the crack of shot and splintering of wood jerked his eye aloft. The spanker gaff had been shot away and the colors were sailing down to deck. A commotion followed upon the quarter-deck section, and no sooner had the colors been hoisted to the mizzenmasthead than the enemy demonstrated both his speed in closing the distance for effective shelling and the power of those 11-inch Dahlgrens. The bulwarks of the *Alabama's* quarter-deck were of a sudden being shot away in sections. The fire continued, deliberate and hot, and Adam found himself too occupied to reach Semmes with a now useless warning.

The yell of battle increased about him. The men seemed too busy to realize that they were scared or that one had to know fear to know courage. They threw their weight against the tackle ropes, hauled up shot and shell, wiped tears evoked by powder smoke, all as they had done in gun drills. The decks continued to recoil from the blast of guns. The only difference, this was real.

Again Semmes cried out jubilantly. A 100-pound percussion shell had lodged in the *Kearsarge's* sternpost near her screw, causing considerable excitement among the Federals. Should it explode, the *Alabama's* victory would be assured. But it did not explode.

Sweat-and-powder-caked, Adam was working up to the 8-inch pivot gun port when an enemy shell struck. The gun, manned by twenty-two men under Lieutenant Wilson, ten men on each side, two captains in the rear, had just been loaded and run out to fire. Adam saw Michael Mars, compressor man, stoop to his knees to retard the recoil. Then the enemy shell came, struck full in the stomach of the first man on portside of the gun, and tore on through him and every man lined up in that row. A moment before serving the gun five men were instantly piled up, with half their bodies shot away, in a mass of blood, flesh, and bone—even before they could close their eyes to the carnage of their dying selves.

As Lieutenant Wilson's hands jerked up involuntarily to close off the ghastly sight, Adam bit his lip until it bled; then recovering, he ordered the mangled trunks thrown overboard and the wounded rushed below. Amid the screams of the latter, the firing continued. Mars shoveled the dead over the side and sanded the deck once more.

To Adam, the taking and not striking back was unendurable. Why didn't the Confederate shells pierce the enemy hull? Was she actually an ironclad in disguise? There was no time to ponder that question or any other, for the exploding shells were ripping great holes along the spar deck, throwing up sunbursts of splinters, driving them into the smoke, into arms and faces. The sulphurous smoke darted off in streamers, then curled and hovered inboard to blind and choke.

A drill was all give, a battle give and take; but this was hell itself.

The thud of shot striking the hull, the rending of wood and harsh grating of metal, the loaders yelling for room and Fireman Christian Pust crying in one last breath for life as the enemy's second 11-inch brought his life to an end and left four others severely wounded— these were the sounds between the thunderclaps of broadsides and the mighty smashing of Federal shells against the brave but outclassed *Alabama*. The sights were as painfully shocking to Adam Cutler, who felt by the moment the added list of his ship from shot holes at the water line. She careened more to starboard now.

"We're being shot to hell!" was all he could say, and that in fearful silence. "Being shot to hell." And a glance at Semmes was a look at a baffled commander whose boarding exercises were going for naught. One short hour earlier he had had in mind to bring about yardarm quarters, fouling and boarding tactics. Repulsed, he remained calm under fire, trapped but not beaten. His darting eyes were searching for a way to victory. In the past he had always won. He might win this time.

And now, mere seconds later, the quartermaster was binding Semmes's bleeding arm. Then both Semmes and Kell tensed and braced themselves as the ship careened more heavily to starboard.

The circling of the ships continued, and Adam read in Semmes's face a decision to make all sail possible once the circuit of the fight placed the ship's head toward the French coast again. But before the commander could voice it, another enemy shell struck the breast of the gun carriage of the 8-inch pivot aft and spun about on deck. Adam picked it up and threw it overboard.

The circling completed to Semmes's satisfaction, he ordered Kell to raise sail and try to run for the French coast. As a sailing emergency existed, it being imperative to get the ship's head off as quickly as possible, and since the *Alabama* did not answer to her helm as quickly as desired, Kell ordered John Roberts, an Englishman of commanding stature and unusual strength, to loose the jib. When Adam made his way forward through the litter of decks, Roberts had executed the order and was moving away.

Adam saw him out on the jib boom, his grin wide and shoulders erect. An instant later Roberts was disemboweled by an enemy shell. He did not fall but, to the amazement of all who saw him, exhibited an unbelievable aftertenacity of life. He clung desperately to the jib boom, worked along the footropes to the topgallant forecastle and down the ladder to the spar deck. There, with successive screams of agony, he clawed at the air above him until he fell in spasms at the port gangway.

The evolution of the ship continued. By righting the sluggish helm, running up the headsails, hauling at the fore trysail sheet, the *Alabama* came around with head pointing toward the French coast and her port battery facing the *Kearsarge*, now running down to place herself between the *Alabama* and shore.

Engineer O'Brien came on deck to report that the apertures knocked in the hull at the water line had brought water in the lower hold, that it sat flush with the furnace fires. Then Miles Freeman appeared with the news that the fires were out and he could no longer work the engines.

Semmes glared at him. A tiger at bay, his teeth dulled, he made it plain by the intensity of his gray eyes that he could not cast hope of victory aside. There had been no pacts, no stirring vows to go down with the ship, but had Semmes in that moment commanded it, Adam believed that every man would have followed him into the deep with "Dixie's Land" ringing. He broke the spell with:

"Mr. Kell, go below and see how long the ship can float."

With Kell, Adam stared at the destruction of the wardroom. There stood Assistant Surgeon Llewellyn with bandage in hand and a blank look on his face. His table and last patient had just been carried away by an 11-inch shell. Water poured into her. Dazed, Adam went on deck, where Kell advised Semmes that the ship could not float ten minutes. Then Adam heard the fate of the great *Alabama* read by her commander in perhaps the bravest words he had ever spoken:

"Cease firing, and haul down the colors."

Next he said it would "never do in this nineteenth century for us to go down, and the decks covered with our gallant wounded."

Adam dropped his glance as they struck the colors. Wanting to cry like a child, he grimaced unduly, wiped dry his eyes, and looked up just as the *Kearsarge* fired another shell.

Anger assailed him then. "Sir," he cried to Kell, "let me take one last shot at the savage!"

"No, Mr. Cutler." To the crew he said, "Stand your quarters and do not flinch. Quartermaster, show a white flag over the stern."

Another blast from the enemy was followed by three more. Five in all after the surrender!

Anger was now justified, though incredulity showed in the faces of all. Adam had scarcely drawn in his glance from the enemy who chose to disregard an inviolate rule of Christian warfare when Matthew O'Brien called his attention to a stream of blood running from his fingertips. A fragment from the last enemy shell had ripped his sleeve. Dr. Galt bound his arm tight below and above the elbow and placed it in a sling.

The pipe was given: "All hands save yourselves."

The ship was settling fast; air hissed and bubbled up through holes in the deck aft and water gurgled through and curled in grim warning. One dinghy had escaped damage and Kell ordered Adam to take the wounded, with Dr. Galt and Master's Mate Fulham, to the *Kearsarge* and advise that the *Alabama* was sinking and ask that boats be sent to save the crew.

Adam took a last look at wounded, toppling spars, a riddled smokestack, and decks turned into kindling wood by bursting shells and laden with wreckage of rigging and empty shell boxes. But she lived. With sail set, the *Alabama* slid slowly on, wounded, dragging, leaving in her wake a trail of wreckage on the sunlit sea.

## 33.   Victor and Vanquished

### 1

ON BOARD THE *KEARSARGE*, Captain Winslow was ordering his ship laid across the *Alabama's* bows for raking with grape and canister shot when a junior officer cried, "She's launching a boat, sir!"

The captain's executive, Lieutenant Commander James Thornton, quickly verified this.

"Another Rebel trick!" cried Lieutenant Hillyer in the same unyielding voice that had drawn the sharp attention of fellow officers since Tuesday. He was unaware of the scalpel-like glances given him, or of Captain Winslow's growing embarrassment at having ordered five shells hurled at a surrendered enemy.

"Enough, Mr. Hillyer!" Winslow sounded crisp. "It is bad enough that we possibly mistook explosions aboard the enemy for cannonading after surrender. I shall not fire on his boat."

The face of Captain Winslow reddened perceptibly with the memory of his own cry after the *Alabama's* ensign was half-masted, union down, "He is playing us a trick. Give him another broadside!" Prior to the end, it had been a cool, rhythmic hammering at an enemy by a highly trained, efficient crew with nothing of a nature to invite criticism. But here, devil take it, was cause for censure.

James was too elated and keyed up to recognize reproof. He stood with telescope up, eying the *Alabama's* deck and surrounding water where heads bobbed like coconuts. How fast his heart was beating. Each bursting shell against the pirate who sank the old *Hatteras* had been a personal blow at Adam and Semmes.

The yacht *Deerhound* was drawing close now, steaming toward the stern of the *Kearsarge* from windward after viewing the show from the royal box, as it were. And the Confederate dinghy was coming on. James's glass fell to the lads at the sweeps, and then to an officer in battle-blackened gray with arm in bloody bandages and sling.

"Adam!"

This was all he could ask for; the day was now complete; revenge was his in cup running over. But nothing came in such full measure. He should remain alert. Aye! By heaven and hell, he would do just that, not once letting his mind forget that stinging Cutler hand at his cheek the night they burned the *Golden Rocket*.

The boat came on until it rode the choppy sea almost under the huge 11-inch Dahlgren that won the Battle of Cherbourg. Standing aft, Adam could hardly remove his eyes from the thin deal which covered, except for marks of the *Alabama's* shells, the chain armor amidships.

"An ironclad!" Adam exclaimed.

Small wonder, he reflected, that the *Alabama's* shot and shell bounded off the Federal's sides, for there under the deal hung plating of sheet chain of 1.17-inch iron. All down her midship section, ripped and torn and battered by shot, lay that armor that spelled the difference in victory and defeat.

Adam felt both sick and resentful.

Slowly his glance lifted. Just abaft the main chains in the gun port stood the captain and several officers. He said, "Confederate States Lieutenant Cutler sent by Captain Semmes to report to Captain Winslow that we are disabled and in sinking condition, and beg that boats be sent quickly to rescue our crew and that you take the wounded we have here aboard of you."

Winslow stroked his beard. "Does Captain Semmes surrender his ship?"

"Yes." Adam's face tightened up. "We struck our colors, sir, and it is charitable to suppose that after we had done so no ship-of-war of a Christian nation would have intentionally fired five times upon us."

Winslow bristled. "You renewed the fight after surrender. So it is I who am charitable for not continuing the shelling until your ship lay under the waves."

Adam could recall no breach of surrender aboard the *Alabama,* but decided that he could gain nothing by contesting the victor at a time when the need of help was imperative.

"May I hand up our wounded, sir, and return with my boat to assist in rescuing the drowning? You have my word of honor that when this is done I shall return to you and surrender."

After a thoughtful moment Winslow said, "Your request is granted, sir."

Only then did Adam see James Hillyer. He emerged from the group of officers partly hidden by the 11-inch monster of destruction and stood with his gaze fixed on Adam.

For a half minute their glances met and held strong. What Adam saw in James's face was more than renewed challenge at a time when victory should have tempered his former anger. It was a look that seemed stripped raw of amenity and made up of exultation and unyielding judgment, such as Adam had never imagined nor ever witnessed. He felt as though James was about to speak his sentence and watch him swing from a yardarm. These things burned too strong in James, and Adam slowly lowered his eyes to the temperate sea.

2

Minutes later Adam was helping men of the *Alabama* out of the water. The yacht *Deerhound* had steamed up to the *Kearsarge* and, after a pause, moved on to gather up the drowning, though not a boat was lowered by the Federal at that time.

Over there in the water young Maffitt was swimming toward Kell. "Take my life preserver, sir!" Kell refused. With the boat loaded with half-drowned sailors, Adam cried for the first officer to swim to him, that he would take to the water. Master's Mate Fulham then drew Adam's attention to his wound. The sight of fresh blood nauseated Adam. Weakened, he asked about Semmes, and learned that he was afloat. A minute later Adam's crew took Semmes out of the water. In a state of exhaustion, the captain was stretched out in the stern sheets. Then, half the survivors of the dinghy clinging to the sides, Kell was heaved aboard.

The *Kearsarge* tardily launched two boats, as though she grudgingly saw fit to adhere to the rules of civilized warfare; or, thought Adam, perhaps she merely wished to claim the survivors as prisoners of war. One of the boats came within hailing distance and her officer asked of Captain Semmes.

"Captain Semmes is dead," Kell said, ordering the dinghy to the *Deerhound*. A few sweeps of the oars, and someone cried, "Look!"

Adam saw the *Alabama* prepare for her watery grave. Down went her stern, under, deeper. The final plunge of the ship that had won the admiration of the world was at hand. Now launching her bows high in the air, she stood nearly straight up, almost half her length out of the water, her spars, guns, wreckage, and everything loose rolling, rumbling, crashing down into the water. Her anchors swung like toys from the cathead and her headsails still bellied in the wind, proving her very much alive and faithfully at work. Then her smokestack hissed under, and her strong mizzenmast was carried away. Higher lifted her fine, clean bows in final salute to a proud life and a proud death. Then she slid under and disappeared from the face of the waters, leaving in her wake another mast and a whirlpool of great size and strength.

The dinghy touched the *Deerhound*'s side.

Adam's head whirled as though he were drunk. He could not remove his eyes from the spot where the *Alabama* was last seen.

Rising, he swayed on his feet. Kell caught him and demanded that he be passed on board the yacht at once.

"No!" Adam roused himself. "No. I promised Captain Winslow—pledged my word of honor—to return——"

The picture of his father appeared just before Adam lost consciousness. There was Joseph Cutler standing before him with finger upraised and wrath on his face; standing there upbraiding him for betraying a pledge, reminding him that a promise was a promise, even if it had been made to a goddamn Yankee.

3

James watched the *Alabama* go down, saw the bobbing heads about her grave drawn under by the suction. Shuddering, he trained his glasses on the boats, and then on the *Deerhound*, now steaming to leeward.

The guns still hammered at his ears and he gave thought to their terrible destructiveness. He had reason to be proud, and his father had reason to boast, for Lieutenant James Hillyer had distinguished himself under fire on this day. Whether or not he received public credit for directing the fire against the enemy's after pivot gun, historians who recorded this, the most important sea fight of the war to date, could only remark on the magnificent American gunnery on this day.

Surgeon Browne came up to report that the three Federal gunners wounded were in good condition; and hearing it, Lieutenant Commander Thornton said, "Something of a record, I'd say. After all we gave, not a man of our crew lost." This turned Winslow's pinched face about for a slow, detached nod of his head and a subsequent jerk at the visor of his cap.

"Indeed, Mr. Thornton, there could hardly be a more ideal victory under more favorable conditions. All Cherbourg watching from the heights and along the bastions and the mole. All plans perfect enough to have been devised by hindsight. We go into action with fires raked perfectly clean and the safety valves lashed down and our speed at its utmost. We take from the enemy twenty-eight shot, one of which, the 100-pounder, could have spelled our doom had it exploded. We are cut up in the rigging, our smokestack is perforated, three of our boats are shattered, and there is other damage."

The speech seemed to have done him good, in that it relieved him of accumulated tension. The officers waited for him to say more;

rather, something in summation. They were not disappointed.

"But I am wondering, gentlemen, if we in the flush of our victory were not lacking in grace. And charity. That Rebel officer's reprimand sticks in my crop. And our dilatory manner of launching rescue boats is——"

"Sir," the executive interposed, "any imputation of inhumanity can never exist in the face of your request to Captain Jones of the *Deerhound*. You implored him to 'save those poor fellows who were struggling in the water for their lives.' "

James suddenly lowered his telescope. Whirling, excitement strong in his face, he said, "Captain, sir, I beg to report the presence of Captain Semmes and Lieutenant Kell aboard the British yacht!"

"Yes, Mr. Hillyer?"

"The *Deerhound* is steaming off to leeward with them. I suggest that a shot be fired to bring the yacht to, sir. May I have your permission to do so?"

"Impossible, Mr. Hillyer. The yacht is simply coming round."

Thornton's brow knit. "Sir, I'm inclined to agree with Mr. Hillyer."

"Consider, Mr. Thornton. Would any gentleman flying the flag of the Royal Yacht Squadron act so?"

A minute passed by and still another. The *Deerhound* moved speedily north, bows pointing for Southampton. Soon all officers were of the opinion that the yacht was running the prize naval catch of the war and his officers to the safety of the English coast. And still Winslow insisted the yacht was simply coming round.

The empty dinghy of the *Alabama* drew James's attention. "Look, sir! There's proof your generosity was abused. That man was Lieutenant Cutler who fired the first merchantman, the man who twice held me prisoner! Shall we let him escape?"

Captain Winslow looked at the dinghy, then over the sunlit sea at the vanishing *Deerhound* and resorted to silence. The yacht steamed on toward the horizon. The continued silence on deck together with the long faces made it evident that the escape of the *Deerhound* and her coveted prize was a source of deep regret. The famed *Alabama* had been destroyed, sent to the bottom, but her commander had escaped. Victory had lost its essence to the conqueror.

James Hillyer's loss far exceeded that of any officer on deck. The destruction of the *Alabama* and the capture of Adam were the two major things he had lived for. They had so dominated his life that with the sinking of the *Alabama* and the dishonorable escape of Adam, he had only his stubborn anger for the latter to cushion his falling spirits. For burning moments it sustained him. Then he found himself with nothing to lean upon.

## 34.   Coconuts and Carriages

1

ADRIA looked up from the account books thinking she would faint. Hastily she rose and walked to a window. Though the air was naturally hot on this afternoon in early July, there was still a sign of the brave south wind at work. Animated festoons of gray moss seemed to lure a gentle breeze her way. Near the window bees droned about the honeysuckle and in the trees and gardens insects sang a lazy summer's song. How drowsy and inviting, she thought; how she would enjoy giving in to it, as she had been able to do a few years earlier, to scatter responsibilities to the winds and lie in the shade of an oak and dream.

She pretended a minute that she was nineteen again, without a care in the world. The minute ran out and she felt again the weight of Bay Oaks and an upriver plantation.

The ledgers told a story that forced her brows together. The frown wrinkles were etched strong in her face and she seemed to know that they would grow deeper. With mounting debts and continued sharp rises in the cost of bare necessities, she could see no way of going on. But, strangely, there was no way of stopping either; the things that made future existence appear impossible kept on pushing one into that future and on into another one. But how could it just go on and on?

Standing over the books, she turned a page and read an entry at random:

Sat. June 18: Five yds. muslin—$160.00
           Two cakes toilet soap—$80.00
(Returned hat and two feathers for same and used credit of $550.00 for two barrels flour.)

Heavens, the terrible things the books revealed! She turned her back and looked at Hopkins eighteen-page *New Orleans 5 Cent Song-Book* atop a stack of discarded magazines. Songs of 1861 were the songs of her heart. Now she wasn't sure she had a heart. Often she listened to Faustine sing the popular love song "Lorena" without so much as thinking of James. And then again when Randall Sherrod drove up singing in his fine tenor voice "Paul Vane," the answer to "Lorena," something warmed and tingled inside her.

"Heaven forbid!" she whispered, feeling the surge of blood at her throat and temples. Why, of late she had looked forward to the coming of the gift-bearing blockade-runner with no more shame than a slave awaiting Santa Claus. Even now she caught herself gazing eagerly out the window. Captain Sherrod was supposed to have returned yesterday.

"God knows we can use what he brings," she said.

That was the admission that hurt. A year earlier it had been possible to look down her nose at a man far beneath her social level. But a year had raised Sherrod's platform and dropped hers. A symbol of it all was the lowly coconut which Adam had cried for in Mobile. She could not afford it, and Sherrod had bought it for him. The thing cost ten dollars!

Joseph came down the stairs and asked if she had seen his last copy of the *Southern Literary Messenger*. She had, though she did not tell him that the magazine had changed so that it could hardly be called literary any more. She said irritably:

"Here it is, Father. But a lot of good it does to hear President Lincoln called the 'Springfield Gorilla.' It doesn't stop that horrible Sherman's march on Atlanta or tend to relieve our sense of shock at his vandalism."

"I know. I know, Adria," Joseph said, resigned, which caused Adria's pity to strike a spark from her temper. Unable to control herself, she said recklessly:

"You know, Father, I'd be willing to order every last row of beans and peas plowed under if I thought it would rouse some of your old spirit." As he stared at her, more hurt than offended, she wanted to run to him and put her arms about his shoulders. Instead, she hurried out of the room, saying, "What this place needs is life and music and laughter."

In the hall, she stared up at the rear fanlight and, closer, at the Doric columns dividing the hall and said in a voice that rang with

challenge, "And that's what this place is going to have real soon—
a party that will be long remembered!"

Oblivious to the hot July sun, she walked on outside without her
bonnet. Down the path to the bluff, she turned and stared at the
one pillar that gleamed a dazzling white. Only one.

"Even if I have to use my paint money," she said, "there's going
to be a party."

Randall Sherrod arrived one hour later. He sat alongside his
largest Negro in the seat of a wagon. Behind him were barrels and
boxes, and tied on aft was his fine black horse hitched to a bright
and shining buggy. At his cry, "Ship ahoy!" Erasmus hobbled on
his cane from the kitchen and Claribel ran down the stairs ahead
of Adam and Faustine. Aunt Eugenia came to the balcony above the
front door and asked what the pirate was peddling.

Sherrod's blue eyes narrowed on her. "Well, well, I thought you
were still in Yankee-held Natchez. Just how did the Yankees get rid
of you?"

"It wasn't easy," Eugenia retorted. "But when I told them I knew
you, they banished me."

From the front gallery, Faustine said, "Aunt Eugenia was actually
banished, but it was for walking out of the services during the
prayer an unwilling preacher was saying for Abe Lincoln."

Sherrod scoffed, "That's what they told her."

As Faustine's laughter joined Sherrod's, Eugenia said, "Faustine
Cutler, at least I'm no Methodist, as you and Elvy. If I was, I
wouldn't admit belonging to a church so violent up North that the
Federal War Department gave Yankee Methodists the right to lay
hands on any Southern Methodist minister."

"That's because you're a lovable old hypocrite," Sherrod retorted,
tossing a bundle of knitting yarn up to her.

Adria arrived at the upstairs balcony door in time to hear her
aunt say she would knit a hangman's noose to fit him and give it
to the Mobile Committee of Public Safety.

Adria knew the story of Sherrod's last brush with the so-called
vigilantes. In late May they had cornered him in a downtown hotel
lobby with a warrant for his arrest as a public nuisance. Despite
the fact that his *Belle of Mobile* had a riddled smokestack and
other marks of Yankee guns, he was publicly accused of treating
with the enemy. Facing the group, who seemed as ready to hang
him as not, Sherrod told them to make up their minds, that he was

due in the Gulf off Pensacola to buy with Southern cotton from a Yankee merchant a boatload of flour, medicines, shoes, and clothing. "At a risk of fifty thousand dollars of *my money*, gentlemen." To which the leader of the group declared that here was proof of his Yankee connections. Sherrod winked an eye at him and said with impunity before walking away, "Handy connection, isn't it, suh?"

Aunt Eugenia knew the story, Adria recalled. For Leland Jarvis had no sooner told it to them than Adria had exclaimed on the spur of the moment, "I could hug him for that!" And Aunt Eugenia had responded with, "I believe you're in your right mind, child."

Adria remembered something else, that in that moment she had been alarmed at her sudden jealousy of Faustine.

Looking down at Sherrod now, she felt a sudden upsurge of the old resentment for him. Perhaps it was because she wished to remain superior to him as in the years gone by and was forced instead to lean upon him. Then again, it could be that the long struggle had placed her in contact with a man stronger than she who simply waited, confidently, for the day when he could buy her body and soul. He had the patience of the tides and winds. And on his side was war, which crept in and corroded everything it touched.

Everything. She looked at Faustine.

In her heart she wished to go to her room and lock herself inside. But there was cotton to haggle over. She had a family and over one hundred slaves to feed. Mustering her strength of will, she drew herself proudly erect and went down to accept his gifts and bargain with him.

## 2

Two hours had gone by. Every minute had been a strenuous adventure to Adria. Every emotion in her had been aroused, she thought. Sherrod had looked her over hungrily. He had dropped a barrel of sugar for the Negro children and all had watched them eat it until one said, "Marse Joseph, it done taste bitter." Sherrod had with war talk and zeal made Joseph "fighting-mad" again. With gifts and blarney, he had caused Annabel to forget war and trouble. He brought wine and cigars and good things to eat. But he looked at Faustine with a sudden lift of a brow as some private memory of her surfaced. Adria had wished at once to both hurt and thank him. He had offered her thirty cents a pound in coin for ten bales of cotton but seemed pleased when she held out for sixty cents in gold on twenty bales, ten cents a pound more than the top price.

Why, she asked herself, should he do this? And why should she demand it?

Sherrod got up from the table, complimented Annabel's meringues, and said he should be going. Looking at Adria, he spoke of selling his black horse and rig at a low price and, despite her repeated statements that she wasn't interested at any price, he finally talked her into riding with him to the river and back. Urging her to drive, he watched her all the way to the crossing, where she reined up and tried to hide her interest in luxuries she could not afford with a casual:

"How much?"

To her great surprise, he said, "They are not for sale, Adria."

She met his steady glance without wavering. Slowly she nodded understanding. "Just how much is your horse worth, Captain Sherrod?"

"Every bit of three thousand Confederate," he replied, searching behind her eyes.

"Or three hundred coconuts," she said, dropping her glance and biting her upper lip thoughtfully.

"Three hundred coconuts, Adria."

Her glance darted back to him in search of mockery or a hint of amusement. She found neither in his expression; rather, she saw a speculative light, perhaps a shaft of suppressed excitement, in his eyes. But she was looking at a gambling man who could laugh at gain or loss alike.

He touched her dress. "Why should you of all the women in the South wear Dixie silk?"

That was what homespun was called, Dixie silk. He knew why she wore it—to save the remnants of real silk and dresses of years past for public gatherings—so she did not bother to reply to so foolish a question.

"I've fetched you silk, Adria," he said.

"Yes," she replied. It had gone to her mother, some of it to Faustine. And right now she was wearing a petticoat made from a piece of his scarlet taffeta. She looked from her folded hands in her lap to a log floating down-river and thought that his color and brand were scarlet. As the color of war was not pink but blood red, so was Sherrod's banner the color of Satan's face.

"Yes," she repeated. "And when this damn war is over, I'll pay you for every yard and inch of it."

"If it had been for sale, I would have sold it. The same as the white paint I'm running in next trip."

"Paint?" She could not check her look of sudden alertness in time.

"For the columns of Bay Oaks." A light laugh escaped him. "As long as they're white—isn't that it, Adria? Your pride is up for show on those pillars. A pretense of past grandeur keeps something alive, doesn't it?"

"What is it to you?" she demanded, anger rising.

"A great deal, Adria," he replied, more serious than she had ever seen him. "You see, it's like this: Anything you want that much I intend to get for you, one way or another."

"Why? What on earth could you possibly hope to get in return?"

His eyes and voice were both calm and reckless with adventure as he said, "You."

She did not dare lift her eyes to him for they would reveal her loathing. She was fastidious beyond his imagination and her flesh crawled at the thought of his nearness. Her hands trembled. She wanted to cry out and tell him she was Mrs. Lawrence Jarvis, the soul of honor. Then she was suddenly afraid of him; afraid, rather of the boldness and mystery of this man who made danger a junior partner in his pursuit of business or pleasure.

He was wise enough to remain silent and to make no movement that might disturb her. Even when she picked up the reins and turned the horse toward the gates of Bay Oaks, he very slowly tugged at the reins and brought the buggy to a halt before turning her face toward his.

"I'm afraid, Captain Sherrod, you've mistaken me for someone else."

"I don't make mistakes like that. However, I'll send a bill of sale for the horse and buggy around tomorrow."

"You mean——?" She stared at him.

"Just a gift. I always bring gifts, don't I?"

His head bent and he touched his lips to hers. Meeting no resistance, just curious study in her fine level eyes, he took her in his arms and covered her mouth with his. She felt the heady weight of passion, and she shrank from it, from the roughness of his cheeks and muscular mouth. But she did not draw too far away from him, because she liked it more than she would ever admit to herself.

Then it was over and she sat trembling and burning with shame at what she had done. He took the reins and said calmly, as though the touch of her did nothing to him, that the horse was called General Magruder, after the most elegant and dashing of Confederate generals.

Adria said nothing. She decided that she had little if anything to regret. After all, she had given precious little for a great deal. Besides, the family and the slaves had to eat, honor or no honor. The horse was worth a lot of money; so was the buggy. And all the pillars of Bay Oaks, not just one, would be white with paint; and there would be a great party.

She took the reins in her hands and said, "Giddap, General Magruder."

## 35. Thunder over Mobile Bay

### 1

ADRIA AND HER MOTHER lowered coffee cups almost in unison and listened. From the south came strange sounds, like thunder. However, thunder over a horizon rumbled and rolled across the line of earth and heaven, while this seemed more like repeated explosions dulled by distance. Besides, the day was clear and sunny.

It was around eight on this August morning when Adria joined her father on the gallery. "Heavy cannon, Adria," he said grimly. "I believe I told you the Yankees landed over a thousand men on Dauphin Island day before yesterday to lay siege to Fort Gaines. The noise down there now means the Federal fleet is probably working between Forts Gaines and Morgan. Old Farragut, you know, is out to do to Mobile what he did to New Orleans two years back.

"But we've got him stopped. Yes, sir, we've got him. Didn't General Joseph Johnston say the defenses of Mobile were the strongest in the Confederacy? And my money helped do it, Adria. Helped build the most powerful ironclad ram afloat—the *Tennessee*—same as the efforts of you and women like you were largely responsible for the gunboats *Selma, Gaines,* and *Morgan,* all Alabama-built. They're down there to stop the damn Federals if they get past the forts."

Joseph talked on, about the forts, the *Tennessee* under Admiral

Buchanan, who had commanded the *Merrimac* (*Virginia*) at Hampton Roads, the barriers of piles and torpedoes in Mobile Bay.

Adria scarcely heard a word her father was saying. She was busy trying to reconcile in her stunned, unbelieving mind the first cannonading she had ever heard. There was in the sound of it something fascinating in a dreadful sense, like judgment day and immortality, for each punctuated rumble was a deliberate, death-dealing blast. The war had cast a lengthening shadow over her land. Now it had come, actually, within hearing distance. Men were being shot at and killed. The terrible things she would hear about tomorrow were happening now. The concussions were jarring the unpainted columns of Bay Oaks, causing her to stare affrighted into the clear southern sky that arched down over the entrance of Mobile Bay, where on that morning of August 5, 1864 . . .

2

The desire of Admiral Farragut to get under way with his fleet of eighteen ships at daylight on the inflowing tide had been thwarted by fog in the night, which delayed the work of forming a battle line. With the first dim hint of day the fog began to lift gradually and present a view of ponderous phantom ships, weird and gray in the false dawn. The delusion of bulk was not a deception, but vessels lashed together in pairs, "balanced to partners," for the run past terrible Fort Morgan. Vessels stripped of top-hamper, boats towed on the portside, gradually got under way, *Brooklyn* in the lead, the flagship *Hartford* next in line. The great fleet of eighteen ships swept on to the attack with four monitors in the starboard column, close inshore, nearest the powerful smoothbores and rifles of the fort. On decks cleared for action, below decks, and in the rigging, men tense, expectant, and prayerful awaited the battle.

So intently were officers and crews watching the fort over the starboard bows and the Confederate fleet ahead that not a Federal so much as suspected that the flotilla had a nineteenth ship.

The long gray *Belle of Mobile*, Stars and Stripes flying, kept pace in the staggered line just abaft an armed side-wheeler which she greatly resembled. Standing his deck in the uniform of an officer of the American Navy, Randall Sherrod looked every bit as efficient as any captain in the fleet.

His only worry of the moment was the day on the rise, which would of course reveal him a single in a parade of paired ships. But worry of a serious nature was something Captain Sherrod seldom indulged in. Rather, in a business made up of risk, he recognized a given danger and dealt with it on a win-or-lose basis. Late on the day before, while running full speed with Havana goods for Mobile, he had discovered the powerful Federal squadron blocking his way and had decided that it was either enter the bay on Farragut's coattail or perhaps lose the chance to ever run into port with a cargo worth close to two hundred thousand dollars in coin.

Suddenly the Federal *Tecumseh* fired a 15-inch shell over Fort Morgan. "Quarter to seven," Sherrod said to his black at the wheel. "Ease her inshore a point. Easy, easy."

At fifteen minutes past eight the fog had lifted and the firing became general. The Confederate fleet was in position to rake the bows-on Federal ships, and Fort Morgan gunners were bringing their guns to bear effectively.

"Cap'n Sherrod, suh," a Negro called from forward, "we ain't got no bizness stayin' heah."

Sherrod ordered the helm shifted to put the ship's head more inshore, reduced his speed again, and raised his deck hands with, "Break out the Stars and Bars flat on the starboard hull!" Gazing at Fort Morgan, her walls belching fire, he said, "I hope to hell General Page conns my side before throwing a shell at me."

He knew where the torpedoes lay, where to thread the piles in the channel, where shallow and good water met, and how close to the spits he could take the *Belle*. Through his glass he saw the monitor *Tecumseh* ranging foolishly into the field of torpedoes. The *Brooklyn* came to a halt that almost brought the whole fleet into collision. Then the *Tecumseh* struck a torpedo and careened. She sank almost instantly, taking with her half her Federal crew. Signals flew and still the *Brooklyn* sat at the head of the column in a state of nautical paralysis. In the lead, she held the whole fleet stationary.

"Like sitting ducks!" Sherrod exclaimed.

The gunners of Fort Morgan and the Confederate gunboats were not blind to the opportunity. The slaughter began in earnest. The decks and bulwarks of the flagship *Hartford* seemed to leap up with debris and mangled bodies. In the circle of Sherrod's glass a gunner lost both legs by a cannon ball, and as he threw up his arms in falling both of them were carried away by a shot. At one of the nine Dahlgrens in broadside a whole gun crew on one side were cut down by shot. Bodies were piled in rows and Sherrod knew that the deck literally ran with blood when they began shoveling mangled flesh and bone over the side.

With the little Confederate *Selma* raking the Federal flagship, cutting her down to size, and Farragut's frantic orders to the *Brooklyn* to move on availing him nothing, the battle was fast approaching a Confederate victory. The *Brooklyn* sat still, blocking the forward progress of the entire fleet. On each side of her lay the torpedoes. To circle her was to gamble with death. So if ever the Yankee had got himself in an awkward spot, Sherrod thought he had done so now. Rather stupid, in fact, caught without being able to bring a gun to bear. There they sat, Federal canvasbacks in Southern waters, absorbing shot, unable to spread their wings.

Then the *Hartford* and her consort, the *Metacomet,* suddenly swung to the left around the *Brooklyn* and over the torpedo ground into what seemed shallow water. The *Selma* stayed directly ahead of the *Hartford* and continued to rake her fore and aft. The *Hartford* was a mile inside the bay before she cut the cables binding her to the fast side-wheeler *Metacomet*. The latter steamed swiftly after the *Selma,* which soon surrendered. Then the *Gaines* ran aground after suffering heavily under the *Hartford*'s guns.

Sherrod frowned. Farragut had made a decision. Buchanan on the *Tennessee* seemed to have missed his moment. The canvasbacks had absorbed the fort's fire, amazing as it was, and were taking wing.

Sherrod saw the Confederate gunboat *Morgan,* a few minutes before grounded on the shoals east of Navy Cove, running like a crippled dove for the shallows near Fort Morgan with two Federal ships in pursuit.

"Which leaves only the mighty *Tennessee,*" Sherrod said, just as his mate came up on the run, pointing frantically toward the wall of the fort.

"Signals, Cap'n! General Page says, 'For God's sake, get the hell out of here!' "

A shell screamed overhead and burst a hundred yards away on the deck of the Yankee *Winnebago*. Then Sherrod found himself caught between fort and Federal, with Farragut's *Monongahela* pulling out of formation to block his forward speed. While breaking line aft, as though to run him down, came the little ship he recognized as the *Galena*.

Amid the thunder of heavy artillery, clouds of acrid powder smoke on every side riding the wind up the bay ahead of stabbing sheets of flame and succeeding curtains of smoke, the *Belle of Mobile* responded to Sherrod's "Full speed ahead!" like a thoroughbred under the touch of a quirt. The blockade-runner rushed to the wheel and shoved the helmsman aside, then swung her head to starboard. Up and under the quarter of the heavily armed *Monongahela,* whose guns blasted back at the fort not five feet above his head, he aimed with mathematical precision for that halfway mark between opposing guns despite his mate's repeated cries of "Ye'll shoal 'er, Cap'n!"

Though light, the *Belle of Mobile* scraped bay bottom once, twice, the last time to a noticeable loss of speed, a dragging and jarring shudder running her length and ending in a play up Sherrod's spine.

A shell burst overhead, a fragment striking like a bell his forward smokestack and ripping open a hole one could crawl through. Something struck the side, bounded off, exploded in a muffled roar aft. Over his left shoulder he saw the *Monongahela* bearing down on the *Tennessee;* incredulous that, a wooden ship ramming a ram. But she did, pouring in a broadside of solid shot as she did so. Then the *Tennessee* emerged no worse off than before, provoking from Sherrod a most amazed "Well, I'll be damned!"

The exclamation served to draw his attention to his own unhealthy spot. Dollar marks danced behind his eyes again; thoughts of medicine and necessities were dwarfed by silks, scented soaps, wines, and other profitable items. Barrels of white paint had to get through.

"Aye!" A hard grin of challenge, the reckless kind that had opened and sustained his adventure, formed and held as he helmed her and brought her graceful clipper bows in a quarter circle from east to due north.

The mate cried above the din of battle, "Ye'll never get through, Cap'n!" Pointing up the bay, he named the reasons why. "Farragut! Torpedoes!"

Farragut was a human being. To match wits with him was a pleasure, Sherrod was thinking. But the other obstacle? He said, "Damn the torpedoes!" It went unheard. When later the same statement became synonymous with Farragut's fame, supposed to have been made as he went around the *Brooklyn,* Sherrod vowed with some justification that the admiral couldn't at the time have made himself heard six inches away.

Steam hissed and oiled cylinders began to work faster. The *Belle of Mobile's* cutwater split the waves and her rakish masts and smokestack seemed to lean farther aft as she laid low and ran like a fox for the channel beyond the Yankee flagship.

As much as Sherrod would have enjoyed watching the battle between the *Tennessee* and the entire Federal fleet, he felt an obligation to the buyers of wines and satins in Mobile. He ran on, skirted the fleet, ran a half mile east of the flagship, now at anchor, and then, "for the very merry hell of it," ran down the Union ensign and hoisted the Confederate colors.

Under his telescope he saw an officer point him out to the admiral. When Farragut raised his glass for a look, Sherrod waved a hand, bowed politely, and said:

"Thanks for the escort, Admiral."

3

As Adria listened, the firing ceased. She looked into the sober faces of her parents and a score of slaves standing on the sunlit gallery. A little later the noise of guns began anew, fainter now, more sporadic. Then the thunder ceased altogether. All was quiet. Deathly quiet. Not even the male cardinal in the bougainvillaea broke the silence.

Joseph and Erasmus went to Mobile that morning. Leland Jarvis returned with them late that night. There was, it seemed, much anxiety in Mobile. The *Tennessee,* the sole hope of the naval South, had been forced to surrender after a gallant stand, after her admiral had been wounded and her rudder chains were pounded apart, so she could no longer mind her helm or aim a gun at the enemy.

"But," Jarvis declared, "that blockade-runnin', speculatin' scoundrel Sherrod slipped in with the Federal fleet."

Adria looked up as he said, "They shot his ship up considerable, all right, but he said they did it after the battle got so monotonous that he decided to dredge for bay oysters in order to stay awake."

Lawrence's father stayed on, adding his long face to those of the Cutlers and their slaves. Three days later Fort Gaines surrendered. The bombardment of Fort Morgan continued by Federals ashore and afloat, and the smell of powder smoke was wafted up the bay by the south wind. Sherrod brought the paint a few days after the sea battle, though he did not remain. Even Faustine's veiled, dark-eyed entreaty could not hold him. He simply left a few barrels of paint and joined the citizens of Mobile who were trying desperately to get together five thousand slaves to throw up breastworks around the city.

Strange indeed, Adria thought, Sherrod's interest in the defenses of Mobile. She shrugged it off as either a false rumor or a paradox of war. The paint remained in the barrels under the shade of a live oak as more than eighty Cutler slaves went to work on the fortifications of Mobile. Erasmus was hobbling about more than ever, and Abel had lumbago. The painting must wait, she decided, until fall, as the party she had continued to postpone.

There was news, mostly bad, though there was talk of peace, of the failure of the "Horace Greeley Peace Conference" in Niagara Falls, Canada, of this statesman's peace plan and that one's, of the Democratic nominee for President of the United States, General McClellan, and the peace outlook after the general election in the fall. Peace! Peace! they said. They got only war.

As hot August advanced, Adria received a letter from Lawrence. He wrote from Camp Douglas Prison, Chicago. The strange note of a caged animal was intermixed with the frantic longing of a man on the verge of crossing a mental boundary as he, a son of the outdoor South, wrote of "starvation and dark, vile dungeons." Months earlier Lawrence had written that few prisoners saw any benefit in revealing their prison troubles; and now this. Something must have snapped inside him.

Atop this, on the twenty-second, one day before General Page surrendered the much gunned and battered Fort Morgan to the Federals, Adam's letter telling of the sinking of the *Alabama* reached Bay Oaks.

Poor, dear, foolish Adam. The very idea of his coming out of consciousness aboard the yacht *Deerhound* with no elation at having escaped, but with a feeling that he had violated a pledge to Yankee Captain Winslow and had no honorable claim to freedom.

As Faustine wept and Annabel tried to soothe her, Joseph thought about it and said Adam was right. Shaking her head and running a hand across her eyes, Adria tried to laugh. It fell flat.

"First Lawrence. Then Adam. And now you. Father! Must I go through life listening to such crazy talk?"

A tugging at her dress drew her attention to Adam's upturned face. "Where my papa, Auntie Adri?"

"Oh, you dear!" she cried, sweeping him up into her arms. Then she said, "He wrote this from Southampton, England. But he says here, 'If I am unable to give myself up to Captain Winslow, I may go to Liverpool and on up to my friends in Waterloo and Barrow-in-Furness until I am well again.'"

Adria said nothing to the family of Adam's account of the meeting with James. She read avidly, again and again, a little fascinated, somewhat puzzled, resentful now, forgiving a minute later. But this memory of James; though it hurt her deeply, she could only add it to her growing responsibilities and shoulder it along with empty sugar and flour barrels and the sight of staring, hungry-eyed colored children.

Slowly Adria struck out alone under the low, bright stars of early evening for the bluff over the river. The night insects sang peacefully, causing her to forget momentarily all problems. Then she was wondering how long Atlanta would hold out against Sherman, Mobile against the siege she felt was sure to follow. She walked on, step after step, asking herself how long she could go on trading the family plate piece by piece for necessities, living on what the land would produce, with scant sowbelly to flavor the dish of master or slave—all because of men like James Hillyer! But they were strong and numerous. They were slowly but surely pushing aside all opposition.

Pausing on the path, she looked up at the summer stars and cried passionately, "I'm licked and I know it! If you asked me now, Randall Sherrod, I'd trade myself right into your arms."

Randall Sherrod came to Bay Oaks a few days later. He seemed tired and worn and he smelled of whisky. After talking business with Adria and her parents in the shade of live oaks near the back of the gallery, he was left alone with Adria. He stared at her boldly over a glass of lemonade and said:

"Better go easy on the lemons. It may be some time before I get through to the tropics."

"I can do without lemons the year round, sir," she replied. "But I can't curb my curiosity. Just why did you work so hard to get niggers for the breastworks?"

"Why?" He shrugged. "If Mobile is taken, I won't have a market for my goods. It's that simple."

Adria's glance was steady, amused and accusing.

"Somebody had to take the initiative," he said. "And listen to me, Adria Cutler——"

"Jarvis," she corrected politely.

"I never will get used to that, ma'am. Jarvis just doesn't ring with Adria."

He rose, finished off the lemonade with a wry grimace, and moved to her side. "See here, Adria, we're in for hard times from now on, times you won't want to or won't be able to meet on your own. Look at a war map if you don't believe me. The Yankees have us licked by land and sea. They have us outnumbered, and their source of supplies is unlimited. They can and will fight on. They——"

"Dear me, Captain, how you talk. You know as well as anyone the Yankees are war-weary."

"Sure, I know it. The Yankees admit it. But they're not desperate, and they know we're fast getting that way, same as they know that for every Southerner they kill or capture they'll starve two and add for good measure some of us good folks back home."

"They'll make peace. Mark my word they will."

"On their terms, Adria. Else they'll admit to losing the war. And no matter how bad off they are, do you think the gang of politicians in Washington are about to vote themselves out of office with peace terms in our favor?"

She moved on up the steps, Sherrod at her side arguing more convincingly than she would admit to herself. Just inside the open hall door he said in low voice, "Your troubles won't get any less, Adria."

Taking her hand in his, he brought her to an abrupt halt and said in a fierce whisper, "Aren't you ready for me to shoulder your troubles?"

Adria thought of the awful ledgers, and the unpainted pillars and fences, and the general state of ill repair at Bay Oaks. With lips parted, she gazed at him spellbound a minute. Then she felt the blood drain from her face and leap up from her neck again hot with her shame. Hurriedly she turned her back to him and stared at the table before her with unseeing eyes. Then she saw a small pair of silver candleholders. Seizing them up from the table, she whirled and faced him with a hard light of defiance in her eyes.

"How much for these, Captain Sherrod, in coin or trade?"

36.    The Destruction of Selma

1

AS THE SUMMER WORE ON INTO AUTUMN, Randall Sherrod's unwelcome prediction rang louder in Adria's mind. Her troubles had by no means lessened. The South had hardly adjusted itself to the fall of Fort Morgan and the sealing off of the port of Mobile to outside supplies than another great disaster was announced. The fall of Atlanta to the hordes of General Sherman meant the loss of the Southern rail center, arms depot, seat of foundries and factories engaged in the war effort, and one of the proudest cities of the Confederacy. The staggering blow was felt in more ways than one. The military loss was followed by a further drop in the value of state and Confederate money.

Adria watched the panic grow. It seemed to sprout up a malignant thing and reach out with long horrible fingers to devour everything in its path. It took hold of a mind, for it held fascinated before one's very eyes the destruction of values and the rise of a wild economy. September was bad, October was worse. By November the rate of exchange on the Confederate dollar was thirty to one. One dollar in gold was worth twenty-five in state currency. Cotton, standard of wealth for generations and the sterling of the South, had lost its value for want of a means to the market. There was nothing solid in the world of material things to fall back on.

One day in the winter Adria sent a cow to market and realized nearly one thousand dollars for it. Before she left Mobile she had spent all of it for one sack of salt, ten yards of calico, two barrels of flour, and a few pounds of imitation coffee. While she was staring hopelessly at these things and wishing she had kept the cow, Leland Jarvis came up and told her that Confederate money would buy twice as much in the interior of Alabama. How she despised him in that moment.

In January, Abel died of pneumonia, and Claribel ran away and married a free Negro who had gone to war as a substitute for a white man from Mobile and recently deserted General Hood's army. Aunt Eugenia lost the use of one leg in December and they had made a bedroom for her downstairs. Annabel, who had not been strong since the siege of pneumonia in 1863, lost more weight that winter. Adria despaired of her and often left her hurriedly in order to hide the threatening flood of tears. Joseph alternately brooded in silence and talked of the old days. There was plenty of wood for fuel, though food was so scarce everyone seemed continually hungry. Pea and bean soup and cabbage and cornbread; an occasional squirrel, though seldom was there enough gunpowder to shoot one in the yard. Adria played chess of nights with Joseph until she wanted to scream.

But always she thought, "Come spring, things will be better."

Only Mammy Rose agreed. She went about her work singing "Pop Goes the Weasel" and the humorous song, "You Are Going to the War, Willie Boy," as though she refused to take the war seriously. "Looky heah, Miss Faustine, better git de cobwebs offen dat blue-back speller and learn little Adam how to spell so he say words right," she would say. Then to Joseph, "What difference do hit make if folks say yo'all is done got exempt from war on account of dat twenty-nigger law? We all knows yo' is too old to fight." And when in a bluster he gave her to know he was not old, she would laugh and say so he could not hear, "Dat ris' him up outen his misery."

There had been a rumor of another Confederate commerce destroyer in the Atlantic before Faustine received a letter from Adam late in January confirming it. Adam had written in October from "off the Island of Madeira, from which we were ordered to depart in the name of his sovereign of Portugal." His letter opened as follows:

On the evening of October 8, 1864, twenty-seven of us met on the Prince's Dock, Liverpool. We were taken aboard a waiting tug to the blockade-runner *Laurel* and were soon standing out to sea. At the same hour, the English ship *Sea King* was casting off from a London dock. A week later, both ships arrived in the harbor of Funchal, Madeira, where officers, arms, ordnance and coal were transferred to the *Sea King*, which a few days later Captain James I. Waddell read into service as "now and forevermore the Confederate States warship *Shenandoah*," her object to prey upon and destroy the whaling fleet of the United States.

While I have lost none of my patriotic zeal, I am more bitter than is good for me. Even with things terrible and real happening at home, I cannot erase from my mind the memory of a pledge made to Captain Winslow of the *Kearsarge* to return in surrender. As long as I live I shall feel the cold, accusing eyes of James Hillyer boring into me. I am a man without honor to his way of thinking. Nor can I soon forget how I humiliated myself before the haughty American Minister in London in an attempt to give myself up to Winslow. So you see, I am sailing to the Pacific under the Stainless Banner to serve the South I love, but only by virtue of Yankee stupidity. . . .

Adria's heart went out to Adam as she tried to cheer Faustine, though in reality Adam's troubles were so foreign and distant to the increasing problems confronting her that she secretly resented his putting them in a letter home. Actually, she was a great deal more concerned over the prolonged absence of Randall Sherrod than Adam's odd sense of remorse. With even necessities getting scarcer and scarcer, she needed as never before the help of the former blockade-runner.

Strange, Sherrod's departure; stranger, his stay. Shortly after the fall of Atlanta he left Mobile with a jaunty "See you around Christmas." The *Belle of Mobile* had remained at her dock with only a watchman aboard since September. Nearly four months. Then one morning she gave Mobile a surprise. She had flown in the night. There followed, of course, the talk a mystery provokes: Sherrod had lost his fortune; had sold his ship after making a deal with the Yankees to let her go to sea; had, himself, slipped into Mobile and run her past the Federals in the dead of night—for he was the king of the men who plied the Nassau–Havana–Mobile trade "on moons," that is, they timed their run past the blockade squadrons to the darkest nights. Despite rumor, few thought Sherrod had met with reverses. In December, when a swarm of small craft began to arrive in Mobile with supplies, the people were quick to blame and bless the scoundrel and saint, Randall Sherrod.

He was constant and bold, Adria admitted on a day in early February of 1865. A wagon creaked to a stop at the back of the house and delivered two boxes. As everyone gathered in the rear parlor, they were opened. Perfumes, vases, lace, silks, fine gloves, a box of cigars for Joseph, snuff for Mammy and chewing tobacco for Erasmus drew exclamations of delight from all but Annabel and Adria.

The more Adria saw, the angrier she became. When at last the boxes were empty, she threw a vase at the mantel and cried out, "Good God a'mighty! Not a bite to eat, nothing we can use! Randall Sherrod, I'll hate you always for this!"

Then Faustine found a note and read it. Looking up, she saw Adria moving out of the room. "Wait, Adria!" she called. "The gifts were sent for Christmas!"

It didn't matter. Then it did matter. Adria brushed a hand across her forehead and sat down on the lower stairs. A sob shook her, though she drove it back, for she knew that once she admitted to needing and actually wanting Sherrod near her she would burst into tears.

As winter turned into spring, Adria learned that it was impossible to obtain seed corn. She found it difficult to accept this alarming fact, for as much as she despised cornbread and lye hominy, the war had made corn the Southern staff of life.

There was no cheering news. Charleston had surrendered. Sher-

man was moving out of Savannah to scorch the earth of the Caro-
linas. Everyone was saying dismally that any hope of peace had
faded with the failure of the conference at Hampton Roads, that
desertion was thinning the ranks of the armies of Lee and Johnston.

At home rumors that evoked fear all fall and winter became facts
in mid-March when the Federals from Pensacola and thirty-two
thousand men under General Canby moved up the east side of Mobile Bay and began the siege of Spanish Fort, seven miles from the
city. The guns thundered louder now, and the sounds, the booming
of cannon by day and night, shook the pillars of Bay Oaks without
surcease.

From upstate came the news that the seventeen thousand cavalrymen picked by Federal General J. H. Wilson were preparing to lay
waste northern and central Alabama. They were picked men, it was
said, men who could and would without any qualms of conscience
operate according to the pattern written a year earlier by General
W. T. Sherman:

*"The government of the United States has in North Alabama any
and all rights which they choose to enforce in war, to take their
lives, their houses, their lands, their everything, because they cannot
deny that war exists there, and war is simply power unrestrained
by constitution or compact. . . ."*

Adria had cried in derision, "The Christian North!" But scorn had
availed her nothing. "The charitable, sword-courageous Sherman"
had with Northern steel ripped open feather beds and with Northern matches set fire to cotton and houses. Northern "bummers,"
scavenging civilians allowed to follow the Yankee army, tortured
Southerners to learn where valuables were hidden.

And in March of 1865 the Cutlers and other Alabamans were
alarmed by the news that "Wilson's Raiders" had been turned loose
by the civilized United States on a land that could not boast of one
Confederate soldier within one hundred and twenty miles.

It was the day of the locust.

2

On an afternoon late in March, Adria stared wide-eyed and unbelieving at the note in her hands. From the plantation up in Clarke
County her father had written:

Adria—I have no time for particulars. Break the news to Annabel
as gently as possible that I'm off for Selma to fight with my friend

General Forrest, who is desperate for men. With nothing but old men and boys to carry guns, God helping me, I'll try to be a boy again.

"Lord in heaven, not this!" Adria slumped to a chair and tried to accept and adjust this surprise in her mind. "Oh, Father, you poor dear."

Then she was thinking of Selma. Faustine was up there visiting her sister. Now where else would the Raiders go but to Selma? Since the fall of Atlanta, the largest arsenal in the South was in Selma, as was the navy yard and naval foundry. There the ram *Tennessee*, the gunboats *Morgan, Selma,* and *Gaines* had been built. The finest cannon were cast there. The foundry alone employed over three thousand men. There, in over one hundred state and Confederate buildings covering fifty acres, most of the fixed ammunition used by Southern armies had been manufactured since 1863.

But all this, Selma, Adria realized with rising panic, was undefended.

With an effort she composed herself long enough to hide Joseph's note in her bosom. Her fears increased as she thought of Adam's son up in Selma. If anything happened to him, she would never forgive Faustine. Never.

But she was imagining much. Wilson might not reach Selma. And perhaps even now Faustine and her son were on their way home.

Faustine felt quite secure in Selma. Had not General Forrest, with several thousand troops, gone in chase of one of Wilson's bands? And the Federal Croxton was reported to be in Tuscaloosa, sixty miles northwest of Selma. Despite the terrible news that he was burning the university up there, no one thought Selma was in immediate danger. With the commandant of the arsenal and his inspectors and superintendents sustaining a calm, the six thousand men, women, and children employed in Selma went about their work as usual until the sudden arrival of the terrorist Wilson and his Raiders on that day in early April.

Faustine's sister Eunice, who made cartridges for small arms at the laboratory, was at work when the Raiders, said to be nine thousand strong, rushed Forrest's small force. As the afternoon wore away, the thunder of battle grew louder. Faustine closed the doors and windows of her sister's house and drew Adam and Eunice's two children to her. There was nothing to fear, she told them.

"Once upon a time there lived a beautiful princess," she began, thinking that the firing drew steadily nearer. Then she was wondering if all Forrest's men were like Joseph Cutler, having never been under fire until this battle. "She had long golden hair, which shone in the sun, and everyone in the castle, even the king who was very sad, brightened when she was near."

The noise of horses at full gallop and the yells of men caused her to run to the door in time to hear retreating soldiers crying, "Stay in your houses! Wilson is coming!"

Faustine felt the blood draining from her face. Eunice's two slaves, Uncle Joe and Mammy Sue, entered trembling and mouthing wishes that Miss Eunice's husband hadn't been killed in the Battle of Atlanta. Quieting them, Faustine looked into the curious faces of the children and forced herself to go on.

"One day the king sent for the princess and told her that a prince from a land far, far away wished to marry her. She——"

A horrible yelling outside grew in volume. Wilson's Raiders were riding in to sack the town. They spread out, sending their horses over lawns and into flower beds. They tore through Eunice's yard, hacking crape myrtle and crying:

"Down with you Rebels! We're here to burn you out!"

Eunice arrived with dress torn in a dozen places, her cheeks, arms, and neck bleeding, and a look of frozen terror on her face. As she fell inside the door in a state of shock, she managed to convey what several of Wilson's men had done to her. Unable to adjust such a crime in her mind, Faustine seized Adam and stared from her sister to the child in her arms.

A pounding of hoofs on the porch was followed by the curses of two soldiers. The door burst open and the pair entered demanding valuables. Faustine gave them her rings, bracelets, and earrings. Unsatisfied, one of them explored the divide of Faustine's bosom and, upon finding a small sack containing two gold coins, struck her across the face with the back of his hand. As he placed the gain in his canteen, Faustine made the mistake of crying out in anger:

"Cowards! Cowards!"

The larger of the pair ordered the other hold Faustine over his lap with dress up to her waist. When Faustine was finally subdued, the raider said to frightened Uncle Joe, "You're free. Now pay the damn Rebel woman for ordering you about." Forcing his sword into the hand of the old slave, he said, "Give her a good dozen with the flat of it across the rump."

The Negro's protest was of no avail. He was forced to strike

Faustine's exposed buttocks a dozen times. Then, when he had finished his terrible job, he cried out in torment to his Lord in heaven and tried to drive the sword through its owner. He died for his trouble.

More soldiers arrived. They hacked the furniture, tore beds apart, ripped dresses into shreds, and tore up the floor and walls in places in their lust for loot and destruction. With vile oaths, they threatened rape despite the howling of the "Rebel brats," and then proceeded to set fire to the house.

Driven outside, Faustine clutched Adam to her bosom and ran as fast as she could go. The night sky was a glaring, leaping yellow and red. Fires burned on every side. Down by the Alabama River a giant blaze held her fascinated gaze. It drew her on against her will, for she seemed to know it was the Selma arsenal. She staggered and ran, oblivious to the charging horses, the flames, the shrieks and moans of victims, and the hellish cries of the drunken soldiers. She continued west on Water Street, telling herself that she would find a boat and escape with Adam down-river.

She was at the intersection of Water and Church Streets when a group of Union officers ordered her to halt. Thinking they wished to abuse her further, she ran north on Church Street for Hinton Alley. She knew that just north of the two-story brick warehouse lay Johnson's Cotton Yard. There she would hide until the horrors of the night ended. But between her and the alley the fire blazed up in that enclosure filled with frame buildings, warehouses, and shops. Beyond the two artesian wells were buildings filled with powder and cartridges.

A strong sense of warning caused her to halt. The cries of the Federal officers behind her impelled her forward. The brick wall hid her from the pursuers. Then the crackle of the flames, punctuated now and then by booming explosions, drowned all sounds of pursuit. She looked back and saw the officers. They were beckoning frantically, waving her back.

"No!" she cried. "My darling Adam, they wish to hurt me, to separate you from me."

They were fools, beasts! Her bottom burned from the forced beating. She had seen men struck down with swords and flying hoofs, women caught up screaming into saddles and carried off to a terrible fate in the night. And the officers in blue thought to wave her back!

She was no longer afraid of them. Adam, wherever he was on the high seas, would be proud of her. That was all that mattered. She loved only Adam. And her son, their son. He was no longer crying, but staring with big eyes wide at the flames licking skyward above and beyond the brick fence.

Suddenly the whole world seemed to leap high in a blinding sunburst. A tremendous explosion shook the very earth. It sent her flying through the air with sharp fingers touching her neck and face and hair. Then she lay still, her arms about Adam. There was no pain, no sound, no sight. Then she could see. Adam was safe in her arms. Slowly she got up, wondering what held her. Bricks, of course. She should have known. Then she felt something. It was wet and sticky and it ran down her and on Adam.

A flash of light revealed its color. Shocked, she felt of her face and let out a scream. Then she was running toward the Union officers. It no longer mattered. Nothing mattered but saving her son. And now she seemed to know why they had tried to stop her.

She reached them, somehow, and told them to send her boy to Bay Oaks. "Please, if ever you did anything good, do this for me."

Before the officer could reply, she fell, shuddered all over, and lay still. The man in blue looked from her to the frightened boy and hurriedly turned young Adam's face away from the brave mother with half a face.

## 37.     By Sword and Flame

### 1

"ERASMUS, what on earth?" Adria asked, pointing at a lone horseman moving toward the gates. "Why, he looks like a soldier—a Yankee!"

As the Union soldier rode closer, with white flag upraised, both Adria and Erasmus recognized the boy in the saddle with him. Adria ran outside without pausing to look in the mirror.

"Adam! My darling!" Meeting the young soldier's glance, she said, "Whatever is the meaning of this, sir?"

Adam came to her arms. Holding him close, Adria listened with

mounting horror and unbelief to the soldier's terse account of the
burning of Selma. "My captain, miss, is from Vermont, but he vowed
the behavior of Wilson's men turned his stomach. It did mine. Anyhow, he saw the boy's mother and tried to stop her. She ran back
to him and begged him to send the boy here. She was brave. We
buried her in the arsenal grounds."

Stunned, Adria tried to swallow. Faustine dead! She looked at little Adam, now running toward Erasmus. Faustine gone; it was impossible.

"My father," she managed to say. "He was with General Forrest."

The Yankee said, "Forrest and a few hundred men escaped."

The strange blue uniform held Adria's attention. "You must be
hungry and tired. There's little to eat, but you're welcome."

Next day Adria feared for the safety of the Northern soldier. The
sack of Selma so infuriated the people of southern Alabama that
women, old men, and mere boys swore eternal vengeance. As detailed accounts of Northern savagery reached down-river, Adria's
anger increased. Wilson's Raiders had destroyed powderworks, army
and navy stores, foundries, and thousands of bales of cotton. War
excused this, but the gods of war could never condone the burning
of homes, the rape of Selma's women, the murder of civilians, the
killing of every horse and mule in the city. The animals were left to
decay in the streets while the Yankees under the Stars and Stripes
continued their pillage and destruction.

Soon word reached Bay Oaks that the Confederates had destroyed
the navy yard near the Sunflower Bend of the Tombigbee to prevent
the enemy from taking it.

Still there was no word from Joseph.

The Federals continued to hammer at the gates of Mobile. Fort
Blakely, above Spanish Fort, defended by thirty-four hundred Confederates, had been assaulted on the second of April by a force of
from twelve to fifteen thousand Federals under General Steele.

With the battle raging within a few miles of Bay Oaks, Leland
Jarvis came down-river to report the burning of Brierlane. Gone
were the fine mansion, barns, gins, houses, cotton, and all that had
made the Jarvis name a proud and honored one. Lawrence's father
was a beaten old man who alternately brooded and cursed heaven
and the destructive God he had once worshiped.

"No, Leland," Annabel countered gently. "Man is destructive.
Your God is a creative God. Remember, Leland, how Joseph used to
gather Adam, Lawrence, Adria, and sometimes Faustine together

and tell them to take the time to marvel at the things God created. I recall once it was a watermelon. Joseph talked of its colors, how the red bled into the pale green rind, how God spaced the seed. No, Leland, don't talk about a destructive God."

Jarvis simply glared at her, as if to tell her that she had not convinced him of anything.

On the day Lawrence's father left for Fort Blakely, an officer of General Maury's staff paused at Bay Oaks and advised Adria to hide all valuables. "Just in case," he said. Adria stared after him, eyes narrowed, mouth open and tense. For the first time, actually, she felt the South had lost the war. There was no argument inside her to put down the sense of defeat. *Defeat!* It was a terrible word, a forerunner of worse words, such as *conquered,* and the bitterest of words, *submission* and *subjugation.*

No, she could not and would not think of defeat. She looked from the untended gardens to the gray pillars of Bay Oaks and made a vow to begin painting them as soon as the mirrors and chandeliers were buried.

On the morning of April the seventh a "flag-of-truce" letter from Douglas Prison, Chicago, arrived at Bay Oaks. Adria read with mixed feelings of pity and alarm Lawrence's account of six thousand deaths among thirty thousand prisoners. He wrote that it was more heroic to endure the horrors than desert the Cause by taking the oath of allegiance to the United States. He rambled at length on the subject of divine interference in favor of the North before declaring that God had purposely altered the principles and motives of human conduct.

Adria destroyed the letter. It would never do for Leland Jarvis to learn of his son's bitterness. Nor did she want her mother or Aunt Eugenia questioning Lawrence's sanity. It was bad enough to live with growing doubt on the score, but not half so bad as sharing it.

Lawrence had brooded too long. He would recover.

But strange things she did not wish to believe were happening. It taxed her credulity to think again of Selma and Faustine and admit actually the destruction of a city and the death of a member of the family. The whole Northern run of successes from the fall of New Orleans to Atlanta seemed unbelievable even now. Impossible things, all. But they were true, and the cumulative effect was nothing short of a warning finger pointing straight and true to the fall of Mobile. After that, God only knew what would happen.

Shuddering, Adria watched the slaves lowering the wrapped mirrors and other valuables into deep holes dug out in the fields behind the house. She dreaded evenings in the halls and twin parlors denuded of finery. It was a selfish thought, she realized a moment later when Annabel's scream reached her ears.

She ran to the house as fast as she could go, with all the slaves racing after her. She knew that something worse than parlors without vases and mirrors had overtaken her. She was being punished, she told herself, even as she begged God to forgive her and spare her more bad news.

Mammy Rose was bathing her mother's head with cool towels, and old Cap'n Hardy of the river boat *Anne* was standing with cap in hand.

"Dat note," Mammy said, "hit from Genrul Forrest hisself."

Adria stared at the sheet of paper. "About—Father?" The blood was fast draining from her face. She sat down and tried to slow the awful spinning sensation. A minute later she picked up the paper and read:

My friend Joseph Cutler was killed in action while defending the breastworks at Selma on April second. Though thrice wounded, he fought gallantly until the end. . . .

Slowly Adria rose and walked to a window. Somehow she managed to fight back the flood of tears and put down a strong desire to just give up and cry and sob until all grief was gone. Something told her that this was the furnace, the crucible, out of which she must emerge as chaff or refined metal. Her remaining parent and aunt and father-in-law and many slaves were depending on her. And she seemed to know a mere straw could in her weakness and sorrow strike her down. Randall Sherrod; if only he were here to take over, to assume the heavy responsibility that was hers, she would throw herself at his feet in complete surrender.

She raised her head in defiance. Sherrod was not here. No, by thunder! The weight continued to fall on her shoulders. The Lord willing, the Lord forgive and help her, she would remain strong.

She closed her eyes in supplication. She opened them in determination. "Have them take Mother upstairs, Mammy," she demanded. "Then send them back to burying the valuables."

"Yassum," Mammy replied, cocking her head and staring in puzzled wonder at her baby.

2

The cannonading continued. Fort Blakely fell and the Yankee monster swallowed up another few thousand Confederate prisoners. Next day Forts Tracy and Huger, the last works guarding the east approach to Mobile, were evacuated. The Union fleet moved up the bay and the armies pressed on toward the city. Confederates in boats escaped up the rivers and hundreds more waded through the marshes. Then General Maury began his northward retreat. The firing ceased. A strange quiet fell over the land.

Mobile had fallen.

Adria met the stragglers and listened attentively as weary old men told of what had happened at Starke's Landing, Catfish Point, in the swamps and in the city. At noon on the twelfth, they said, Yankee General Granger lowered the Confederate flag and raised the Stars and Stripes over Mobile.

Soon even the stragglers departed. Not a boat plied the river. The awful quiet continued. For more than three weeks there had been no news of events in Virginia. Some said Lee was doomed. Others said Johnston's army was ready to engage Sherman's. Adria did not know what to believe. She seemed to live in a state of expectancy, of waiting for the inevitable, seemed to live in constant fear of destruction. She placed a watch on the bluff overlooking the river and the road. Every minute of the day a slave boy waited to warn them of the approach of Yankees.

Adria was supervising the weeding of the vegetable garden behind the house on the afternoon the slave boy came up panting and told of the approach of bluecoats.

With heart beating fast, Adria ran to the house and looked out the parlor window at a long line of Federal cavalrymen. In no hurry, they came on and halted. Their lanky, mustached leader relaxed in the saddle and looked the place over in silence before urging his horse up the steps and to the door. There he booted the glass out of a side light and yelled:

"Come out, Rebels, before we smoke you out."

Adria walked to the door with head high and eyes flashing anger. "Sir, the glass you broke came from England. I'll have you——"

The Federal drowned her demands with a guffaw. Then he ordered a thorough search of the place.

They came in droves, laughing, cursing. They pushed Adria aside.

Against the wall, she saw them divide into groups. But worse, the leader entered, not afoot but on his horse, and directed the looting from his perch in the saddle. With sword upraised, he ordered the occupants outside. Soon Adria saw her frightened mother and Aunt Eugenia in the arms of soldiers.

"They're sick!" she cried, forcing her way to the leader.

"They're Rebels," he replied. Then he looked her over again. "Corporal Faye, seize this spitfire and take her outside."

"Git yo' hands offen her! Jest touch her once, Yankee white trash!"

Adria stared, amazed. Mammy Rose stood a few feet away swinging a Yankee sword she had somehow managed to obtain.

The Federal raised his voice with, "Crazy nigger, don't you know you're free?"

"I don't want to be free! Now git on outen heah befo' I starts carvin' on yo'all!"

With Mammy suddenly disarmed, the corporal caught up Adria's hands behind her. He was pushing her toward the door when the leader decided that the "hotheaded Rebel wench" should stay inside to "watch the progress of the war."

For more than an hour Adria was forced to witness the work of the enemy. She closed her eyes in horror when they slashed the curtains from the windows and in the next strokes of their sabers hacked fine pieces of imported rosewood and mahogany into kindling wood. She bit her lip and writhed inwardly when the graceful balustrade of the staircase cracked and splintered before dangling from landing to hall floor in ruins. Terror, anger, madness, and frustration descended upon her in swift succession, overpowering her, suffocating her as sabers split the brocade of a Sheraton sofa and boots tore ragged lengths in the Aubusson rugs.

A burly man wearing a sergeant's stripes stumbled down the stairs crying, "Captain Black, look! Gold!"

Adria gazed unbelievingly at the coins. Her father must have hidden them. She covered her face with her hands and cried out in despair. Opening her eyes, she watched two men slit a feather bed on the landing and scatter down on the stairs and into the hall. A portrait of Joseph on the wall of the parlor drew the captain's attention. Drawing his pistol, he placed a bullet directly between the pair of eyes and replaced the gun with a grin of satisfaction on his face.

The looting ended with a raid on the smokehouse. The few sides of bacon and small hams hanging there for curing were sampled and thrown away. Then the soldiers came inside the house with a large washpot of soft soap and a barrel of molasses. They split open the barrel and mixed syrup and soap over the floor of the hall and dining room.

When Adria was ushered outside to join her mother, aunt, and the household slaves, she saw her piano being converted into a horse trough. This seemed too much to bear. But always one act of vandalism was followed by another, and the last burned deeper into her memory. She thought the uncalled-for burning of the small Negro church the worst of all when the captain said to Erasmus, "There goes your damned old gospel shop." This too seemed far in the primitive past when the captain ordered the horses of all officers quartered in the drawing room while the plunder was piled up for assessment and division.

Thinking that the invader could do nothing more to surprise her, she found herself staring in wide-open astonishment when the loot was divided as follows: one fifth to the commander-in-chief and staff; one fifth to the field officers of the regiments; and two fifths to the company. The captain said, "When we get through with southern Alabama, the general will be almost as rich as Sherman. Why, Sherman's share in gold watches and chains alone at Columbia, South Carolina, was 275."

Adria turned away, fell to her mother's side, and implored her to stop weeping. Aunt Eugenia sat up, flushed of face, her anger greater than her pain as she spoke her opinion of any government that gave its armies unrestricted license to plunder and burn.

"Shut your mouth, you old Rebel crone," Captain Black replied. "We've stripped you down to your goddamn pride. Want us to take that?"

"If you think you can, you poor, depraved specimen of a low-down dirty Yankee son of a bitch!"

"No, Aunt Eugenia!" Adria cried, but not in time. The captain strode to Eugenia and snatched the earrings from her ears, leaving two ragged bleeding wounds.

In all her life Eugenia had never met her match. This fact, her very domineering past, the awful shock of the present, all seemed to leap up in her startled eyes for Adria to see as Eugenia clapped hands at her ears. A moment later she stared at bloody palms and Adria seemed to know that her aunt would never again be the same.

Turning to Adria, the captain said, "Pretty soon we'll see if you're hiding any valuables." Beckoning to his top officer, he said, "First, we'll teach the proud Rebel a lesson. Get the horses outside and dip the cotton balls in turpentine."

Leering at Adria, he said, "You don't want a wrecked house, do you, honey? So we'll just burn it."

The left wing of Bay Oaks was lighting up the late afternoon sky when Captain Black ordered the slaves set free and made ready for the upriver march with his cavalrymen. The captain then turned to Adria and demanded that she bare her breasts and raise her skirts if she wished to avoid a most thorough search of her person. He desired only valuables, he said, but he could change his mind if she showed further resistance.

Adria replied by spitting in his face.

He had partially uncovered Adria's bosom and was preparing to fulfill his threat when two horsemen galloped up and came to a halt ahead of a cavalry unit. One of the men wore the insignia of a Federal general, which sent a buzzing through the ranks of the plunderers.

"Stop this, boys," said General Canby. "You there, Captain, what sort of a soldier are you to attack a woman?"

Adria scarcely heard Canby. Her dizzy, whirling senses seemed to be deceiving her with a vision of something she wished greatly to see. Then she managed to narrow her eyes into focus on the general's companion. He was dressed as she had seen him last, in sea cap and merchantman's coat of blue. She wanted to cry out a welcome and at the same time upbraid him for not returning in time to prevent the sacking of Bay Oaks. She did neither, but watched him in fascination as he dismounted and approached Captain Black in casual manner.

Why he was riding with a Yankee general did not pose a question in her mind. Whether as imp of Satan or Unionist, all that mattered was his presence. Her heart cheered him.

He did not meet her glance then, but turned to Canby. "General," he said, "I'll consider it a personal favor if you'll order the troops to put out the fire before it consumes my favorite Southern mansion."

Only then did Sherrod look at Adria. His glance did not waver when General Canby granted his request. "Just a moment, Captain," he said, his eyes resting speculatively on her almost naked breast. Without any hurry or outward interest in her, he raised the torn dress to her shoulder, then smiled at the Yankee spoiler.

Adria felt her blood run strong and defiant again as Sherrod said in a voice Canby could not hear, "Captain, I'll lay odds ten to one you don't live through the night."

## 38.    The Weeping Waves

### 1

ADAM turned his gaze from the lofty snow-clad mountains to the whaling ship on the edge of the ice field ahead. He glanced at the waiting gunner, at the 12-pounder, and up at the Russian ensign at the *Shenandoah's* masthead before giving the order to fire a warning shot.

The Sea of Okhotsk was a cold and lonely hunting ground for the Confederate commerce destroyer. But by virtue of a laconic order from the Richmond government, the *Shenandoah* had stood up the Pacific from Melbourne to her position on this day late in May of 1865 off the bleak coast of Siberia. The written order sounded every bit as terse as a ship's log and seemed more a mapped course executed in detachment, until the object in mind gave it a red-blooded climax.

The *Shenandoah* should intercept the North Pacific whaling fleet bound to Oahu with the products of the summer cruise.

Adam watched the Stars and Stripes break out atop the ship ahead. There, she had identified herself, and in so doing had signed her own death warrant.

The capture of another whaler evoked little excitement aboard. Officers and crew alike were more curious as to the type of trade goods she carried. This one, the *Abigail* of New Bedford, shipped half a hundred barrels of good red whisky, a great deal to send up in flames.

The whaler lit up the northern sea that night and too much whisky aboard the Confederate nearly caused another of many misunderstandings between fretful Waddell and some of the officers. Adam remained aloof. Captain Waddell's stock remark, "Mr. Cutler, I had to talk to somebody," caused Adam to realize for the thousandth time that he did not sail under another Semmes. When the disparity loomed up so strong that even old impressions had to fall away like the waves, there appeared, as if by sheer exposure, qualities in Waddell that excused his weaknesses. Constant fear was a part of him, though his ability to carry on in spite of it was proof of bravery. The fact that he took his great responsibility too seriously proved his almost fanatical loyalty to a cause and a trust. Also, in his favor was another factor one could not argue against: success. So Adam shrugged it off, grinned wearily out over the frozen waste, and went below to raise a beaker of hot rum punch and drink the seaman's choice toast, "Sweethearts and wives."

The sun rose at three in the morning and set at nine. Where they were going the days would grow longer. They made their way on east and north through hissing onslaughts of snow and rain, through squalls in seas filled with dangerous ice floes. A far cry from the tropic seas and the receptions down in Melbourne. At times the *Shenandoah* found her way blocked on all sides by jagged floes and towering icebergs. Somehow she found a passage and met the morning sun with braces, blocks, yards, sails, and her running rigging encrusted with ice. And minds seeking diversion smiled up at a ship of sugar, her masts penciled with dazzling blue-white gems. Lieutenant Lee, nephew of Robert E. Lee, saw a silver ship set with rhinestones and Adam saw a jewel-bright pin with tiny masts at Faustine's bosom.

As the men dislodged the ice with billets of wood, Adam continued to dream of Faustine. Marriage had worked a great change in him. As much as his physical self demanded Faustine in his arms, he did not feel dominated by a purely physical relationship as such, but was able to put it in its place as a gesture of love without symbolism; something to unite him to his wife in a completeness beyond a bachelor's understanding.

A man thought deep and long at sea—too deep, too long, Adam supposed—about this and that, mistakes, promises, one promise in particular, a pledge to an enemy and victor to return in surrender. As the days went by, his sense of guilt seemed magnified by the vast empty bulk of the Pacific. Reason told him he had been unable to return to Winslow of the *Kearsarge*, but reason didn't enter into it. Just honor, the kind Southern planters instilled in their sons.

A man dreamed of home, saw in the waves and distant ice hummocks loved ones. And when he wasn't dreaming he was wondering. There was little or no news. The progress of the war ended with the last batch of captured newspapers, always months and months old. The South was winning, the South was losing. You picked your shell and hoped your choice was a good one. So it was with events at

Bay Oaks, he supposed. Had the place run down or had his father kept it up; how healthy was his son Adam, now three years and two months old; did Adria love Lawrence or did she continue to think of James Hillyer?

Questions all. The sea and the wind off the sea gently or roaringly came on to mock him.

A cracking southwester struck the *Shenandoah* and drove her northeast, up and on up into the Bering Sea and the land of the midnight sun, where a day was six months long, where subzero weather and snow squalls were constant companions.

It was late in June when they overhauled the *Susan Abigail* of San Francisco. There were newspapers containing dispatches of war. Waddell and his officers read of Lee's surrender to Grant on the ninth of April, of the evacuation of Richmond, the flight of President Davis and his Cabinet, the assassination of Lincoln on April fourteenth.

Their moans were audible, and such stanch and brave men as Matt O'Brien, once of the *Alabama*, and Senior Officer Lieutenant Whittle shed tears without shame. There was a ray of hope, however, a slim one, for a portion of Lee's army had escaped and joined General Johnston in North Carolina, and President Davis had issued a proclamation declaring that despite reverses, the war would be carried on with renewed vigor.

"What shall we do?" Waddell asked. Following the vote of the officers, he thanked them and said they should proceed with the cruise.

That day the Yankee *Susan Abigail*, trader with a cargo of Yankee gewgaws likely to draw furs, sealskins, and walrus tusks from the eager Eskimos, was burned level with the sea. As she sobbed under and left the world of living ships and men, the *Shenandoah* pointed her bow north and steamed ahead toward the northern lights.

Three days later the decks came alive with the "Sail ho!" The lookout's cry lifted the eyebrows of Lieutenants Grimball and Cutler. The lad up there could, they thought, be on the balmy side, else drunk, for he had cried not one but six of sail.

"Grim destruction, Mr. Cutler," said Grimball. "You know, I'm getting a sick stomach from it."

Adam smiled it off as a jest, since he too felt somewhat surfeited. "The order is to destroy the Federal whaling fleet," he said. "Seems we've reached the place to do it."

The sea was calm. The covey could not fly. The *Nye*, the *Nimrod*, and the *Catherine*, all of New Bedford, were quickly captured and set afire. The crews of all three were placed into twelve whaleboats and towed by the *Shenandoah*. In her wake the flames of three whalers lit up the icebergs. The next vessel was ransomed to transport the two hundred and fifty prisoners back to the States, but the *Gipsey* and *Isabella* were sent to Davy Jones, charred and blackened.

"Not a bad day." The remark ran the length of the *Shenandoah*. "Not at all bad," the reply ran back.

Next morning Adam heard to his amazement the same lookout cry the deck with, "Eleven of sail!" To Lieutenants Lee and Chew he said, "I'll go aloft and verify it."

In utter astonishment, Adam gripped the icy ropes near the lookout's perch and counted eleven ships. Narrowing his gaze over the choppy sea, he felt his heart beat fast with the sudden realization that ahead to the northward, stretched before his very eyes, was perhaps the very backbone of all that was left of the American whaling marine.

"To destroy it——!" he said, eyes burning with a light that caused the lookout to swallow hard.

"Ahoy, up there!" came the cry from deck. "Shall I loose a warning shot?"

"Hold your fire, Mr. Chew," Adam replied. He hurried down to deck and on past the officers without a word. Minutes later he was addressing a surprised and somewhat overwhelmed Waddell. "Sir, a fleet like that is worth waiting days for. If we are able to stand by unrecognized until a calm sets in, we can strike a blow at the enemy from which he will never recover." He talked on. "If we should bank our fires, lower the telescopic smokestack, and slip into their midst like a wolf in the fold . . ."

Next morning a dead calm fell over the sea. In water as still as a lagoon the Confederate steamed in under the American flag and joined the unsuspecting fleet. Five boarding crews were detailed at once, one for each of the boats. As they made off in unison for the five nearest whalers, the Confederate flag was hoisted to the *Shenandoah's* masthead.

The wolf had entered. Little groups gathered on whaling decks and gazed from the "pirate" to their useless sails hanging limp in the Arctic air. Soon the whalers lowered their flags in surrender. Even the Confederates agreed that war was a cruel thing.

The *James Maury* and the *Nile* were ransomed to return the three hundred prisoners to San Francisco. By the time the sun dipped its cheerless face for only a few minutes behind the northern horizon that night, the barks *Waverly, Martha, Favorite, Covington,* and *Congress* were given the torch along with the ships *Hillman, Nassau, Brunswick,* and *Isaac Howland.*

In the still of night over the Bering Sea the *Shenandoah* stood safely apart from the greatest conflagration ever to light up the seas.

Adam leaned on the rail, eyes narrowed against the glare from the flames of nine whalers. The spectacle rivaled the brilliance of the aurora borealis, and the drifting ice picked up and reflected from tall bergs that seemed on fire the glow of destruction in all its colors of reds and yellows, its bursts of flame and dying embers. The sea mirrored it and the sky cast its quivering mask of unearthly light down upon the cold water. A strange roaring and hissing, like a hundred monsters of the deep in the throes of death, was made more inhuman by the echoes that were thrown back by the ice into the sounding box of an Arctic sea. Adam saw in memory the burning of the *Golden Rocket,* only this was nine times as big and on a scale to stun the imagination.

He felt suddenly sick, and he turned his back on the fury and the sound and the hell of war.

2

The ice was closing in fast when the *Shenandoah* steamed for the Aleutians, her mission now to run south and lie in wait for United States commerce on the California–Panama track. On she ran, down to where ice and snow were memories and pea jackets and heavy underwear were items for the chests.

On the thirteenth of July the officers were celebrating Waddell's birthday, when the captain revealed a madcap scheme to capture the city of San Francisco. According to the papers, only the ironclad *Saginaw* protected the city and bay. Senior Officer Whittle and Sidney Smith Lee looked at Adam, who lowered his gaze. Francis Chew frowned. The captain—well, he had more than twenty years to his credit in the Old Navy. He had been the assistant professor of navigation at Annapolis. These things were respected.

"It's like this, gentlemen," said Waddell. "We'll steam into San Francisco Bay in the night, hurl boarding parties on the *Saginaw's* deck, and capture the ship before the Federals know what struck them. Next morning two ships could train broadsides on the city."

The officers voted to adopt the audacious plan. They wished, however, to be sure that the *Saginaw* had not been reinforced. In order to determine this, they sailed in search of a sail outward bound from San Francisco.

On the second of August they overhauled the British bark *Barracouta*, thirteen days out of San Francisco. She carried newspapers and she sailed her way, leaving in the ribbon from her stern a group of men who had suddenly no hope left in them and no reason to carry on.

The war had ended in April. The solid collapse of the Confederacy had come in May, almost two months before the destruction of the Yankee whaling marine. The officers were not prepared for the crushing blow. They met together, faces long as they looked into the past at a lost cause. They stared at each other in confounded manner as they considered their present position. What had happened to them was unprecedented in all naval history. There was no pattern to follow. They were men without country or flag aboard a ship without a nation.

The grave situation was touched with a grim bit of humor; they would not capture San Francisco.

The officers agreed that they had no right to carry arms. Their guns were hurriedly swung below and all rifles, pistols, and cutlasses were locked away. The Confederate cruiser had become a merchantman, a veritable derelict without aim or course, without a home port.

But they sailed on because they could not root to the sea. And in their minds were the things the captain of the *Barracouta* told them: "You are branded in every port as pirates. President Johnson of the United States has issued a proclamation of outlawry against you and has his warships scouring the sea for the *Shenandoah*."

The officers were divided on the course to take. Sydney or Liverpool? They met and argued. Waddell lacked decision, and gradually the Sydney faction swayed him. Then one night he called Adam to his quarters and said, "I hate to take this crew to Australia and leave them penniless."

"Then don't do it, sir," Adam replied. "The Yankees will be looking for us in the Pacific, so if we can slip around the Horn we can take the ship to Liverpool and surrender to our British friends."

After many meetings, near mutinies, and arguments, Captain Waddell resolved to follow the plan and, almost in secret, set his course for England, seventeen thousand miles away.

The days slipped past slowly as the vessel under sail tried out her topgallants and crowded on sail until she ran a fleet sixteen knots despite the heavy crust of barnacles on her copper. Prompted by Adam, Waddell abandoned his conservative and extraprudent type of sailing by night and sent her along like a free thing with all sails set to the winds.

Faces remained troubled and discipline became harder to enforce. Her officers were caught smoking on the night watches, but worse than the deeds aboard were pictures of the future. Squalls came and calms stood them still, as though anchored to their shadow. They slid on down to the trade winds, stood down the Pacific for Cape Horn, working ship and hauling sheets and taking this tack and that, but always with the dread awareness that they were men of the crushed and beaten South.

Finally they reached down to the west winds and sailed deep below the South American coast for a rounding of Cape Horn. Then they slanted up into the South Atlantic.

Lookouts continued to scan the horizons, though not for prizes now; rather, to avoid any and all vessels.

Adam tasted the very dregs of defeat one afternoon in September when there was no avoiding a huge three-sticker flying the British red ensign. She came on, bound down for a circling of the Horn, heeling until her copper flashed golden in the sunlight, her colors dipping in salute. She flew, drove on, her officer aft staring curiously at the disguised *Shenandoah,* as if to ask why the stranger failed to return the courtesy of the deep stream. Why, indeed?

There was a reason why. It hurt deep, and Adam hung his head. His ship had no colors to dip other than the flag of a nation which no longer existed.

3

On the morning of November fifth Captain Waddell and his officers gazed nervously into the wall of fog and winced at the repeated blasts of the *Shenandoah's* whistle. Muted echoes out of the gray pall did nothing to break the tension.

Engineer O'Brien said, "The firemen are scraping the bottom of the bunkers, Mr. Bulloch. You'd better show us some land."

Lieutenant Lee said pensively, "Land. We haven't seen land since —when?"

"The Aleutian Islands," Adam replied dolefully. "Twenty-three thousand miles from here." He added, "That is if Mr. Bulloch can guarantee we're actually near the British Isles."

"In this fog we may be on the coast," Bulloch drawled with enough anxiety in his voice to dispel all humor.

They trusted his navigation, however, despite the fact that he seemed forced to sail as much by guess as by accuracy. There had been no chance to rate the chronometers, so he was relying on the patent log, instinct, and whistle.

Slowly the fog thinned and straining eyes made out all sorts of ghostly shapes. As it furred and lifted in ragged streamers, the land opened up. The coast of Ireland drew a cheer. They steamed on toward Holyhead that day and entered St. George's Channel.

Early next day a pilot boat came alongside and a wrinkled, lobster-red pilot came over the side with, "A fine good mornin' to ye, gentlemen." Taking in the deck and rigging with a practiced eye, he said, "And what ship might this be?"

Mr. Whittle looked his lieutenants over and nodded to Adam, who replied, "The Confederate States cruiser *Shenandoah.*"

The pilot started. With a cock of his head and a squint of an eye, he exclaimed, "The hell you say!" Somewhat skeptical, he said, "The ship ye speak of is in the Arctic. That is, the papers say she is."

"We were there," Adam replied.

"Then how did ye get by the Yankee warships they have out lookin' for ye? And if ye're what ye say, where's yer flag?"

Adam looked at the officers, at Captain Waddell. "Shall we raise it, sir, this last time?"

A silence gathered and the old pilot shook his head impatiently as Waddell said, "We swore allegiance to it. Run it up, Mr. Cutler."

The Confederate colors were soon hoisted to the peak. As the flag whipped and straightened in the breeze for the last time over land or sea, the old barnacled pilot raised a pair of surprised eyes and said in his excitement:

"Lo and behold, 'tis the outlawed banner!"

39.     By Whom Remembered . . .

1

ADRIA looked up at the bleak February sky and drew her wrap tighter about her neck before picking up the ax again. Adjusting the rags tied to her palms inside the remains of a pair of elbow-length gloves, she began chopping at the ruins of a fence. The night promised a chill wind and the fireplaces on the tenable side of Bay Oaks made demands on her, the only person on the place who could swing an ax. Poor Mammy was "ailin'" and Erasmus was lucky to move about. The Yankees had scattered the remaining slaves.

On her left, the charred planks of the slave hospital brought frightful memories of the day the Federals came. But that had been all of ten months earlier. The "bummers" arrived a few days later to loot and jeer and threaten before moving on to make room for other scavengers of war. Roving bands of Negroes, former slaves from near and far, came and camped and held their gospel meetings and fought and drank in their efforts to adjust themselves to the new freedom. They were like children; to them freedom was something like a promise of paradise, a state in which hunger or cold or a spoken command was unknown. A dog and gun and a new wife for the old one, plenty of pigs and chickens for the taking, made up the new life. But they soon tired of it, and nine hundred ex-slaves met in Mobile in the fall of 1865 and voted seven hundred to two hundred to return to their former masters.

Adria knew there were good Negroes, and she had only to look toward the river road or pay the slightest attention to the jeering laughter to realize that there were also bad ones.

Claribel was one. She sat atop a fence post near a man she claimed to be her third husband, a big black in a faded Yankee uniform. "How do it feel, Adri, to chop yo' own kindlin' wood?" she cried. "Don't like the law o' June twenty-sebben, what makes me good as yo'all, does yo'?"

Adria knew to ignore Claribel. To drive her away would serve to bring down the wrath of the Freedman's Bureau and the Negro Federal troops. The last time Mammy Rose had chased Claribel away with a bucket of hot coals, Adria had been arrested and tried on a charge of assault preferred by Claribel. The degradation seemed unbearable. Thrown with drunken soldiers and lewd women who crowded Mobile's streets, she had been forced to submit to a lecture by a Negro official. And upon leaving the court, she had been arrested again for refusing to walk under a United States flag over the sidewalk.

Lowering her ax, Adria caught her breath and stared at Lawrence. In the field behind the garden, he leaned on a hoe and gazed forlornly at the sky. She was used to this, used to his eternal silence and brooding, his spells of coughing and his sitting out days in one place as though he were still a prisoner at Camp Douglas. Nor did he seem to be improving. Constantly weakened by the racking cough, he continued to lose weight and stamina.

Adria looked again at the low sky. Mist was beginning to sift down out of the pall. Claribel and her man were getting atop a gray mule. Down the road a bearded stranger stood with battered hat in hand staring at Bay Oaks.

"Another bummer or outlaw," Adria said, eying the loaded rifle hidden in the brush a few feet away.

The rifle was a gift from Randall Sherrod. The day they had arrested her for refusing to walk under the flag, he had appeared out of nowhere to stand grinning as she defended herself before General Woods himself. How she had stood up to the Federal and his court! A wonder, she reflected, they hadn't seized Bay Oaks when she called them "savages trying to enforce laws that were a crime against civilization."

"Which of our laws are crimes, Mrs. Jarvis?" the prosecutor asked.

"Most all of them, sir," Adria replied hotly. Head high, she went on to say, "In order to get permission to sell enough cotton or vegetables to buy necessities, one must take the Oath of Amnesty. Imagine my surprise when I learned that a Cutler could not take the oath, that our plantations are called 'abandoned' by the Treasury Department and were not to be restored because my brother, who sailed aboard the *Shenandoah*, was considered a pirate at sea in defiance of the United States.

"So I was not allowed to sell anything. Your most benevolent country decrees that I and my family shall starve and remain at the mercy of plundering niggers, outlaws, bummers, and Federal soldiers, while the commonest outlaw, as you know, can commit murder, rob and burn, and be released by your courts if he calls himself a Unionist.

"Really, gentlemen, do you expect me to respect a flag that reduces me, a victim of war, to a state beneath a murderer?"

The noble court had raised its brows, all right, she remembered, and General Woods had said he was tired of being snubbed by Southern ladies; and she had risked banishment or worse by saying on the impulse of the moment, "What can you expect, sir?"

She gathered up the kindling and started for the house. The unkempt stranger, an outlaw or river thief, no doubt, was walking through the gap left open by the bummers who stole the scrollwork gates. Pausing, she cried out to him:

"Better not come any closer. I've got a loaded gun."

The man stopped and looked at her. With hat in hand, he seemed more spellbound and meek than dangerous. But one never could tell. She called Mammy Rose to come get the kindling. When free of it, she picked up the rifle and took a few steps toward the stranger.

"Where's your father, ma'am?" the man asked.

"Killed in battle. But there's a man about."

He was a long time silent. "Where's your mother?"

"Upstairs sick in bed, if it's any of your business."

Adria's eyes widened and she lowered the gun a trifle. "Your voice! You—you couldn't be——" Her cry rang loud, "Adam!" and she was running to him.

"Careful, Adria, I'm still a fugitive," he said, holding her close. Slowly he raised her head and looked searchingly into her face, into the four and one half years that had elapsed since he left for England. He saw the girl of twenty he had last seen now a matured woman of almost twenty-five. She seemed at once older and younger than her age, though there was no telling in her face what she had lost or gained. War was a cruel thing.

"So Father had to fight. Tell me about it."

As Adria told the story, Adam's gaze dwelled on the half-burned, smoke-darkened, and weather-beaten mansion. The gallery roof on the burned side dipped down as if trying to touch the corner pillar that thrust only half its length into the air.

Adam blinked his eyes to rid them of the mist. "That was Father, all right," he said. Almost timidly, he ventured a question. "Is Faustine at home?"

Then he saw Lawrence moving slowly toward the house and said in amazement, "That can't be Lawrence."

"Yes, Adam. It's worse than just being sick. He—he won't forget any of it." Sighing, she smiled hopefully. "Maybe you can help him recover."

"I told you I'm still a fugitive."

"Why, Adam? Why, when you can take the oath?"

He began with the return of the *Shenandoah* to England. He told of the run up the Mersey, of the old pilot's saying that all England would be "set on her merry beam ends," of how true his words had been. When Captain Waddell surrendered and sent the word to London, the officers and crew had been ordered to remain aboard as prisoners of war until Her Majesty's pleasure was forthcoming. England was agog. Lord Clarendon of the Foreign Office could find no parallel in history to aid in a decision. The London *Times* deplored their return as "an untoward and unwelcomed event," and the debates continued until the evening of November eighth.

"The British officer came on deck," Adam said, "and asked for a muster of all men. But prior to this we had been informed to answer to the roll call with our nationality, and that every native of the South was to be set free. So Englishmen, Scot, and Scandinavian responded with, 'Southerner.'"

"Then you are free," Adria declared.

Adam's face fell. "No. Every man of us aboard the *Shenandoah* was specifically excluded from the terms of the post-war general amnesty. Some say it will be ten years before we can return home. I am on my way to South America, Adria. I just couldn't help risking a visit home——"

He looked eagerly toward the house. "I had to see you and Mother —and Faustine."

Adria's mouth trembled. She could not take her eyes off him. "Adam, better brace yourself. It's about Faustine."

He listened, his eyes boring into hers at first, his mouth so tight it trembled. Then he lowered his head and turned the hat in his hand around and around, oblivious to the tears running down his cheeks. He stood there, with Adria's hand gripping his, in a silence that seemed without end. His life with Faustine ran before his mind's eye again in panoramic detail—that which was given, that which was taken; a flower in bloom, a thorn and a bleeding wound that would never heal; a ray of hope and a memory, a pretty one.

Her hair was so black, and her eyes so vibrant in joy, curiosity, and defense, so——

He raised his head and swallowed hard. The mist was wiped from his washed eyes and he looked again at the half pillar and the sagging roof and asked himself how long the roof could hang there without dropping to the column. Something big was dead, gone; charred and parted, leaving him and Adria, and all, suspended in a void like that between the roof and the column, between the glorious past and the uncertain future.

Faustine, the old days, the cheering and the bands playing—these things were. They had been. They were gone. Gone forever.

For something to say, Adam said, "How did you put out the fire?"

How? She felt sorry for him. What did it matter how the fire had been put out? She looked toward the distant trees and back to the house.

"Adam," she said, "look standing in the front door. It's only two weeks until his birthday."

Adam's eyes underwent a slow but sure change from sorrow to interest to hope and then to subdued joy; subdued, Adria knew, for fear that his son, too, might disappear like everything else. But something new was being born in Adam and it was good to see, to know. It was like a shoot sprouting green out of barren soil.

Watching Adam going to his son, Adria said aloud, "Stop that, Mr. Yankee, if you can."

With the wrap about her neck and lower face, she moved toward the ax again. Adam was home. There was a little liquor in the bottle Sherrod had brought Aunt Eugenia, she recalled. Poor dear Auntie, near deaf and on crutches. Enough liquor to spread a little cheer. The sudden brightness of the day turned her surprised face toward the west.

The sun was breaking through the gray curtain of clouds. There it came, free at last. Well, almost. As she watched, it painted the clouds in colors of gold and crimson, then found a tiny slit in the curtain and bathed for a moment the grim world of Bay Oaks in mellow light.

Simultaneous with that shaft of sunlight, Mammy Rose yelled, "Marse Adam!" Her shrieks of delight continued as she swept Adam to her bosom.

Adria compressed her lips, wiped her eyes, and brushed stray locks of hair from her forehead. A minute later all the old fear returned. A carriage halted at the gateway and a tall man got out.

He wore the blue of the Union Navy, and he stood there shaking his bare head in despair as he gazed at the ruins of Bay Oaks.

There was something very familiar about him. A naval uniform of the Old Navy. The stance. Almost it went beyond horror and hate to the wonderful days. Yes, there was something very familiar about the Union officer. His hair! Adria thought she would faint. Then she was running toward the house as fast as her legs would carry her, for he was, of all people, no doubt about it, James Hillyer.

2

Adria could not define her feelings as she entered the house and cried, "Adam, hide!" Then she was taking the steps three at a time in a dash to the room she shared with her mother. She supposed she still hated James. But strange sensations were running through her, warming her, flooding her bosom. Perhaps all she despised was his uniform. She could not be sure.

She breathed a sigh of relief upon finding her mother asleep. At least she would not be called upon to explain her reasons for getting into that old rose silk ball gown she had worn the night she met James. Heavens, that had been more than five years in the past!

As Adria hurriedly changed her dress, downstairs Mammy Rose turned from a window with a scowl and, " 'Nuther one o' dem Yankees, Marse Adam. Now where did my honey chile leave dat rifle gun?"

Adam continued to stare at the visitor, wishing as he did so that he were anyone other than James. The gulf between them was too deep and too wide. They were not strangers, but former friends, close friends who had separated to become strong enemies. One was the spirit of the North, the other of the South. One was now the conqueror. Adam realized that he had only his pride left. He should run from possible arrest, but somehow he could not. Not from James. His pride!

Minutes slipped by before James Hillyer sauntered up the steps and stood with a frozen look of incredulity on his face. What had happened here, the ruin, the contrast, seemed unbelievable. It did not at first occur to him that men in blue, like himself, were responsible for this crime. And when there was no avoiding an admission of the fact, he recalled with a stab of shame his own desires aboard the *Kearsarge* to fire on the enemy who were escaping aboard an English yacht.

Then he was staring up at the balcony, back into the holidays of 1860. It was as though she were up there now, a vision in pale rose, and he was seeing her for the first time. He lowered his head and closed his eyes. Hammering at his brain were the lines of a verse:

> *You were born to love, to hate and die*
> *And war will do it faster.*

A moment later James rapped at the scarred door of Bay Oaks.

"Admit him, Mammy," Adam said, moving to the fire. He stood there until he felt James's presence behind him. Then he turned.

They met again in silence, with all that had stood between them in their eyes clashing moment and another, then with all that had drawn them together before the war surfacing and rising and falling away in succeeding awkward moments. A difference in their appearance angered Adam. He put down his resentment and composed himself.

"Have a chair, Lieutenant Hillyer."

James winced. "I thought it was you I saw leaving that British ship, Adam. I followed."

"What do you want?" Adam asked coldly.

James's face softened. "What I've wanted for a long time." He stared from Adam into the fire. "Ever since your letter reached Captain Winslow, I've wanted to apologize."

Adam's eyes were black, steady, and accusing. They did not leave James's face in the long minute of silence.

"I know how you must feel, Adam. I know what you're seeing now. It's that look I gave you when your boat came up to the *Kearsarge*. Well, victory erased it. I don't mean it the way it sounds, Adam. I'm not gloating. You see, at Cherbourg I learned that it was I who was defeated."

James's hands joined behind his back. He looked embarrassed. Lowering his gaze to deep marks of horses hoofs in the floor, he said falteringly, "Thank the Lord it's all over."

Adam squared his shoulders. "Is it now? I lived through hell to get home. I'm wanted as a pirate."

"I know." James rubbed his jaw disconsolately. "The navy men recognized you. I asked for the honor of capturing you, Adam."

Suddenly Adria stood in the doorway with rifle up. "You won't have the honor of bringing him in!" she cried.

Adam said crisply, "Put that gun down, Adria. What happens between the lieutenant and me is none of your business."

Confounded, Adria gave the rifle to Mammy Rose and preened herself. She felt James's admiring eyes upon her, his attention strong as he looked from the wrinkled ball gown of 1860 to her neck and face and hair. Under his scrutiny, she felt herself turn from hot to cold. Her emotions ran the gamut, and she knew it. She loved this man; she hated him; she both loved and hated at once. Then she heard herself saying:

"Mammy, we have a guest for dinner."

The Negress looked puzzled. She realized that Adria knew there was scant food in the house and that of the commonest sort. She shook her head in despair as Adria said, "Now bring the bourbon bottle from upstairs."

Adam took his son in his arms and introduced him to James. "Imagine me with a fine fellow like this and just now meeting him for the first time." Under the strong flood of happiness, Adam came close to adding, "Admiral Co-Co." Instead, he sobered instantly and spoke of the little time left him for striking up an acquaintance with his own flesh and blood.

At the door to the hall, he turned and faced James. "Don't worry, Lieutenant Hillyer, I won't run away." Seeing James wince, he added, "Any more than I'll submit meekly to arrest."

For a second and another, the old malice enveloped them. Then Adam said in a voice strangely lacking in resentment or defiance, "There's too much at stake."

Adam walked away, and James found himself making every effort to regain his composure before looking at Adria. Their glances met and he forgot Adam, forgot everything but the lovely picture before his eyes. To him she was the embodiment of his dreams. He thrilled to the sight of her. She was older, yes, but becomingly so; mature and more radiantly alive and desirable. Trouble shone through her wide-set eyes. It lingered about her firm mouth, grim and scarcely masked by her pride. He saw her then a fitting symbol of the glorious, proud South and the final tragedy that had befallen a way of life.

Adria put her back to him. "Sir, I trust you have fared well all these years."

It sounded so foreign. He frowned. "Why—er—yes."

"Pray be seated, Lieutenant. Dinner——"

"Adria!" James sounded gruff. As she whirled and looked at him, despite her sudden vow to appear disinterested, he blurted out, "I still love you, Adria!"

Adria stood aghast. Then, suddenly all that had happened since his departure rose up to testify against him, to indict him. He was in the instant tried and judged and she was reading sentence.

"How very apropos your declaration, sir. With a bayonet at my brother's back, you pause to convey your sentiments to me. How very chivalrous! It comes of wearing the blue, I'm sure."

With wrath kindling a dancing, exultant fire in her eyes, she paced back and forth between what was left of a Sheraton sofa and the fireplace, her mocking and defiant glances alternately falling to the floor and lifting to his face.

"But you are out of character, Mr. Hillyer. Now had you followed the Yankee pattern and entered Bay Oaks with sword drawn and hacking away at what is left, your remark might have sounded honest. Of course——"

"Adria, stop it!" he commanded.

Ignoring him, she continued. "One gets used to such things, as a look about the parlor must verify. So don't hold back. There is a single unbroken vase atop the corner table over there." She pointed. "Now why don't you smash it into a million pieces and then speak of love?"

"Adria, I don't condone pillage and destruction. I didn't believe the things I heard were possible."

Adria scoffed. "Don't let your Turkish-minded fellow officers hear you talk so. Not your Yankee cousins who shot my father, tore the earrings from my aunt's ears, and killed Faustine."

James looked stunned. "Faustine?"

"First they forced a slave to beat her." Adria came to a stop before James and eyed him accusingly. "They did worse to her sister."

As she talked on, James looked beyond her and then down at his boots. Her anger and scorn were enough, though the things she told him evoked shame for the uniform he wore. His glance lifted only when she said:

"You chose tyranny over me back in 1861. And yet after such crimes by your people, you return to tell me you still love me. You dare to say this to me!"

He caught her hands and held them tightly in his grasp. "Yes, I dare it," he replied gruffly. "Because I can't stop loving you."

The suddenness of his doing took her by surprise, and his reply and dark look held her transfixed. Then feeling came back with a rush and her first instinct was to free her hands and strike out at him. She might have done just this had he not renewed the initiative by saying, "Surely you can't blame the outrages of our armies on me—any more than you can actually hate me, Adria."

She could not look away from him. For all his preposterous talk, there was in that moment something of the James who had proposed to her. Here was the man she had once given her heart to, and it was as though there had been no parting, no separation, no guns, no war.

He repeated his statement. She did not answer.

She thought he was going to take her in his arms and kiss her. He wanted to do this, his eyes said. If he did, she would know her heart, she told herself. But he was wavering. As the James of old, he could not make up his mind. Then the opportunity was gone and he was saying:

"Adria, you don't despise me. You love me."

Her mouth fell open and she said, as if in debate, "I don't know." Hastily she recovered and stepped back from him. "No! I could never love you!"

A minute later James stood utterly confounded. Entering the parlor was Lawrence Jarvis. A ghost, thought James; the tall, emaciated, hostile ghost of the man who had embarrassed him here back in 1860 and whom he had thought dead.

"Another goddamn Yankee," Lawrence was saying. "You know what they do to me. I don't want a Yankee around the place. I keep telling you I don't want to see another one."

"Why, Lawrence," Adria scolded gently, "your manners! You remember Lieutenant Hillyer."

"Sure." Lawrence's eyes were mere sunken pinpoints. "Could I ever forget him? Now get rid of him before——"

Adria came between him and James, removed a knotty cane from his hand, and said, "Sit down, Lawrence. Over there." As he obeyed, still glaring at James, she said, "He was in a Federal prison." She added grimly, "Too long."

Suddenly she said, "But he is my husband, Lieutenant Hillyer."

James dropped his gaze and said in bitter tones, "Forgive me, Adria. I heard in Mobile that you were a widow."

"Most soldiers' wives are," she said. "But don't let it bother you." Her anxious glance left Lawrence and improved greatly as it fell on James. "Strange, isn't it, your return to Bay Oaks after five years?" She waited for his quizzical eyes to lift before saying, "For the purpose of taking Adam prisoner."

"Prisoner?" James's smile was spontaneous and all too brief. "Why, Adria, surely you realize that I couldn't do it. Adam is going to escape before he reaches Mobile."

Adria supposed she should convey her thanks and sudden relief, though she found herself thinking how inconsistent the invading Yankee really was. Pillage on Friday, favors on Saturday. Suddenly a commotion in the hall drew her attention. She listened and heard:

"Look here, nigger, what the devil are you doing with a few drops of raw whisky when Randall Sherrod has brought chilled champagne? And look in this bag, will you."

Mammy's laughter echoed from the walls. "Lawdy Lawd! Honest-to-goodness flour! And, praise God, look at dem fo' fat fryers! Cap'n, I could kiss yo'all!"

"Belay, and show lively with fried chicken and gravy. And fetch the supplies in out of the wagon. Miss Annabel will be wanting her oyster stew right off."

Sherrod came to a halt just inside the room. Eyes sharp as a scalpel coasted the length of James, then Adria, before thawing under a mocking grin that spread slowly over his face. Advancing unhurriedly, he stood before James.

"Well, well, if it isn't the shadow of Admiral Farragut. Last time I saw you was—don't tell me—Havana, wasn't it, Lieutenant? Sure now, that it was. You ran off with a lady's slipper."

Turning to Adria, he said, "Yours."

To Sherrod's evident pleasure, James colored from the neck up and cast a sidewise glance at Adria. Then he started at what he saw in her face as she looked at the schoonerman and ex-blockade-runner. If her expression in any way indicated her sentiments, the rakehell was more than welcome in this house. Things had changed here, had come to a pretty pass. War was a monstrous thing. A wave of anger, terrible and impatient, flooded James.

Mammy arrived with a tray of tall glasses, part of the crystal buried a year earlier, and Sherrod popped the cock. He gave Adria a glass, poured another for Lawrence, who refused it, and then presented it to James. With a glass for himself, he stood before the fire.

"To the past," he said, bending stiffly toward James, the blue of his eyes flashing. "And all we hope to forget."

It was the way he said it.

As James drew himself up to his full height and showed resentment at the barb unmistakably directed at him, Sherrod bowed slowly before Adria, his glance holding hers. "To the future without a past," he said.

In the instant, he released her eyes and darted a glance, all too significant, at the silent husband. And then, with mocking disdain in his face, he looked at the visitor in blue and threw his glass into the fire.

To Adria the moment was electric. Sherrod's gesture had been open, bold and deliberate, and the resulting tension was strong. It shone in the intent eyes of James Hillyer, and as she looked from the offender to the offended, she felt that time itself, from the deep, dark beginning of things, had struggled through the ages for the sole purpose of casting aside the curtain on this moment.

Lawrence began to cough violently. He seemed to be tearing himself to pieces. Little time was left for Lawrence, though it could be measured by long weeks or months of suffering, Adria realized, as against the swift passing moment of the present, in which she felt herself caught up between two fires, both raging. She was unable to spare Lawrence a sympathetic glance.

She scarcely heard Sherrod's mocking "Cheer up, Lieutenant. After all, you did win the war," though she felt his speculative eyes on her as he said, "But the South will make a fair wind of it." He added, grinning wickedly at her, "Of course, she will require a lot of patience—and paint."

Adria was not blind to his meaning, and her anger almost flared into the open.

Then she looked at James and her heart seemed to stand still as she relived in glorious seconds the memories of his courtship. As she turned her glance on the impudent adventurer and mysterious wartime provider, any anger for him fell away and her heart leaped up and beat with more than simple gratitude. In James's place minutes before, Sherrod would have kissed her without hesitation. A trivial thing, that thought. Then it was big for what it revealed.

Two men, James Hillyer and Randall Sherrod. She could not love both of them; only one. She knew which one.

As though it mattered which! The racking cough continued. It mocked her, shamed her. She turned her back to fight back the tears threatening to push through, to hide from one of the visitors her great longing for him and from the other the fact that her heart could never respond to a man lacking in decision. A minute more and she lifted her head high and walked proudly across the room and stood by the chair where Lawrence sat.

Then she was looking toward her guests, both of them, smiling at them, even as she ran nervous fingers tenderly through her husband's hair.

85